Cursed Truths

Blood of a Guardian

M. J. Harper

Cursed Truths: Blood of a Guardian

ISBN: 978-1-7374366-0-7

PROLOGUE

MONTEREY COUNTY, CALIFORNIA
July 04, 2008

The thunderous boom of the rockets, the dazzling finale to the town's firework display erupting behind Daryl Metzger, masked the click of the latch. Specks of strontium carbonate burning red in the atmosphere reflected in the glass of the French windows as Daryl Metzger opened them and stepped from the balcony to the bedroom. She would need to be quick if she was to carry out her plan before the others arrived.

Kneeling by the child's bed, Daryl reached into the pocket of her black, hooded jacket and removed a syringe and a pair of tubes. The child's breathing was shallow and rapid. Her arms twitched, spurred by some nightmarish dream. Whatever the girl was imagining, it could not be worse than the path laid out before her. Lifting the child's foot, Daryl pressed the needle between her toes and filled the first tube. Listening for sounds from downstairs, Daryl swapped tubes, filling the second one and pocketing them before removing the needle. One down, one to go.

Leaving Skylar to her nightmares, Daryl silently crossed the hallway to Sawyer's room, adjusting the cloth over her face as she went. The cloudless sky bathed the manor's backyard in moonlight, making it easy to spot Lukai's assault team through the hallway's floor to ceiling windows. Moving swiftly, Daryl twisted the doorknob, wincing at the loud click, and stepped into the second bedroom.

The boy was awake.

Rubbing his eyes, Sawyer sat up in bed. If he screamed, the entire operation was ruined. Hers and Lukai's. Wasting no time, Daryl closed the gap to his bed and clamped her hand over his mouth. Startled by the move, the boy lashed out, his arms flailing uselessly as Daryl gripped his shoulders with her other arm and twisted. The boy was scheduled to die anyway; what difference did a few minutes make?

With another two tubes filled, Daryl dropped the boy's useless corpse on the floor and headed for the parents' room. Let Lukai's first assault team tackle Jeremy. Their inevitable deaths meant nothing to Daryl and would buy her enough time to complete her own task before helping them with theirs.

Daryl stiffened, hand on the doorknob to Joanne and Mark Sinclair's room, as the unmistakable sound of glass shattering echoed around the house.

Fools, Daryl thought as she threw open the door. The gung-ho idiots were not supposed to blow the bloody doors off. Then again, stealth was never a strong suit for Lukai or his goons.

Joanne was already up and heading for the door, launching herself at Daryl with a hellish scream as soon as their eyes met. The two women collapsed into the hallway in a tangle of limbs as Joanne threw all her weight against the intruder. For all her fury, the woman was no match for Daryl. Grabbing Joanne by the shoulders, Daryl threw her off, sending her back into the room and knocking her husband from his feet as he rushed to Joanne's aid.

"You'll pay for that," Joanne said as she pulled herself to her feet.

Daryl smiled beneath her mask and lowered the hood of her jacket, revealing her punkish, short, black hair and keeping Joanne distracted as the balcony door slid silently open. The glint of moonlight on the cluster of earrings in Daryl's left ear was enough to hold Joanne's attention as two goons crept into the room, blades raised.

Mark screamed, drawing Joanne from their battle of wills, as the first goon slashed at his neck. Amazed that such an easy kill could be botched so badly, Daryl stepped into the room as Mark fell to the floor, arm raised to ward off a follow-up strike. Recognizing the most pressing threat, despite wanting to rush to her husband's aid, Joanne kicked out at the door to delay Daryl, but her reactions were too slow. Daryl slipped into the room as the door slammed against the frame, bouncing ajar from the force of the impact. With Daryl blocking the hallway door and Lukai's goons blocking the balcony door, there was no escape for the Sinclairs.

Daryl tilted her head slightly at the sound of footsteps in the hallway. The girl. No threat there. Mistaking Daryl's hesitation for weakness, Joanne launched herself at Daryl with an easily blocked right hook and a casually sidestepped left uppercut. Against a normal opponent, the rapid attack sequence might have worked.

Listening to the combat downstairs, Daryl blocked another strike as Mark, struggling from the blood loss, finally succumbed to the kicks and punches of Lukai's goons. A kill that was needlessly drawn out so that the two men could revel in the physical violence. The same could not be said for the fighting on the first floor. From the sound of it, Jeremy would be done with Lukai's crew in short order.

Tired of kicking a corpse, the goons turned their attention to their next victim. Daryl stepped back, leaning against the wall, and flicked her head in the direction of Lukai's men. Warily, Joanne took the hint and switched her focus. Mark was an easy target, untrained in the art of self-defense. Joanne deserved some retribution before breathing her last.

Snarling behind the ski mask that obscured his face, the first of the goons, the one that slashed her husband, grabbed for Joanne. Like his master, he assumed that might was all he needed to carry out his aims. Joanne made him pay for his arrogance with a perfectly timed punch to the throat. Daryl was neither surprised nor dismayed. There was no allowance for incompetence in her mind.

Capitalizing on the man's inability to breathe, Joanne drove her knee into his stomach and hurled him away from her, forcing the other man to dodge as his comrade fell at his feet. There was no denying Joanne's ferocity or skill. Had she been anything other than human, Joanne may have been a viable threat. As it stood, only Lukai's men needed to worry about those quick hands and powerful legs.

The battle was everything Daryl expected. With the second goon on the defensive, Joanne was quick to press her advantage, kicking at the man's knee while swinging a fist at his temple. Less quick to judge his opponent by her size, the man-made a better effort to kill his prey than the first goon, scoring several blows on Joanne. Fueled by rage at the assault and desperate to save her family, it was not enough to slow Joanne's attack.

As Lukai's second man fell, Daryl pushed herself off the wall and walked to the center of the room, giving herself a clear path to the balcony. The thud of a body in the hallway downstairs signaled Jeremy was getting closer.

"How dare you violate the treaty?" Joanne asked through gritted teeth. "You'll rot in hell for this."

"Oh, Joanne," replied Daryl in her rich, Australian accent. "You and your kind don't even know what hell is. I would be more than happy to teach you about it if you wish."

"Get fucked, vampire whore," said Joanne, her eyes darting to the hallway. "You cannot come into my home, attack my family, and expect to escape retribution."

Daryl resisted the urge to look to the door. As tempting as it was to think Joanne was planning to make a run for it, Daryl knew she was stalling for time.

"If this is the day I die," Joanne continued, "I'm taking you down with me."

Daryl fended off Joanne's wild lunge, listening to Jeremy's footsteps as he reached the top of the stairs. Would he go for the child or risk everything to save the mother? Readying herself to dash for the balcony, Daryl forced Joanne back. The door crept open another inch as Jeremy's footsteps reached the bedroom door. Pulling her hood back over her head, Daryl swept forward with a barrage of punches too quick for Joanne to defend against, driving the woman to her knees and making it clear there was no hope of victory before drawing back. There was no sense in drawing Jeremy into the fight when she already had the blood of the children.

Daryl smiled beneath her mask at the look of relief on Joanne's face. Not for herself, but for her daughter. Keeping her face turned to the floor, Daryl stepped behind Joanne and placed an arm around her neck.

"You're too late," Joanne whispered through a mouthful of blood.

"Am I?" asked Daryl, twisting Joanne's head until her neck snapped as Jeremy raced along the hallway with the child, his footsteps fading as he bounded down the stairs.

With the threat of Jeremy's interference gone, Daryl opened her jacket and removed another syringe. With no need for subtlety, Daryl jabbed the needle into Joanne's arm and began filling another pair of tubes. Sounds of combat echoed from downstairs as Jeremy fought his way through the second squad with Skylar. Exactly why her master needed the girl to escape, Daryl did not know. The fact that it would upset Lukai was reason enough for Daryl.

Her work complete, Daryl grabbed the fallen goons and hoisted their cooling bodies over her shoulders. In the manor's entrance hall, three members of the second squad were still drawing breath. Severely wounded, they struggled to their feet as a young man, flanked by two muscular brutes, strode through the open front door. Lukai Golovkin, with his expensive suit and slicked-back hair, surveyed the damage as Daryl descended the stairs.

"Ladies and gentlemen," Lukai announced as Daryl dumped the bodies at the foot of the stairs and joined the survivors of the second squad, "you have failed me."

Daryl, stood in line before the sixteen-year-old vampire whelp, resented playing the part of a regular soldier. Soon, the council would learn to fear her more than Jeremy and the other monks.

"Master, how do you mean?" a woman from the squad asked as the other two glanced at each other in confusion.

"You let Outteridge escape," replied Lukai, his lip curling up in a snarl at Jeremy's name. "Outteridge, and the girl."

"The girl is not an immediate threat," an unmasked man at the end of the line stated. "The son is dead. I killed him myself."

Daryl blinked slowly, unconcerned by the man's false claim for she knew what would come next. The look of pride faded as Lukai rounded on him, his eyes wild.

"Your impudence will not be tolerated, Tamaz."

Before Tamaz could react, the heel of Lukai's hand thrust into the man's jugular. Daryl heard the tearing of flesh and muscle, along with snaps and cracks of breaking bones, as she cast a sidelong glance at Tamaz. The show of strength had the desired effect on the other two members of second squad as they watched, horrified.

"Now, does anyone else want to contradict me?" Lukai screamed, veins in his forehead and temples bulging. The other members of second squad looked down at their toes and shook their heads.

"Good. Now, can anyone explain to me why letting Outteridge and the girl go is a problem?"

"He took the girl," replied Daryl, eager to get Lukai's showboating over with, "because she's important enough to risk his life saving. The bloodlines have to be protected or the guardians die out."

"But girls can't be guardians, can they?" the third member of second squad asked, making the other woman flinch.

Instantly, Lukai was before the man, twisting his neck up and back and letting him fall to the ground, his head practically turned around.

"Get these out of here," Lukai commanded his brutes before straightening the lapels of his jacket and stepping in front of the woman from second squad. "Take them to the van outside. Put them in the back. As for you, Outteridge and the Sinclair girl should never have been allowed to escape. Any remaining bloodline is a threat. The girl may not be a guardian, but she can birth one. I now have a substantial mess to clean up."

Daryl smirked as the woman, knowing what to expect, parried Lukai's hand and reached toward him, her fist striking his cheek as her jaw began to elongate. Before the force of the blow could make itself known, Lukai had her hand locked in his grip. Despite her bestial nature, the woman was no match for a vampire lord. Twisting her wrist, Lukai forced the woman to her knees, howling in pain. Daryl waited dispassionately as he grabbed her shoulders and drove his knee into her chest, stopping her heart with the blow.

Daryl forced herself to look interested as, adjusting his tie, Lukai stepped in front of her. She had always wondered what it would be like to tear out the throat of one of the masters.

"Track them, follow them, but do not act against them until instructed to do so," Lukai ordered. Daryl nodded as if that was not what she already intended. "First, burn all this down."

-1-

LOS ANGELES COUNTY, CALIFORNIA
March 15, 2029

Mariela Michaelis unfolded the letter, an actual pen and paper letter and not an email or instant message, and began to read. Ink on paper was a novelty in a time when everything was digital and there for the taking. Even the slickest computer expert could not hack a hard copy, and a message this risqué needed to be secure. The letter had been sent by special courier, a trusted associate from the motherland, rather than left to chance by using the postal service. The sensitive nature of the documents warranted the extra effort.

Mariela had known the moment she had looked at the surveillance feed and seen him waiting for a response to his polite but firm knocking that the courier brought news from home. Despite having lived in California for so many years, more years than she had spent in the motherland, Mariela still considered Belarus her home. Her family's estate, a few miles outside Minsk, had been gifted by the tsar many generations ago, and Mariela would one day inherit the estate, returning home to take up her family duties. Until then she would enjoy the life she had made for herself in Los Angeles.

Opening the door, Mariela found the man to be much older than she had first thought. The tight bunch of lines at the corners of his eyes suggested a maturity in years that was easily missed at first glance thanks, in part, to his long dark curls, pulled back into a ponytail. As she opened the door, the man removed the letter from the inside pocket of his navy-blue suit jacket and handed the letter to Mariela. No words were spoken, or needed, just the slightest of nods as the letter changed hands.

7

The man had left immediately, leaving Mariela to withdraw to her study, calling briefly to her husband that she was going to do a little reading.

"Okay dear," Dave shouted back from the kitchen. "Let me know when you want something to eat."

Mariela read the letter a second time.

M,

We need to step up the operation. N and I are in agreement that the current pace is unacceptable. An agent acting in our interest has devised a plan that will provide us with an opportunity beyond compare. Be ready to act. N has instructed her operatives to capture and stockpile as much new resource as possible the moment the signal is given. Your influence with the local authorities has been instrumental to our efforts within Los Angeles and the state of California. As such, you are charged with ensuring that this continues to be the case as we expand our operations. All local operatives, mine and N's, will take orders from you going forward. Succeed and you will be officially inducted into our organization. Failure will not be tolerated.

L

Mariela leaned back in her chair and twisted her dark-blonde hair around her index finger, a wry smile spreading across her thin lips. Her highlights would need re-doing soon, but right now there were more important matters, years of careful manipulation were about to pay off. Naturally, the letter contained no detail on the nature of the signal or the stock that Nikola's operatives were cataloging, just in case it did fall into the wrong hands. Nothing in the letter would enable the enemy to decipher their agenda or identify the people involved.

Even so, Mariela pulled a lighter from one of the drawers in the writing bureau, a nineteenth-century mahogany piece that she had acquired at auction for a very respectable price, and set the flame it produced to the letter. As the flames licked their way toward her fingers, Mariela moved her hand over the wastebasket, holding the burning paper a fraction too long before dropping it into the can. With the evidence disposed of, Mariela gently sucked the tips of her singed fingers as she pulled up her cousin's number on her phone.

"Vasily," Mariela said the moment he answered, standing and crossing the room. "We need to meet. Be at the marina on Sunday. I expect to see you at the yacht for lunch."

"Can it wait until Monday? I was going to take Brianna down to Maneadero for the weekend to see her niece," came Vasily's mumbled reply.

"It wasn't a request, cousin," Mariela replied sharply as she pulled a bottle of single malt from the small drinks cabinet she kept in the study.

The range of drinks available was vastly inferior to the main cabinet situated in the drawing room, but Mariela found it convenient to keep a bottle or five close at hand. "Be there."

Ending the call before Vasily had a chance to comment further, Mariela poured herself a generous measure of whiskey and took a small sip, savoring the earthy aroma and the peaty warmth of the whiskey as it slipped down her throat.

Mariela's study was entirely hers; not even her husband entered her sanctuary. It was the one room in the house where she could completely relax with no expectations of her. No playing the host or maintaining an appearance for the benefit of others. One downside of being the mayor's wife was that all eyes were on her during public events. Not so in this room.

Releasing a breath she had not realized she was holding, Mariela wondered what form the signal would take. Knowing Lukai, it would not be subtle.

2

SANTA BARBARA COUNTY, CALIFORNIA
March 16, 2029

The sound of tearing metal seemed to last forever. There was no way that would polish out.

"I'm going to have to call you back, Annie," said Alex as he steered his Mustang over to the central reservation. "The car in front braked suddenly."

"Oh my god," came Annalise's voice over the sound system. "Are you okay? Is there anything I can do?"

Alex shook his head as the car rolled to a stop. Annalise was a sweet girl but ditzy at times. "Not from where you are. Look, I'll call you later."

"Okay. Missing you."

Alex killed the line without replying as his victim stepped out of her car and marched to inspect the damage. Everything about her, from the determined stride to her tightly pursed lips, suggested this was going to cost him. While she checked her car, Alex reached into the glove compartment for his insurance papers. A pack of gum, some old tissues, his friend's beanie, and a book Annalise had left behind. No documents.

"Crap," he muttered, closing the door and checking behind the sun visor, just in case they were there. He was going to have to call Skylar. His sister would be so pissed.

Stepping from his vehicle, Alex raised two fingers to the other driver to indicate he would be with her shortly and thumbed through his contacts. Resting one foot on the sill and his thick, brawny forearm on the open door, he hit the dial icon and waited for his sister to pick up.

Even at this early hour, the California sun was making its presence felt. Eager to be done with the mildest, driest winter on record, mother nature was pushing hard for spring to begin in earnest. They were barely halfway through March, and the weather stations were warning of droughts and heatwaves. If the sunlight on the bare, dark-olive skin of his bulging biceps was anything to go by, another year of water restrictions was inevitable.

"Yo. What's baking, little bro?" Skylar called down the phone. The background noise gave Alex hope. It sounded like his sister was still on the road. Hopefully, not too far into her commute.

"Me," Alex replied, regretting not wearing a cap as he ran his fingers through his thick, black hair. "Any idea where my insurance papers are? Or who I'm with?"

It did not take much effort to imagine Skylar shaking her head and cursing under her breath in the moment of silence before answering. "What have you done this time, Xing-Fu?"

The use of his birth name confirmed Skylar's disappointment. Born in Hong Kong as Zhang Xing-Fu, Alex was an orphan with no record of who his real parents were. Zhang was a common surname, and the fact that Alex could not be certain it was his parents' name or just the one provided by the orphanage made finding his parents near impossible. That was why he had hired a private investigator. As grateful as Alex was to Skylar and her uncle for adopting him, not knowing who he was and where he came from left Alex feeling incomplete.

Alex's Chinese heritage was easy to overlook. The dark tone of his skin made people assume he was a mixed-race African-American. Considering his sister's pale, European complexion it was not a massive leap of logic to think one of his parents was white. Skylar would bristle at that assumption as if it was some sort of personal insult that people thought he was what he looked like. It made no difference to Alex. The body he was born with was not about to change shape or color to suit the world view of other people. His time was better spent working on aspects he could change and improve. Right now, he had a situation in dire need of improvement.

"Where are you?" Skylar demanded once he had explained his predicament.

Alex was on the outskirts of Santa Barbara, heading northwest to Santa Maria. Any later and his sister would have already been heading east on the 101 to her office in Los Angeles. As it stood, Skylar was running late and still heading to the highway from their home in Santa Paula.

"Okay, I'll be there as soon as I can."

"Thanks, sis," Alex replied, but she was already gone.

Slipping his phone back into his pocket, Alex went to inspect the damage to his car. He must have caught it at exactly the wrong angle as the entire front wing of the car was hanging off. The other driver had finished inspecting and photographing the damage to her car, a broken taillight and buckled panels were the only visible issues, and was heading his way.

"What gives?" The woman asked as Alex tried pushing the wing back into place. "Did you not see me braking?"

Alex released the buckled sheet of metal. Even if it had stayed in place, it would have made no difference. There was no air in the tire. Something must have torn the sidewall as he swerved to avoid the collision.

"Don't you try and intimidate me, rolling your shoulders like that," she snapped. Alex looked at the woman with confusion at her accusation. He was unaware he had rolled his shoulders in an intimidating manner. "You think just because you're a man, flashing your muscles in that tank top, you can bully me into letting you get away with ramming my car. Well, you've got another coming."

Alex crossed his arms and sat down on the hood of his car. "I was going to suggest you take down my name and number, as I don't have my insurance details with me. That way, you could continue your journey while I sit here waiting for a recovery truck. Now, I'm not so sure that's a good idea. That sounded a lot like an attack. I'm not sure I want to provide my details to somebody prepared to openly attack me in broad daylight like that."

The woman's mouth opened and closed as she stammered a few buts at Alex's unexpected response.

"Perhaps we should call the police and let them take care of this," Alex continued, regretting the decision to perch on the car as the heat stored in the black metal panel radiated through his shorts. "I know I would feel a whole lot safer with a police officer present. You know, to make sure I'm not subjected to another verbal assault motivated by discrimination."

"But I have to get to a meeting," the woman replied, losing some of her bluster at the suggestion that she was being sexist and racist. "I can't afford to wait here for the police to arrive."

"Sucks to be you. I'm in no rush to be anywhere," Alex lied, pulling his phone from his pocket as if to make good on his proposal.

"Wait," the woman said, waving her hands at Alex to emphasize her request.

Alex recoiled, playing to the victim role as if he was afraid she was reaching out to strike him. Unsettled by a big, strong man reacting in such a way, the woman immediately backed away.

"Please, I didn't mean to offend," said the woman, glancing around as if she was worried somebody had recorded her actions. "I've been under a lot of stress lately. My firm is on the verge of securing this big contract that will secure my promotion to VP of sales. I let it get the better of me. I'm sorry. I'm sure you're a very fine person. I didn't mean to imply you are violent just because you're a man."

Alex suppressed a smile as he returned to a more relaxed position, using it as an opportunity to get off the hood of the car. He had only intended to highlight her stereotypical attitude toward men of his build. The retraction and apology were unexpected.

"Look," the woman continued, looking over at Alex's crumpled wing, "the damage to my car isn't very much. What do you say to the idea that we forget this ever happened? Nobody is hurt, and the damage to your car is punishment enough for not paying attention. I can still make it to my meeting, and you can do whatever it is you need to do. Deal?"

Alex pretended to think about it. There was no way he was going to pass up the opportunity to avoid the hassle of dealing with the insurers, even if it did mean funding repairs himself, but he wanted to make her sweat for being so abrasive.

"Okay," he replied before the woman became too flustered. "I think I can overlook your attack since it didn't get physical. Sticks and stones as they say."

Relieved, the woman thanked him for his understanding and hurried back to her car. Alex waited until she had re-joined the traffic and was hurtling toward Sacramento before examining the damage again. This would make for an entertaining story when Skylar arrived.

Explaining why he was heading to Santa Maria would be more challenging.

3

VENTURA COUNTY, CALIFORNIA
March 16, 2029

Alex watched his sister's face for a reaction as he described his roadside ordeal. Her midnight-black hair was pulled back into a basic ponytail, making it easy to scrutinize her expression. There was no tell-tale twitch in the corner of her mouth. Apart from a brief admonishment upon arrival, her full lips had remained pursed for their journey back to Santa Paula. Her focused but cool, blue eyes remained fixed on the road ahead of them. A slight nostril flare was the only indicator of her displeasure at his behavior.

"I don't know whether to be impressed or disgusted, Batman," she said after considering his story for a moment. Alex's fondness for all things related to the caped crusader had earned him the nickname only his sister used. "I can't condone playing the victim card, but turning her attitude back on herself must have been satisfying."

It was. Seeing her grapple with the concept that she was being intolerant almost made up for the aborted journey. Almost. With his car off the road, there was no way he would make it to Reika before she left for Tacoma.

Of all the private eyes Alex had contacted, Reika Pfeiffer was the best investigator by far. Although talented, none of the other candidates had the impressive international experience Reika wielded. Given his circumstances, Alex considered that experience vital. Gazing out at his Mustang, perched on the back of the truck ahead of them, Alex regretted not going to meet her earlier in the week.

"Why Santa Maria?" Skylar asked, swiping at the stalk to indicate her intention to turn off the 101 for Santa Paula.

It was the question Alex was dreading. "I thought I'd take the weekend to go hiking up around Orcutt."

Alex was a hopeless liar when it came to deceiving his sister. A career built on extracting information from suspects outmatched Alex's career of lifting weights and goofing around. He tried to look casual. The trick was to act like nothing was wrong. If she caught him watching her from the corner of his eye, Skylar would suspect something. Instead, Alex turned his head back to her and waited. Her eyes darted in his direction before returning to the road. He wanted to shift attention to another topic, but that would raise her suspicion, not dispel it.

Act natural, he thought as the seconds ticked by. *Don't stare*.

Turning to face the front again, Alex pulled out his phone. Checking for messages was a perfectly natural thing to do. Staying silent was not.

"At least you get a day off work," he said, sliding his phone back into his pocket. Skylar would be expecting a flippant or sarcastic comment. Taking everything seriously was her job, not his.

"It doesn't work like that, Alex," Skylar replied, casting another sidelong glance in his direction. Rather than avert his gaze at being caught watching her through peripheral vision, Alex turned and smiled.

"Come on. You could do with a break after working so hard for this promotion. Since my day is ruined, why don't we chill out in the pool?"

"It doesn't work like that," Skylar repeated with a sigh. "Although, it is tempting."

Alex clapped his hands together, careful not to overdo it. Although it seemed like he had avoided the interrogation, it was possible his sister was luring him into a false sense of security.

"That's decided then. Pull into the market on the way through town, and I'll run in and get some steaks for a barbecue."

Skylar hesitated. "I can't, Alex. Besides, there's steak in the house."

"Suit yourself."

Alex turned away and watched the countryside roll by as he contemplated his next move. Patches of yellow and brown tarnished the greenery of the emerging spring, making it seem like high summer outside the air-conditioned car. He watched Skylar's reflection in the window as she reached forward and adjusted the radio, turning the volume up as some old rock song started playing. People were often surprised to discover that the stern, no-nonsense Skylar Sinclair-Blake, looking like the stereotypical special agent in her graphite business suit, was a metalhead.

"Don't you have any easy listening stations, Sky? Riding with you is audio assault and battery. I'm going to need therapy after this."

Blood of a Guardian

"The word is aural. Aural assault and battery. And 'Number of the Beast' is a classic. Don't dis the Irons."

"I thought oral was... You know," Alex replied as he made an obscene gesture with his hand and mouth.

"Aural, with an 'a' and a 'u' in it, not oral. Now, are you going to tell me what's in Santa Maria?"

"People, houses, dogs, cats," Alex replied, turning and flashing Skylar a cheeky grin. "Gypsies, tramps and thieves."

"Okay, Alex. I'll stop asking questions if you stop trying to sing."

"Ouch. That stings," Alex replied with mock offense, grateful that his sister was dropping the interrogation. He did not relish the idea of confessing he was meeting with Reika.

Skylar had taken an instant dislike to Reika. She failed to see the irony that, in Alex's eyes, the pair were similar in so many ways. Skylar claimed that Reika was too cold and logical, uncaring of Alex's feelings in her search for answers, all the while ignoring the fact that she could be just as harsh when she forgot to switch her work brain off.

Alex took another long look at his damaged car. The torn panel was flapping in the wind as the recovery truck trundled down the highway. Hopefully, Reika could reschedule their meeting.

"You, know," Skylar began, turning the radio down a touch to make it easier to be heard, "this is a great example of your problem, Alex."

Alex tuned out, half-listening to his sister's lecture on fulfilling his potential and making the occasional "uh-huh" to sound like he was taking it all in. He knew that she knew he wasn't listening, but Skylar pressed on regardless. Alex had heard it all before. He enjoyed his job as assistant manager at the local gym, but Skylar thought he was underselling himself. It came from a place of love, but being the high-flyer she thought he could be did not appeal to Alex. Sure, he wanted to better himself, but becoming president, ending disease or solving world hunger did not appear on his radar.

"I'm happy doing what I do," Alex said when he realized his sister had finished. "I've got my health, friends and a comfortable lifestyle. Why should I put myself through stress I don't need?"

Skylar sighed, allowing herself a moment's distraction to look him in the eye before turning her attention back to the road.

"If you say so, bro. I just want you to get the most out of life. As long as you're happy. That's what counts."

"Happier than a dancing penguin," Alex replied, grinning as his sister cracked a smile for the first time that morning.

The grin faded as Alex checked his phone. Still no reply from Reika. As much as Skylar wanted him to consider his future, Alex could not

16

relinquish his past. Not until he knew who he was.

-4-

LOS ANGELES COUNTY, CALIFORNIA
March 16, 2029

"This place is lame!"

Shay was positive she had misheard Karen over the pounding bass that filled the club. After queuing for two hours, gaining access to Emerald was the highlight of Shay's young life. A homage to some old film Shay had no interest in watching, Emerald was rapidly establishing itself as the hottest of hotspots among Santa Monica's influencers. Any moment now, socialites and celebrities would be pouring into the club's VIP section, passing Shay and Karen's strategically selected position by the stairs as they did so. It was unthinkable that Karen would scoff at such an opportunity.

"It's not so bad," Shay said with a smile, tossing her lustrous brown locks, professionally styled for tonight, as she held up her phone. "Got a guy's number."

Shay flicked her eyes down the room and watched Karen scan the available talent like a couple at a farmer's market, seeking out the best cut of beef.

"The Latino guy or the hunk of dark chocolate in the trilby," Karen shouted in Shay's ear, her voice sounding like a whisper.

"Neither," Shay replied, unsure what a trilby was but assuming it wasn't the name for the tribal artwork snaking up the arms of the muscular stud at the end of the bar. "To the right. No, my right. Tattoo Boy."

Karen looked again. "Going for a creamy latte instead of a dark Americano, huh?"

"Girl, that ain't white," Shay replied, putting her arm around the shoulders of the petite girl that had just walked up to them. "This is white."

"What?" Emily shouted, teasing a rogue blonde curl back into position. "I can't hear you over this noise. Too much bass, no treble."

Shay and Emily were inseparable from kindergarten until her parents moved away last year. The small fortune they made off the sale of their Santa Monica property allowed them to buy a house in Pasadena outright, taking early retirement and living off the surplus from the sale. Determined not to let the move ruin their friendship, Shay and Emily talked daily, by phone and video chat, but it wasn't the same as being in a room together. Having Emily around on Shay's first club night made the occasion extra special.

"I was just saying to Karen that Tattoo Boy down there ain't white."

"Who cares?" Emily replied with a dismissive shrug. "Where's Beth?"

Bethany was the one who had scored them their fake IDs for tonight's outing. Shay glanced around, suddenly aware that Bethany had been absent for ages. Knowing her, she was in a bathroom stall, skirt hiked up around her waist, getting filled by the first guy to buy her a drink.

"There," said Shay with a knowing grin as she spotted Bethany coming back from the bathroom. Her smile faded as she saw how frail her friend looked. Tapping Karen on the arm, Shay moved to intercept.

"Wassup?" asked Karen as they escorted Bethany to an unoccupied booth in a quieter section of the club.

"Nothing," Bethany said, giving the group a small smile. "Just can't get going today."

Blooms of sweat were spreading across Bethany's dress, and her face was flushed as she clutched her stomach, fighting the sickness that churned inside.

"This night's done," Karen stated, folding her arms across her chest as if there would be no discussion. "There is no way you're okay. We're getting you home."

"What? No," Shay protested. "You just need a drink, right, Beth?"

"Executive decision," Karen insisted. "We're getting Beth home."

Shay glanced at the others. Bethany was putting a brave face on, insisting she just needed to sit down for a minute. Emily wasn't falling for her nonsense and sided with Karen.

"I'll call a taxi," Emily said, getting up and heading for the door.

"Come with," Shay said, leaving the others at the table to go outside with Emily.

It was unseasonably warm for March but felt cool after the heat of the club, forcing Shay to suppress a shiver as she stepped outside. Emily tapped away on her phone as Shay pulled out a pack of cigarettes, stared longingly at the packet for a moment, then put them back in her purse before taking out her e-cigarette instead. Karen was forever preaching about the harmful effects of smoking, eventually convincing Shay to make a show of giving up, just to stop her nagging.

"Done," Emily said, putting her phone away. "Car's on its way."

"All because Beth's a lightweight," Shay sneered, her words coming out nastier than intended.

"Harsh. Girl can't help being sick."

"Sorry, Em. I was having such a great night was all. Now it's over."

"Tell you what, why don't we suggest a sleepover? You, me and Karen? I was going to stay with a cousin up in the Palisades, but I can cancel that and swing by as soon as Beth's safely home."

"No harm in asking," Shay said, looking back at the club. "Here she comes now."

Emily pitched the idea to Karen as they waited for the taxi to turn up, working out details and getting address information so Emily could book a car back to Karen's after dropping Bethany off. With a new plan in place, the girls returned to the club. It was hardly the glamorous night of reckless abandon that Shay intended, but it was clear from Bethany's spaced-out expression that staying out was not an option. Feeling a pang of guilt at her earlier obstinance, Shay wished Bethany the best with a gentle hug as they made to leave, despite Bethany advising against it.

"We've been with you for hours. We'll all be bedridden with the flu by Monday," Shay explained. "You get better, there will be other Emerald nights."

Leaving Emily to supervise Bethany, Shay and Karen opted to walk home from Emerald. The night was clear, and Karen's house was only a mile away. Besides, it gave them a chance to talk about the girls at school. By the time Shay had finished telling her about giving all the guys at the club her archrival's number in exchange for drinks, they were outside Karen's house.

"If only Emily had pulled that trick, I wouldn't have had to pay for half her drinks," Karen said, taking her keys out of her purse.

"Ah, so you're the one she conned into covering her debt," Shay replied as she checked her phone, hoping that Tattoo Boy wasn't one of those three-day-rule guys.

"What do you mean? She told me she had credit card fraud."

"That's one way to put it. She's the fraud for thinking she's richer than she actually is. Beth told me she maxed out her card on clothes."

"Sneaky bitch," Karen said with a laugh. "Good job we're the same size, she'll be lending me some of those new clothes when we go out next in that case."

Shay smiled and hugged Karen before setting off for her house.

As she strolled down the street, without the distraction of talking to Karen, Shay regretted not wearing a longer dress or bringing a sweater. The air had become decidedly cooler since leaving the club, providing a faintly dramatic touch that made Shay feel an unusual need to hurry. Picking up the pace, she reached into her purse for her e-cigarette. Her hand brushed against the cigarette packet. A moment's hesitation followed. Taking a cigarette from the pack, Shay rummaged around for her lighter. Vaping may have been the big trend, but Shay still felt the draw of a proper cigarette, that nicotine buzz that only a pack of menthols gave her.

Shay's house came into view as she held the lighter up to her face. As soon as she flicked the metal wheel on her lighter, the streetlamp above her head flicked off. No sound, no warning. Shay froze as the world fell away from the flame that sprang up in front of her face. The flickering light made the world beyond it darker as her cigarette waited expectantly for its touch.

It's only a streetlamp, she thought as she lit and took a drag of her cigarette. *Relax, Shay.*

After a brief pause and a few long drags on her cigarette to steady her nerves, Shay took a few tentative steps, chiding herself for being such a chickenshit. This was not some horror movie where a bulb blowing meant you were about to get attacked by some creature of the night. Shay dropped the half-smoked cigarette and reached into her purse for her keys.

A light came on in the upstairs window of her house. That was good. No risk of waking her mother up with the sound of the shower. She'd need one to clean off the cigarette smell. Shay was in no mood for one of Karen's lectures. As she stamped out the cigarette with her heel, Shay's phone rang.

"That was quick," Shay said, dropping her keys in her rush to answer the phone to Tattoo Boy. "Missed me already, eh?"

"Not quite."

His voice sounded in stereo. It came from behind her, not the receiver. A hand clamped over her mouth as strong arms gripped her tight. Shay's mind raced against the panic that gripped her. She had heard the tales, warnings about girls being dragged off the street and assaulted, but never once thought it would happen to her. Not so close to home.

Shay kicked and struggled, trying to scream through his hand. It was no use.

5

LOS ANGELES COUNTY, CALIFORNIA
March 17, 2029

Francis Eckhart watched nervously, rubbing his dark, mustache-less goatee with his left hand, as another steel barrier was lowered into place at the junction of Saticoy and Topanga Canyon Boulevard. What began as a handful of suspected food poisoning cases at the start of the evening had escalated into a full-scale medical emergency as thousands of citizens descended on the city's hospitals with extreme flu-like symptoms. The Centers for Disease Control and Prevention were quick to react, establishing a quarantine zone when people started vomiting blood.

One hundred miles of these barricades needed to be installed by yesterday, turning most of the southern half of Los Angeles County into a prison for the estimated ten million people inside the quarantine. As terrible as the idea was, it paled in comparison to the horrific consequences of not taking such extreme precautions. Eckhart hoped it was enough.

"Hey," a woman called out from beyond the barrier as the next segment of the barricade was lifted off the truck. "What's going on?"

"Nothing to worry about, miss…" Eckhart paused and fixed the woman with his soft, hazel eyes until she announced herself as Miss Turner. "Return to your home and sleep easy."

It was okay for Miss Turner; she was on the right side of the barrier. For the poor souls trapped on Eckhart's side, the only rest would be the sleep of the dead. Eckhart rubbed his furrowed brow as another segment of barrier touched down, keeping Miss Turner safe and moving Eckhart another step closer to captivity. The temptation to slip through the blockade before it was erected was strong. Having witnessed the death that awaited, nobody would blame him.

Eckhart doubted that the sight that greeted him upon arriving at the emergency room of the UCLA Medical Center would ever leave his mind. The sight of hundreds of people crowding the hospital, wailing in agony as sores wept pus and blood, while the beleaguered nurses and doctors attempted to establish some form of order was like something from a disaster movie. Officers in hazmat gear were brought in to suppress the sporadic fighting that broke out as patients became desperate for medical attention.

The true horror of the situation was captured perfectly when a young boy, no more than six years of age, fell to his knees at the entrance to the hospital and vomited all over the sidewalk before collapsing into the spreading pool of bile and blood. Rather than helping the child, people continued to force their way into the already packed waiting room, trampling the child to death. Knowing that the boy's fate was already sealed did nothing to alleviate the gut-wrenching terror of seeing his frail, pox-ridden body crushed beneath the boots of frightened adults. Until that moment, Eckhart doubted the CDC's call for a quarantine was warranted. Now, it seemed like the only rational course of action.

"I prayed we wouldn't need these," an officer said as Eckhart marched up the line.

Every few junctions, another section of the barricade was being started. Drones hovered above them, mapping the progress of the barricade and downloading position data to the cranes below. The precision with which the cranes placed each section, enabling each line to join without gaps in the barrier, amazed Eckhart. When people talked about machines replacing humans, he thought of robotic arms assembling vehicles and television sets, not heavy machinery imprisoning citizens in a plague-ridden city. As troubling as the image was, Eckhart was impressed by the speed at which the barrier was being erected. At this rate, they might have the full perimeter in place by sunrise. Then they could turn their attention to helping those unfortunate enough to be within the quarantine.

"A necessary evil," Eckhart said to the officer as a group of citizens approached. "If this outbreak is as deadly as the CDC predicts, we need to stop it from spreading."

Eckhart turned his attention from the barriers, a product of the last mayor's response to the 2024 riots, and gestured to the officers equipped with riot gear to ready themselves. Although commissioning the barriers in response to the riots was beyond excessive, Eckhart was grateful the

LAPD had them. If ever there was a need for such drastic measures, this was it.

"Citizens," Eckhart called out as he tucked his cap under his arm. He had elected to stick with a standard police uniform instead of donning full riot gear, to avoid projecting a militaristic look. "How can I help you?"

"You can start by telling us what's going on," a burly man in white pajamas, covered by a flannel robe, shouted in response. His demand was backed up by a chorus of enthusiastic cries from the eleven people gathered around him.

"We need to erect these safety barriers for some work being carried out," Eckhart replied with the calm yet authoritative voice that made him such a powerful speaker as well as the deputy chief of the LAPD.

"Why?"

It was a reasonable question, although Eckhart did not see who shouted it, and one that he had dreaded answering. The official line was to say nothing and avoid a panic. Internet and phone signals were down all over the county to slow the circulation of news and misinformation that could create a panicked uprising before a proper containment was in place. Eckhart knew that saying nothing would not prevent a panic. People would concoct their own theories and make wild assumptions. Although the likelihood of those assumptions being worse than the reality of being trapped inside a walled city with a deadly outbreak was slim, Eckhart could not allow rumors to go unaddressed.

"For the safety of the citizens of LA," Eckhart replied. As explanations went, it ranked only slightly higher than "because...reasons" on the scale of vagueness, but it was all he had. "Now, I suggest you try and get a good night's sleep. I'll inform my officers to keep the noise to a minimum. Hopefully, we'll be out of your way before too long."

Eckhart stood with arms folded across his powerful chest as the group debated with itself. It was hard to gauge which way they would go, especially at such an early hour in the morning.

"I must admit," said Eckhart, uncrossing his arms and adopting a relaxed posture to win them over, "I envy you. I really do."

His words were tantalizing enough to distract the group from their discussions. A reticent hush fell over the crowd as they waited to find out why the deputy chief was envious of a group of nervous citizens being corralled by the LAPD.

"I am so tired," Eckhart began, slowly shaking his bald head to emphasize the despondency in his voice. "I started my shift nineteen hours ago. Nineteen hours. I should be in bed right now. That's why I'm jealous of you good folks. Jealous of the warm beds that are just a brisk walk away. Jealous that you can curl up next to your loved ones while I'm out here, watching over these vehicles to make sure they cause as little disruption to your lives as possible."

Faces turned to each other in a mix of sympathy and confusion. Eckhart seized on the opportunity by singling out a woman at the edge of the group. The way she clutched a teenage boy, lines of worry on her brow, identified her as one of the least confrontational members of the group.

"You, miss," Eckhart called out, nodding when the woman anxiously gestured that she wanted to remain a faceless part of the mob. "Can I interest you in taking the rest of my shift? It's really easy. Follow these vehicles and make sure they place these barriers in a straight line. They should be done in another six to eight hours. That way, I can go home, climb into bed next to my loving wife, and get a good night's sleep."

The woman shook her head vigorously as she shrank back into the throng, dragging her son with her. Unimpressed with the prospect of being called upon to take Eckhart's shift, she was not the only one to shy away from the deputy chief.

"Guess I'm here until the job's done," said Eckhart, replacing his hat and adopting an authoritative stance. "You're more than welcome to stand around and observe, but watching these cranes does get boring very quickly. Personally, I'd come back in the daylight, having had a good night's sleep, and watch us dismantle them."

Eckhart turned and marched back to the barrier, stopping before the sergeant of the riot suppression team. The look on the sergeant's face suggested Eckhart's gamble had paid off.

"Well played, sir. Half of them have turned back. The others don't appear to have any fight in them."

"For now," Eckhart replied, resisting the urge to look back over his shoulder. "The day is young."

6

VENTURA COUNTY, CALIFORNIA
March 17, 2029

"Where did I put that file?" Skylar muttered to herself as she moved papers out of the way on the desk she had squeezed behind. The events of yesterday evening had her operating out of her old office at the Ventura County Resident Agency. Her old office stood empty for three years, ever since she transferred, and it was easy to see why nobody rushed to claim the space. The claustrophobic closet was a far cry from her beautiful Los Angeles office. It felt like going back to a high school desk.

"Hold on guys. I need to get my bearings here. I'm not in my normal office space."

"Understood, Sinclair," said the bald man on the left screen. Skylar had his name written down. Somewhere. Ah, yes. Agent Victor Adams of the Federal Emergency Management Agency.

The first conference call of the day. Since the city of Los Angeles was declared a quarantined zone in the middle of the night, Skylar's life was set to be one endless stream of reports and conference calls. Everyone was on call until they figured out what was going on. Skylar hoped this call would bring answers. She didn't hold much faith in getting them from the two clowns from FEMA.

The man on the right let out a *tsk* and whispered to someone off-screen, forgetting that the microphone on his computer would still pick up his voice. "So wasteful. Who even uses paper these days?"

"Okay," Skylar said as she located her briefing papers, pretending not to notice the remark about her preference for paper copies. She had no doubt the agent would provide an opportunity for payback during the call. "I'm all set. Doctor Lewis. Would you mind starting us off with our current status?"

Doctor Taylor Lewis from the CDC was an old friend of Skylar's from university, but they had not kept in touch beyond the annual Christmas card. By the time Skylar returned from training in Quantico, Taylor was starting a career at the CDC in New York. Even so, his name on the list of attendees was a welcome sight. Skylar knew that she would not be the only one looking to cut through all the bureaucratic crap and get the job done. There was too much that did not add up to be wasting time on red tape.

"It's still early stages," Taylor replied, eyes scanning a set of notes on a second screen as he spoke. "We're running all the tests we can to get a definite cause, but everything so far is pointing to an, as yet, unidentified strain of anthrax. Early symptoms include skin ulcers and blisters, usually accompanied by swelling and itching sensations around the face, head, and neck."

Taylor paused to make sure everyone was keeping up.

"What about degradation symptoms? Nausea, heartburn, indigestion, upset stomach, diarrhea?" Skylar asked with no hint of sarcasm. Taylor cracked a brief smile, unable to contain himself.

"Easy bleeding, easy bruising, fever, the works," he said, snapping back into serious business mode. "Chills, flushed skin, fainting, bloody vomiting, diarrhea-"

"Christ help us," Victor interrupted. Skylar whipped her head to glare at him.

"-and death as a result of what looks to be brain hemorrhaging," Taylor continued, ignoring the outburst. "Usually between eight and twenty-four hours after. In about half the cases we've logged so far the victims begin bleeding out of every orifice as the body shuts down."

"Oof. This thing is a beast," Skylar said as Taylor finished his gruesome list. The FEMA agents looked like they were about to puke.

"It is," Taylor said, looking grim. "We're facing a very, very high mortality rate."

"Is it airborne, Taylor?" Skylar asked, unable to keep a note of nervousness from her voice.

A shake of Taylor's head was reassuring. Rubbing her forehead, Skylar looked away from the screens for a moment. Not for the first time, she thanked the stars that her detour to collect Alex on Friday resulted in her working from home. If this thing was as dangerous as Taylor claimed it would wreak havoc as an airborne contagion. Correction, more havoc. News that it was not airborne would not be much to the citizens within LA, but it would calm some of the neighboring counties.

"So, what is this? The next Ebola?" the man on the right asked. Skylar sighed and checked her notepad. Colin Klein. Pen in hand, Skylar scribbled the word "dipshit" next to his name.

Taylor was drumming his fingers on his desk in annoyance, out of sight of the webcam. "Not even close. It doesn't have an obvious source, and it doesn't have the traditional signs of being a true epidemic. It's very concentrated. We're trying to figure out why. As soon as we know what we are dealing with, we can stop it."

"That's why we're on this call, agent," Skylar quipped, leaning her head into her hand and giving Colin her most exasperated look. "At least, now, we've got some means of identifying the infected. That'll make managing the quarantine a little easier."

"Not necessarily, Sinclair," Taylor replied before taking a sip of coffee. He always was a bean freak. Dealing with this outbreak would have him chain drinking. "It could take several days for those affected to show any symptoms."

"Oh, Christ help us," Victor blurted again. That guy had watched way too many disaster movies before taking this job. "We need to send out evacuation alerts. Have you, uh, contacted the Emergency Operations Center, Sinclair?"

What a plonker, Skylar thought as Taylor raised an eyebrow at the camera. She opened her mouth to rip him a new one, but Taylor cut in.

"Who would we be evacuating, Victor? I just said it can take days for symptoms to manifest. That means seemingly healthy people could be carrying whatever this is."

"Okay, boys," Skylar said as Victor began to speak, ending the debate before it gained any momentum. Her voice dropped lower. "So, we need to secure and maintain the quarantines. We also need to get supplies to the points of dispensing. Doctor Lewis?"

"It will be another thirty-six hours before we can scrounge up enough information on how to adequately treat this. Like I said, it's still early stages. What we can do is prep every anthrax countermeasure we have in our arsenal for the PODs."

"Brilliant. Thanks, Taylor," Skylar replied before giving each of the FEMA bozos a stern glare. "Now here's what I need you two to do. Have your New York emergency response coordinators send me their reports, along with relief effort strategies. Employ the STARCC principles. Conduct resource assessments using the National Response Framework and get inventory STAT. The city needs to know where it can pick up whatever countermeasures the CDC can provide. Until then I need every scientist and health surveillance employee you have glued to this task. And have you even bothered to contact any private sector agencies for input, or do I have to spoon-feed that to you too?"

Victor sat there, dumbstruck. Colin conferred with whoever he had in the room with him. Skylar waited for an answer, growing even more impatient with their inability to provide answers promptly. Taylor was smirking. She was not having any more of their wishy-washy bullshit today. *Contact the EOC? What am I, an intern?*

"Any time fellas. It's not like we've got a state of emergency to deal with or anything," Skylar reprimanded, tapping her pen against the desk as she spoke.

Their discussion became more hurried. Skylar waited until Colin was just about to answer what she thought was a simple question before hitting him with a metaphorical slap.

"Perhaps if you wrote down some notes before attending a meeting, you wouldn't have so much difficulty answering questions. Next time, grab yourself a pen and paper and take some notes. Now, have you done what I asked?"

"We have, from our office," Taylor said raising his cup and tipping it at her to show the reason for Skylar's dig had not gone unnoticed. "We're on top of things here."

"Thanks, Taylor," Skylar replied, putting her pen down before addressing the FEMA agents. "As a precaution, I need you two to draw up a risk assessment and contingency plans for the adjacent counties, including plans for a potential evacuation, and a list of resources you can bring to bear."

That should keep them busy.

"Will do, Sinclair," Victor answered, eager to make amends for his earlier missteps. "We'll start that right away."

"Meeting adjourned."

Skylar hit the button to end the meeting and sat back in her chair. There were too many unknowns concerning this outbreak for her liking. That would change.

7

VENTURA COUNTY, CALIFORNIA
March 17, 2029

Skylar's cell rang almost immediately after she ended the meeting.

"Now, I may be stepping out of my bounds here," Taylor began the moment she answered, "but that may have been a bit harsh."

"Seriously?" replied Skylar, her voice rising with each syllable. "People are dying. We're less than a day into this mess, and so far, the evidence is taking a fat dump on all our theories. It bears all the hallmarks of a terrorist attack but no terrorist group has taken ownership. Twenty cities around the world have been hit, with nothing to link them. We have no idea what this outbreak's origin is, and the news is even saying that it's the Armageddon virus. We've got the media up our asses for details. The number of people dead is already staggering. I need to crack down on these assholes as much as I can. Without them turning this into the next big zombie apocalypse franchise."

"Well, the news has it wrong. Anthrax isn't a virus."

Skylar grinned. Trust Taylor to pick out that correction within her rant. "I'll leave you the honor of telling them that they need to be calling it the Armageddon Infection to stoke the correct level of panic, Doctor Lewis."

"Thanks. Seriously though, know that the CDC is throwing everything we have into finding out what this son-of-a-bitch is."

Skylar did not doubt it. Her frustration was not with Taylor or the CDC. She wanted answers. Something she could build an action plan around.

"I know," Taylor replied when Skylar explained her position.

"You're an impatient woman. When you say jump, heaven help anyone who wastes time asking 'how high.' On a more positive note, at least you're outside the quarantine. Gives you some flexibility."

Skylar nodded at the stroke of fortune that she happened to be outside the city when the outbreak struck. Talk about a blessing in disguise. As a precaution, the FBI scheduled an emergency check-up on arrival at the office and gave her the all-clear. Taylor wasn't so lucky. He was in Manhattan when the quarantine of New York was announced. Skylar looked down at the list of affected cities. Beijing, Bogota, Buenos Aires, Cairo, Delhi, Dhaka, Jakarta, Karachi, Kinshasa, Kolkata, Lagos, Los Angeles, Manila, Mexico City, Mumbai, New York City, Rio De Janeiro, Sao Paulo, Shanghai and Tokyo.

"Do you have a safe place to go?" she asked, pulling at the cuffs of her suit as she pondered why those twenty were targeted.

"The lab is the safest place to be right now," he said, rubbing his cheek as he glanced across at something outside the view of the camera. "I transported the wife here yesterday. We have enough food and medical supplies. We should be fine."

"You will be. Vigilance, Taylor."

With a salute, Skylar signed out of the meeting. One down, an endless amount to go.

Skylar sighed and stretched before grabbing her mug and walking out of her broom closet of an office. The aroma of fresh coffee drew Skylar to the break room and a steaming glass pot. Next to it was a note. *Figured you might need this.* Diana's handiwork, bless her heart. That woman's caffeine addiction bordered on incurable. Not that Skylar was complaining. It meant a fresh batch was never far away.

Fresh cup in hand, Skylar walked back to her office to discover a new stack of reports in her inbox. How anybody managed to find time to do any actual investigation work with so many emails to contend with was a mystery to her.

"Soon," Skylar whispered, reminding herself she was in spitting distance of a senior position.

Looking up from her screen, Skylar groaned at the cramped conditions she was stuck with until that promotion was official. There was enough room for two people to sit and have a conversation, but it was hardly conducive to a productive working environment. There wasn't even a window, just a row of glass blocks instead of bricks eight inches from the ceiling. Her office in LA had three windows and enough room to comfortably sit another twelve agents, without them being so close they could file sexual harassment claims.

Skylar's computer beeped, bringing an end to her fantasizing about office space. The sun-beaten face of Jerry Horner appeared above an incoming video call notification. Jerry was assistant director of the counterterrorism division and Skylar's mentor, of sorts. Upon completing her training in Quantico, Skylar was asked to present her dissertation and thesis on criminal profiling and extremist mentalities to Jerry and the executive director. It seemed an odd request at the time. It was only when she received her first promotion that Jerry revealed there was a real possibility of Skylar being selected to take his place when he retired. All Skylar's progress since that day was with that goal in mind.

Skylar reached out and hit the accept button to start the video call.

"I can't make our call this morning," Jerry blurted, skipping formalities and niceties. It was one of the things Skylar admired about him. When things needed doing, he didn't waste time checking how your goldfish felt about it. There was a time and a place for small talk and high fives. This wasn't it. "Can you run the meeting?"

"Of course," she replied, struggling to hide her excitement at being given such an opportunity. "It's no problem. Anything else you need from me?"

"No, just keep up the good work. I'll send you my notes shortly. I made some inquiries about getting you assigned to counterterrorism full-time. There will be eyes watching how you handle the LA situation."

That caught Skylar by surprise. Before she could reply, Jerry ended the call and left her staring at a growing collection of emails.

In the midst of all the tragedy, that bit of news was enough to keep her going for weeks.

8

LOS ANGELES COUNTY, CALIFORNIA
March 17, 2029

Shay blinked away the fuzziness, waking from her drug-induced sleep to find her bones and muscles ached from being left on the floor. As details came into focus, she became aware of bars around her, lit by the ruddy, yellow light of the high ceiling lamps. Shay counted four lights above her, lighting what appeared to be a large barn. Or perhaps a warehouse. Lifting herself onto her elbows, she tried to get a better look at her surroundings. Her head swam, forcing her back onto the floor.

"It takes a few minutes to get your bearings," a voice gently called out to her. "Don't rush, it will just make you sick."

It smelt like somebody already had. The room stank of sweat, piss and vomit. Shay discreetly checked she wasn't the reason for the smell of urine. She had no idea what was going on, but there was small relief in the fact that she had retained control of her bladder. As the fog cleared from her mind though, the reality of the bars set in and forced her to attempt to sit up again.

Shay found herself trapped in a cage that, despite being spacious, was just a little too short to allow her to stand fully. Probably intended for transporting circus animals. The combination of rising and inhaling the horrid smelling air made Shay retch, forcing her to suppress the sickness. Even so, a little made it to her throat and left a lingering taste of puke in her mouth as she swallowed down the need to empty her stomach all over the floor of her cage.

In a cage, about six feet to her left, sat a boy around her age, maybe a little older, but certainly still in his teenage years. His unkempt hair partially hid a scattering of acne across his forehead, confirming his youth to Shay. This must have been the owner of the voice she had heard as the occupant of the cage opposite her was a younger boy who appeared to still be unconscious. In the cage next to his was a girl, possibly a little younger than Shay, who looked terrified. She was huddled in the corner of her cage, staring out like a rabbit in headlights.

"Where are we? What's going on?" Shay asked, sitting back down and trying to stop her stomach from rolling.

She recalled leaving Karen's house and walking home to get some things for a sleepover, stopping to smoke a cigarette on the way. The girls' night out had proven to be a farce. Shay remembered a streetlight going out as her memories began to fall in line, the bulb burning out as she entered its circle of light.

She patted her pockets to confirm her keys were not there. She had dropped them outside her house, rushing to answer her phone, and that was when somebody had grabbed her. Not just anybody, she recognized the tattoos on the arms that had grabbed her. It was the creep from the bar. She had given him her number, thinking he was cute, but now she began to think Karen was right and that boys were jerks. When he grabbed her, Shay was sure she was going to be raped or murdered. Or both.

There was a black car outside her house that she had not really noticed as she strolled home. When he had taken her, Tattoo Boy had drugged her and thrown her in the car. How long ago had that been? Her phone had been taken from her, along with her purse, and she felt lost and alone without it.

"I'm not sure what's going on," the boy replied. "There were some others here when I awoke, but they were taken out an hour or so ago, when you were brought in, and nobody has been back since. I'm Adam by the way."

Shay did not care what his name was. She was not here by choice and definitely wasn't here to make friends. She just wanted to get out and go home. Removing a hair clip, Shay shuffled up to the cage door and reached around to the lock. Wiggling the clip back and forth she managed to get it into the keyhole but was unable to turn the latch. Escaping from a locked cage was not as easy as it appeared in the movies. Reluctantly, Shay pulled the hairclip back out of the lock, but only half the clip came out.

"Shit," she cursed her luck.

During her walk home, Shay had thought about how much of a disaster the night had been but, in that moment, she would have given anything to be back home, safe in a nice warm sleeping bag on Karen's bedroom floor. If only she had not insisted on going home to fetch some things and just stayed at Karen's as they planned.

"So, when did they grab you? I'm assuming you were snatched from the street like me?" Adam continued trying to make conversation. "Was it a client?"

Shay ignored him, partly because she did not care and partly because she was unsure what he meant. There were some windows toward the top of the warehouse walls, about fifteen feet up, but Shay could not see anything that she could climb to get to them. She assumed just strolling out of the door was not an option. First, she had to figure out how to get out of this cage though.

"I thought I'd struck it lucky," Adam said, shifting his weight and leaning against the bars of his cage. "Rich looking dude, looking for a little excitement and a touch on the curious side. Five hundred bucks for a quick tug. Easy money, I thought. But when I opened the car door there was another dude in the back seat. Grabbed me and jabbed a needle in my arm. Next thing I knew I was waking up here."

"Wait, you're a prostitute?" Shay asked, suddenly putting two and two together and arriving at four.

"Yeah, I mean, aren't you?"

"You cheeky prick," Shay exclaimed. "How dare you call me some cheap slut?"

"I'm sorry, I just assumed by the way you're dressed that we were in the same line of business."

"No, I am not," Shay replied, tugging at her dress to make it seem longer. "This happens to be the height of fashion for young girls on a night out."

"Aren't you a bit young to be on a night out?" Adam asked, further infuriating Shay.

Her parents were constantly telling her the same thing. Shay was too angry at his assumption that she was a hooker to dignify Adam's question with a response. Besides, explaining that a bunch of seventeen-year-old girls had managed to obtain fake ID's and get into a nightclub would not result in her getting out of the cage.

There was a small part of Shay's frantically racing mind that was clinging to the hope that this was just a sick game, concocted for someone's amusement. Or perhaps a test, like those sick torture porn movies that were all the rage back in her parents' day. Shay looked around but couldn't spot any cameras and there was no sign of any ventriloquist's dummies anywhere. Perhaps the key to escaping required her cellmates after all.

"What's your name, honey?" Shay asked the girl across from Adam.

After what he had said, there was no way she was going to start by talking to that jerk. The girl just stared at Shay with that terrified look. Shay kept a slight smile on her face to ease her feelings.

"E-E-Emma," the girl said, just as Shay was beginning to think the girl was too traumatized to talk.

"Hey, Emma," Shay replied in the most soothing voice she could manage. "Is there anything near you that we could use to get out of these cages?"

Emma looked around her cell then shook her head. It seemed she would have to talk to Adam after all. Unfortunately, the effort was just as fruitless and Shay was left figuratively scratching her head as she tried to come up with a solution. She lost track of exactly how much time had passed and still had not figured out a way of getting out of the cage when the door to the warehouse opened. Shay almost leaped in excitement at the sight of a police officer in the open doorway and called out to him in earnest.

"What's going on here?" the officer called as he walked up to the cages. "why are you kids in there?"

"We don't know, officer," Shay replied.

We woke up here," Adam added.

"Woke up here?" the officer repeated as he looked back to the door. "How on earth did you get here?"

"I was grabbed by a guy outside my house," Shay replied before Adam could say anything more. "I was on my way home from a friend's house when he took me and drugged me. We were all snatched from somewhere."

"I see," the officer replied, turning to Shay but making no effort to open the cages. "And have you been mistreated at all?"

"We're in cages!" yelled Shay. "If this isn't mistreatment, what is?"

"I mean, nobody has..." the officer stopped mid-sentence as the door opened again and a pair of men entered. Shay noticed their gloved hands and figured these must be the ones who grabbed Adam. Neither of them looked like Tattoo Boy but it was safe to assume they were working together.

"Morning, Officer. What can we do for you today?" Asked the man on the left, reaching up to scratch his chin. His dark, almost black, beard was close-cropped but lacked the attention to detail required to call it designer stubble.

Even though there were two of them, the officer seemed unconcerned. His hand rested lightly on his service pistol, holstered but unclipped to allow for a quick draw if the need arose. Stepping away from Shay's cage to stand more central to the room, the officer removed his hat and tucked it under his arm.

"Do you mind explaining why there are kids in these cages?"

"We feel the need," it was the blonde man on the right's turn to talk, his accent foreign but unrecognizable to Shay, "to feed. We have a deal with your boss so run along now, mister policeman."

Shay's heart skipped a beat at the sound of those words. If it was true, these cannibals were taking children and eating them, and the head of the LAPD knew about it. Suddenly the police officer's calm demeanor made a lot more sense.

"Spare me the crappy puns. The deal was that you clean up the streets, slowly and quietly, and we turn a blind eye. The homeless, destitute, gangbangers and drug dealers. Not kids taken from the streets. It was bad enough when you started taking people with terminal illnesses, at least we could pretend it was for the best and that their suffering would stop. This is a step too far. We can't just make this disappear. We're talking about children for Christ's sake."

"Haven't you heard? There's a pandemic. Children are dying by the droves all across Los Angeles, we're just saving them the trouble of getting ill first," the bearded man replied. "We're being good Samaritans."

"New orders from our boss. I suggest you take it up with yours," the blonde man cut in before the officer could reply, scowling at his partner's flippant answer.

"I will," the officer replied, looking around the room one last time. He tried to avoid eye contact, but Shay managed to catch his gaze and held it for the briefest of moments. All hope of rescue drained from her at the sight of his expression, eyes filled with disgust at the situation but devoid of hope that he could do anything to help them. "In the meantime, get these children some proper accommodation, this place stinks worse than a farm. And make sure none of them are harmed."

Shay watched in dismay as the officer left, the two kidnappers stepping aside as he passed between them. As her captors conversed in a language she did not recognize, Shay looked around at her fellow captives. Impossibly, Emma seemed to have retreated even further into the corner of her cage while Adam's bravado and forced calm had shattered, tears rolling down his face as he silently cried at the thought that this was not some elaborate ransom scheme after all.

9

LOS ANGELES COUNTY, CALIFORNIA
March 17, 2029

Eckhart winced as the bulletproof shields lining the barricade rattled from the sustained impact of hundreds of bullets. At least the assault rifles were keeping the mob back. Nobody wanted to get hit by a stray round while attempting to breach the barrier. With communication networks restored, social media erupted, angrily protesting the fascist government and its dehumanizing treatment of its citizens. Those protests soon gathered momentum and became a rallying cry, prompting small mobs to seek revenge against the perceived mistreatment and breach the quarantine.

Eckhart, stood atop the barricade in a hazmat suit, sympathized with the people. Waking to find themselves shuttered behind a one-hundred-mile wall of reinforced steel and bulletproof shielding was a scenario that should only take place in Hollywood, not around it.

"We need to silence those guns," shouted a lieutenant in SWAT gear to Eckhart's right. "Where are our snipers?"

Eckhart was the only one on the nearly two-mile-long stretch of barrier between the I-5 and the 118 to be wearing a hazmat suit, a stark reminder that he was as much a prisoner of the quarantine as the scared citizens attempting to escape under the bridge below him. His position within the LAPD granted him special dispensation to man the barriers, provided he did not jeopardize the security of the containment.

"Non-lethal force, lieutenant," Eckhart called out, pushing the thought that he may also be infected from his mind. "We have our orders. I expect you to follow them."

"Seriously? They are firing at us!"

"We have our orders," Eckhart repeated, slamming his hand against the bulletproof shielding as a short, stocky man made his way along the barricade to Eckhart's position. "These barriers were designed for heavier fire than this. Until our orders change, be ready with the water cannons."

Avoiding further discussion on the matter, Eckhart turned and moved to intercept the man heading his way. The way his head pivoted nervously from side to side suggested this was his first combat mission.

"Deputy Chief Eckhart, I presume?" The man asked, thrusting out a hand.

"Yes," Eckhart replied, glancing at the outstretched hand but refusing to shake it. "What can I do for you?"

"I'm Meldon Brown, from the Occupational Safety and Health Administration. I'm here to carry out an assessment of the quarantine," the man replied, withdrawing his offer of a handshake and tapping on a screen he carried in his other hand. "Make sure everything is in order and you're fully equipped."

"Great," Eckhart replied, stepping aside to let the man continue along the barricade. "Once you've confirmed everyone here is wearing the proper respirators, perhaps you would like to go and tell those gunmen that shooting at us poses an occupational safety risk?"

"There's no need to be like that," Meldon began, but Eckhart was already advancing down the barricade to check the situation at the Rinaldi Street bridge. With the assault rifles discouraging people from approaching the barrier, a large number of citizens were spotted heading north on Sepulveda Boulevard, presumably to try their luck at Exit 72.

Realizing that gunfire would not gain them their freedom, the citizens attacking the barrier on Rinaldi Street were employing more creative methods. After attempting to ram the blockade in the tunnel with an armored van, a series of buses and trucks were being strategically positioned along the road to create a chicane path to minimize exposure to the water cannon situated above the bridge.

Admiring an ingenuity not normally associated with the mob mentality, Eckhart arrived at the bridge in time to see a telehandler, with ropes hanging from its forks, being maneuvered through the maze of trucks and buses.

"What do they hope to achieve with that?" Eckhart asked with incredulity as the FBI agent managing the defense of the bridge walked over and grasped his hand.

"Hey, Frank. I heard you were avoiding the riots downtown."

Eckhart shrugged as Michael Blake of the FBI's Critical Incident

Response Group squeezed his hand and shook it like a child trying to guess a Christmas present. The riots in the city were nothing more than the antics of opportunistic looters. Stretched thin by the fact that half of the LAPD were infected with whatever was sweeping through the city, Eckhart and Chief Parker agreed that maintaining the quarantine was the top priority. At least until reinforcements arrived.

"And I heard they sent your sorry ass over to lend a hand," Eckhart replied, gripping Mike's hand with equal vigor. "Thought I'd best check your team had enough pacifiers and blankies to go around."

"Why?" asked Mike as the forks of the telehandler struck the top of the barricade. "Did the LAPD leave theirs at the station?"

"No," said Eckhart as the water cannon blasted a torrent of water down onto the street, discouraging the citizens from attempting to scale the ropes attached to the telehandler. "As always, the FBI came in and took charge of the entire case. Pacifiers, blankies. Even the safety pins for the diapers. I guess you go through a lot of diapers over on Wilshire."

"More than I'd like to admit," Mike replied with a chuckle. "Now, what are we going to do about that forklift truck?"

"Telehandler."

"Okay, smartass. What are we going to do about that posh forklift?"

Eckhart reached over and tapped the shoulder of one of the agents operating the water cannon and gestured to the telehandler. "Get the rental company on the phone. Tell them we need access to the remote override of that vehicle. Stow the forks and lock it down."

The agent glanced at Mike for confirmation of the order, receiving a nod to proceed. Eckhart's wife, Daisy-Marie, was a South Dakota farm girl, and some of the knowledge about the vehicles her father taught her to operate had permeated Eckhart's brain. Surprised that the information proved useful, Eckhart gave Mike a brief explanation of the model's anti-theft software, feeling none of the excitement Daisy-Marie exhibited when she talked about geofencing and remote automation of the vehicle. How she got so worked up over some things was a mystery to Eckhart. To him, the vehicle was just a tool for lifting.

As the citizens retreated from another blast of the water cannon's powerful jets, Eckhart gave thanks that Daisy-Marie was outside the quarantine. Having moved to Baldwin Park straight after New Year's, their home was barely two miles beyond the eastern edge of the quarantine zone. It was a move that Eckhart had opposed for many months, preferring to move closer to Downtown and the office, but Daisy-Marie's enthusiasm for the house they eventually purchased won him over. In hindsight, it was the best decision they ever made. As rough as things were, they were less than twenty-four hours into the quarantine.

The real violence was still to come.

10

KYOTO PREFECTURE, JAPAN
March 17, 2029

With deft strokes of a pen, Daryl Metzger wrote the date on a label before tucking the pen behind her ear. On the bench before her, a large white rat squeaked as it clawed at the bars of its cage. Beside the cage, a stopwatch steadily cycled through the thirty-eighth minute. So far, so good. Daryl's hand drifted to the cluster of gold rings in her left ear as she lifted a soda can to her lips and sipped.

"Progress?" her master asked as he descended the stairs to Daryl's laboratory.

There was no sound as Mitsuhide crossed the room, coming to a stop behind her chair. No telltale clink or squeak of his boots on the tiled, polished floor. No rustle or clang of his all-encompassing samurai armor as he moved. Mitsuhide was the embodiment of stealth, a black hole of sound.

"Too early to tell," Daryl replied without taking her eyes off the rat. Its breathing was becoming labored. Daryl placed her soda can on her desk and reached for her pen.

"Dosage?" Mitsuhide asked.

Daryl's pen hovered over the sheet of labels. "180mg. Weight, 302.8g."

"About 12 times the lethal dose," said Mitsuhide, telling Daryl nothing she did not already know as the rat flopped onto its side and began convulsing.

Daryl's eyes flitted to the stopwatch as the rat gave one last pitiful breath, spasmed and died. Forty-four minutes was impressive, but not the highest survival time. Noting the time, Daryl peeled the label off the waxy backing paper and reached for a glass tube from a rack to her left. Careful to ensure it was parallel to the lip and centered on the test tube, she affixed the label and smoothed it flat.

"How many subjects?" Mitsuhide asked as Daryl stood, moved the sheet of labels aside, and reached for a syringe.

"With this one, thirty-five," replied Daryl, lifting the rat from its cage and pushing the needle into its limp body. "Average survival time of forty minutes, twenty-eight seconds."

Mitsuhide stepped to the side as Daryl half-filled the test tube with blood and forced a rubber bung into its top. Ignoring the samurai, Daryl crossed the room and opened one of three freezers against the side wall. At this rate, it would not be long before she needed a fourth. Each of the shelves was filled with racks holding blood-filled tubes. Finding a space at the top of the freezer, Daryl placed the tube in the freezer and returned to her desk. The laboratory was well equipped, there was no denying that. Mitsuhide provided anything she asked. Even the fridge under the desk for sodas. Daryl thought she was pushing her luck when she requested that.

Emptying her can before taking another blood sample, Daryl piped a drop of blood onto a microscope slide and slid her chair over to the microscope at the end of her desk. Dropping into her chair, Daryl placed the slide under the microscope and twisted the dials to bring the image into focus.

"What is it?" Mitsuhide asked after a moment.

Daryl moved the slide, examining the sample until she was sure of the result before pushing back and standing up. "See for yourself."

As Mitsuhide stepped over to the microscope and bowed his masked face to the lenses, Daryl shrugged out of her lab coat and placed it over the back of her chair.

"I don't see anything," Mitsuhide replied as Daryl lifted her grey, flannel shirt from a coat peg.

"Precisely," Daryl replied as she pulled the shirt on over her black vest top. "The blood is normal."

"Yet the rat's immunity was boosted," mused Mitsuhide, folding his arms as he straightened up. "Interesting."

Daryl crossed the room to the wall opposite the freezers. Shelves filled with cages stretched the entire length of the wall, each cage labeled with dates, dosage levels, and quantities.

"All of these," said Daryl, gesturing to a shelf, "have been given a dosage of six times the lethal amount. Some of them, multiple times. A single dose at seven times the lethal amount is the tipping point. So far, three have died from a single dosage at that level. Eight have died after multiple dosages."

"And they all show no cellular metamorphosis?"

Daryl nodded. It was not the result she was looking for, but a few applications for her findings sprang to mind.

"What next?" Mitsuhide asked.

"I'll send this formula over to the doctor for testing. Then, I'll need another donor."

11

VENTURA COUNTY, CALIFORNIA
March 17, 2029

The afternoon brought a slew of meetings, interagency calls and giving all the numpties inspirational "let's go, team" speeches, when all Skylar wanted was to tell them to get their heads out of their asses and buy a clue. By far, Skylar's highlight of the day was her meeting with counterterrorism. The meeting itself was a predictable exchange of questions without answers, she expected that, but what delighted her about the meeting was the ready acceptance of an outsider at the head of the meeting. Jerry's team was the definition of professional in their approach. They exchanged ideas like old friends at brunch and established a credible plan of action for uncovering the perpetrators behind what was increasingly looking like a targeted attack.

Mid-afternoon, Skylar received a text from Director Horner. In true Jerry fashion, it was as short and informative as needed. A simple "thumbs-up" emoji. Skylar didn't consider herself to be as delicate as others of her generation, constantly seeking praise for turning up, but that acknowledgment of a job well done struck a chord that put her on a high for the rest of the day.

"Get home safe, Diana," Skylar said as she passed through reception with a certifiable spring in her step.

Diana Hemsworth was Skylar's favorite secretary, and easily the FBI's best. Skylar defied any other office telling her they had a better record keeper and organizer. When she left the VCRA to take up a special agent in charge position at the LA office, Skylar tried to get Diana to move there with her. Skylar knew her skills would be invaluable in dealing with the admin, but Diana refused to move to the city. In hindsight, that was the smartest thing she had ever done.

"Before you go, soon-to-be Assistant Director Sinclair," she said before slurping from a giant coffee mug that said "World's Best Aunt" in red Comic Sans.

Skylar turned back, waiting for her to finish the sentence. As the seconds slipped by, Skylar began to wonder if Diana had discovered a bottomless mug.

"When you're ready, Diana."

Still draining the mug, Diana lifted a giant stack of papers with her free hand and held them out to Skylar. The file was so big her hand shook from the strain of holding it out one-handed. Skylar let out an aggravated groan and grabbed the papers from her, flipping through them at a rapid-fire pace. As if there weren't enough reports clogging her inbox.

"Are you serious? Did these really just come in?" Skylar asked, not even trying to keep the irritation out of her voice as she looked through the hasty scribbles on each file. The dates only went back to yesterday. Skylar flipped past the initial briefing to see several missing child reports, along with a colorful mix of headshots.

"It's from the Los Angeles Police Department," Diana said, her voice faltering. "We just filed them."

"Crap," Skylar muttered. As if on command, her cell phone rang. Skylar perched on the edge of Diana's desk and pressed Accept. "Sinclair."

It came out snappy. Holding the file to her chest, Skylar took a deep breath, calming her thoughts, before looking back down at the papers.

"Good evening, Sinclair. This is Chief Darren Parker with the LAPD," said a gruff male voice on the other end of the line.

"Hello, Chief," Skylar replied with a measure of civility. "What prompted you to call me, if I may ask?"

"We're facing a major problem, a crime wave if you will. The LAPD has been working on some cases, and I'm following up on the bulk case file I sent this afternoon. We could use some federal assistance down here."

Bulk case file was right. Skylar put the stack of paperwork back down on the desk. Holding it was starting to make her wrist ache.

"I have it here. I literally spent thirteen seconds skimming it before you called. What are you expecting from me?"

"Manpower, Sinclair. We are under-resourced for this crime wave. Keeping order is next to impossible."

"Chief, I would love to send my people down to you, but have you been briefed on what we're dealing with here? I have all my agents working on this outbreak case. We're even looking at options for deputizing ex-servicemen. Any extra people we get are being assigned to the quarantine. I can't spare anyone for a few missing kids right now." Skylar flipped back through the first few entries in the file. "Especially given that they have been missing for less than a day, Chief. I'm sorry."

"Agent, I think if you see the numbers, you'll find that this needs some attention. I understand there are outbreak casualties that include minors, but these kids aren't on any hospital admission records. This is different. The amount of kids I have as reported missing has skyrocketed since last night. This situation isn't from the outbreak-"

"Okay, okay," Skylar interrupted, overlooking his use of "agent" for her title, and reached into her bag. She pulled out her wallet, flipped open the black leather flap, and reached in for a pair of business cards. Skylar eyed them both then chose the one on top. "I know some people who are in LA right now. They can't get back home because of the quarantine. This would give them something to do."

"With all due respect, agent, I need trained support," Chief Parker answered. Skylar's grip on her phone tightened at the attitude creeping into his voice, "not some friends who happened to pick a shitty time to visit the city."

"Excuse me?" Skylar snapped, standing and pacing the room. "With all due respect, chief, I haven't been an agent for quite some time now. Check your attitude at the door before addressing me in future. This isn't the sniffles and a cough I'm dealing with here. Now, do you want my help or not?"

Silence.

"I do," the chief said.

Skylar stopped pacing and took a deep breath, letting the chief stew a moment.

"The two people in question are private investigators. They're highly trained in their fields and will be great assets to your investigation. Just the type of people we're looking to deputize. You take them or find other help. Do I make myself clear?"

The chief grunted an acknowledgment, unhappy at being shot down but grateful for a compromise that allowed him to save face.

"I'll have the boys head down to the precinct in the morning, chief. In the meantime, send me a report on your plans to help manage this quarantine," Skylar said, hanging up before Parker could reply.

One fire at a time, she thought as she walked back to the reception desk and examined the file again.

As terrible as these cases were, Skylar could not afford to be dragged into a city police matter. Not when she had a duty to the country to find out who was responsible for the outbreak. It was a shitty position to be in. Ordinarily, Skylar would gladly support the LAPD with finding these missing children.

There was nothing ordinary about today.

12

LOS ANGELES COUNTY, CALIFORNIA
March 17, 2029

When Mariela first started dating Dave Michaelis, people had mistaken her for some sort of mail-order bride. Dave was more than twenty years her senior and thoroughly average in his appearance, the type of person who blended into a crowd or could duck out of a party without his absence being noticed. Even now, as Mayor of Los Angeles, people regularly mistook him for being any one of the smartly dressed businessmen in the city at first glance. Mariela, on the other hand, was considered quite the young beauty, and time had not diminished her allure in the sixteen years they had been together.

"Are you ready to eat, dear?" Dave asked as Mariela entered the kitchen, a large open plan room that was separated from the main dining space by a long breakfast bar.

"Famished," she replied, taking a seat at the breakfast bar and kicking off her shoes. "Deborah didn't come around earlier so I skipped tea. What did you have in mind?"

"Well," said Dave, going to the fridge and taking a brief look inside. "Would you like some sausage?"

"Hmm," Mariela purred, slowly licking her lips. "Maybe after dinner. Impress me with a good stir fry first."

Dave's extremely dry delivery of some of the most barefaced innuendo had tripped Mariela up a few times when they first started dating. She quickly managed to weed out some of his more blatant puns and recognize them for what they were, but every so often he would come up with some quip, delivered with the straightest face possible, that caught her unawares. Not just her either, on more than one occasion Mariela had caught him disguising suggestive comments in normal conversation with friends without them spotting it.

"I'm assuming Deb has shuttered herself in her house because of this outbreak," said Dave as he began chopping vegetables for the stir fry. "Can't say as I blame her, it's looking pretty rough out there."

Although she paid little attention to the details on the news, Mariela was aware of the violence at the city border. Dave spoke far more freely about work than he really should, knowing that Mariela would keep it in the strictest confidence. In that regard, she had a personal source for local news.

As Dave described events out at the I-405, Mariela sipped at her whiskey and pondered her next move. Listening with one ear to details about injuries sustained as civilians attempted to storm the cordon and escape the quarantined city, Mariela wondered what new game Nikola was playing.

Although she technically worked for Nikola, having moved to the United States with her parents to broker a deal and end a century and a half long feud, Mariela's true loyalty lay with Lukai. Her family had supported his cause for generations, acting as human informants and operatives both at home and abroad. The promise of eternal life was always denied them, but Mariela's ancestors had been richly rewarded for their service, ensuring a very comfortable lifestyle. Mariela was the first of her line to be given the chance to join Lukai's undying cohort. If achieving that meant working to further Nikola's schemes also then so be it.

"Your friend Skylar is heading up the FBI operations on this one," Dave added, focusing Mariela's attention on his words.

"Naturally," Mariela replied, finishing off the whiskey. "She is the assistant director for the area."

"Acting assistant director," Dave corrected her. "At least until the paperwork is filed. There isn't a better candidate for the job as I see it, but that's not what I meant. She's also handling the terrorism investigation. Agent Lovelace reckons she's being groomed for a role in the counterterrorism division and that this is her initiation test or something."

Mariela thought for a moment before replying. She had known Skylar for five years, a fresh-faced recruit working security for a charity event that Dave and Mariela were attending. That was the night that Dave had announced he was running for mayor, and Skylar was subsequently assigned to security detail for quite a few of his candidacy rallies. They had become fast friends during that time thanks to a shared love of whiskey and rock music, despite Skylar's musical appetite being on the lighter side of the spectrum.

Like Mariela, Skylar came from money but was raised to appreciate the hard work it took to get to that position. A wealthy, well-educated woman, Skylar could have adopted the life of luxury, but she shared Mariela's distaste for the pretentious socialites and sycophants drawn to people like Dave and Mariela. Unlike Mariela, Skylar had yet to harness their desires and turn them to her own ends.

Considering how difficult Skylar could be, having her occupied with a counterterrorism investigation may be advantageous to Mariela, keeping her from asking questions about other activities. There was no way of predicting how she might react if Mariela needed to persuade Skylar to see things her way.

"That's good, isn't it?" Mariela eventually replied. "I know Skylar is keen to get to the top of the tree and serve as a role model for all the young girls out there who still feel it's a man's world. A job in counterterrorism would set her up nicely on the national stage wouldn't it?"

"Certainly won't harm her career ambitions," said Dave as he poured Mariela another glass of whiskey albeit it not quite as generous a serving as her first, "just her social life. She'll be stuck in meetings from here to eternity. And if that wasn't enough, the LAPD has only gone and sent across a whole bunch of fresh missing person cases. Kids no less."

"What? For Skylar?" Mariela asked, immediately jumping to the conclusion that a sudden surge in missing person cases was probably Nikola's handiwork. This might be a problem, one for which Mariela would have to drag the chief of police over the coals.

"Yep, well sort of. They are looking for FBI support in general, not specifically her help."

"And?" Mariela urged, trying to sound curious rather than concerned.

"Well, she threw it back to the LAPD. FBI resources are stretched just as thin because of this outbreak, and that takes priority for them. Leave local policing to the local police, basically."

Mariela took a longer swig of her whiskey to hide her relief and compose herself. Nikola must be kidnapping and stockpiling children to serve as a literal blood bank. It would not be the first time she had initiated a scheme and not updated Mariela. That explained some of the riddle of Lukai's letter at least. It was not the move Mariela would have played. Too risky. Safer to stick to the homeless and the infirm to avoid detailed scrutiny. However, with a substantial reserve in place, stepping up her own operations became far easier for Mariela to orchestrate.

"She did suggest a couple of private investigators though," Dave added, serving up food and interrupting Mariela's planning.

"Really?" Mariela mused, taking the chopsticks that Dave proffered. Before Dave became mayor, he worked for a major multinational, spending weeks at a time in Asia and becoming quite adept with the use of chopsticks. Something Mariela had never quite mastered. "That's a somewhat novel approach."

"That's what I thought," Dave replied between mouthfuls. "Not afraid to think outside the box to get results, that girl. Always been the same, ever since she was little. Did I tell you I used to do some work for her father?"

Mariela nodded in response, all the while pondering how to work the scenario to her advantage. If she did not act quickly, all the deals and arrangements made over the last eight years could unravel before her eyes. The remainder of her meal was eaten in silence as she contemplated her options.

"Don't forget, I'm taking a trip down to the marina in the morning," Mariela stated, swallowing the last bite and dropping the chopsticks into the bowl. "With everything that's going on, it'll likely be the last chance I get to take the yacht out for a spin before we become housebound."

"Are you sure that's wise?" Dave asked, his face a mask of concern.

"I'll take one of the autonomous cars and get Vasily to prep the yacht before I arrive. No need to risk encountering anyone who might be infected."

Dave sighed. "I know there's no stopping you so just be careful, okay?"

"Absolutely correct, nothing is going to change my mind on this," Mariela stated, standing up and walking to the hallway door before turning back to Dave and adding, in an innocuous tone that would make him proud, "you know how much I love getting wet."

-13-

VENTURA COUNTY, CALIFORNIA
March 17, 2029

"Doing some therapy, Sky?" Jeremy asked as he strolled into her home gym. Skylar paused her routine, giving the Wing Chun dummy a well-earned break.

Uncle Jeremy had Skylar practicing Taekwondo from an early age. He told her the discipline required to master the techniques would help her understand and cope with losing her parents and brother. It sounded strange but proved to be true. Skylar couldn't explain it, but the practice sessions allowed her to find an inner calm.

By the age of ten, Skylar was good enough to compete in tournaments and still had the bronze medal from the only tournament she took part in. Competing made it feel like she was doing it for other people, and studying martial arts was something Skylar wanted to do for herself. Instead of competitions, Skylar began training in other disciplines. The dummy she habitually took out her aggression on was a thirteenth birthday present from Jeremy. A gift to help her hone her skills and work through her troubles.

"Aye. Therapy," replied Skylar, using the interruption to rehydrate. "Or something like that, uncle. Off to work out?"

Skylar realized how dumb a question it was as soon as she said it. Jeremy was wearing a matching sweatsuit, complete with headband, and an old-fashioned music player clipped to his waist. What else would he be doing dressed like that, fly fishing?

"Yes, Sky, need to clear my head a bit," he said with such resignation that Skylar's mood seemed positively upbeat by comparison. "Some fresh air will do me good."

His face looked haggard. For a retired scholar living rent-free in her house, Jeremy had a knack for being disproportionately stressed. Whatever was weighing him down must have been brutal. Maybe the old librarian in town had asked him why he didn't just buy an e-reader.

"Why don't you spar with me, uncle," Skylar said, tossing him a rattan baston. "It's been a while since I had an eskrima partner."

He caught the baston and struck as Skylar reached for hers. It was all she could do to bring the stick up in time and deflect his strike.

"Be on guard at all times, Sky. That's a given," he said as Skylar retaliated, their session starting in earnest.

Skylar's attacks were precise and unrelenting, forcing Jeremy to shift his weight. The crack of rattan against rattan filled the room. She pressed her advantage, only for him to catch Skylar's arm and throw her off-balance. For an aging man, her uncle was quick. Jeremy followed up with a palm strike to her forehead before she could recover. Skylar twisted away. Too slow. The plane of his hand caught her temple. Not hard enough to do damage, but hard enough to send a message. Skylar spun out and readied herself for whatever he threw next.

"You won't let me catch a break, will you?" Skylar forced out through clenched teeth. "This is a little more than a sparring session."

"Sorry, Sky. I got carried away. It's been a rough day."

"Yeah, tell me about it. I even had the LAPD trying to…" Skylar screwed up her eyes and shook her head. "Shit. I need to call Tate and Tanner."

"I'll leave you to it," Jeremy replied with a slight bow.

Skylar put the bastons away and returned the bow. Manners cost nothing.

As Jeremy strode out of the room, she pulled out her unofficial contact cards and plugged Tate's number into her phone. Tate and Tanner Turner were some of the most darling people she knew. If the word "darling" was a subset of "little shits." They rode with Midnight Flight, the Santa Paula biker club that did more than ride and drink beer on pit stops. Skylar gave them an easy ride in exchange for digging up dirt on local investigations when official channels ran dry.

It was a good trade, and right now she needed them. Skylar needed everyone she could muster.

"Tate Turner," a voice answered, saving her the misery of an automated message. Skylar wanted to be greeted by a real person, not some robot voice telling her to press one for sales, two for accounts or three to go boil your head.

"Hey Tater Tot, I'm sending you to the precinct."

"Good lord," the low voice said back to her. "I am drowning in these freelance quarantine assignments. There was no one else you could call, eh?"

"Nope," Skylar replied, resting her elbow on one of the dummy's wooden arms. "Besides, I know how much you and Tanner love the fuzz. Look, the number of missing kids in Los Angeles has climbed into the hundreds in the last twenty-four hours. I need you to mitigate, even if it's a few hospital visits or youth center drop-ins. I don't expect it to be too intense, but you owe me."

The silence when Skylar finished talking lasted too long.

"You owe me, Turner. You and Tanner both do. Get your asses over to the station first thing in the morning, or I'll have some of our local officers swing by that shed of yours. You know, the one with an excessive power consumption."

"Fine. First thing, we'll jump down to the PD. And for the record, I have no idea what shed you are talking about."

"I don't care, because I heard nothing. Ask no questions, hear no lies."

Ending the call, Skylar studied the other business card in her wallet.

Not today, she thought, returning it to her wallet. *Not today*.

-14-

LOS ANGELES COUNTY, CALIFORNIA
March 18, 2029

Mariela's journey to the marina was, for the most part, surprisingly uneventful. The way the media had portrayed events in the city was akin to some futuristic dystopia, in which, the degenerate masses ran amok while plotting to escape the confines of a city turned prison and overthrow civilized society. Mariela wondered if she had missed the announcement that the commander-in-chief had signed directive seventeen into law, condemning the citizens of Los Angeles.

The city was what it always had been, just quieter. Out of fear of exposure, many citizens were securing themselves in their homes and avoiding contact with anyone. A sensible measure but one that would prove to be futile should the disease be transmitted through any means other than proximity to the infected. The chances of that seemed slim though.

Dave had revealed that the CDC's initial assessment was leaning toward anthrax and the possibility of a targeted infection. It explained the lack of traceable origin that was characteristic of a natural pandemic, but the selection of targets was baffling. New York and Los Angeles were the only US cities affected with Mexico City the only other city in North America ravaged by the infection.

The lands on the other side of the Pacific Ocean were similarly afflicted with Tokyo, Shanghai, Beijing, Manila and Jakarta all resorting to quarantines to manage the outbreaks. The speed with which local authorities acted and national containment procedures were implemented made a staggering difference to the ability to maintain peace, and the violence seen in Los Angeles paled in comparison to the full-scale rioting that was occurring in Mumbai and Dhaka. The Indian government had successfully imposed and maintained quarantine around Delhi but control over Kolkata was beginning to slip.

India and Bangladesh weren't the only countries struggling to maintain order. The Pakistani government was struggling to appease public outcry over the handling of the infected in Karachi and the threat of war loomed in Africa over the mishandling of confinement in Kinshasa. News on the state of affairs in Lagos had ceased only hours after the Nigerian government had ordered the city quarantined, fueling speculation that the city was lost.

Cairo, Rio De Janeiro, Sao Paulo, Buenos Aires and Bogota rounded out the list of affected cities, each barely managing to keep control in the face of panic, death and violence.

Mariela assumed the council had somehow staged the whole thing to look like a terror attack to hide their true activities but could not see the logic behind their city selection. Perhaps that was their intent, to keep the world guessing. Any number of conspiracy theories were likely to arise from this, providing perfect cover by disguising an unlikely truth amongst plausible lies. It wouldn't be the first event in history to be orchestrated by the council in such a way as to generate myriad theories surrounding its origin.

As she watched from the bulletproof windows of the autonomous, nondescript sedan that carried her to the marina, Mariela contemplated the path being set before her. Dave was a big advocate of driverless vehicles, despite criticism from some technology fearing groups over deaths caused by autonomous cars. The truth was that driverless deaths accounted for a fraction of a percent compared to fatalities caused by cars with a person behind the wheel. At one meeting on the subject, an erstwhile statistician even went so far as to counter anti-autonomy arguments by highlighting the number in 2027 was even exceeded by fatalities caused by cars with canines behind the wheel.

Mariela had argued for something more stylish than the grey sedan when picking out a car but Dave had won that particular debate. The understated luxury allowed for a degree of anonymity when they wanted to travel without drawing attention. Reclining in the comfort of its leather-clad interior, Mariela admitted to herself, and not for the first time, that she was impressed with Dave's choice.

The first sign of any real trouble was just outside the marina when Mariela had to wait in line to be ushered through the blockade. Many of the city's more affluent inhabitants were attempting to flee the city via boat, forcing the police to set-up roadblocks on the access roads to the marina, ensuring only those with legitimate business entered. This was one of those occasions where using her husband's title would not sit well with influential voters, those being turned away by the police officers manning the blockade. Better to wait in line and pass through discreetly.

"Name and purpose," the officer at the barrier stated, for what sounded like the millionth time that morning, as Mariela reached the barrier. It was clear from his tone that he had heard more pleading and begging since the quarantine was enforced than he could handle, a warning not to test his patience with some sob story.

"Mariela Michaelis, here on business regarding shipments of goods into LA," Mariela calmly replied. The officer looked at her as if to question why she was at the marina and not the port of LA. "My cousin runs one of the shipping companies and we are having lunch at my yacht to go over some strategies for ensuring the city is well supplied during this quarantine. We figured it was safer than going to his offices downtown."

"Well, you're right about not wanting to go downtown," the officer replied. "Rioting broke out again this morning, and we don't have the manpower to maintain the quarantine and suppress the rioting and looting."

"What's wrong with people," Mariela said with a sigh. "You'd think they would be avoiding exposure, not courting death to get some free sneakers."

"No idea," he replied with a shrug, stopping short of commenting on the stupidity of some people. "LA county officers are shoring up the border, and we've got more inbound from the neighboring counties, so we can get things under control before they call in the national guard."

Deciding that Mariela's business was legitimate enough, possibly as a result of the Michaelis name, the officer waved for his colleague to let her through. Mariela fidgeted with her engagement ring, hooking the large diamond with her nail and slowly wiggling it from side to side while she waited for her path to be cleared. The act was an ingrained habit, and Dave had learned to quickly change the subject when he saw her do it or risk losing her interest, interjecting whenever a dinner guest was talking about something she had no desire to discuss.

"A word of warning," the officer added before stepping aside and allowing Mariela through. "The coast guard is enforcing the quarantine with orders to use any and all measures to stop anyone trying to leave by boat. If you don't want your yacht to be holier than your Bible, I suggest you don't stray too far."

Mariela nodded in affirmation and instructed the car to proceed through the now open barrier, down to the berth where her yacht was docked. The wind sweeping in off the ocean brought with it a crisp freshness and a rich saltiness that Mariela soaked in through her lungs as she stepped from the car. A text message from Vasily came through as she stood, staring out over the water, saying he was at the blockade and would be there shortly.

Vasily Malinovskyi had been born in the US and lived in several states before settling in California. His father had moved to Chicago on business and, after meeting Vasily's mother while working on a contract in Peoria, embarked on a whirlwind romance that resulted in Vasily. Upon hearing the news that his new girlfriend was pregnant, Vasily's father decided to make his stay more permanent, angering some among the older generation who felt he had a duty to the family estate. The family had disowned Vasily's father when he told them he would not return to the motherland and so Vasily had never known the home that Mariela would one day inherit.

None of the generations that had deprived Vasily of his inheritance were still alive, leaving nobody to object to Mariela gifting the estate that should rightfully have been his back to Vasily when it passed to her. Vasily, Mariela, her father, and her grandfather were the last of the line, and Mariela had no interest in upholding a grudge based purely on aristocratic pride. Not when there were so many other horrific acts that had taken place in her family that were unreservedly worthy of her contempt.

The work Vasily performed for Mariela had earned him a great deal of respect. Her cousin had been instrumental so far in ensuring that their plans ran smoothly. He would be instrumental in ensuring they continued to do so.

"This is unacceptable," Mariela raged the moment he arrived. "Children, Vasily. Children. I cannot accept this unless we have strict rules and enforce them rigorously."

"Nice to see you too," Vasily replied, taking a seat below deck. His towering physique, the result of college football and an intense workout regime layered on an already impressive natural size, seemed to fill the cabin. "I'm already dealing with the grunts who think they can just grab whoever they take a fancy to. None of the boys and girls that are taken will be forced to do anything they don't want to do."

"Thank you. We have a job to do, but we don't need to be monsters to do it. I want a program in place to draw blood from the children safely and in limited quantities. It will mean more subjects, but I would prefer mild discomfort for many to needless pain for a few."

Mariela stood up and began pacing in the limited space available below deck to disguise how badly she was shaking. Although the yacht was one of the more luxurious yachts in the Marina it was still a yacht, lacking an abundance of space in comparison to her estate. Dave had suggested they upgrade to a larger craft, but Mariela wasn't interested in owning one of the monstrosities that were commonly associated with the likes of CEO's, Wall Street kingpins and the flashiest of celebrities. Mariela wanted her yacht to be an escape from the world. Bringing all the trappings of excess with her when she went out on the ocean to scream at the waves did not match her description of escapism. The only reason her yacht contained as much luxury as it did was that she still needed to maintain a certain image.

Dave and Mariela were considered by many to be at the cutting edge of technology and fashion and were regularly approached by style magazines to discuss their latest soiree or ideas on technology for better living. It became tiresome, but it helped to push through legislation, such as clean fuel initiatives, when the Michaelis family were seen to be practicing what they preached. They had become the poster children for what could be achieved with hard work and commitment.

"Consider it done. What do you want to do about those who wish to engage in the..." Vasily hesitated, seeking the best choice of words to finish his sentence, "...less savory appetites of our clientele?"

"If they comply freely then so be it, I won't stand in the way of those who choose such debauchery. As for the others, pick out the candidates best suited to our plans for Los Angeles and send those with limited potential to our operation in the valley. I have no objection to manual labor when it's the alternative."

Before they could discuss any further plans, Mariela's phone rang. As tempting as it was to ignore it, she glanced at the screen and saw Darren Parker's name.

"I have to take this."

Vasily nodded and went above deck as Mariela accepted the call.

"Chief Parker, I believe you owe me an apology."

"What?" the chief exclaimed, caught off guard by Mariela's abruptness. "I've just arrived at the marina. I take it you're at your yacht."

"Indeed I am. Be quick."

Mariela ended the call and exhaled sharply. If the chief expected any sort of leniency then he was sorely mistaken. Chief Darren Parker was as straight a cop as she had ever met, and it had taken some extreme measures to ensure he toed the line. Where other officers had been swayed to her cause through bribery, threats or just careful manipulation, the chief posed a challenge. Like most people, however, the chief had a weakness. His daughter.

"What on Earth are you playing at?" the chief demanded the moment he arrived.

Mariela, calm and composed following her conversation with Vasily, a conversation that had skated far too close to the thin ice of her past, had taken a seat.

"How dare you question me, Darren? I call the shots, and you follow orders."

The chief noticeably withered in the face of her fury. He had come expecting to unleash righteous condemnation only to be hurled back from the offset.

"But, but," he stammered, his carefully planned speech derailed. "These are children you're taking."

"Don't tell me my own business, chief," Mariela snapped, loading as much disdain for his title into the word as possible. "I am well aware of what is going on. I have just instructed my subordinates to ensure our new guests are treated with the utmost respect. This is not a simple clean-up operation to feed the swine. I am beginning a new phase of the plan to save our city, and you will fall in line.

"I am not a monster but if you dare come here again expecting me to bow and scrape to you because you find something distasteful then you will quickly see that I am not a woman to be trifled with. You work for me, and don't you ever forget that or I will personally ensure your daughter does not."

"I'm sorry, Mrs. Michaelis," Chief Parker groveled, suddenly contrite at the vague threat aimed at his daughter. "I was distraught and understandably angry at the revelation that things had changed without explanation. Please don't hurt my Sophie."

"Provided you give me no reason to change my mind, your daughter will remain safe in my care. Now get out."

Chief Parker, lost for words at being scolded, turned and headed for the exit.

"I hear a report was filed with the FBI," Mariela added before the chief could escape her. "I want it buried and an example made of the man responsible for getting your office to issue it. Don't fail me."

Mariela relaxed a little as the chief hurried from the yacht. Playing the tyrant was always a chore. Mariela much preferred a subtler approach to getting her way.

"Do I need to take care of him?" Vasily asked as he returned to the cabin.

"No, I have others who can deal with him should the need arise. Now, tell me how things are looking with our shipments."

-15-

"Pompous, arrogant, conceited, conniving, stuck-up, fucking bitch," the chief cursed as he slumped into the comfortable embrace of his leather desk chair.

The surface was worn smooth from years of heavy use but, despite Eckhart's insistence, Darren refused to replace it. He liked to think that after so much time attached to his butt, the chair had adapted to suit his posterior. No amount of jostling from health and safety would convince him a new chair would provide equal or greater comfort. They may take his life but they would never take his chair.

"I take it things didn't go too well," Eckhart stated, rubbing the back of his hand over his dark stubble as the echo of the slammed door receded.

Francis Eckhart had worked a beat with Darren, back in the day, and, although their simultaneous rise through the ranks meant they frequently ended up working different precincts, Darren had more trust in Eckhart than anyone else on his staff.

"As well as can be expected," Darren said with a groan. "They aren't going to stop and they know they have me over a barrel. To make things worse, she knows somebody tipped off the feds and wants the culprit made an example of."

Darren sighed as he settled back into his chair. As soon as officer Jenkins had returned from the warehouse with reports that the vampire scum had started taking children, the chief began looking for a way of resolving the situation for good. Unfortunately, there were too many who were aiding the vampires voluntarily, and Darren could not be sure if they would all share Jenkins' distaste at the change in strategy. There might have been sympathizers of which the Chief was unaware, watching his every move and reporting back to their undead masters.

While the vampires were picking off criminals, they had amassed a fair degree of influence throughout the force. As their methods became more distasteful, seeking out people that could easily be written off or made to disappear, such as terminally ill patients and illegal immigrants, and the true nature of their predatory behavior became clear, the vampires tightened their hold on the police. Early dissidents were quickly eliminated in the most gruesome ways possible, a clear warning to any officers who knew the truth to fall in line or be the next example.

For some, it was not fear for their safety that forced them into compliance but fear for the ones they loved most. Darren himself fell into that category. His daughter, Sophie, was one of the first to be taken, providing the vampires with leverage over him and, as a result of his compromise, a route into the police force. In a demonstration of intent, they had forged her death certificate, making it look like she had died in the crash that had taken her mother just over twelve months earlier. If he refused their demands his daughter would be lost to him forever.

Eliminating career criminals to protect his daughter was an easy decision to make. If he had known where it would lead, Darren wondered if he would still make the same decision. Sacrificing criminals was one thing, but now other families, other people's children, were suffering because he tried to save his own. The only thing that kept him in check was the periodic video updates from his daughter, delivered by Mariela's henchmen and deleted immediately after viewing.

His daughter's captivity stopped him from taking direct action against the vampires and their human agents, like Mariela and Officer Jenkins, but Darren had been sure that leaking the case file on the missing children to the FBI would expose them and force them back into the shadows. He had even taken it straight to the top, just in case the FBI was also compromised.

The chief had only met Skylar once, but she had a reputation for being true to the cause of justice. His encounter had left him thinking she was a bit of a snob, highly demanding and somewhat dismissive of those outside her immediate circle of friends and associates. It was like people were tools to her that she could just pick up and use to get a job done. Her colleagues at the FBI had nothing but praise for her though, so either the chief had misread her or he had caught her on an off day.

His phone call to follow up on the case file had most certainly been at the worst time on her worst off-day. It was no accident that the vampires had changed their game plan to coincide with the outbreak. Even if he could trust the police entirely, his team was so overwhelmed that dealing with the missing children, the quarantine, and the pockets of rioting that were breaking out was impossible.

The strain was easing slightly as more reinforcements arrived from the neighboring counties, but it was a small reprieve. Officers from Ventura had arrived around noon to take over the quarantine along the 27, allowing the chief to redirect his people to the rioting downtown, with San Bernardino officers arriving to support the Orange County officers already manning the quarantine on the 605 soon after.

Given the risk of infection, only those officers in LA at the time of the outbreak were allowed to enter the city itself. Support from the neighboring counties, although greatly appreciated, was confined to the border. As a result, the FBI had committed not just the Critical Incident Response Group to the outbreak but every available agent in the city.

The vampires must have predicted such a response, rendering any push back against their plans unfeasible. Darren could not deny that it was a practical move as rioting was likely to get worse before it got better. Continued violence would result in the deployment of the national guard. Only timely intervention by the mayor in securing the support of neighboring counties had prevented that scenario from becoming a reality already.

"We could use Jenkins as an example," Eckhart offered, flexing his fingers as he took a seat across from the chief.

"No," Darren replied, leaning forward and resting his elbows on the desk. "There are precious few people I know who are willing to stand up against the vampires. I'm not going to throw someone under the bus just for expressing concern over the way they are acting, even though he supported them when they were offing criminals. I need people willing to question their behavior."

"You misunderstand me, chief. Jenkins died this morning. It appears he was among the infected. We could spin it to Mariela that he was behind the leak, but the disease got him before we could act. Problem solved."

Darren thought for a moment. It could work. Nobody would need to suffer. Outwardly, Jenkins would be recognized as a brave officer taken out by a terrible infection while answering the call to duty. They would only need to besmirch his name to Mariela, and doing so would save another from her wrath so it would hardly be a stain on his honor. Nothing compared to his willing compliance with the vampires before they started going after children. There was just one problem.

"Until she discovers how deeply I'm involved."

"Not necessarily," Eckhart answered. "You were simply appeasing officer Jenkins, safe in the knowledge that you could make it disappear once he was taken care of."

"But I phoned Skylar directly."

"And how did that conversation go? From what you told me it sounds like it resulted in the case being thrown back over the fence."

To all intent and purposes, it had. Tate and Tanner had arrived at the station bright and early. Pleasant enough lads, but they had not inspired Darren with confidence in their ability to get to the bottom of this and expose the whole damn mess. The web of deceit and intrigue the vampires had spent years weaving was hardly in the same league as finding a lost puppy.

"True, true," Darren conceded. "but I didn't want it thrown back, I wanted support. I can't live with myself if I allow this to carry on. I know I'll be damning myself and Sophie, but I must blow the whistle on this. I just need to find someone who will listen."

"Leave it with me, chief," Eckhart replied as he rose from his seat. "Don't do anything rash while I'm gone."

-16-

VENTURA COUNTY, CALIFORNIA
March 23, 2029

Alex closed his eyes and let the setting sun beat down on his face, enjoying the serenity of Serra Cross Park in relative isolation. The indistinct chatter and unmistakable scent of weed wafted over from a group of teens at the edge of the park, disturbing the otherwise tranquil atmosphere, but Alex was otherwise alone to enjoy the park. Only once had Alex ever tried smoking, during a college graduation party nearly ten years ago, and it was not an experience he intended to repeat.

Following the outbreak, the park was inundated with people seeking comfort or guidance. Many residents of Ventura had friends or family in Los Angeles and came to the cross to pray. Alex did not blame them. Serra Cross Park was a favorite spot of his to contemplate life, faith and the universe, with its stunning view over the houses below and the Pacific Ocean beyond.

Alex had avoided the park during the immediate aftermath, shunning the crowds for private contemplation. As the infection burned a path through the population, exhausting its supply of fresh victims, the people of Ventura turned from public prayer to private mourning. Returning to a normal level of activity, the park once more provided Alex with the space he sought without feeling secluded.

As much as he loved spending time with Skylar, living in her house had its drawbacks. The house was big enough, with its seven bedrooms and five bathrooms, that it never felt like they were in each other's way, but it did feel crowded at times. Occasionally, Alex just wanted to be left alone. Reclining on the park's freshly cut grass was the closest he came to peace and quiet.

"Penny for your thoughts?" a light, lilting voice asked as a shadow engulfed Alex. He opened his eyes to see the figure of a woman at his feet, silhouetted against the setting sun. "You look very contented. Wanna share your secret?"

"Depends who's asking," said Alex, glancing around. The teenagers were still loitering at the edge of the park, although a couple of them had drifted away from the group, and an elderly couple was walking their dog. Nothing out of the ordinary.

Being suspicious of strangers was a side effect of living with two FBI agents and being raised by a man who saw danger around every corner. A side effect Alex despised and intended to overcome. For Mike and Skylar, it was a professional habit, but Jeremy's paranoia was hard to explain away as a by-product of the trade. Alex could not make the connection between Jeremy's ultra-cautious, super-suspicious persona and his career as a museum curator. Caring for exhibits was hardly the knife-edge lifestyle of a soldier or federal agent at its pinnacle of excitement, and Jeremy had been retired for around ten years now.

Curious as to what Jeremy did that warranted such discretion, Alex had followed him on three separate occasions as he went about his daily routine. There was no better word to describe Jeremy's behavior than routine. Breakfast at six, shower at seven, morning run, another shower and into town for twelve. His afternoons maintained the monotony, spending four hours at the library following a light lunch. Only when the evening rolled around did Jeremy mix things up. Sometimes he would go see a movie, sometimes he would drive or cycle around for hours, taking in the scenic routes of California. After the third attempt to discover his adopted uncle's secret, Alex gave up and concluded there was no logic to Jeremy's fondness for security and secrecy.

"The name's Phoebe, Phoebe Stuart," said the woman, drawing Alex's attention back to her. "My father volunteers at the park. He's a gardener."

"Okay," Alex replied, not sure what this woman was expecting but determined to not treat her like an outcast.

"Can I sit with you?"

"It's a free country," said Alex, putting his hands behind his head as he returned to his prone position on the grass.

No longer silhouetted by the setting sun as she sat cross-legged beside him, Alex could make out Phoebe's features. The smoothness of her skin and the gentle twinkle of her smile suggested she was younger than him by around ten years, putting her in her late teens, with genuine warmth and affection for people.

"Did you know, Father Serra planted the first cross on this site nearly 250 years ago?" said Phoebe, gently tucking her long blonde hair behind her ears. "This cross has stood here for nearly 90 years."

Alex chose not to contest her claim. Although Father Serra was credited with erecting a cross to guide pilgrims to the San Buenaventura mission, there was some doubt over the location of the original cross. Some argued that it was closer to the mission and moved to the hill at a later date.

"Do you believe in our Lord Jesus Christ?"

Alex scanned her face for any sign that Phoebe was jesting. Her soft, innocent eyes revealed nothing but curiosity.

"I do," Alex replied with a hint of reluctance. He was not ashamed of his faith, but he did not want to get drawn into a lengthy debate on the subject with this stranger.

"He died for our sins, you know," Phoebe continued, almost as if Alex had not spoken. "Only by allowing the Lord into your heart can you find your way to Heaven. 'I am the way, and the truth, and the life; no one comes to the Father but through Me.' John 14:6."

A wistful note crept into her voice as she recited the quote. The words differed slightly from the version Alex knew, but the meaning was the same. They were the words charlatans used to con people into throwing money at them, equating their churches with the Lord and offering His salvation in exchange for donations. As with the thief on the cross, Alex knew that he did not need the blessing of a church, only the love and acceptance of Christ.

"He is easier to find than you think," Alex said, suspecting her melancholy stemmed from doubt. 'For where two or three are gathered together in my name, there am I in the midst of them.'"

"You should state the passage when quoting the Bible," replied Phoebe, smiling as she lay on the grass beside him. "The references are important. There is strength in numbers."

Alex sighed. "I don't think that's the correct use of that phrase."

A tense silence fell over them as they each explored their own thoughts. More than once, Alex caught a glimpse of Phoebe looking over at him, her expression serene yet full of wonder. She appeared content to lie there and wait for him to pick up the conversation. For Alex, silent contemplation was ample.

"I hope I'm not interrupting anything," a familiar voice stated as the minutes dragged on without a word from Phoebe.

Alex tilted his head back, the grass tickling the back of his neck as he did so, to see Jeremy towering over him. A sly grin spread across his ancient cheeks as he held out a hand. Alex declined to take it, opting to roll his weight onto his shoulders and flip himself up onto his feet.

"Not at all," said Phoebe, taking Jeremy's hand and rising to her feet. "Such a gentleman. I'm Phoebe. Phoebe Stuart. And you are?"

"This troublemaker's uncle," Jeremy replied before turning to Alex. "What brings you all the way up here, Alex? Avoiding your sister perchance?"

Alex gave Phoebe a meaningful look. It took a moment for her to receive his unspoken instruction.

"I'll give you two some space," she said upon grasping the reason for the ominous silence. "Maybe I'll see you around. I'd like to know more about your thoughts on salvation."

"Giving sermons on the mount now, are you, Alex?" Jeremy asked as soon as Phoebe was out of earshot.

Alex looked into Jeremy's eyes. In the fading sunlight, he appeared much older than a man in his mid-fifties. It could have been exhaustion, but Alex suspected there was a weight Jeremy was carrying that was not physical.

"You know me, uncle," Alex said with a grin, taking in Jeremy's headband and faded sweatsuit. "Always time to talk to a pretty lady. I take it you're out for a run. You should be taking it easy at your age. You might break one of those brittle old shin bones if you keep running marathons like that."

"I'm in better shape than you are, Alex," Jeremy said, performing a few stretches. "I could beat you back to the house, that's for sure."

"On foot? Probably. But why would I race you on foot when the Mustang's parked down on the street? Besides, I'm not heading back yet. Not because I'm avoiding Sky, before you go there, but because I have a life that doesn't revolve around her."

Alex regretted the words as soon as they were spoken. They came out more testily than intended.

"Anything I can help with?" asked Jeremy, immediately seizing on the subtext.

Alex shook his head. Bringing Jeremy in on his situation was worse than including Skylar. Merriam-Webster would need to create a new word to describe how overprotective Jeremy could be.

"I'm good," Alex replied, hoping to change the subject. "As good as can be expected when there's a city full of suffering on your doorstep."

"Yes, Alex," said Jeremy, turning his head in the direction of Los Angeles as if he could see the city from their vantage point. "It's a curious state of affairs. Very curious."

"Uncle?" said Alex, surprised at the contemplative tone of voice and anxious expression on Jeremy's face.

"Oh, I was just thinking how challenging it will be for your sister to bring the people behind this attack to justice. Quite the puzzle the terrorists have left," said Jeremy, the anxiety in his demeanor replaced with forced jolliness as he turned and smiled at Alex. "Ah well, nothing we can do about it. Not at my time of life, at least."

"No," Alex replied, the serenity draining from him, replaced by a creeping dread. "Nothing we can do but pray."

-17-

VENTURA COUNTY, CALIFORNIA
March 24, 2029

Skylar stifled a yawn and wiped her hands over her face as the agents on her conference call droned on. A week into the quarantine, almost everyone in the city of Los Angeles had been admitted to hospital, filling the CDC's emergency field surgeries. Just as Doctor Lewis warned, the supposedly healthy started to drop after a few days. Many didn't make it to a medical professional and died at home or on the way, causing panic in the surrounding counties. The lull in the violence as people ceased attempting to escape the quarantine made some of the so-called professionals turn their attention to self-aggrandizement.

"I know, but we can't pull funds from FEMA's flood insurance program," Skylar heard Lauren Diaz, the FEMA team leader, whine into the phone as she worked her way through a backlog of reports.

"Why not? There are too many fires in California. We need to pull out more stops," somebody said from another line.

The call with Diaz's team and the local fire and police departments was Skylar's third call of the day. They had been arguing like that for fifteen minutes. Drowning in bureaucracy, Skylar's tolerance of what was sounding increasingly like a FEMA dick-swinging contest was wearing thin, forcing her to mute her line to the meeting ten minutes into the call and focus her energies on the terrorism investigation. So far, not a single person had noticed her absence.

Half listening for a reason to rejoin the call, Skylar could not help but think that Diaz was pulled into the mix to meet a quota. If that was the case, somebody needed firing. It was truly sad that so many exceptional women passed on opportunities to rise to the top of their professions. Having to put up with incompetent, token promotions like Diaz added insult to injury.

Where the Los Angeles relief efforts were being bogged down with interagency politics, the terrorism investigation was stalling from a lack of leads. The CIA's intel provided nothing tangible to build a case around, and surveillance shared by America's allies was equally devoid of usable information. Despite their assurances, the agents Jerry had assigned from his division were also drawing blanks. Every report Skylar read offered nothing that she had not already worked out for herself.

Sighing heavily, Skylar filed Agent Houston's latest report and glanced at her watch, eager for the morning to be over. 1:12 p.m., no wonder she was feeling hungry. Having skipped breakfast, a granola bar from the vending machine at the end of the corridor was Skylar's only source of sustenance. That and an excess of coffee that was doing nothing to stave off her exhaustion.

Needing something to distract from the bickering on the call, Skylar opened another report and stared at her screen until the words became blurry black smudges. After several minutes of re-reading the report's synopsis, a chorus of reluctant mumblings as FEMA and the fire department struck a compromise drew Skylar back to the call.

Summing up the dying flame of her enthusiasm, she unmuted her line.

"Excellent job, everyone," said Skylar, desperately trying to not sound patronizing. "I know I can count on FEMA's support while we figure out exactly what we're dealing with. I expect you to join the CDC delegates on-site and make your assessments first hand."

No way are they getting away with sitting pretty in their offices while the rest of us are getting our hands dirty, Skylar thought, leaving the command hanging over them. They may not have liked it, but the edict was handed down from the very top that all agencies would follow her lead until order was restored.

The mounting silence broke Diaz and her team, forcing them to sound their agreements in turn as they realized there was to be no further discussion on the matter.

"Finally," Skylar muttered, ending the call and immediately dialing the office reception desk. Time for lunch.

"Hey, Diana, is that salad place still open? You know, the one three blocks over. Just after the gas station? I wanna say, The California Salad Café."

After wading through calls and reports, Skylar figured she deserved a treat.

"Nope. They turned it into a bank."

"Well, shit," Skylar replied, a little crestfallen. "Guess it's that other one for lunch. Oh, what is it called? You know, the one two blocks further on."

"That place with the short Spanish waiter that barely spoke any English, right? They were closed down. Health inspector found a Siberian hamster running loose when he dined there one evening."

"A Siberian hamster?" asked Skylar, picking up her pen and giving it a few clicks. "Wait, I don't even want to know. Where's the best place to get a spinach salad, no bacon, with just a sprinkle of parmesan and an Italian dressing, in that case?"

Diana chuckled at Skylar's specifics. "There's a new place called Cali Salads that does deliveries. It's three blocks away. I'll phone it through."

Skylar thanked Diana and slipped on her suit jacket. Some open space beckoned, a welcome relief from the four walls of that old office, even if it was only a walk around the block while waiting for lunch to be delivered.

Squinting as she left the building, the spring sun beating down on her face, Skylar regretted leaving her glasses in the office. Not that they would be very effective given the sun's brightness. Still, as ineffectual as her photoreactive lenses were on such a clear day, they would do more good if she remembered to wear them from time to time. As she stepped into the shadow of the office block, Skylar heard Jeremy's voice in her head, telling her that her eyes would only get worse if she did not wear her glasses. The way he fretted, anyone would think she had severe corneal dystrophy rather than being slightly farsighted in one eye.

As Skylar completed her second lap of the block, she spotted a guy in surf shorts and an unbuttoned shirt exiting reception. Assuming that was her delivery, Skylar smacked her lips and quickened her pace in anticipation. The walk had done wonders for clearing the cobwebs from her head, not that any breakthroughs had moved in to replace them, and sharpened her appetite to a keen edge.

"Better Cal-Sal," Diana called out, holding up Skylar's lunch as she entered the building. The bizarreness of Diana's statement stopped Skylar in her tracks.

"What?"

"The name of the salad place that the health inspector shut down. It was called Better Cal-Sal," Diana clarified without a hint of sarcasm in her voice.

Skylar blinked twice, convinced that Diana's intel could not be right but unsure what to say in response. Deciding against saying anything on the subject, Skylar thanked Diana for the lunch order and retired to the cafeteria, where a fresh pot of coffee would be waiting.

"Wait," Diana shouted as Skylar grabbed the door handle to the back rooms. "The Los Angeles deputy chief of police has been trying to get hold of you about those missing kiddies. I've also got some requisition forms I need you to sign."

Skylar sighed at the prospect of more forms. Looking down at the brown paper bag and the promise of food within, she could not help but think fate was conspiring against her.

"Okay, Diana, remind me after lunch," Skylar said, defying fate and heading through the door. "Mama's gotta eat."

With the endorphins released by her lunchtime stroll wearing off, Skylar took the sight of an empty coffee pot as she entered the cafeteria as another middle finger from the hand of fate. That Agent Miner, the only person in the office able to rival Diana for caffeine addiction, had finished lunch only moments before her was circumstantial evidence. Slinging the old paper filter in the trash, Skylar refilled the coffee machine and set it to brew another batch.

"Ugh," Skylar groaned through a mouthful of limp spinach as she tucked into her lunch. "Turns out new isn't always better."

Swallowing the soggy mess, Skylar considered tossing the salad and getting some fried chicken from the store across the road. The thought of all that grease forced her to reconsider. As crappy as the salad was, at least it was organic.

With ten minutes of her lunchbreak remaining, Skylar poured a mug of the freshly brewed coffee and transferred the rest to the empty carafe, ready for the next agent in need of a boost. Blowing across the top of her steaming coffee, Skylar's thoughts on whether to do another lap of the block were rudely interrupted by the incessant cry of her phone. Looking at the number, Skylar concluded that fate would only be denied for so long.

"Hello, chief," she said dryly, forgetting Diana's words as she put the phone on speaker.

"Not yet, Mrs. Sinclair-Blake. Deputy Chief Francis Eckhart here. I'm calling to inform you that your friends were a useful addition to our investigation. Thank you."

"Good," Skylar replied, heading back to her office. "I'm glad to hear Tate and Tanner provided proper assistance."

"They did. Unfortunately, with so many officers dead from the virus-"

"Infection," Skylar interrupted, unsure why she sought to correct that detail.

"With so many officers dead or occupied with maintaining the quarantine, we don't have the personnel to follow up on any of the leads."

"I understand the LAPD is struggling, Francis, but you're not alone in that regard. Do you honestly believe I have agents sitting around playing Galaga while things go to Hell in a handbasket?"

"Of course not," Eckhart replied as Skylar arrived at the door to her office. "But I did hope you might have some trick up your sleeve that would alleviate the burden and allow us to turn our attention to enforcing the law instead of your quarantine."

Skylar looked from the phone in her left hand to the coffee mug in her right. Why did the door have to have a knob instead of a lever she could operate with her knee or her butt?

"Deputy," Skylar said, trying to keep her composure in the face of his groveling. "We are doing everything we can to establish a forward operating base and get the city back on track. As shitty as it may sound, based on the report you've given me, your case is not that critical. You don't need more federal help."

"But, Mrs. Sinclair-Blake-"

"Enough," Skylar snapped, abandoning her attempt to twist the knob without dropping the phone as Eckhart's pleading tone grated her last nerve. "I'm not here to handle your basic 101 shit. You're a grown-up, and you're the deputy chief. Why am I doing all your investigative work for you?"

"Now, listen here, we're all civil servants," Eckhart growled into the phone. "I'm trying to protect the people, just like you are. You have no reason to reprimand me at a time like this."

"Watch me," Skylar said, loading the words with menace. "Don't show such mediocrity, Francis. Put on your big boy pants and recruit people yourself. I don't care if you have to pull survivors off the streets, assemble some sort of force and get this done."

Ending the call with a huff, not waiting for the deputy chief's response, Skylar stashed her phone and threw her office door open. As the door slammed against the coat stand behind it, Skylar bowed her head and sighed. She could hardly blame Eckhart. If the roles were reversed, she would be doing everything to find those children too.

Taking a seat at her desk, Skylar considered that Eckhart was not the source of her frustration, he was the straw that broke her. Activating her screen, Skylar dialed the number on the open report.

"Sergeant Anderson," she said, addressing the subject that had put her on edge. "Let's discuss your proposals for mobilizing the national guard."

-18-

LOS ANGELES COUNTY, CALIFORNIA
March 25, 2029

"This is not a good time," said Mariela, stepping to the window of the drawing room and looking out over the garden.

Dave was soaking up the sun and putting the miniature golf course to good use, or he would have been if he hadn't paused his game to take a call. Mariela gave him a little wave as he gave her an exaggerated shrug with one arm. No doubt some lobbyist was wasting his Sunday afternoon by bending Dave's ear to wrangle cash from the city budget. Cash that should be spent on restoring the city to some semblance of order.

There was no fear Dave would misuse the city's funds. As a shrewd businessman with a detailed grasp of economics and a noted philanthropist with a keen sense of public opinion, Dave Michaelis was able to temper the more frivolous spending demands of lobbyists without alienating the left-leaning voters he relied on for re-election. It was a difficult task, but the early polling numbers suggested that, in the absence of a more favorable Democrat opponent, his centrist policies had enough support to secure another term.

"Forgive me, cousin," Vasily replied, "but you told me to call you the moment the transfer was complete. Everything is in order."

"Good," said Mariela, turning back to the drawing room. "My calendar is up-to-date. Prepare a report and schedule a review by the end of the week. I want to understand our projections now our supply issue is resolved."

Mariela ended the call and lowered herself into the armchair before the fireplace. The leather was worn, but she was loath to part with it or have it reupholstered. Sitting in the armchair reminded Mariela of those rare, happy evenings when her mother would sit and read with her before the open fire. There wasn't much need for lighting the fire in California, but the open hearth was a central feature of the drawing room nonetheless. Of all the rooms in the house, the drawing room, with its oak-paneled walls and cream-colored, woolen carpet, was the only one modeled on Mariela's childhood home.

Mariela's thoughts briefly turned to her mother as she glanced wistfully at the logs in the fireplace. Her mother had the soul of a poet and wrote many short stories of young girls defying their elders and making their own way in the world. Mariela read every one, offering suggestions for names and places the plucky heroines could visit. One day, Mariela would return home and recover her mother's manuscripts so that others might find solace in them. Until that day, there was business to attend.

"Now, Frank, where were we?"

Following Chief Parker's discretionary slip, Mariela thought it wise to lean on his second-in-command. Leveraging Francis Eckhart's desire to elevate himself was far more preferable to Mariela than using the chief's daughter to apply pressure.

"You had just confirmed the details of the clean-up operation and were about to ask something," Eckhart replied with impassive calm.

Mariela found Eckhart to be a hard man to read. If she did not know better, she would swear his skills were honed at high-stakes tables on the Las Vegas strip, not working a beat on the streets of Los Angeles. His dark eyes revealed nothing as she studied his expression. There was no twitch to indicate approval or disgust at Mariela's orders, and his lips remained pursed but not tense.

"Yes," said Mariela, taking her glass of peach juice from the small table alongside her armchair as she watched Eckhart. "I trust you can carry out my request with more tact than your boss."

"I suspect we would not be having this conversation if you thought otherwise," Eckhart replied, hands held in his lap without so much as a hint of his thoughts on the task at hand or the slight at Chief Parker.

"I've heard good things about you, Frank. I predict big things in your future if you can deliver on this. I fear our illustrious chief of police has lost his nerve."

"Your trust is well placed," Eckhart replied with a note of pride. "However, Chief Parker deserves more credit. Upon discovering that one of our officers had sent a report to the FBI, he promptly quashed it."

Mariela gave Eckhart an unconvinced look. If that was Parker's attempt at throwing the FBI off the scent, Mariela dreaded to think what his efforts to shine a light on her dealings would look like. As much as she detested the idea, Mariela needed Sophie Parker as an ace up her sleeve.

"I'm sure you've heard that he went straight to Mrs. Sinclair-Blake," Eckhart continued, receiving the slightest of nods to confirm his statement. "A calculated move, designed to antagonize our friends at the FBI and have them throw the file straight back to us."

"A lucky break."

Skylar loathed it when people expected her to do something they were perfectly capable of doing themselves. For that reason alone, the chief's gambit produced a desirable outcome.

"Calculated," Eckhart repeated flatly. "As evidenced by the results. Rest assured, the officer responsible shall be making no such mistake again."

Mariela drew a deep breath and exhaled slowly. Eckhart's confidence was reassuring, but she knew Skylar too well. The distraction of the outbreak would only work in Mariela's favor for so long. The risk that Skylar would turn her attention back to the kidnap cases when things died down was too great.

"Skylar is tenacious. If she gets involved in this, it will not end well."

Eckhart rubbed one hand over his shaved head and down the back of his neck. "Let's call a spade a spade. You don't think Chief Parker is up to the task, do you?"

"The man is lucky to be alive," Mariela replied. Even though Mariela intended to elevate Eckhart, it would not harm her to remind him that his position relied on her goodwill. "When you're as careless as the chief, accidents become more frequent."

"Perhaps," Eckhart replied, rising to his feet. "I suspect he has yet to fulfill his potential. I shall ensure your plans are not impeded either way."

"Good," said Mariela, rising and gesturing to the door. "It would be unfortunate if I needed to take drastic measures to achieve the utopian vision I have for this city."

Eckhart nodded and allowed Mariela to usher him from her house. The man seemed more pliable than Parker, but his demeanor left Mariela with a knot in her gut. Needing more to work with, Mariela decided to get Vasily to unearth some of Frank's skeletons as soon as he returned from Death Valley.

"Your utopian vision?" came a voice from the hallway as Eckhart's car made its way down the cobblestone drive.

Mariela closed the front door and turned to face the owner of the silky, Australian accent. Her hair was cut short in the style of the punk-emo crossover youths of the early part of the century. Her baggy clothes, a dark flannel shirt and urban camo pants, hid the muscular physique Mariela knew was under those layers. Daryl Metzger; the council's top enforcer.

"What was your take?" Mariela asked, returning to the drawing room and finishing her glass of juice. Dealing with Daryl would require something stronger. "Can we trust him?"

"I don't trust any of you," said Daryl as she followed Mariela into the room and half-heartedly inspected the décor. "So long as you do the council's work, I tolerate you."

"Charming," Mariela muttered under her breath as she poured herself a glass of bourbon.

"I'm not here to be charming," Daryl replied, making Mariela wince at the realization Daryl had heard her. "I'm here to collect intel and report back to the council."

"Well," said Mariela, downing her drink and pouring another before turning to face Daryl, "you can inform Lukai and Nikola that everything is going to plan. Better, in fact. Not only am I on target for this month's shipment, I have managed to increase turnover at our Death Valley operation."

"And?" Daryl asked when it became clear Mariela had finished.

"And that's a good thing," Mariela said, biting back a retort about how obvious that should have been. The inability of the council to realize when they were onto a winner was a frequent occurrence, especially with Nikola, but it still caught Mariela by surprise.

"Have you found anything in Death Valley?" Daryl asked as she fiddled with the cluster of earrings in her left ear. Her dismissive tone made the question seem as inconsequential as an inquiry about next week's weather.

"Well, no," Mariela replied, her voice rising slightly in response to Daryl's attitude. "But it is only a matter of time. If the council's intel is correct, that is."

"Results are everything," said Daryl, fixing Mariela with a cold stare. "The rest is bullshit. In future, deliver results before bragging about how well you are doing."

Mariela clenched her fist, an act that did not go unnoticed by Daryl, the woman's thin lips curling into a smirk at the gesture, before opening a cupboard and pulling out a manila envelope.

"If results are what get you wet, you may want to read this," Mariela replied, holding the file out.

Mariela held her grip for a moment too long as Daryl reached out to take the file, releasing it only when Daryl's shifty eyes narrowed slightly.

Even though the woman could snap her like a twig, Mariela was determined to push back against her attempts at intimidation.

"This," Daryl said as she flipped through the contents of the envelope, "is something you can take pride in. This is something I can use."

"Yes, well, sometimes you need to know what you're doing to get results. Now, are we done?"

Daryl stuffed the papers back in the envelope and tucked it into the front of her pants before covering it with her shirt. "For now. Nikola has a lot riding on this scheme of yours. Pray your utopia isn't a hollow dream."

Mariela slowly sipped her bourbon to avoid speaking, watching Daryl over the top of the glass. Satisfied with her appraisal, Daryl marched from the room without a goodbye. If Mariela never saw the woman again, it would be too soon. There would be no place for Daryl in Mariela's new world. Suppressing a shudder, Mariela walked over to the window and watched as Dave tapped a bright yellow golf ball into the hole on the putting green. For a man presiding over the biggest catastrophe to hit Los Angeles in living memory, he seemed unusually at ease.

Mariela took a deep breath and emptied her glass.

"All in good time," she whispered to herself as she watched the world turn. Judgment could wait for another day.

-19-

LOS ANGELES COUNTY, CALIFORNIA
April 02, 2029

The second week of the quarantine was ending on a grim note for Michael Blake. Although the worst of the violence appeared to be behind them, keeping control of the city was taking its toll.

"CDC convoy inbound. ETA 9:05," Deputy Grayling said as Mike swiped at the 3D projection of Los Angeles that hovered over his screen. "Requesting permission to approach."

Claire Grayling was one of the deputized ex-soldiers aiding with the quarantine effort. A veteran of two Iraq wars, Claire's thirty years of communications and tactical response experience in protracted, hostile circumstances was a welcome addition to the team. Although Mike's CIRG training and experience meant he was no novice in coordinating missions, he was always willing to learn from the expertise of others.

"Granted," Mike replied before turning to the other officer in the command bunker, a pimped out portable building at the junction of the 118 and the I-405. "Shaw. Take Agents Vickery and Helms and join Officer Martinez at the inspection point. Let's get these CDC folks on their way. The sooner they're gone, the sooner they can return with more supplies."

"Yes, sir," Officer Shaw replied, saluting smartly before marching out through the open door.

Having completed their studies of the infection, the CDC was confident that their latest concoction would serve as both an antibiotic for the infected and an inoculation for the wider population. Despite heavy lobbying for the medication to be distributed to the neighboring counties first, it was President King's mandate that every surviving citizen inside the New York and Los Angeles quarantine must be treated before general distribution commenced.

"They look up to you," said Claire as she adjusted her headset, a superior version of the wireless earpiece-microphone combination used by entertainers. "The PD, I mean."

Mike gave Claire a bemused look, wondering where her line of reasoning was going.

"I expected more of an FBI versus LAPD mentality."

"You watch too many rebel cop movies," Mike replied as he placed his fingers over a flashing area of the map and flicked them open to zoom in.

"Are you trying to tell me the FBI doesn't rock up to precincts and tell the cop with a hunch they'll be taking the case from here?" Claire asked, stepping closer to the map and examining the alert.

"Well, maybe. Sometimes," Mike replied, pulling the map back slightly to study the area around the flagged incident. "How else are we meant to motivate them to do something reckless or comedic for the entertainment of others?"

Claire smirked at Mike's dryly delivered sarcasm as she nodded to the map. "You want me to get Whittaker's squad to address that?"

"No," said Mike after weighing his options, tapping the data stream alongside the map as he spoke. "It's low-level looting in a sparsely populated area. Inform Chief Parker to mobilize some squad cars, and have Whittaker on standby. In case it escalates. I'm stepping outside for a few. Anything else crops up, I trust you to make the call."

Claire nodded, returning to her post to contact the LAPD as Mike pulled out his cellphone. His wife's number was saved as "A Skylar" to make sure she was always top of his contacts. When Mike pointed out it was an unnecessary gesture as he had her on speed dial, Skylar's response was to poke out her tongue and give him the middle finger. In response, Mike saved his number to her phone as "AA Mike" as a constant reminder he was not *a* Mike, but *the* Mike. It was a move that backfired on him when his birthday rolled around and all he received from her was a sobriety chip.

Skylar had been a fixture in Mike's life for longer than he could remember. Mike's father worked security for Skylar's grandfather back when George Sinclair was still alive. As Skylar's parents were frequently away on business trips, Skylar and her brother, Sawyer, spent a lot of their youth at her grandfather's Santa Paula estate, and Mike took every opportunity he could to visit the Sinclair children. As an only child, life could get lonesome at times.

Mike's opportunities to play with Skylar became less frequent after her brother died. Following the Fourth of July accident that claimed the lives of Sawyer and his parents, Skylar relocated to Wales. It was a move that came as a surprise to Mike, who expected the six-year-old orphan to move in with her grandfather full-time. It was not until they started dating, fifteen years later, that Mike learned the frightening truth behind the decision.

"How's it going, love?" Skylar said as her welcome visage appeared on Mike's screen.

"Working from home today?" Mike replied, taking a pair of sunglasses from his pocket and sliding them on to reduce the sun's glare and make the screen easier to see.

"Jealous?" Skylar asked, rubbing the fleecy collar of her robe against her cheek and purring contentedly to spark a reaction.

"Not really," said Mike, refusing to rise to the bait. "Why would I want to be home with you when I can spend twelve hours as the king of my castle, glaring down at my subjects from the battlements?"

Mike glanced up to the highway and the ominous wall of reinforced steel that made Los Angeles a prison as he spoke. It was no wonder there was so much rioting. Treat people like criminals for long enough and, sooner or later, they will start behaving like criminals.

I dunno, Mike," Skylar replied, adjusting her camera angle and opening her robe to expose her cleavage, "I can think of two reasons."

"Only two?" asked Mike, flashing Skylar a mischievous grin.

"How many were you thinking?" asked Skylar as she reached into her robe with her free hand and began massaging her breast.

"I'm sure you can think of a third reason."

Skylar angled the camera back to her face and pressed a finger to her bottom lip. As Mike watched, his heartbeat quickening as he imagined the things he would do with his wife that night, Skylar slowly wrapped her tongue around the tip of her finger and drew it into her mouth.

"What about a fourth?" Mike asked as Skylar slowly slid her finger in and out of her mouth, curling her tongue around her digit.

Skylar grinned wickedly as she slipped another finger into her mouth and ran her tongue between them.

"No fair," Mike said with a laugh. "That doesn't count, and you know it."

"Maybe I'll record a video of where they go next," Skylar replied, pulling her robe closed again. "Business first."

"Okay, how much for an hour?"

"Oi, cheeky," Skylar said, giggling as she tucked her hair behind her ears. "What's the status with you?"

"Not so good," Mike said, scratching at the five o'clock shadow that dusted his cheeks, softening his razor-sharp jawline in the morning sun. "We've had people approaching the perimeter again in the early hours, begging us to let them leave this city of death. The agents on the perimeter have been turning them back, but it's hard to watch, you know?"

"That's because you care. I can't help feeling a twinge of fear for you all, though. Fear and respect. Fear, respect, and guilt for not being down there with you."

Mike gave a slight smile and nodded, taking a breath and pursing his lips together as if to hold back a sigh. "At least we're not getting hit as hard as New York. Eight hundred civilians gunned down at a protest gone wrong. What did they expect calling in the national guard would do? They better not try that down here."

"Yeah, about that," said Skylar, drawing out the words.

"No. No fucking way," Mike stated, receiving a nod from Skylar in response. "You've gotta be fucking kidding me. Why would you surrender command to the guard? They'll turn the city into a warzone!"

"I haven't, and we'll make sure it doesn't come to that," Skylar replied, her voice taking on an authoritative tone. "It took some haggling, but I've agreed that the guard will take up position on the wall, under the command of the FBI. That will free up all our agents and the LAPD's officers to move into the city and restore order."

Mike turned his gaze toward Thousand Oaks, expecting to see tanks and armored personnel carriers trundling down the highway. As much as he welcomed the opportunity to bring the quarantine to an end and get the city back on track, the thought of the national guard being involved filled him with dread.

-20-

VENTURA COUNTY, CALIFORNIA
April 08, 2029

The water rattled against Skylar's window as a gust of wind blew the gently falling raindrops sideways. California had experienced one of the driest winters of the century. Some April rain was a welcome change. A light fog crept across the yard, hiding the furthest corners of the avocado orchard, and trapped the warmth like a blanket for the earth.

"New infection cases are dropping rapidly. Survival rates for the infected are steadily climbing."

Taylor's words were welcome, a much-needed boost after so much devastation. The combined efforts of every agency, every effort spent in making sure everyone received medical care, was finally amounting to something.

"What are the numbers?" Skylar asked, resting her head against the glass of the study window.

The branches of the avocado trees below her swayed in the breeze, the rustling leaves catching the moonlight and reflecting in turn, sending a coded message in their blinks and flashes. She had no idea what the flicker of reflected light was trying to tell her, but she felt it was a message of reassurance, affirming Taylor's news that the worst was behind them.

"Before these treatments, we were looking at a mortality rate of seventy-seven percent. Even if there had been enough medication during those first few days, it would have made little difference. The death toll among the treated and untreated was near identical. In the few cases where the antibiotics did have an effect, the toxins released into the body proved more lethal than the actual infection. With the new medication, our prediction is high single-digit mortality."

"Pretend I'm not a medical expert, Taylor. What does that compare with?"

"Pneumonia," Taylor replied after a brief pause. "The milder cases, that is. Provided treatment is administered before the toxins build up."

Heaving a combined sigh of relief and exasperation, Skylar raised her head and rubbed at the smudge she left on the glass with the sleeve of her nightshirt. As Taylor continued to recount his findings, Mike's hand appeared next to hers, making her jump as he gently moved her away from the window.

"Sorry," she whispered, covering the receiver with her hand. Although he was understanding of the twenty-four-hour nature of her job, Skylar tried to keep the late-night calls from interrupting his sleep.

As Mike began cleaning the blemish from the window, using a cloth and small canister of lens cleaner from her desk, Taylor concluded his report. The findings left Skylar with a sick feeling in her stomach like all the wind had been knocked out of her.

"Do you have any more developments on its movement patterns?" asked Skylar as she paced the room.

Dealing with the aftermath of the attack had taken its toll on Taylor and his colleagues at the CDC. The worst nightmare for someone like Taylor, a man that had dedicated his life to preventing unnecessary illness, was an unfathomable plague. As crucial as treating the infection was, a cure was only half the problem. The sigh he uttered carried an entire week's worth of stress that emphasized that sentiment.

"If you mean its origin, no. This thing came from nowhere. No further outbreaks since. The small number of infected victims outside quarantine were traced back to the city on the day of the outbreak."

Small mercies. Knowing the quarantine was not in vain made Skylar feel like her contribution mattered.

"I suppose we're in a decent position, all things considered," she said, taking a seat at her desk to avoid wearing a path in the carpet. "I can imagine the various agencies are already disagreeing on how best to proceed. As soon as this assessment is circulated, I'll be back to refereeing a giant pissing contest. Just as I was making progress too."

Mike chuckled at her comment, all too familiar with Skylar's rants about the latest power plays by the likes of Diaz. She was too close to restoring order to let them screw it up with their bureaucratic games.

"Hence the heads up," Taylor replied. "I'll be issuing my report in three hours, recommending that treated citizens be permitted to leave the city. The quarantine can be lifted the moment every citizen is treated."

With the smudge gone, Mike threw the cloth back on her desk and kissed Skylar's cheek before heading back to the bedroom, tapping the wall clock on his way. 3:01 a.m.

"Won't be long," she told him before addressing Taylor again. "By the way, you're the only person that takes the 'call day or night' offer seriously. I appreciate the advance notice, don't get me wrong, but this is way beyond the witching hour."

"Hey, you're the one that made it an option," Taylor said, slurping something loud enough that Skylar heard it at her end of the call. "One more heads-up, FEMA wants to begin clean up and have started harassing us over it."

That did not surprise Skylar. Since the CDC first started treating people, Diaz was pushing for unrestricted access to the city, despite the CDC issuing a statement that they were unable to guarantee the success of any vaccination. Anyone entering the city would not be allowed back out. Without that specter looming over her, Diaz would no doubt increase her efforts to take over the operation. Forcing the FEMA agents to come down to the quarantine had backfired on Skylar where Diaz was concerned. Where the experience had humbled the others and shocked them into action, Diaz came out of the affair with the notion that it somehow put her in charge of the operation. More than once, Skylar had to remind Diaz she was not the Brian Johnson to her Bon Scott.

"I get that the city needs to be re-opened, but I'm not risking lives so FEMA can hit some arbitrary deadline."

"I know, just giving you the heads up. I know you'll be a bit more surgical than this…" Taylor paused as he consulted his notes, "Lauren Diaz."

"Roger that. I'll relay that to my people tomorrow. It's too early in the morning to talk to anyone here."

Taylor took the hint, wishing Skylar a good night as he ended the call. Tomorrow promised to be a long day.

-21-

LOS ANGELES COUNTY, CALIFORNIA
April 13, 2029

As Shay pulled her white cotton socks over her feet she reflected on the bizarreness of the last few weeks. To think she would go from obtaining a fake ID and sneaking out to a nightclub to this was, well, unthinkable. Her time in the cage was short-lived, thank God. Although the creeps that took them ignored the police officer, they snapped to attention and rushed to make Adam, Caleb, Emma and Shay comfortable when the giant foreign man arrived and started barking orders. Shay was under no illusions that the giant was there to free them, but he showed concern for their welfare that was sadly lacking in their captors. Granted, the hospitality he showed them meant their ankles were chained to a bed instead of being in a cage, but it was still a bed.

The chains were a temporary measure to ensure their safety. According to the giant, a man Shay discovered was named Vasily, Los Angeles was under attack. Vasily worked for a secret organization dedicated to protecting people and delivering them to a new world of peace and prosperity. His people were told to gather as many young people as possible to populate the new world. Unfortunately, their methods left a lot to be desired.

It all sounded far-fetched to Shay, like one of those dystopia books that Hollywood kept making schlocky movies about, but what choice did she have? She either joined the fifth wave of divergent, maze running teens or die tomorrow, when the war began.

Those who wished it could leave Los Angeles. Although the police had quarantined the city, Vasily was helping to smuggle people to a secret base they were building in Death Valley. If they were willing to help in the construction, they would be permitted to take refuge there. For those unable or unwilling to help the construction efforts, there were opportunities to assist in the underground movement to retake Los Angeles. The alternative was to go it alone. Each of them had a choice to make.

Despite being shown news footage of riots in the city and police officers attacking civilians with water cannons at the barricades, some people chose to leave. Emma, Adam and Caleb were amongst them. As they waited to be released, Vasily told them of a thirteen-year-old girl who chose to leave, choking up a little when he described finding her broken body before the day was over. It was enough to make Caleb and Emma change their minds.

Of the remaining options, Caleb chose Death Valley. The thought of clogged pores and rough, callused hands from shoveling rubble and pouring concrete did not appeal to Shay or Emma. That just left servitude. For many, this was no more onerous than donating blood. The rebels fighting to overthrow their corrupt oppressors could not rely on aid from hospitals, the outlets of propaganda from big pharma, which, in turn, was a weapon in the arsenal of tyranny. They relied on blood from the brave boys and girls that would one day claim the world for justice. For some, there were other ways of serving the cause.

"It's just, oh, I don't know how to explain it," A Latina named Alejandra told Shay when she asked about the more intimate options available. "It hurts at first, but once they're in it feels good. In a weird, different sort of way. I was nervous at first, but one of the boys told me he tried and nearly came from it. You should give it a go."

Unconvinced but willing to try anything to improve her position, Shay agreed. But only if Alejandra came with her. Although Alejandra vouched for her master, Shay did not feel comfortable visiting him for something so sensual alone. After obtaining assurances that he would take it slow and make sure Shay was comfortable before progressing further, they were finally doing it.

Slipping her shoes over her heels, Shay took a deep breath and looked across at Alejandra, barely noticing how accustomed to her surroundings she had become. After the inhumane conditions of the cage, the converted factory that served as home was almost luxurious. Plain, cinder block walls, coated in discolored beige paint, rose to a corrugated steel roof. To alleviate the heat, an ancient air-conditioning unit strained to pump cool air into the facility, fighting against the heat generated by the Neolithic fluorescent tube lights suspended from the rafters. Although the building was split down the middle, separating the girls from the boys, Shay had no personal space or privacy.

Out of curiosity, Shay had once counted the beds and determined that there were three-hundred and forty-three bunk beds in the girls' side of the factory alone. Her guess, ninety percent were occupied.

"Are we really doing this?" Emma asked, sidling over to Shay and Alejandra as Shay smoothed down her skirt.

Although they were far from fashionable, Vasily ensured that each of the brave souls under his protection was provided with serviceable clothes. The skirt that Shay picked out for that night was the best of a bad bunch. Although she would never admit it, the skirt was a size too small, pinching at the flesh of her hips, and the vibrancy of the red fabric was lost to repeated washing. Her dull-white, sleeveless blouse was barely an improvement. Being a size too large, it hung loosely from her, disguising the curves of which she was so proud and making her look frumpish. All she needed was a knitted cardigan and a thermos flask.

By comparison, Alejandra looked amazing in her skintight jeans, midriff revealing crop top, and half-length denim jacket. That was one advantage of having a sponsor, it granted access to better things, and Shay could not deny that was a major factor in her decision to go through with her plan.

"*We* are not doing anything," Shay said to Emma. "You're only fourteen."

Shay could not be certain if it was the similarity between the names Emma and Emily or just a big sister instinct that made her protective of the younger girl. Apart from being rakishly thin, there was little that Emma had in common with Shay's best friend. Her hair was brown, not blonde, and her face was rounder than Emily's ghost-like visage. Maybe it was her mousy nervousness that made Emma a substitute for Emily. There was nothing Shay could do for her friend, so protecting Emma was the next best thing.

"Look around," said Alejandra, cutting off Emma's protest as she gestured around the room. "We're all niñas here, chica. We do what we must. Let's have some fun while we do it."

Shay glanced down, reluctantly accepting Alejandra's point. Despite her womanly figure, she was just as much a child as Emma in the eyes of the law, no matter how much she pretended otherwise.

"Okay," Shay said putting her hand on Emma's scrawny shoulder. "Together then. Today we stop being niñas and... What's Spanish for 'women' again?"

"Las mujeres," Emma replied, nervously glancing at Alejandra to check her pronunciation.

"Mujeres," said Shay, resigning herself to the fact that Emma was going through with it. "Today we become mujeres."

At least Shay would be there to make sure Emma was protected.

-22-

LOS ANGELES COUNTY, CALIFORNIA
April 13, 2029

Despite Mike's reservations, relinquishing the border to the national guard was proving effective. Although they had no live ammunition, the sheer presence and militaristic nature of the national guard was enough to make the average citizen think twice about assailing the barricades. With more CDC convoys arriving in the city, attacks against the FBI and LAPD were also becoming less frequent. After weeks of oppression, public opinion was beginning to shift from seeing the government as gatekeepers to one of relief bringers.

"How are we doing for time, sergeant?" Mike asked as he stepped into the air-conditioned office.

Having surrendered his command post to the guard, Mike's base of operations was moved to the reception area of an office building off the junction of San Fernando Mission Boulevard and Langdon Avenue, within spitting distance of the CDC processing center on Orion Avenue. With so many people wanting to leave the city, it was easier to administer treatment at the designated CDC access points on the border and ship them straight out than treat them at the field surgeries and hospitals within the city and process them again at the border. For those who were happy to stay, treatment was also available at any major hospital.

"I've told you a hundred times, I haven't been a sergeant for some time now, sir," Claire replied, switching displays and pulling up data on the treatment schedules.

"And I've told you a hundred and one times, Mike is fine," he said as he stepped around the reception desk Claire was using as a monitoring station to get a better look at the data.

"We're going to miss the senate's deadline by just over twenty-eight hours," said Claire, scrolling through updates on one screen as she reached over to open an alarm notification on another.

"Still?" Mike asked, peering at the details of the alarm.

"Looks that way," Claire replied, switching screens again to bring up details on agent placement. It was an improvement on the thirty-five hours from which they started, but there was only so much time that could be squeezed from the treatment schedule. "I can't see us improving further on that."

"It is what it is," Mike said with a shake of his head as Claire flagged three groups for support. "That's what happens when politicians who don't understand the details set deadlines. Flag Hancock's team as well."

Claire cast Mike a questioning look as she tapped on the agent directory tab. Grimacing, he nodded and opened the additional details on the alarm.

"This guy here," said Mike, opening a mugshot under the alarm. "Mark Ewing. Real troublemaker. His followers don't appreciate the irony of fighting fascism with fascism. If he's with the group heading this way, we're dealing with the heavy mob."

Claire nodded in understanding and flagged Agent Hancock for support. "Sergeant Hopkins is moving additional troops to the gate as well."

With a slight nod, Mike turned and headed back outside. As tempting as staying in the air-conditioned building was, keeping tensions in check was going to be difficult with Ewing stirring up his followers. Pre-emptive de-escalation was in order.

Mark Ewing was one of the instigators, if not the primary cause, of violence during the 2024 debacle, turning the protests into a full-scale riot. To his followers, he was a determined champion in the fight against the fascist, alt-right regime threatening to consume government and turn the States into the Fourth Reich. In reality, he was an anarchist who found a pliable audience to imprint with his ideology of violence. It was possible his recent, eighteen-month prison sentence turned Ewing into a rehabilitated citizen. Mike was not going to chance it.

Turning to his right, Mike examined the queues waiting for treatment. Every hour, more citizens arrived to replace those who filed through the CDC's field surgery. To prevent things from getting out of hand, each citizen was allocated a processing time for their surgery of choice. It was the easiest way to manage the rush that would otherwise ensue as people clamored to get treatment.

"Where do you want us, sir?" came a voice from behind Mike, drawing his attention from the soldiers moving into position on the bridge where San Fernando Mission Boulevard passed under the highway.

"The main group is coming up Langdon," Mike replied, turning to Agent Haskell. "Place some additional barriers across the road and take up position behind them."

Haskell nodded and signaled to her team to get moving. They were just in time. No sooner had they dragged some barriers into place, the crowd of protestors came into view.

"Okay, team, you know the drill by now," Haskell shouted as her agents locked shields.

"Claire," Mike called into his earpiece. "How long 'til the other teams arrive?"

"Franklin is three minutes out. The others are eight and ten."

"We don't have three minutes," Mike replied, turning to see more protestors marching down San Fernando Mission Boulevard as the group on Langdon came to a halt in front of Haskell's team, shouting abuse and brandishing a variety of homemade signs telling the fascists to do the world a favor and kill themselves.

"Sergeant Hopkins is offering support," said Claire, emerging from the office to get a visual on the situation. "Permission to allow the guard into the city, sir?"

Mike turned from one group of protestors to the other, weighing his options. Enlisting the support of the guard may be enough to put a match to the kindling for those among the crowd that already saw the police as a glorified militia, enforcing the will of the state. Without them, their position would be overrun. Judging by the rhetoric on the placards, violence was highly likely, regardless of Mike's decision.

"Do it," Mike replied, turning his attention to the civilians waiting for treatment. After everything they had gone through, he had to do everything in his power to get them over this last hurdle.

As the protestors began beating their signs against the riot shields of Haskell's team, Mike unclipped his transponder and cycled through the options. De-escalation was looking increasingly unlikely, but delaying further action was still within his reach. Syncing his headset to the speaker system installed at the junction, Mike prayed for a miracle.

"Citizens of Los Angeles, I hear your frustrations. Please, aid us in administering treatment as smoothly and efficiently as possible by joining the queues at your designated time. And remember, a peaceful protest is a respected protest."

Cries of "bullshit," "fascist" and "liar" rang out as the crowd eased their attack. The moment was short-lived, the assault against the riot shields redoubling as those at the back spurred the front row of protestors onward. So much for reasoning with them.

"Sir," cried Claire as the high-pitched whirr of an electric motor cut through the sound of the protests.

As Mike turned to the direction of the sound, the force against his back knocked him from his feet. The pain in his shoulder barely registered over the sickening, dull crunch of metal hitting a body. The crack of glass, followed by the thud of flesh on asphalt echoed in Mike's ears as the world spun. His mind raced to make sense of what happened, recognizing that a car raced by as a fire hydrant brought Mike to a sudden stop. Feet from the queue of startled citizens awaiting treatment, one of the guard's armored carriers charged into the fray, forcefully bringing the car to a halt and averting further damage.

Pulling himself up to rest against the hydrant, Mike turned his attention to Claire. Her vacant stare burned itself into his mind as blood trickled from her nose. With protestors racing down the road and soldiers deploying to stop them, Mike hauled himself to his feet, ignoring the tearing pain in his shoulder, and rushed to Claire's side. The awkward angle of her neck was evidence enough that it was too late, but Mike cradled her head and begged her to move, regardless.

A pair of motorbikes hurtled by as Mike desperately tugged at Claire's body, the pain in his shoulder making it impossible to hoist her up. Bursting through the national guard's shield wall as two soldiers grabbed Mike and Claire, the bikers were knocked from their vehicles by precision blasts of the water cannons on the wall.

"Get those men in cuffs," Agent Franklin shouted, arriving on the scene as the shield wall closed behind Mike and Claire. "Use everything short of lethal force to stop those protestors."

Hurling themselves against the riot shields as Franklin's team joined the guard, the protestors rained down blows and hurled projectiles over the defenders' heads, glass shattering as it hit the floor.

"Fall back," Mike shouted as the unmistakable smell of gasoline assailed his nostrils.

Struggling to withdraw while maintaining a functional battle line, several of the soldiers were engulfed in flames as a Molotov cocktail ignited the gasoline. The shrieks of pain from protestors caught in the blaze filled the air as any semblance of an orderly retreat collapsed. Equipped with fire retardant riot gear, the soldiers and agents fared better than the protestors, regrouping behind the wall of burning gasoline. As more bottles were hurled into the spreading fire, Mike's eyes were drawn to Claire and the flames caressing her lifeless body.

"Where's Ewing?" Mike demanded, turning to Franklin with vengeance in his eyes.

-23-

LOS ANGELES COUNTY, CALIFORNIA
April 13, 2029

Stepping from the silver 4x4 that was sent to collect them, Shay felt a surge of homesickness at the salty aroma of the Pacific Ocean. Not that there was anything for her at home. The plague unleashed on Los Angeles claimed the lives of her friends and family. Glad to be spared the suffering, Shay looked down at the beach and the retreating tide, wondering why she was chosen as Alejandra and Emma joined her on the sidewalk. Why not Emily, with her financial connections? Or Karen, with her dizzying intellect? Even Bethany, dumb, whorish Bethany, had the advantage of political connections? What privilege did Shay have?

"Are you ready?" Alejandra asked, smiling at Shay and Emma as she pushed open the gate to the beach house.

Turning her attention from the golden sand to the sun-bleached wood of the house, Shay nodded and followed Alejandra into the garden. Wiping her clammy palms on her skirt, Shay looked back over her shoulder to see the nervous excitement on Emma's face. Her eyes were wide with wonder, soaking in the sights of the garden, with its palm trees and statues of heroic men and women, as she followed Shay and Alejandra. It was obvious to Shay that the potential pain of their upcoming experience paled in comparison to the prospect of heightened pleasure. It made Shay wonder if Emma was also a virgin or if she had more experience in the pleasures of the flesh. The closest Shay had come to a sexual encounter was having Bobby Knightley clumsily poke two fingers in her before filling his underwear. When Alejandra described her encounters as being better than sex, Shay did not have a very good baseline with which to compare.

The concern must have been clear on Shay's face, prompting Alejandra to put her arm around her shoulders as they reached the front door.

"Don't worry," Alejandra said as she pressed the doorbell. "Relax, and it will be fine. Carlos knows how to treat a woman. Besides, the boss lady would cut off his head if she found out he forced himself on us."

Shay's throat clenched. All her concerns were centered around the prospect of not enjoying herself or wanting to change her mind the moment he penetrated her. Alejandra had sung his praises so highly that the thought he might force himself upon her had not crossed Shay's mind.

"Let's go," said Emma as the door swung open. "I can't wait to find out if it's as good as you say it is."

Embarrassed into action by Emma's enthusiasm, Shay followed Alejandra into the house and up the stairs.

"Motors," Alejandra said as the door swung closed behind them, making Shay jump. "The house is rigged with cameras and actuators to allow guests to enter and exit without disturbing the master."

"So, why ring the doorbell?" Emma asked, one foot on the staircase.

Alejandra paused, almost at the top. "I… don't know. Habit, I guess."

Shay nodded in understanding. Sick of people leaving lights on around the house, her father installed sensor-operated lighting last year. It did not stop Shay from reaching for the switch every time she entered a room. There was no such lighting in the beach house. The passage at the top of the stairs was cloaked in darkness, the scant light from downstairs barely illuminating Alejandra's profile as she stepped off the stairs.

Reaching the top of the stairs, Shay's eyes adjusted to the gloom enough to make out four doorways, two to each side. Straining to make out any further detail, Shay almost jumped out of her skin as something brushed against her hand. Her uncharacteristic confidence finally buckling, Emma gripped Shay's hand tightly.

"I don't want to do this," Emma said, her voice barely audible in the oppressive darkness. "I've changed my mind."

"That's quite alright, child," a man's voice called out, its owner cast in silhouette as he opened the door at the end of the left-hand corridor. "You are free to change your mind at any time. Although, I encourage you to see for yourself before you make a final decision."

Shay watched as Alejandra hugged Carlos, her face pressed against his bare, sculpted chest as he gently cradled her in his arms. Emma's grip slackened, allowing blood to once more flow to Shay's fingers, as Carlos released Alejandra from their embrace and stepped aside.

"How are things at the academy?" Carlos asked as Alejandra stepped past him. "Not pushing you too hard, I hope."

In addition to her visits with Carlos, Alejandra was signed up for the organization's combat academy, where those who wanted to play a more active role in liberating Los Angeles from the yoke of tyranny were trained to become the next generation of freedom fighters.

"Only as hard as needed to ensure our success," Alejandra replied, shrugging off her jacket and tensing her toned biceps. "Soon, I'll be strong enough to defend us from the oppressors."

Wrapping his fingers around Alejandra's arm, Carlos smiled and gently squeezed her taut muscles. "Very good. I pity the man who follows you down a dark alley. And what of our friends? How are you supporting our community and making our leader's vision a reality?"

Every one of the children in Vasily's care was given basic self-defense training, but being on the front line held no appeal for Shay. Faced with Carlos' warm, encouraging smile, Shay began to question the wisdom of her decision.

"I give blood," said Emma, releasing Shay's hand and moving toward Carlos. "I'm too weak to fight."

"Nobody is weak if their heart has a purpose," Carlos replied, running his hand through Emma's hair and cupping her chin. "Together, as one, we are strong. And what of my ebony princess?"

Shay swallowed and stepped forward at being addressed directly. "I want to help, but I'm not much of a fighter."

"You don't need to be a fighter to serve the cause," said Carlos, extending his hand to Shay as Emma joined Alejandra on the room's three-seat sofa. "We need people with strength of mind as well as body if we are to educate those who fear our way of life. I sense you have the strength of mind that will make you a powerful leader of our new world."

Shay bowed her head, unable to look Carlos in the eye for fear of exposing her truth. She was not powerful. Everybody knew that. Stupid, naïve, ignorant, childish and self-absorbed. That was the person people knew. And they made sure Shay knew it.

"No," Carlos said, gently lifting her chin. "Hold your head high. You are one of us now. You, are a winner."

Shay looked into Carlos' eyes. And Alejandra's. And Emma's. They all stared back with admiration. They were all enthralled by the power inside her. A power that was there her entire life, waiting for Shay to harness it. Carlos nodded, his smile growing wider as he witnessed Shay's awakening.

"Shall we begin?" he asked, leading Shay to the sofa.

Sat between Emma and Alejandra, Shay took in the details of the room. Besides the sofa, there was an armchair, upholstered in the same faded crimson fabric, and a small table that separated the two. A curtain divided the room, making it appear much cozier than it should, and a roller cabinet stood behind the door. It was far from the display of grandeur Shay expected before her arrival but perfectly in keeping with the humility Carlos exuded.

"I think Shay should go first," said Alejandra, patting Shay's knee as Carlos opened the roller top and poured them each a drink. "As any true leader should."

Carlos looked serious for a moment as he handed each of them a shot of bourbon. "Only if that is the heart's desire. We don't pressure anybody into doing anything."

"It is," said Shay, the words leaving her mouth before she realized it was everything she wanted. She turned to Emma. "I want to be first. To show Emma that it will be alright."

Taking his seat in the armchair, Carlos beckoned for Shay to join him. With the girls watching, their expressions a mix of jealousy and anticipation, Shay sat upon Carlos' knee and angled her body toward him.

"Relax," he told her. "You're so tense. Here, let me massage your shoulders."

Shay watched Alejandra's face as Carlos worked her shoulders, the tension draining from her body. There was a perverse pleasure in seeing Alejandra's breathing quicken, her mouth opening slightly as she struggled to contain herself. Emma, too, was not immune to the mesmerizing effect of Carlos' technique.

"I want to taste you," he whispered in Shay's ear. The gentle breeze created by the words sent shivers down her spine.

Pulling her hair to one side, Shay tilted her head to expose her neck. The signal was not ignored, and Carlos pressed his lips to her flesh.

"I need you to say it," he said as he kissed from her shoulder to her jaw. "Command me."

Shay closed her eyes, savoring the feeling of having him hanging on her word. "Take me."

Inflamed with desire, Shay barely felt the sharp sting as Carlos sank his teeth into her neck. In a flash, the pain was gone, just as Alejandra promised, swept away by waves of pleasure as he lapped at the drops of ruby red liquid that rose on her neck. Her pulse quickened as he pulled her closer. His muscular frame pushed against her back, one hand on her arm while the other held her shoulder. She pressed back, encouraging him to go further.

It was all over too soon. Just as Shay was beginning to lose herself in the euphoric sensations that coursed through her body, he released her, licking his lips. Alejandra was before her, begging Shay to allow her to share in the joy. The temptation to refuse her was strong, but what sort of leader kept the joys of this world for themselves.

In that moment, realization dawned. Shay understood what utopia looked like.

-24-

LOS ANGELES COUNTY, CALIFORNIA
April 13, 2029

Violence begets violence. Mike repeated the phrase, determined to not let his anger get the better of him as Mark Ewing was dragged into the office. The memory of Claire's empty stare made it a futile gesture.

One volunteer, two soldiers, and sixteen civilians no longer drew breath because Ewing wanted to turn fear and distrust into a weapon against law and order.

"Resisted arrest," Agent Haskell said by way of explanation for Ewing's appearance.

Mike nodded. Claire made a lot of friends supporting the quarantine, Haskell included. Ewing was lucky she found him first. If it was Mike, Ewing would have resisted a lot harder. With the fire threatening to engulf them, Ewing's mob scattered to the wind, leaving their leader at the mercy of the FBI. Discovered hiding in a gas station washroom, his journey to justice was not as rough as he deserved.

"I wish to file a complaint about police brutality," Ewing mumbled through broken teeth, blood dripping from his chin.

"Of course," Mike replied turning to Agent Haskell. "Your bodycam footage will corroborate Mr. Ewing's story, won't it?"

"Damaged in the riot, sir," Agent Haskell said with a perfect poker face.

"Hmm," Mike said, turning back to Ewing. "That's the problem with riots. Things get broken."

The crunch of cartilage as Ewing's nose was flattened against his face would not bring Claire back, but it did relieve some tension.

"Get this terrorist over to lockup," said Mike, wiping the blood from his fist. "And get me a working bodycam. Mine's broken."

"The Pharaohs called Moses a terrorist. Look at him now."

Mike grabbed Ewing by the throat, forcing him to the floor and planting a knee on his chest.

"You dare to compare the cowardly acts of violence you commit to scripture? You're no freedom fighter. You're not liberating slaves. You're just a psychopath, intent on destroying lives. Well, not anymore."

Releasing Ewing's throat when he realized the man could not breathe, Mike stepped back and let Haskell take the creep away. The temptation to beat Ewing to a bloody pulp was strong, but Mike had to believe justice would prevail. Otherwise, Ewing won.

Sitting at the console, Mike allowed a tear to run down his cheek. Claire's coffee was still on the side, a milk skin floating on its cold surface.

"I smoked for twenty years," Mike remembered her saying when he suggested she lay off the full-fat milk. "Drank hard liquor for thirty. If that don't kill me, nothing will. Especially not the juice from a cow's tit."

Mike picked up the mug, drew a deep breath, and hurled it at the wall.

"Fuck," he muttered through clenched teeth, unsure if it was the tearing in his shoulder or the rage in his heart that prompted the outburst. Why did she have to push him out of harm's way?

"Sir?" Sergeant Torre asked, glancing at the coffee streaks on the wall as he entered the reception area.

"It's nothing," Mike replied, standing up and making to leave. "I need to go see Sergeant Hopkins."

"Not unless I say so," said Torre, placing his hand against Mike's chest.

"Need I remind you, the guard answers to the FBI here. As your commanding officer, I order you to step aside."

"And as a medical officer," Torre replied, undaunted by Mike's words, "I order you to cut the tough guy act and let me examine that shoulder."

Mike glowered at Torre's defiant expression, counting to ten in his head before relenting. There was no hiding the fact that his collision with the hydrant damaged something. With every passing minute, the pain ratcheted up another notch, making it harder to move.

"Separated shoulder," Torre concluded after a brief examination. "We need to get you to a hospital to be certain, but it doesn't look too serious. Who's next in command?"

"Deputy Gray…" Mike began, habit moving his mouth before his brain engaged gears. "Uh, Agent Hancock. He's overseeing the cleanup outside."

"Okay, sit tight. We'll have you checked out and drugged up soon enough. Until then, keep that shoulder still."

Mike nodded. Even if he could, he doubted he had enough fight left to argue against Torre's instructions.

-25-

VENTURA COUNTY, CALIFORNIA
April 27, 2029

"I don't want to see that."

Alex glanced sideways at the sound of Mike's voice. It was enough of a distraction to get Alex killed. Heavy machine-gun fire tore through him as he caught the edge of the wall to which he was dashing, falling to the ground in a bloody mess instead of reaching the relative safety of the stone edifice.

"Sorry, guys," said Alex as a chorus of complaints and jeers came over his headset. "Some clown distracted me. Going AFK a sec."

"Aw, did my little orphan-in-law get a booboo?" said Mike, curling his bottom lip down and theatrically rubbing beneath his eyes.

"I dunno. Does my eyes bleeding from that thing on your face count as a booboo?"

Mike raised his chin as if deep in thought and stroked the short, stubbly beard he was starting to grow out. No longer than the close-cropped, ash-brown crew cut Mike sported, Alex could not resist pointing out that the wiry fuzz around his jaw made him look like a kiwifruit.

"Nothing wrong with a bit of facial hair. You'll learn that yourself when you grow up," Mike said, looking around the room. "You planning to put that thing away anytime soon?"

"I've only just logged on." Alex waved his gamepad in the air for emphasis as he removed his headset. "First mission. Honest, squire."

"Don't you squire me. And I was referring to your other joystick."

Alex lifted his vest to reveal more of his bare flesh and slapped his exposed buttock. "You're just jealous I've got something to expose. Besides, my jeans are in the wash."

"Along with your only pair of boxer shorts, I assume. Your sister will lose her shit if she sees you free balling it on her sofa."

Alex did not doubt that for a second.

"Don't panic, dude," he replied with a smirk as Mike flipped over a cushion and checked behind the armchair. "I'm not dumb enough to risk the wrath of Skylar by free balling it. I put an old rag down. Don't want my nut sack sticking to the leather."

"I don't want your nut sack in the house. Don't you have anywhere else you can be? Your sister needs a break, something to take her mind off work. I'm cooking up a bit of a treat for her, and I don't want you waving your junk around the place, even if you do need binoculars to see it."

Alex scratched his knee as he thought for a moment. "Most of the boys are in San Fran for Wes' stag party. I could give Maria a ring, I suppose. See what she's up to while they're away."

Mike stopped and turned to Alex. "Who's Maria? What happened to Annalise?"

"She was too clingy. Maria is Wes' aunt."

Mike raised an eyebrow. "Trying your luck with an older woman? Respect."

Alex shook his head. "Late pregnancy. Maria's only a year older than Wes."

"Ah. Wes has a randy granny. Gotcha. How come you didn't go with them to San Fran?"

"I only know him because he's friends with Tanner," said Alex, logging out of the game as Mike dropped into the armchair, frustrated by his fruitless search. "Besides, I'm off to Newark on Sunday, remember?"

Mike looked nonplussed at the news that Alex was going away. "I probably wasn't listening. What's in Newark?"

"Parks, trees, a functioning sewer system. They've got it made. Do you seriously not remember?"

Mike held his hands out and shrugged as he gave Alex a look that suggested it was the first time they were having this conversation.

Alex ran a hand over his face in frustration. "I've got a meeting with Reika. She's found some information on my parents that she thinks has some potential. I know we've had this conversation before because I made you swear not to tell Sky. You know she's not keen on me hiring Reika, but I've got to find out what happened and why I was abandoned."

Mike nodded and waved his hand to suggest Alex should lower his voice. The increase in volume and sharpening of Alex's tone was involuntary. The idea that answers were out there and he could not find them made it hard to keep his emotions under control. The news that Reika had found something was the first solid clue since the missed meeting in March.

"Yeah, I remember now. As far as Sky is concerned, you're meeting up with an old college friend. I get that you don't want to upset her or make her think you don't feel part of the family, but I wish you would talk to her and straighten things out."

Alex sighed at Mike's words and the slightly desperate plea conveyed by their tone. The subject of family was a difficult one. Since the age of six, Alex and Jeremy were the only family Skylar knew. Their shared plight was the furnace in which their friendship was forged, and Alex could not help but feel his attempts to find his real family were some sort of betrayal in Skylar's eyes. Family was the most important thing to Skylar. It was why Alex and Jeremy lived with them. It was also a painful fact that the importance Skylar placed on family didn't extend to Alex's search for his birth family.

"Now isn't the right time," Alex replied after careful consideration. "As you said, she's got a lot on with work that is stressing her out. She doesn't need the extra burden of my problems right now."

"I hope you know what you're doing, kid. I can't shake the feeling this quest of yours is going to end badly."

"That's actually reassuring," Alex said with a grin. "What with your track record of never being right."

"You may have a point there," Mike replied, favoring his injured shoulder as he pulled himself up from the chair. "Case in point, I could have sworn I left my shirt in here. You know, the fancy one Sky bought me for Christmas."

"You did," said Alex, lifting himself slightly and pulling a crumpled shirt from beneath him. "You may want to wash it."

Mike's expletive-filled response as Alex threw the garment over to him brought a smile to Alex's face. A smile that faded once Alex was alone. For all the promise that Reika's lead offered, Mike's concerns over Skylar's reaction when she inevitably found out could not be ignored.

-26-

VENTURA COUNTY, CALIFORNIA
April 27, 2029

With the quarantine finally lifted, civil unrest remained but no longer manifested in the form of armed mobs. Provided the protests and calls for action didn't become violent, Skylar could live with that. For once, the light at the end of the tunnel didn't feel like it was the lamp of an oncoming train.

The lessening of the load in California coincided with an increased focus on counterterrorism's investigation into the origin at the most inconvenient of times for Jerry. His wife of thirty-three years was rushed into hospital shortly after one of his agents unearthed a potential lead, leaving Skylar to hold the fort while he took a brief absence. Things were coming together. Almost. There was still a backload of local cases that needed clearing.

After another day of case reviews and talent searches, Skylar's spirit was running on fumes. As she entered her kitchen, the smell of garlic mashed potatoes in the oven provided a momentary boost. Mike always used a dash of horseradish in his potatoes, his secret recipe, and her mouth watered at the thought of tucking into the meal that would be served.

"Mariela, that's not a good idea," said Mike, phone cradled between his head and shoulder.

The roll of Mike's eyes as he crossed the room told her it had been a long call. Skylar slid onto one of the barstools and kicked her shoes off as he switched to speakerphone.

"I get that, Mariela, but isn't sending a 'business as usual' message going to come across as indelicate?" Mike asked, putting the phone on the counter and pouring Skylar a glass of wine.

Skylar swirled the wine gently, taking a gentle sniff to get a sense of the aromas before inhaling deeply. There was a smokiness to it that she struggled to place, hidden behind the rich, spicy aroma of the fruit.

"We cannot live in fear, Michael. If we do, then this virus will have claimed more than lives," Mariela declared, unaware she was now talking to both of them. Skylar mouthed the words "Not a virus" to Mike, eliciting a chuckle as Mariela continued. "I won't let it take our spirit. I'm designing the formal invites. Please, say you'll come."

For as long as Skylar had known her, Mariela epitomized the glamorous, wealthy housewife with a flair for style. Her extravagant parties were always well attended because everybody wanted to be seen attending a Michaelis event. Mike and Skylar's names regularly appeared on the guestlist for Mariela's events. Skylar's family inheritance was one factor, a substantial fortune that began with a lucky ancestor during the California gold rush, but it was her friendship with Mariela that ensured she was a regular attendee.

"Okay, okay," Mike answered as he turned on the heat beneath a skillet of salmon. "Send over the invitations. We'll work something out."

"Very well. We can talk more in a couple of weeks. Say hi to Sky for me."

Skylar took a sip of her wine, letting the first sip linger a while before taking a second, smaller sip. There was a good balance there with a pleasant fruitiness.

"Is this that Tempranillo from Paso?" she asked as soon as the line went dead. Mike nodded his affirmation as he returned the phone to its cradle. "I take it Mariela was following up on the invite I received from Dave."

"Yeah. Some fancy gala she wants to throw."

Dave Michaelis had called Skylar on her way home from the office about dinner with some of Los Angeles' business leaders and the deputy police chief at Casa Michaelis. He wanted to have a brainstorm about ways to honor the dead and fund some restoration projects. It did not sound that fancy.

"Yeah, that's something else," Mike said when Skylar told him Dave's plans. "Perhaps this gala Mariela was on about is one of those fundraisers."

It was possible. It would be just like Mariela to start planning the fundraiser before Dave had even planned what they were raising funds for.

"If I'm being dragged along to two of Mariela's parties, I'm definitely wearing jeans," Mike continued, flipping the salmon and sprinkling some steak seasoning over it. "How come Eckhart is going? Parker can't make it?"

"I don't know, Mike. Although, I'm glad he's not going. That guy's on my shit list."

"Still no joy with finding those children?"

"Most of the names are on the outbreak's casualty lists," said Skylar with a shake of her head as Mike slid the fish from the skillet. "Parker's making out like my decision to not throw resource at his case makes it my fault if more kids turn up dead."

"What? That's ridiculous."

"I know. Like I don't have enough shit to deal with," she replied before giving him an expletive-filled account of her day.

"And there's nobody else who can fill in for Jerry or sort out recruitment?" Mike asked, emptying his plate as she finished her tale. "The suits should be all over this."

"I know," Skylar replied, plucking a grape from a dish sitting in the center of the island. She tossed it into her mouth and bit down, the skin snapping between her teeth. "I considered taking it to Banks but thought that might not be the best career move."

Mike sighed and nodded as he filled a glass with water.

"How's the shoulder today, Mike?" Skylar asked, eager to change the topic during the lull in conversation.

Mike did not like talking about the attack on the border that resulted in his separated shoulder. Skylar didn't push him on it, focusing instead on his recovery. Although surgery was avoided, physiotherapy would keep him off active duty for a while.

"Oh, this won't kill me," he said, tapping his shoulder as Skylar's husky, Cali, padded into the kitchen in search of table scraps. "Probably find myself stuck with a desk job when I get back. At least I'll be able to join you for all those steak dinners at fancy restaurants when I become a desk jockey."

"Yeah, right. You can see what my life is really like. Reports and meetings. Meetings and reports. Not that I'm jealous but, if my life was a soap opera, people would be screaming 'fuck the conference calls, show us what's happening in LA!' at their screens."

Cali put her paws on the counter to beg for attention, giving Skylar a pleading look. Skylar buckled, unable to resist those gorgeous eyes, and gave her a treat from the jar in the center of the island.

"Why do you think I've never gone for promotion?" Mike asked, clearing the plates and loading them into the dishwasher. "What you do is important, but I wouldn't want to swap being in the midst of the action for all that admin."

"I know, I know," Skylar sighed, taking another sip of wine and sucking air over the red liquid. "I guess I'm just nostalgic for all the romance of strapping on a vest and getting stuck in. I feel like I'm trapped in a TV show that has squandered its budget and is making do by having everything happen off-screen."

"Yeah," Mike said with a nod. "Then have the characters spend all their screen time talking about it."

Skylar raised an eyebrow and bit her lip as Mike reached into the cupboard. Her eyes traced every inch of his body as his shirt lifted to reveal the skin beneath.

"You still hungry?" he asked hopefully, lifting down a pair of dessert bowls and crossing over to the refrigerator. "I made some of that blueberry cheesecake you like."

Skylar stood up and stepped over to where he was standing. There was no greater aphrodisiac than a man showing enthusiasm in catering for his wife. Emptying her glass, she pressed her body to his back and rested her cheek on his good shoulder.

"I am, but not for food," she whispered as she wrapped one arm around his stomach.

Mike's abs tightened as Skylar gently splayed her fingers over his body. He flinched at her gentle touch, eliciting a sharp breath as his body quivered. She slowly rotated her wrist, the tips of her fingers sliding under his waistband, as she kissed his shoulder. He turned around and took the empty glass from her hand before reaching for the bottle.

"I want you to finish this," he said as he filled her glass almost to the top.

"Finish what, Mike?"

"Dirty girl. Come on."

He took her hand and held it over her head, signaling for Skylar to do a twirl. Eager to please, she spun through 360 degrees, spilling some of the wine as she did so. Skylar did not care. Butterflies danced in her stomach as he squeezed her hand. Who knew married life could still make her feel like a schoolgirl?

Walking her over to the couch as she finished the wine, Mike spun her again and grabbed her by the waist. Whispering in her ear, he dipped Skylar down, the empty wine glass tumbling from her hand, and rested his face between her breasts. Skylar's flesh tingled as he blew gently, the warmth of his breath sending shivers down her body.

The world was swimming, intoxicated as she was by the wine and her husband's touch. She felt her lips spread into a slow, satisfied smile as Mike lowered her to the couch and sat down next to her. He went to kiss her cheek, his hand rising to cup her face, but Skylar leaned in and put her teeth on his neck, eliciting a gasp as she bit down.

"You, Skylar Sinclair, need to relax," he said as his fingers massaged small circles on her thighs. They traveled up, his touch becoming gentler, and her toes curled.

"Relaxing is not in my nature. But you do a pretty decent job of helping me do so."

Mike looked at her, his eyes gazing into hers as he placed one hand on her collarbone, the other still caressing her thigh.

"Pretty decent?" he said, a slow smile spreading across his face as he pushed her back until she was led on the couch. "Put me on a pedestal, why don't you?"

Lowering his body, not once taking his eyes off hers, he nuzzled her collarbone as his hand caressed her neck.

"Oh, hush," Skylar purred, raking her hands through his hair. "Relax me."

Skylar's hands roamed across his back as he alternated between forcefully kissing the nape of her neck and gingerly flicking his tongue up toward her jaw. Her passion was rising. She grasped his tight ass with one hand as he moved up to tease her ear, gently biting and teasing as he whispered sweet nothings. She could feel him, hard and intent, pressing against her stomach as he leaned down to her. He moved his hand from her thigh to her waist. Higher. His hand inched toward her breast. She teased his neck with her tongue, gently sucking the skin.

"Hey," he said, his voice gone husky. "Don't leave a hickey."

Skylar grinned. "Do I ever?"

He grinned back, a big boyish smile, and leaned in to bite her neck. Gasping, Skylar's fingers found his waistband and grabbed on. Her heart was racing, the anticipation becoming unbearable as he continued to tease, kissing her just how she liked it and touching her just where she wanted. Skylar rubbed the front of his pants, feeling the hardness there, and knew he was desperate for release.

Sliding her hand down the front of his pants, Skylar's nails teased the tip of his manhood as she kissed from his shoulder to the cleave of his muscular chest. She strained to get a better grip, but his pants were a hindrance. They had to go. Mike was one step ahead, lifting his frame to provide better access and taking the opportunity to unbutton her blouse as she unzipped his pants. Released from the constricting material, his thick, throbbing penis sprang free.

"Archduke Tally-Whacker, reporting for duty," he said, groaning as she quickly took hold and massaged his swollen dick.

Mike's hand pressed against her right breast, gently teasing her nipple. His erection pulsed as she kissed him hard, thrusting her tongue into his mouth. She knew he was getting close. Her expert touch was too much for him. The thought of him being powerless to resist made Skylar even more aroused.

Mike had other plans, however, and shifted position to put himself outside her reach. She stretched down, but he blocked her by grabbing hold of her pants and yanking at the button. Lifting her hips, Skylar wriggled free as he slid her pants down her legs and cast them aside. She parted her thighs in anticipation, moaning in expectation for a thrust that did not come. Instead of sliding inside her, Mike began kissing his way down her body as his fingers curled around the elastic of her underwear.

Weaving slowly downward, Mike inched closer to his target. Skylar cried out for him and arched her back slightly. His lips found their way between her thighs. She grabbed his hair as he began sucking and licking at her wetness. She was getting close. With short gasps that drew a tickling breeze over her clitoris, Mike continued until she shuddered, climaxing hard against his face.

"I want to feel you inside me," Skylar whispered as Mike surfaced for air, leaning back against the couch.

In the throes of ecstasy, it took her a moment to realize that he was in agony.

"I just need a moment," he whispered through gritted teeth.

There was no hiding the pain that their exertions had inflicted on his injured shoulder. He knew how stressed she was. Despite the hurt, he did his utmost to bring her a moment of blessed relief. That was the kind of man he was, putting her pleasure above his pain. That devotion needed rewarding.

"Just relax," Skylar whispered as she sat up, sliding her thigh over his. "I have ways to take your mind off the pain."

When Jeremy walked in an hour later, Mike and Skylar were sat at the kitchen table, scraping cheesecake remains from the dessert bowls, decent and presentable. Without a word, he filled his water bottle before heading into the living room, leaving them to their moment of silent companionship.

"Why is there a wine glass under the table?" He called out after a minute or two.

Mike and Skylar looked at each other and grinned.

-27-

ESSEX COUNTY, NEW JERSEY
May 01, 2029

The reception area outside Reika's office had all the hallmarks of a dentist's waiting room. The sterile coldness and pragmatic design of the room was everything Alex expected from a woman who dealt in hard logic and ruthless efficiency. Stuck for entertainment, Alex found himself mentally redecorating the room after scanning the two magazines left as a token gesture for alleviating boredom. It was a small improvement over the first time he had visited Reika's office. The idea that people might not want to sit alone with their thoughts in a plain, white room while waiting to see her had not entered Reika's mind until Alex suggested it.

Having decided a forest green color scheme with rich, purple seating would be a more appropriate décor, Alex turned his attention to the view from the office window. Located on the third floor of a cookie-cutter office block on the edge of Newark, there was little to see but traffic and other boxy, red brick buildings. That Alex had made it to Newark without interrogation still surprised him. There was no way Jeremy had bought Alex's story about needing a break, but his uncle did not pursue the matter. That in itself was odd enough. Skylar's complete disinterest in his activity only furthered Alex's surprise. Rarely did she become so single-minded in her focus that she lost sight of the big picture. The shift made Alex wonder if being promoted was the best thing for her.

"Mr. Zhang," Reika called from the doorway, drawing Alex's thoughts away from his sister and back to his present situation. "I'm ready."

Alex had never known a woman more intimidating than Reika Pfeiffer. In her pinstripe suit and half-rimmed glasses, she looked every inch the authoritarian figure, ready to broker a multibillion-dollar deal or sign into effect a sweeping reform of the welfare system. Alex had never heard her swear or raise her voice, yet she radiated menace. Looking at her, with her blonde hair pinned in a high tail, put Alex in mind of the still waters of a crocodile-infested lake.

"I like what you've done with the place," said Alex, gesturing to the magazines.

"Good," replied Reika, killing his attempt to inject some levity into the meeting. "Come."

The image of a PVC-clad Reika, riding crop in hand, burst to the front of Alex's mind. Shaking off the image of Reika ordering her slaves around, Alex followed her into her office. The room was almost as utilitarian as the waiting room, with its white walls and minimal furniture. At least the chairs were more comfortable. Alex could not resist spinning through 360 degrees the moment he was in the swivel chair in front of Reika's desk.

"Finished?" she asked as Alex came to a stop facing her.

"Nope," he replied with a grin before kicking his feet out and spinning the chair in the opposite direction. The calm, impassive expression on Reika's face discouraged him from making the third cycle.

Alex shifted in his seat as Reika stared at him. "Sorry."

"Let us begin. I have made some progress since you failed to attend our last meeting. Your grandfather is dead."

Skylar had warned him that dealing with Reika would result in heartache. Reika's delivery of information was the primary reason the two women had fallen out when, during the early part of the investigation, she announced his father's passing in a similarly brutal fashion. The lack of sugar-coating was a culture shock, but Skylar needed to give him more credit when it came to what offended him or not.

"Does that mean you know who my mother is?"

"Kendra Williams. Nassau born. Her father, Henry Williams, served in the British Navy and was stationed there in his late teens. He married your grandmother, Mary Gibson, and became a lieutenant commander in the RBDF when Kendra was a baby. Moved to-"

"Wait," Alex interrupted, racing to keep up with the barrage of facts. "RBDF?"

"Royal Bahamas Defense Force," Reika replied, interlocking her fingers as she leaned back in her chair. "Formed in 1980. Your grandfather served with the RBDF until the end of the cold war then moved to Hong Kong. He re-enlisted in the British Navy and served for nearly three years, retiring from service in 1994 when Mary passed away. Kendra was fifteen at the time."

"Okay, slow down," said Alex, amazed that Reika was reeling off personal details of strangers in rapid succession without once glancing at her notes. "So, my father is Chinese, and my mother is British-Bahamian?"

"Yes. Kendra is a fifth-generation Bahamian. I couldn't go back any further as it appears your family entered the Bahamas as American slaves freed by the British."

Alex ran his hands over his head as he processed the information. The gaps in the picture that made up Alex Zhang were getting smaller, but there was still so much to learn.

"Wait," said Alex, leaning forward as he seized on an important detail. "You said 'is' fifth-generation. Does that mean my mother's still alive?"

"To the best of my knowledge," Reika replied, leaning forward and placing one hand on the file on her desk. "The trail goes cold after your father's death. What little evidence there is suggests they planned to marry and relocate to the mainland. There is nothing to indicate your mother went to the mainland without him, and I cannot find her on the island."

Reika pushed the file across the desk and allowed Alex to scan through it before continuing. "There are other sources I could utilize, but they come at a price. I have provided an estimate in the file, along with my fees for pursuing such a course of action."

"I see," Alex said after examining the quote for a moment. Raising such a princely sum would take some effort. "I'll need to review my finances."

Reika nodded and leaned back in her chair as if she expected such a response. "You have my number."

"I do," Alex said standing and reaching out to shake Reika's hand before remembering that she avoided physical contact wherever possible. "I'll work out something and get back to you with the details."

KURSK OBLAST, CENTRAL FEDERAL DISTRICT
May 03, 2029

The Golovkin estate was a sprawling maze of labyrinthine tunnels beneath the baroque mansion where Lukai's tale began. Iosif Malinovskyi knew many variations of the tale that resulted in his master's ascension to the aristocracy of the night. It was likely none of the stories were accurate, but the most repeated version saw young Lukai outsmart the legendary Dracula himself. When asked for his heart's desire as a reward for his ingenuity, Lukai informed the lord of vampires that he wanted to cure his sister of her terminal illness. His wish was granted when, that evening, Dracula turned both Lukai and his sister into vampires.

Forever in his debt, Lukai swore allegiance to Dracula and became the first member of his high council. However, Lukai's joy was short-lived. Hearing of her miraculous recovery, the town priests came to investigate his sister. Blinded to the blessing of life by their piety, they condemned her to death.

Regardless of the truth, Iosif's family had long served the Golovkin family, and Lukai's transformation into a vampire lord did nothing to change that.

"Wait here," Erik ordered, holding his hand out in front of Iosif as they reached a large metal door, several floors beneath the mansion.

No lights lined the subterranean walls or ceilings. Their reassuring glow was unnecessary for people like Erik, Lukai's top lieutenant, and the other creatures that patrolled the grounds, forcing Iosif to use the light on his phone to see. There was no chance of Iosif joining Erik in

Lukai's undead army, but he could still serve the cause. The freedom to operate in the human world often proved invaluable.

A steady drip, the result of an underground stream exerting its influence on the tunnel, filled the silence, occasionally punctuated by a soft thud from behind the door.

"Who fucked up?" Iosif asked.

"None of your concern," Erik replied, arms crossed as he waited for their master.

"Anything I can help with?"

Erik turned his harsh, taciturn stare on Iosif. Iosif was no scrawny runt, being naturally tall and having served in the military, but compared to Erik's broad frame he felt insignificant. Turning his gaze to the floor, Iosif waited in silence for the door to open.

"Ah, there you are, Erik," Lukai said as he emerged from the torture chamber, licking blood from his knuckles. "Nikola trains her agents well. Not a word from this one on what she hoped to achieve by deviating from the plan. Find me another. I will learn the truth."

"Yes, my lord, but first, I have Iosif for you."

Lukai turned his attention to Iosif as if seeing him for the first time. "Ah, yes. I have a mission for you. One that could be highly advantageous for your family."

Iosif flinched involuntarily as Lukai reached up and put his arm around Iosif's shoulders. Guided from the labyrinth by his master, Iosif heard the thick squelch of tenderized meat dragged through its juices as Erik removed Nikola's former agent from the room behind them.

"I'm feeling generous," Lukai continued. "I'm going to give you the opportunity to get revenge on the monks. One of their kind is doing a book tour this summer. I want you to book him for an appearance then slip him a poison I've been working on."

"Thank you, master," Iosif replied, slouching to bring his shoulders closer to Lukai's. "There's one problem. I have nowhere to host this book signing."

Lukai huffed, the disappointment that Iosif thought that problem was not already handled evident in his action. "You do now. A little place outside Odesa. I had my team persuade the owner of the town's bookstore to sell up. Success will see your family elevated to its once great status in our society."

Iosif winced as Lukai grasped his shoulder, fingers digging into the muscles. "Fail, and your daughter will bear the consequences of your actions."

"You can count on me," said Iosif, his muscles tightening at the prospect of failing Mariela again.

"Good," Lukai replied, stopping and turning to face Iosif. "I knew you would rise to the occasion, which is why I have a bonus for you. Consider it a down payment for your services."

With unnecessary force, Lukai grabbed Iosif's phone and pressed his thumb to the glass to unlock it. Leaving Iosif to suck away the pain of having his thumb crushed against the glass, Lukai tapped away at the screen before handing the phone back.

"What is this?" Iosif asked as he moved the map around the address Lukai loaded into his phone.

"The last known address of your father," Lukai responded as he turned and walked away. "He was sighted there last week. I suggest you hurry if you want to catch him."

-29-

VENTURA COUNTY, CALIFORNIA
May 06, 2029

With the last ounce of his reserve energy, Alex pushed upward, muscles straining as his arms straightened. He preferred the gym first thing in the morning as there were few people around. A few runners occupied the treadmills in the hall next door, but the weight room was abandoned.

"Good show," Tate said, taking the barbell from Alex and placing it on the rack as Alex sat up. "Not your best. Need to shake off that holiday haze."

Tate Turner was an excellent work out partner. Everything was a "good show" with room for improvement. Some people needed trainers that embodied the pain and gain mantra and were unrelenting in their pressure to go further. Alex preferred the softer approach. It worked because Tate would put his money where his mouth was and go the extra round. If he asked Alex for another five reps, Tate would do those reps as well. He had the physique for it.

To say Tate towered over Alex would be stretching the definition. There was a height advantage. And a bicep diameter advantage. And a chest size advantage. In almost every way, Tate was at least one step further along the path to becoming Mr. Olympia than Alex, but he never belittled Alex for it. They each had an ideal physique in mind.

"Too much booze, not enough snooze," Alex replied with a chuckle. His mind was still turning over the events of Tuesday's meeting with Reika, examining it from every angle. "Partying the night away. Speaking of which, I hear you got into a little trouble in Old Francisco."

"You say it like I got busted balls deep in an old man's rectum," said

Tate, taking his place on the bench as Alex moved to spot him. "I wasn't even the one in the wrong."

"I dunno," said Alex marking off each of Tate's lifts on his fingers. "Getting hauled in by the cops sounds serious."

Tate shook his head, his breathing becoming more labored as he powered through the reps. There was no doubt he would exceed Alex's count. The question was by how many.

"I'm sure whatever those clowns told you is wrong," Tate replied, racking the weight after surpassing Alex by five reps with energy to spare. "We were at this bar, about six pints into the evening, when this drunk girl comes up and decides to get a good handful of my magic flute."

"Tickled your kazoo was the phrase Maria used," Alex said as Tate stepped to the side to stretch. "I'm surprised she found it."

"Oh, she found it alright. It's an easy target. I didn't give her a chance to play a tune though."

"And that's where things got interesting?" Alex asked as he settled into place for another set.

"No. I pushed her away, got a drink thrown in my face, and she stormed off. Didn't think anything of it until the police turned up about an hour later. They asked me to come down to the station to answer some questions about a sexual assault. I told them there was no need as I wasn't pressing charges. That's when I discovered she was accusing me."

"As if you'd ever touch a woman inappropriately," Alex said through clenched teeth. His muscles burned as he pushed the barbell off his chest, determined to match Tate's reps.

"I know, right?" Tate replied, helping Alex rack the weights on the final lift. "The police came to the same conclusion, eventually. The others thought it would be funny to pretend they hadn't seen anything, making it my word against hers. Until the cops got hold of the CCTV footage. Proof it was her, not me."

"Did they arrest her?" asked Alex, grabbing a towel and patting himself down. "For wasting police time."

"I didn't want the hassle of submitting a complaint," said Tate, gripping the bar for his second set. "I just wanted to get from there. They let her go with a warning."

Alex counted as Tate added another five reps to the set as silent encouragement to push further. On any other day, the act would be met with a stubborn determination to keep pace. With Reika's financial challenge weighing on his mind, Alex was ill-prepared to meet Tate's target. Unlike his sister, Alex had no sizeable income or inherited wealth from which he could draw funds. For the first time in his life, Alex found his comfortable lifestyle lacking.

"Problem?" Tate asked, taking the bar from Alex as he failed to complete half the set.

"Not really," Alex replied, drawing an appreciative whistle from Tate as he described Reika's quote.

"That's a tall order," said Tate, nodding in greeting as his brother entered the hall. "Sky's good for it though. Can't she loan you the cash?"

Alex shook his head as Tanner strutted over to them. It was easy to see that Tate and Tanner were brothers with their dark hair and eyes and a strong, angular jawline straight out of the golden age of comics. However, their differences were numerous enough that one could be forgiven for not realizing they were twins. Tanner shared a fondness for the gym but not the weights. Where Tate pushed himself harder than Alex, Tanner was content with maintaining a toned, fighter's physique. The three of them together looked like an advertisement for protein shakes, illustrating years one, two and three of a vigorous training regimen.

The majority of Tanner's gym membership was spent in the pool and the sauna. Or in front of the mirror. Alex took the simple approach to grooming and removed his facial hair each day. Tate's approach of shaving his head and trimming his stubble every three days required even less effort. Tanner took things in the other direction, trimming and styling his appearance for up to an hour each day.

"Hotties inbound," whispered Tanner, gently raking a small, steel comb through his sideburns.

No sooner had Tanner uttered the words than a pair of women in tight Lycra entered the weight room. A redhead with a pixie cut, wearing mid-thigh shorts and a black sports bra, accompanied by a brunette in charcoal yoga pants and a loose vest top.

"What do you reckon?" Tanner continued, giving a surreptitious nod toward the women as they stretched. "Cuffs match the collar?"

Alex gave Tanner a withering glare as Tate huffed with indignation. In response, Tanner shrugged and smiled. "Can't deny you want to find out. I mean, you split with Annalise weeks ago and you're not getting anywhere with Maria, are you? Time you buried your worm in a juicy red apple."

"Bro," said Tate, keeping his voice low. "You can't say shit like that. It's disrespectful to women."

Tanner grinned as he adjusted the settings of the leg press machine that sat alongside the bench press. "If finding a woman attractive is disrespectful then I'm guilty as charged."

Alex zoned out as Tate made a foolhardy attempt to explain to his brother why commenting on a woman's beauty was unacceptable. It was an old argument that never went away. As someone who worked hard to achieve his figure, Alex struggled to understand what was disrespectful about recognizing and complimenting such effort. At no point had he felt insulted when somebody told him his hours in the gym were paying off.

"Well?" said Tanner, clapping his hand on Alex's shoulder and shocking him out of his daydream. "You going to talk to her?"

Alex shook his head. "Got too much on my mind."

"For once I agree with my baby brother," said Tate. "Not his words, but his intentions. Shuttering yourself away doesn't seem to be working for you. At least go have a conversation with another human being. Let me look into this cash problem of yours. You go distract yourself. Who knows, you might find yourself enjoying it."

"Fourteen minutes, dude. That's all there is between us," Tanner said with mock indignation about the baby brother jibe, stroking his neatly trimmed beard as he switched his attention to Alex. "Tate's right though. Go tap that ass. What have you got to lose?"

-30-

VENTURA COUNTY, CALIFORNIA
May 06, 2029

"I still don't get why you have to go in person," Mike said as Skylar dropped her purse on the table and patted down her pockets. "You've managed fine by video conference so far."

"It's political," Skylar replied, checking her purse for the third time. "If I'm going to be in charge of Jerry's team until he returns, I need to make an appearance. Have you seen my glasses?"

The call came in while Mike and Skylar were out at lunch. Jerry's wife passed away during the early hours of the morning after a clot managed to break free and lodge itself in her lung, triggering a pulmonary embolism. Unsurprisingly, Jerry was not returning to work anytime soon after such a shock.

"Tits," said Mike as he cleared the level on the video game he had spent the last hour playing.

"What? Oh," Skylar replied, unhooking her glasses from her vest and putting them in their case.

"What if he doesn't come back?" Mike asked as he waited for the starting flag on the next track. "I mean, he was hinting at early retirement anyway, wasn't he?"

"He was," Skylar replied as she headed out to the hallway. Jerry made no secret that President King would be the last president he served under, giving him another three years if she did not get a second term. That gave Skylar three years to prove herself worthy of filling his boots. Knowing Jerry, he probably asked for her to cover him specifically to bulk out her résumé.

"But a lot of his plans involved cruising the Caribbean with Maddy," Skylar continued, returning to the living room with her suitcase. "He might delay retirement now she's gone."

"Maybe," said Mike, his car spinning off the track as he overcorrected a bad turn. "Or he might say fuck it. Remember what happened with Tom when his wife died? Made him realize life was too short to work 'til you drop."

"Burn that bridge when we come to it," Skylar replied, unwilling to admit to being disappointed that it would delay her promotion plans if Jerry's replacement was further from retirement. Sulking over her career plans being setback when a man just lost his wife left her wanting to take a shower.

"What flight did you get after?"

"Uh, nine thirty-something, I think," Skylar replied, forcing her dress shoes into her case.

"That's not so bad," Mike replied, skidding across the grass on the same corner. "I half expected you to be on an ass crack of dawn flight, waking everybody up at three in the morning as you clomp around the kitchen."

"Nine something tonight," Skylar corrected, pressing down on her bag with one knee to get the zipper to close.

"What?" Mike asked, crashing the car as he turned to look at her. "I was going to give you a going-away present."

"Really?" said Skylar, looking up from her case. "What kind of present?"

"The kind that takes more than the twenty minutes you have if you're going to get to the airport on time."

"Oh," Skylar said, closing her case and standing up. "So, not sex then."

Grinning, Mike shook his head and turned his attention back to the television as Skylar whipped off her vest and pulled on the rock T-shirt she left on the sofa.

"Do I need to arrange for anyone to come around and check on you while I'm gone? I don't want you and Alex wasting away playing video games all week. Where is the little twerp anyway? It feels like I haven't seen him in weeks."

"Not sure," Mike replied, easing the car around the corner that was giving him so much trouble. Taking it that slow, Skylar knew he would struggle to finish in the top five. "I think he went to see Annalise."

"Are they back together?" asked Skylar as she pocketed her phone.

"I don't think so. He was sorting some of the trash in his room earlier. Probably found some of her stuff beneath the mountain of laundry."

Skylar shrugged, filing that one away for when she next saw her brother. There was something she was forgetting. Her glasses and wallet were in her purse, along with the car keys. Her phone was in her pocket, mobile boarding pass ready to go. Shirts, pants and underwear were in her bag along with some basic toiletries. Between the hotel and the facilities at the new headquarters, she would not be left wanting in that department. As tempting as it was to take her hairdryer and some extra clothes, Skylar was reticent to check any bags and deal with the carousel.

"Okay, I'm off," she said, leaning in to kiss Mike's cheek. No doubt she would remember what she was missing halfway to Los Angeles.

"Ah, Sky, you made me crash," Mike cried slumping back on the sofa and tossing the control on the cushion. "Blocking my view with the face of an angel."

Raising an eyebrow, Skylar stood on the couch, placing a foot on either side of Mike's legs, and pinning his arms down with her knees.

"Complaining about the view, huh?" she said, slowly sliding her knees along his arms until her thighs were pressed against the top of his chest, stopping him from lowering his head. "I don't recall you complaining about this view last night."

"Because it wasn't this view," Mike replied, struggling to move his jaw as Skylar gently circled her hips. "There wasn't so much clothing to ruin the scene. And I think you were a touch higher."

"Here?" asked Skylar, adjusting her position.

"Hmmm-mmm mmm hmm," said Mike, his voice muffled by Skylar's shorts.

Springing off him, Skylar dropped off the sofa and gave the erection tenting his shorts a flick.

"You are a cruel, cruel woman, Skylar Sinclair."

"What can I say? I'm good at being bad. Now, I really need to go."

"And what am I supposed to do with this?" Mike asked, grabbing his crotch and grinning mischievously.

"Pretend you're a teenager again and work it out."

"What? Literally?"

"Unless you wanna risk your life asking Alex to give you a hand," Skylar replied as she grabbed her purse and bag. "Just don't whittle it away to nothing. I'm expecting a bloody good pounding when I get back."

"Yes, ma'am."

Leaving Mike to imagine the things she would do to him when she returned, Skylar wheeled her carry-on bag to the door, fishing her car keys from her purse as she went. As much as she hated being away from him, the opportunity to cement her eventual promotion was too good to ignore.

"Mariela?" Skylar exclaimed, opening the door as her friend stepped onto the porch. "Shit. That's what I was forgetting."

"Change of plans?" Mariela asked, brandishing a bottle of expensive wine.

"Yeah," Skylar replied, dragging her case outside as Mariela stepped aside. "Off to Maryland for the week."

"Nothing serious, I hope."

"Personal issue. One of the bosses is taking some time off so I need to go and make sure the wheels don't fall off while he's gone."

"What about my personal issue?" Mariela asked with a smile as she leaned against the doorframe. "Who's going to help me drink this?"

Mike's home alone," Skylar replied, strolling over to the car as the trunk swung open. "He'll be glad of the company. You can show him how to race."

Mariela nodded as she straightened up to give Skylar a farewell hug. "A girl's gotta do what a girl's gotta do. Guess I'm getting drunk with Mike tonight."

"I'll make it up to you when I get back," Skylar said, releasing Mariela from her embrace. "Proper knees up."

"Deal," Mariela replied stepping into the house as Skylar headed to the car.

"Oh, Mariela," Skylar called, remembering the state she left Mike in. Her racing heart slowed as Mariela reappeared in the doorway. "Knock before you go in. Just in case he's bashing the bishop."

-31-

VENTURA COUNTY, CALIFORNIA
May 06, 2029

"No, don't pull out."

Too late. Alex was already out, his semen splashing harmlessly over her landing strip. Panting from the exertion, Alex lifted himself up, kneeling between her toned, athletic thighs. If Alex had a type, Kim was it. Confident, determined and imbued with a no-nonsense attitude. Her lean physique, pretty face, and casual sex appeal did nothing to diminish that. That he had just described his sister did not cross Alex's mind.

"I'm not done with you," said Kim, pushing Alex onto his back and straddling him. "Make me cum."

Alex was rendered mute with pleasure as she took hold of his still erect penis and lowered herself onto him, her wetness allowing her to take his entire length with ease. Grinding against him, Kim raked her hands through her long, brown hair and moaned with pleasure, biting her lower lip as her clit rubbed against his crotch. Wanting to see more, Alex ran his hands over her hips and began lifting the loose vest top that somehow remained on her when they got back from the gym.

Before he could reveal her breasts, Kim grabbed Alex's wrists and forced his hands to her legs. Alex did not need to be told twice and began kneading her thighs as she lifted her top to expose her midriff. He felt his balls tighten again at the sight of her exposed flesh, her pussy tightening around his dick. Desperate to hold out for her orgasm, Alex tried to focus on something other than the beautiful woman riding him. Raking her fingers over her mound, Kim gathered up the trails of semen clinging to her pubic hair and pressed her sticky fingers against Alex's lips.

"Fuck," Kim cried out as her fingers slid into his mouth. "I'm going to cum."

Alex grunted, tasting the strange saltiness of her fingers as he concentrated on not biting down to delay his orgasm. With one hand on his bare chest, Kim gripped his jaw and pushed down hard on his dick, desperately seeking deeper penetration as she ground against him.

"I'm going to cum again," Alex whimpered as her thighs pressed against him. He tried to lift her off, but Kim grabbed his wrists and forced them down.

"No," she said, the word sounding strained as her orgasm overtook her. "Don't stop."

Moved by her rhythmic gyrations, Alex felt the rush of release as he spasmed inside her. Undeterred, Kim continued to grind, her pace gradually slowing as she came down from her orgasm.

"Woo," Kim said, panting heavily as she lifted herself off him and placed a hand over her crotch. "That hit the spot. Open wide."

Alex shook his head, afraid of what she would do next. As intense as their session was, he was beginning to have second thoughts about this woman.

"Spoilsport," said Kim, scooping up a handful of their fluids and wiping her hand over his bare chest. "I'm Kim, by the way."

Alex watched in stunned silence as she climbed off the bed and wiped herself with a towel that was hanging on her bedroom radiator, amazed that she had forgotten introducing herself at the gym. His mind recalled the tales of conquest that Tanner would tell on a Sunday morning of women left in empty beds, earning a scowl from his brother. Alex always imagined those women scrubbing themselves clean after being used for the night. It never occurred to him that it could go the other way.

"Phone," Kim instructed, hanging the soiled towel back on the radiator and holding out her hand.

Before he knew it, Alex was handing her his phone. There was something about the way she spoke the words that made it sound like refusal was not an option.

"Unlocked," she ordered, thrusting his phone at him. "How else am I supposed to put my number in there?"

Unable to decide if Kim scared or excited him, Alex took his phone, unlocked it, and handed it back to her.

"Good boy," she said, typing her number into his contacts and saving his number in hers before throwing his phone on the bed. "I'll make a man of you before you know it. First, I'm taking a shower. Don't be here when I get back. I'll call you when I need you."

Alex waited until Kim entered the bathroom before moving, assuming that she would have told him if she wanted him to clear out quicker. As soon as he heard the gentle patter of water on ceramic, he slid off the bed, wiped himself with the towel, and yanked his tank top over his head. As he searched for his pants, Alex thought back to the last time he had to scramble to get out of a girl's bedroom. The woman's name escaped him, but he remembered her roommate returned home early after her date turned out to be a catfish. Whereas that night ended with Alex getting lucky with both women, he doubted being in the room when Kim returned would prove as fortuitous.

Alex paused, aware that something was different. It took him a few seconds to realize the sound of falling water had stopped. Grabbing his phone and shoes, Alex dashed from the apartment, hearing the bathroom door open as he pulled the front door shut behind him. Pausing for breath, Alex thought back to how his day had started and realized Tate and Tanner were right. The distraction did him good. If only all his problems could be resolved so easily.

-32-

VENTURA COUNTY, CALIFORNIA
May 11, 2029

"Staring at it won't fix it," Mariela shouted as she stepped out of the car outside Skylar's house.

Alex glanced over his shoulder and flashed her a tired but welcoming smile before turning back to his motorbike. "I was about to head out, but I must have hit a nail last ride. Bugger me sideways if I can find where the hole is."

"Put it in a trough of water and try inflating the tire," said Mariela, stepping beside Alex and glancing at the bike over the top of her sunglasses. "Look for the bubbles, not the hole."

"There's a pun in there somewhere," Alex replied as he took hold of the handlebars and pushed his bike back into the garage. "Job for another day."

"The pun or the puncture?" Mariela asked as she casually kicked one of the pebbles on Skylar's drive back into its home in the border. Pretty as it was, the decorative stone border separating Skylar's drive from her front lawn was not to Mariela's taste. Apart from her avocado orchard, Skylar put little effort into her garden, leaving Mariela saddened that so much space was under-utilized.

"Both," Alex replied with a mirthless chuckle. "Not feeling it today. Hence wanting to take the bike out for a cruise up the coast. Guess I'll settle for killing a few hours at the movies instead."

"Don't tell me you've pranged the Mustang again," said Mariela as she drew her eyes away from the bland, green lawn and fixed Alex with a mischievous grin.

"She told you about that?" Alex asked, wiping his hands on a rag and tossing it into a basket before closing the garage door. "It went in for a service this morning. Skylar's only just got home, by the way. Her flight back from D.C. was delayed."

"I thought she was due back yesterday," Mariela said as Alex pulled out his phone and scrolled through his contacts.

"Like I said, delayed," said Alex as he raised his phone to his ear. "Don't get too drunk. Oh, hey, Tate. Fancy catching a movie? You'll need to pick me up though."

Mariela gave Alex a warm smile and left him to make arrangements to be elsewhere. His comings and goings held little interest for Mariela at this point. Her interest lay in what news Skylar brought back from Maryland. Alex's revelation that Skylar had only just arrived home was hardly news. Mariela knew the flight was delayed and planned accordingly. Catching Skylar before she settled in was part of the plan.

Lifting the ornate brass knocker on an otherwise mundane front door, Mariela knocked three times and waited. Any other time, she would have let herself in and called out from the hallway, just as Skylar did when she visited Mariela. Forcing Skylar to come to the door would further disrupt her and make it easier to pry information from her.

"Mariela," said Skylar, making the word almost sound like a question as she opened the door. "What are you doing here?"

"Oh, is this a bad time?" Mariela asked, removing her sunglasses and hooking them onto the waistband of her jeans. "I thought we agreed to meet up when you got back."

"We did," Skylar replied, quickly rallying from her initial confusion. "I thought we'd schedule something specific, like a trip to Goleta."

"Well, I'm here now," said Mariela as Alex briefly drew Skylar's attention by shouting that he was heading into town. "Unless you'd rather I came back another time."

"What? No," Skylar replied, turning her attention back to Mariela. "Come on in. There's a bottle of white in the fridge or you can open that new bottle of prosecco in the rack. I'm going to go get changed out of this."

Mariela assumed that the navy suit Skylar tugged to emphasize her point was the one Skylar wore home and did not blame her for wanting to get out of it. Mariela felt the same after an hour in one of her evening gowns.

Left to her own devices, Mariela strolled to the kitchen and took a bag of ice from the freezer. The ice bucket took a little more effort as someone had not put it back in its usual place in the high cupboard alongside the freezer. Discovering it under the kitchen sink, Mariela emptied the ice into the bucket and opened the refrigerator door. One look at the label on the wine bottle confirmed that it was a bad option. Sliding onto a stool at the island counter that dominated Skylar's kitchen, Mariela instead opted for the prosecco.

The label was not one Mariela recognized, hardly surprising since prosecco didn't feature on her list of preferred beverages, and she took a moment to study it before placing the bottle in the ice. As partial as Mariela was to her spirits, there was no denying that a glass of fine wine was a welcome change. Hopefully, Skylar's selection would not disappoint.

From her seat at the counter, Mariela had a partial view of the back yard and the avocado orchard that dominated one half of the garden. Mariela would consider it a frightful waste of space were it not for the fact that Skylar donated ninety percent of the fruit to local schools. Still, Mariela could think of fifty better uses for the garden without breaking a sweat.

"Your trees need pruning," Mariela said as Skylar strolled into the kitchen wearing a pair of shorts that revealed how little time Skylar spent in the sun and a loose, technicolored shawl top that sat somewhere along the spectrum between poncho and fishing net.

"I know, Mar," Skylar replied, lifting a pair of wine glasses down from the cupboard and placing them on the counter. "I've not had time to take a shit in peace, let alone thin out this year's fruit."

"The joys of management," said Mariela, shaking her head as Skylar offered to put ice in her glass. "It's why I have other people do things for me. I take it the position's official now you've been to head office."

"No," Skylar replied with a sigh as she opened the prosecco and poured. "This trip was all counterterrorism work. Although, I have taken a page out of your book, Mar."

"How so?" asked Mariela as she sipped the wine. There was an elegance to its composition that made it tolerable. Not something Mariela would select for herself.

"Got me a team doing the grunt work," Skylar said with a grin. "Seriously though, Jerry put together a good team for this one. It's a shame the leads are few and far between. What we do have is showing some real promise though."

Mariela gave Skylar a sympathetic look as she took another sip of the prosecco, allowing the wine to linger a while before swallowing. The taste was marginally better than the news that Skylar seemed to have a handle on the outbreak investigation. There was no doubt in Mariela's mind that, if the council was behind the outbreak, no investigation by the FBI would expose their involvement in the attack. Mariela's concern lay in Skylar's ability to multitask.

VENTURA COUNTY, CALIFORNIA
May 11, 2029

Skylar's journey home was a nightmare. After getting stuck in traffic for over an hour, discovering a group of activists had brought the airport to a standstill tipped her over the edge. Learning that the next available flight out of any of the local airports was the following day was the rancid cherry on top of a shit sundae. Helping airport security to bring the troublemakers to task took the edge off her frustration, but it only went so far. Being stuck in D.C., away from her husband for a night longer than intended, was a difficult inconvenience to offset. As Mariela looked on with mild amusement at her tale, Skylar's first sip of wine emptied the glass.

"What do you think?" Skylar asked as she poured herself another glass. "Better than the cat piss in the fridge."

"Yes, I was quite surprised to see such inferior wine in your collection," Mariela replied as Skylar sniffed the wine, taking a moment to appreciate it this time. "Your standards are slipping."

"Not my standards, Mar. One of Alex's friends left it here. One taste and it's easy to see why."

Mariela smiled and nodded as if that was all the explanation required. Exactly who Alex had around while she was away, Skylar had yet to find out. It sometimes felt like Skylar was running a youth hostel with all his friends coming and going. With Alex being out so much these last few months, Skylar kind of missed it.

"He seemed to be in a hurry to leave," Mariela said as she reached across the counter for one of the sable grapes in Skylar's fruit bowl.

"Nothing wrong, I hope."

Skylar opened her mouth to dismiss the notion but paused before the words formed in her throat. "No. I don't think so."

With the outbreak consuming so much of her attention, Skylar felt a pang of guilt over not spending enough time with her family. She needed to rectify that.

"Good," Mariela replied, swallowing the grape and reaching for another. "I can't even begin to imagine how much of a drain on your time this outbreak has been. Speaking of which, I haven't had your RSVP for the benefit dinner. It's only four weeks away and Dave is starting to fret over the food. You know how he likes to have everything planned well in advance."

Skylar sighed and tugged her hairband off, letting her hair fall over her shoulders. "Sorry, Mar. We'll be there. Tell Dave we'll have whatever. He knows what food we will and won't eat. Worrying about entrée's seems so trivial right now."

"Hey, I get it," Mariela replied, reaching across the counter and placing her hand over Skylar's. "It's been a tough few weeks. I'd understand if you want to give it a miss and spend time with your family. I'm sure you could do with a break after all this."

"No, we'll be there. A dose of normal sounds good right about now."

Skylar looked into Mariela's concern-filled eyes and smiled. It was a weak smile, dredged up from the depths of her being, battling through the stress and exhaustion to make itself known. Rather than soothing Mariela's fears, her worried expression grew.

"I hate to ask, but is everything okay. At work? With you and Mike?"

Skylar laughed, the sound coming more freely than the smile as Mariela's questioning chipped away at the tension in her muscles.

"Oh, Mariela. You have a knack for cutting right to the core. But yes, everything is fine. More than fine. In fact, Mike's support in all this has given me the strength to keep going. As for work, the sooner we can replenish our ranks, the sooner it will feel like I'm not running a one-man-band. Without a doubt, that has been the biggest hindrance for getting shit done. Anyway, enough about work. You're supposed to be helping me take my mind off all that, not making me regret going for the director's job."

"Fair point," Mariela conceded, plucking another grape and tossing it into the air, only for it to go bouncing across the kitchen floor when it missed her mouth. "Any thoughts on when that new summer house you've been promising yourself is going up?"

The long-overdue summer house was to be Skylar's first foray into architectural design. Buying a ready-made log cabin and having it dropped into place at the back of the garden would have given her a woodland refuge three years ago, but Skylar wanted to add a personal touch to her sanctuary.

Halfway through Skylar's description of the proposed eco-building, a two-floor hobbit-hole built into the hill at the far-left corner of her garden, Jeremy arrived home. Joining them briefly to sample the second bottle of prosecco and some cheese and crackers Skylar had put out, he quickly made his excuses and disappeared into his office down the hall.

"What do you suppose he's doing in there?" Mariela asked, gesturing to the hallway with her wine glass.

"Napping, most probably," Skylar replied, leaning back to glance down the hallway at the sound of the front door. "Jeremy is nearly sixty after all."

"So is Dave," said Mariela, topping up her glass with the dregs of the second bottle. "Won't catch him napping in the afternoon though."

"That's because you won't let him get away with it, Mar."

Both women chuckled as Mike entered the kitchen and placed his motorcycle helmet on the counter. When Mike looked at them, Skylar waved her hand to indicate they were not laughing at him.

"So, Mariela," said Mike as he reached over and picked up Skylar's glass. "Is this my wine or yours?"

"Yours, Michael. Who else's would I be drinking?"

"Figures," Mike replied, nodding at the flavor with mild enthusiasm. "I'm watching you, Mariela. I'll have my revenge when we come around your house next. Doesn't taste like one of ours."

"It's the prosecco from that new vineyard over in Simi," said Skylar, handing Mike a full bottle. "Do us a favor and top us up."

Shaking his head, Mike opened the bottle and filled each of their glasses regardless. "I'll stick to the bourbon. Going to take a shower if anybody needs me."

"Is that an invitation?" Mariela asked, winking at Skylar before sipping her wine.

Mike grinned and strolled out of the room only to be called back by Skylar. Collecting his helmet, he once again bid them farewell and disappeared upstairs.

"And you say I've got Dave whipped," said Mariela, stabbing a piece of cheese with a cocktail stick.

"What can I say?" said Skylar as she nibbled on a cracker. The lack of real food was beginning to take its toll. "He knows who's boss."

Halfway through the fourth bottle, Mariela called it quits, bundling herself into the back of her car and instructing it to take her home. It was not the same as driving, but Skylar had to admit the autonomous vehicles had a distinct advantage over both her Cadillac and the Porsche when it came to getting home after a bottle or two.

Swaying gently as she returned to the kitchen, Skylar emptied her glass and grabbed the half-empty bottle. Chilling with Mariela did wonders for taking her mind off the mountain of emails waiting for her back in the office, but there was a pocket of tension that Mariela was unable to do anything about.

"Hey, Mike," Skylar said as she burst into her bedroom, bottle in hand. "Summon the Archduke. My ramparts need storming."

-34-

KHARKIV OBLAST, UKRAINE
May 30, 2029

Iosif's father, the man that had betrayed them and destroyed Iosif's family, was a strong man. Soviet special forces, KGB, a man to be feared. When Iosif had confronted his father over the things that had been done to his daughter, his father had demonstrated his physical superiority, not just beating him, but humiliating him as he lay defenseless, barely conscious from the thrashing he had received.

Iosif failed Mariela that day and the pain of that failure hurt more than what his father had done to him. Going to the police was not an option, his father was too influential to be brought to trial for his barbarous acts, and so Iosif had fled the motherland with his family, finally settling in the United States of America.

With his family safe, Iosif began planning his vengeance. He tracked his father across the former Soviet territories, closing in on him with each passing year. Iosif intended to make his father suffer for what he had done. With Lukai's help, that day had finally arrived.

Watching from the safety of the dilapidated barn at the far end of the field, Iosif spent the entire day monitoring the old farmhouse for activity. Not a single person arrived or left. With darkness closing in, Iosif hoped that the glow of a lightbulb or the flicker of a candle would betray his father's presence, but the house remained as dark as the world around it.

Despite following the trail of clues here as soon as he received the lead from Lukai, there was no guarantee his father was still at the farmhouse. The old man may have left the KGB, but the KGB never left him. For over a decade he evaded Iosif, even going so far as to mock his late arrivals by leaving warnings for Iosif to abandon his quest. Arriving at his father's penthouse suite in Tbilisi four years ago, he almost did.

Having come close to catching his father on two occasions, Iosif overplayed his hand in Tbilisi. Despite Iosif's caution, his father knew he was coming and planned accordingly. Disguised as a delivery driver, Iosif ascended to the penthouse and picked the lock. Much like tonight, there was no indication that his father was present, but the lobby attendant had no record of him leaving.

Silently, Iosif crept into the penthouse, weapon drawn and ready. The killing blow had to be delivered swiftly. Any hesitation and Iosif's father would turn the tables, sending Iosif to meet the angels. The living room was clear, the smell of cigar smoke fresh enough to confirm that his father was close. The dirty dishes in the kitchen were no indicator that his father was home. Cleaning was always something he left to the maids.

Moving to the first bedroom, Iosif heard the gentle patter of water coming from one of the en suite showers. Iosif carefully opened the first door. The sound grew no louder. Moving to the second bedroom, Iosif listened carefully for sounds of movement. Pressed against the wall, he could hear the shower but nothing more. Turning the doorknob, Iosif paused at the gentle click of the latch springing free. Still no movement.

Pushing open the door, Iosif entered the bedroom, weapon raised. His father's suit lay neatly folded on the bed, ready for when he finished in the shower. Iosif's eyes were drawn to the black leather holster and the weapon inside. His father's Makarov pistol. With one eye on the bathroom door, Iosif lifted his father's pistol from its holster and slid it under the bed. It was a clear signal that his father was here as he always carried his pistol with him when he went out.

The cadence of the water from the en suite shower was relentless. No change in its pattern or splashing as his father moved beneath the steady rain. Did he know Iosif was here? There was no other door to the bathroom. Iosif's father would have had to pass Iosif to escape. Taking a second to dry his palms on his pants, Iosif shifted his grip on his pistol and approached the bathroom door. Crouching slightly, arm outstretched, Iosif grasped the handle and twisted, yanking the bathroom door open.

Despite being fitted with a suppressor, the rapid release of two rounds as the naked body burst from the bathroom felt unnaturally loud to Iosif. It was an act of instinct. One round through the shoulder. Another through the chest. Kill or be killed. Except, the body was not his father's.

The bathroom was clear. Satisfied there was no immediate danger, Iosif turned his attention to the woman. Her skin was cold. Her muscles were stiff. No blood flowed from the blackened bullet holes, scorched by the close-range gunfire. His father had struck again.

"Don't move. Drop the weapon."

Iosif did as instructed as the security team burst into the room. The trap was sprung perfectly. Somewhere in the room, there was a camera. From the other end of its feed, Iosif's father had watched the whole thing unfold and alerted security. Iosif imagined him smiling as his son was taken into custody. That same smug, domineering, unapologetic smile he wore when Iosif confronted him over his abuse of Mariela.

It took six months for Iosif's case to go to court. Another three for a jury eager to convict to reach a verdict. The girl was a promising student, years ahead of her classmates in her grasp of science and mathematics, and beloved in the community for her support of the local church. Hearing the prosecution read out the list of horrific crimes committed on her adolescent body, mind and soul sickened Iosif. The beatings, the rape, the physical and mental torture inflicted on her were intended as a message to Iosif.

As the case proceeded, Iosif found himself believing the prosecution. The more he considered it, the more he realized he was to blame. If he had not pursued his father to Tbilisi, his father would not have set the trap. He would not have used the girl for bait. Her blood would not be on Iosif's hands. He may not have tied her wrists, cut her flesh, or forced himself upon her, but Iosif deserved to be punished for her suffering. He deserved to pay for not protecting his daughter and her unborn baby.

Fate had other ideas.

Convicted for his father's crimes, Iosif never made it to prison. Lukai saw to that. Mariela's rise through the ranks secured Iosif's release. She wanted her grandfather dead, and Iosif would be the man to do it.

Opening the door to the farmhouse, Iosif feared the events in Tbilisi were about to play out again. The ground floor was clear. Dishes in the sink. The smell of cigar smoke lingered. Silence filled the house. Iosif heard no running water as he ascended the stairs, but the smell of decay wafted from the nearest bedroom. Iosif hesitated. There was no security team on standby and he would hear the approach of any police vehicles. Not that it would help him much in such a remote location.

Pressing on, Iosif swallowed his fears and opened the bedroom door. It was too late to save his father's latest victim. Iosif could not undo his crimes. All he could do was bear witness.

Deciding that his father's trap was no longer avoidable, Iosif took out a flashlight and scanned the room. There on the bed was a body. Despite being stripped and mutilated, his genitals removed and discarded, Iosif recognized the corpse as his father. To further remove any doubt, the old man's intestines had been pulled out and arranged around him to spell out his crimes. Iosif hoped his father had still been alive when it happened.

Standing over his father's ruined body, Iosif took out his phone and called California.

"It's done."

-35-

LOS ANGELES COUNTY, CALIFORNIA
May 30, 2029

"Show me," said Mariela.

There was no sense of relief at seeing her grandfather's mutilated corpse on the jerky video connection. No sense of closure. His reign of terror was done, but it left Mariela feeling hollow.

"Thank you," Mariela said as her father ended the video feed. "Call me when you're next in California."

The sun was at its zenith as Mariela placed her phone next to her sketchbook on the glass table. Her garden design included a cluster of gazebos, each located in its own isolated patch, and it was there she had spent the morning, sketching interior designs. Grapevines sprawled over the trellis separating each gazebo from the next. Ensnared by those grapevines, Mariela wondered what this meant for her plans. There were others like him, that was for sure, but her grandfather's actions were such a major influence on her motivations that she wondered if she had the strength to continue without his specter looming over her.

Mariela was still contemplating her next move when Dave arrived home, five hours later.

"That rough?" he asked as he turned Mariela's sketchbook to face him.

The restaurant chain that Mariela owned was overdue for a makeover. Despite filling half the sketchbook, Mariela was still undecided on the new look. It had to be something with flair and style, but not so much that it discouraged the casual, well-paid diner from frequenting the establishment. It was the budget brand after all. Save all the pretentious snobbery for the assholes who thought splashing out a thousand bucks on a steak dinner somehow made them better than her. If they were arrogant enough to spend it, Mariela would happily take their money. And use it to bury them.

"This one," said Dave, spinning the sketchbook to face Mariela and tapping one of her earlier sketches. "Refined, but restrained."

"He's dead," said Mariela, wiping away the solitary tear in the corner of her eye.

"Who?" Dave asked. Mariela's blank expression could not hide the pain behind her eyes. "Oh. How do you feel?"

Mariela's lip began to quiver as her husband took a seat and placed his hands around hers. Dave knew what her grandfather did. For six years. Every sordid detail. He knew the reason they would never have children. He did not know the pain.

Shuddering at the memory of her grandfather's beating, Mariela placed a hand over her ruined womb and wept for the child she lost. The tears came slowly to begin with, the first drips of water seeping through a cracked dam. With every one that fell, the flow of water multiplied, the broken stone no longer able to withstand the pressure.

"I'm fine," Mariela replied, choking off the tears and looking into Dave's doubtful eyes. "Honestly. It was twenty-five years ago. Knowing he has finally paid for what he did has left me feeling a little overwhelmed, that's all."

Dave looked at her, the worry written large across his brow. "Okay. But if you ever want to talk about it…"

Mariela nodded and grasped Dave's hands as his sentence trailed off. Despite the sun's relentless assault upon the earth, Mariela felt cold.

"Really, I'm fine," said Mariela, taking a pencil and thickening up one of the lines in her sketch. "You don't think it's too generic, do you?"

"This is for Ella's Charhouse, right?" Dave asked, knowing when to let a topic rest. "A little generic won't hurt."

Mariela nodded. The restaurant had been the first of many successful business ventures for Mariela. Her profits provided Dave with the freedom to leave his job and run for election in the 2026 mayoral elections, leaving Mariela to funnel her inherited fortune into supporting the council and securing a place at the helm of a new world.

"I can't wait to see the finished product," Dave said as Mariela put the pencil down and used her phone to photograph the sketch. As much as she enjoyed working with paper and pencils, the final design would be fully rendered in software. "It's about time the place had a look that matched the name."

"Is that your way of telling me you want something fresh and bright instead of old and worn?"

"When it comes to restaurants," Dave replied, studying Mariela's face for signs of jest, "it makes a difference. As for the love of my life, I'll get back to you with a decision when you're old and worn."

Mariela chuckled. Dave always knew how to coax her out of her darkest moments. "You'll be there long before me."

"Old? Certainly," Dave said as he removed his suit jacket and loosened his tie. "Worn depends on how hard you work me."

"Really?" Mariela replied, furiously shoveling dirt over the shallow grave of her past as she looked into his eyes. "I can work you very hard."

"Oh," said Dave, catching the meaningful look she gave him. "That pun was actually accidental."

"That's a shame," said Mariela, closing the sketchbook and putting it to one side. "I could really do with being shown some love right now."

"Hey," said Dave, rising from his seat, "I never said I wouldn't let you work me hard."

"Then why are you leaving?" Mariela asked as he headed for the house.

"I, uh," Dave stammered, gesturing to the house as Mariela placed one foot on the table and the other on the bench beside her.

"Kneel and worship at the cult of Mariela."

Squeezing into the space between table and bench, Dave dropped to his knees as Mariela unbuttoned her jeans. "You did say cult, didn't you?"

Mariela smiled and settled back against the cushions. "You're going to have to work extra hard to please me today. I hope you're hungry."

-36-

VENTURA COUNTY, CALIFORNIA
June 03, 2029

Alex watched as Kim buttoned her shirt and adjusted her hip holster. It was pointless asking her to stay, night shift or not. Kim had made it clear that first night that this was just sex. Four weeks of incredible sex. It was probably better that way. Alex's last three relationships had fizzled out when it came to committing to the long haul, a pattern Alex attributed to his misgivings about family. A situation that would soon be resolved.

As promised, Tate came through with the cash, incentivizing Reika to continue pulling levers until she got the answers Alex needed. Good or bad, those answers would bring some much-needed closure. Every message he received that was not from Reika made the waiting that much more painful. Alex had barely slept knowing that Reika was in Hong Kong and could contact him at any time with a breakthrough. Reika was not one to factor time zones into her communications, arguing that it was up to him to not answer a call or text at two in the morning. She failed to appreciate that the knowledge that a text could arrive in the middle of the night was enough to keep him awake.

"What are you doing Thursday?" Alex asked as Kim took her navy-blue jacket and shrugged it on.

"Working," replied Kim as she adjusted her collar. "I'm off Sunday if you're up for it."

"Definitely."

"Cool," said Kim, grabbing her phone from the bedside cabinet. "I'll bring some handcuffs home from work. Let yourself out."

"Don't be here when you get home," Alex added, settling back for a power nap as she crossed the room. "I know the drill."

There were no goodbyes from Kim. If it did not suit Alex's needs, it would cheapen the experience, leaving him feeling used. In his current mood, the lack of intimacy and affection was helpful. They shared a carnal experience while remaining disconnected from each other and the world. It allowed Alex to drop a façade of boisterous enthusiasm that was getting harder to maintain. The constant fear of his sister discovering how hollow he felt meant he had barely seen her since returning from Newark.

Acting classes helped with masking his emotions. Alex was eight weeks into an evening class that dragged potential stars away from the illustrious world of waitressing that they sought when moving to Los Angeles. To his friends and family, it was a fun and interesting hobby that allowed him to meet other outgoing people. In truth, Alex was finessing his skills in anticipation of needing to charm his way across Hong Kong.

There was still a possibility that Reika would find Kendra and bring her to California. However, the chances were slim, and Alex was prepared to fly anywhere in the world to meet his mother. He just needed Reika's call.

As if responding to his thoughts, Alex's phone vibrated on the nightstand.

"Hey, Reika, what do you have for me?"

"Good news and bad news," Reika's distorted voice replied, tinny from the bad connection. "I've tracked down your mother, but I need to return to the US to take care of some urgent business."

"Okay," Alex replied, drawing the word out as he considered the implications of Reika's news. "Where does that leave me?"

"I'll need three days," said Reika. Alex wondered if she had heard his question or not. "Four at most. Can you get a flight to Hong Kong for Thursday?"

"Probably," Alex replied as he slid off the bed.

There was a pause, the ever-present crackle of the line the only indication the connection was still live. Even so, Alex glanced at the screen to check his call status. Catching sight of himself in the screen's reflective surface, Alex thought about what he said. This was the chance he had waited for his entire life.

"Yes," Alex said, his voice filled with determination. "I'll be there. Even if I have to drive to San Fran and fly from there."

Static. Alex checked his phone, missing Reika's reply.

"Sorry, Reika. Missed that. I just heard something about a flight."

"Text me when you've booked your flight," Reika repeated. "If I can't get back here Wednesday, I'll aim to arrive around the same time as you."

"Sure thing," said Alex, parting the curtains slightly and glancing out at the city as night descended. "I'll get on that as soon as I get home. What about my mother? What if we lose her again while you're in the US?"

"I doubt she'll be going anywhere," Reika replied. Her matter of fact delivery made the words sound too menacing for Alex. "I've got someone watching her. Just in case."

"Is she okay?" Alex asked, but Reika was gone.

Unsure if she ended the call by choice or if they were cut off, Alex hesitated to call Reika back. Had something happened to his mother? If there was a problem, Reika would have told him. That much, Alex was certain. Deciding Reika had told him all she intended to reveal over the phone, Alex pulled on his clothes and left Kim's apartment, unable to shake the feeling that something was amiss.

SANTA BARBARA COUNTY, CALIFORNIA
June 06, 2029

"We're going to be late," said Mike as he overtook Skylar's motorcycle, pumping his fist in the air as he did so. "Dave and Mariela will be there by now."

"Cool your jets," Skylar replied through the intercom built into her helmet, a sunburst orange full-face design to go with the two-tone amber and black of her Triumph Daytona. "You know Mariela will be fashionably late."

"Not as late as we are."

Skylar and Mike were thirty miles out of Santa Barbara, eastbound on the 101. The sun was already dropping toward the horizon behind them as Skylar opened the throttle and pulled alongside Mike on his Screaming Eagle V-Rod. No matter how much she tried, Skylar could not get him to ride anything but a Harley. Cars were one thing, but his bike had to be American.

"You're the one that made us late, Mike," Skylar said as Mike gunned the engine and pulled ahead again.

"Me? It was you parading around the bedroom topless."

"I was trying to get ready," Skylar replied. Taking the lead so he could see her clearly, Skylar raised her hand in a loosely clenched fist and shook it from side to side. "Unlike somebody I could mention."

"I couldn't get my leathers on with it in the way," said Mike as Skylar accelerated away. "Besides, I told you it would go down quicker if you gave me a hand."

"Like I was going to fall for that one. Now quit your chopsing and get a move on. We're going to be late."

"Why you…" replied Mike, his sentence devolving into a merry chuckle as he chased her along the highway.

As they rolled into the parking lot shared between the restaurant and wine bar, Skylar scoured the car park for Mariela's car. It appeared that twenty minutes late was not fashionable enough. Finding a spot in plain sight of the entrance, so Mariela would see them when she arrived, Skylar and Mike parked up. The attendant who walked out as they dismounted had other ideas.

"You can't park your bikes here."

Skylar lifted her helmet off and looked the girl up and down. She looked to be fresh out of high school, probably her first real job, and a recent hire. Skylar spent enough time visiting the establishment to be familiar with the regular staff. None of them ever said they could not park their bikes there.

"Excuse me?" Mike asked gruffly, tucking his helmet under one arm.

"Uh, well," she stammered, gathering her thoughts before continuing in a shakier voice, stripped of the authoritative tone it previously held. Skylar had never seen anybody who didn't know Mike not be taken aback. "There's a parking lot down the hill you could use."

"That's unacceptable. I think I'll have to take this up with management."

The girl was visibly shaken now, faced with the decision to back down and slink away or hold her ground against a man that could probably crush her twig-like body in one hand.

"There's no need for that," she said, attempting to rally and brave the coming storm.

The rest of her sentence went unsaid as one of the sommeliers walked out and caught Mike's eye. Melvin Chisholm was one of the old guard, having been with the company for as long as Skylar could remember, and knew them as regulars. He also knew how to handle Mike's bluff and bluster.

"Hey, busboy. What's all this about us not being able to park our bikes and enjoy one of your fine beverages?"

Melvin turned, saw who he was dealing with, and smiled. "Gotta keep the riff-raff out somehow."

"Riff-raff?" said Skylar, deciding to wade into the conversation with feigned irritation. "I'll have you know we're not just any old riff-raff. We're grade-A gutter trash. Career winos and proud of it."

"I can believe that," Melvin replied with a grin so wide it threatened to slice his ears off. "How the devil are you both?"

"Oh, you know," said Mike, stroking his windpipe. "Hungry.

Thirsty."

"I bet," Melvin said before turning to the girl who was now standing around, looking like a spare prick at an orgy. "It's okay Hanna, they're regulars. Do me a favor and go let Renee know the Blake's are here. "

"Will do," she replied, eager for an excuse to retreat.

"No sign of the Michaelis'?" Skylar asked as Melvin showed them to a table.

"Not today. I take it you're booked in at the restaurant."

"We are," Skylar replied, plucking the wine list from the table as she sat down. "Couldn't come all this way and not have a cheeky drink at the bar first though."

"Of course, of course," said Melvin. "We've got a new red you might enjoy. Strong aroma of violet. Do you want me to add it to a taster flight? Complimentary, of course."

Always happy to try out a new red, Skylar agreed to a sample. If Mariela missed out on the free wine that was her fault for arriving late. By fluke or by design, Hanna ended up serving their table, allowing her to get to know the real Mike. With a glass in hand, he turned on the charm and soon knew the girl's life story. Everywhere he went, Mike would strike up a conversation and get people talking about things like the weather, their pets or even their love life. He had a knack for making people feel comfortable enough around him to talk freely about a range of subjects, when he wasn't toying with their confidence. Although, it did prove annoying when you needed the waiter to take your order. Skylar almost felt bad for interrupting to order a second drink.

"I have something for you," came a familiar voice from behind as Skylar sipped a rather peculiar Malbec.

Putting her glass down, Skylar craned her head back over her shoulder to see Renee, owner of the familiar voice and manager of the wine bar, looking down at her with a warm smile.

"Is it yummy?" Skylar asked, getting up and giving Renee a huge hug.

"Of course," said Renee as she walked away, motioning for Mike and Skylar to follow her to the back room. "But you'll have to buy a whole case of it. Might even give your Tempranillo a run for its money."

"I doubt that," said Skylar as Mike emptied his glass and stood up, freeing Hanna to assist other customers.

Skylar had sampled a few wines in her time, good and bad, but nothing came close to the Tempranillo that Diablo Paso produced. That was the pinnacle of winemaking in her eyes. Every vintage was perfection, with its rich fruitiness and full nose, to which words failed to do justice. Although Renee always gave great advice on the latest wines,

Skylar had yet to find a wine that could match it.

"And what if I don't like it?" Mike asked.

"Then I'll repurchase it from you. At a discount."

Renee knew Skylar well enough to know that was not a likely scenario as she pulled a bottle of Cabernet from the rack. It was better than the Malbec, sweeter but dry at the same time, with a slightly herbal aroma. Not enough to knock the Tempranillo from the top spot, but that did not stop Skylar from ordering two cases.

"I understand you've got a dinner reservation over at the steakhouse," Renee said as she processed the payment. "Do you want me to get these sent up to your room for you? I take it you're staying at the hotel tonight, yeah?"

"We are," said Skylar, sliding her card back in her purse. "There's no way we'll be in any state to ride home later. Dave and Mariela are meant to be joining us for an overdue wine night. Although, they are taking the piss a little with the time. I hope nothing's happened."

-38-

VENTURA COUNTY, CALIFORNIA
June 06, 2029

"Penny for your thoughts?"

"Afternoon, Phoebe," Alex replied without opening his eyes. She had tried masking her voice, mimicking a gruff, male tone, but to no avail. Every time she spotted him in the park, she opened with the same line.

"Is it?" she asked, her voice a lot closer as she sat down next to him. "Or is it now evening?"

"evening is technically after noon," said Alex, emphasizing the space between after and noon.

"True. I've always thought we should have a word for the hours in between afternoon and evening."

"We do. Teatime."

"Teatime?"

"It's an English thing."

"They have a specific time of day for drinking tea?" Phoebe asked, lying down next to Alex. "And they use it to separate afternoon from evening? And I thought Portland was weird. Why don't they call it something else and drink tea whenever they want?"

"Post meridiem, Phoebe," Alex replied, opening his eyes to observe her reaction.

Phoebe's brow furrowed for a moment as she tried to decipher Alex's statement. On the handful of occasions Alex had visited Serra Cross Park over the last few months, he had failed to appreciate how cute Phoebe was. Her rakish frame had a certain elegance, despite not being Alex's personal preference, and her lightly tanned skin had a rare smoothness to it. There was nothing particularly outstanding about her appearance, but the slight overbite as she thought gave her otherwise plain face a pleasing aspect.

"I take it you're from Portland," Alex asked, providing Phoebe with an excuse to move on from his previous comment.

"Originally," said Phoebe, the cute little overbite becoming less noticeable as her brain switched to a topic with which she was at ease. "We moved to Ventura three years ago when my aunt got sick. Leukemia. She's dead now."

"I'm sorry. Must have been tough, seeing her go through that."

"Oh, no. She enrolled on an experimental drug trial that put her into remission. It was the outbreak in March that killed her. Terrible way to go."

Alex thought back to his first encounter with Phoebe and her questions about salvation. "Is that why you came here? Back when we first met, I mean."

"I come here quite often. I find it soothing. It's a good place to sit and watch the world go by. Although, I would be lying if I said her death didn't play a part in me seeking comfort with a fellow Christian. What about you? What's your reason for seeking the Lord's guidance?"

Alex sighed. "Family drama. I have the opportunity to visit the mother I never knew, but I can't tell my sister that I'm going. With everything going on at work, it's difficult to talk about my issues without feeling like I'm piling on her. I've kept it secret for so long she'll probably freak if she finds out. It'll look like I'm trying to run away from home."

"Is that what you want?"

"No. I would never abandon my sister. We've been through so much together. And she knows that. Deep down, she knows that."

"Sometimes," said Phoebe after a thoughtful pause, "just being is enough. The Lord does not need to come around for lunch to share his light. Your sister does not need you to follow her around to know you are there for her. Does she not want to visit your mother?"

Alex shook his head. "No. We're adopted. Her mother died when Sky was little."

"Sky. What a beautiful name. Is your mother far? Letting Sky share in the joy of your reunion may help with whatever difficulty she is going through."

"Hong Kong."

"Ah. Not a day out at the Santa Monica pier then."

"Not quite. I've booked an open ticket as I'm not sure how long I'll be gone. It depends how things go."

"Ah," Phoebe said as she turned onto her side to see him more easily. "And that's why Sky will think you're abandoning her. A one-way ticket to Hong Kong doesn't sound so good."

Alex nodded. He knew it sent the wrong message, but he did not want to cut short his time with his mother to jump on a plane if it could be avoided.

"When do you leave?"

"Tomorrow afternoon," said Alex as he turned his head skyward and closed his eyes. "Before my sister gets back from Goleta."

-39-

SANTA BARBARA COUNTY, CALIFORNIA
June 06, 2029

"Better late than never," said Dave as the car glided into the car park. "Can't be helped."

Mariela remained silent as the car came to a stop. Arriving late was of no concern to her after Vasily's news. She was still trying to wrap her head around it. Six percent. That was the survival rate for stage three lung cancer. To survive the outbreak only to receive that diagnosis was proof that this world was cruel beyond belief. The sooner Mariela swept away the corrupt institutions and replaced them with a compassion filled society where everyone protected each other, the better. There had to be a way to accelerate her timeline. For Brianna's sake.

Given the uncertainty over her future, Brianna and Vasily were moving up their plans to get married. There would be no grand ceremony, just a simple wedding as soon as they could get a date. On top of the cancer, having to sacrifice their plans for an elaborate wedding was adding insult to an already considerable injury. Weddings were meant to mark the beginning of a new era of joy, not an end to happiness.

"Are you getting out?" Dave said, ducking down to peer in through the open car door.

Mariela spared one last thought for her future cousin-in-law's cruel fate and turned to Dave, a bright smile on her face. "As soon as you get my door."

"You can get your own door," said Dave as he forced a wry smile. "Wouldn't want you thinking I'm some sort of sexist."

Mariela pushed open her door and waited for Dave to join her, hooking her arm through his as the car locked itself. "I'll settle for some sort of sexy."

"I think I can manage that," said Dave as they crossed the car park and entered the bar. "Depending on how many you're planning to have."

"More than enough to make a mess in the back of the car during the journey home," Mariela replied as she scanned the room for Mike and Skylar.

"I hope you're not referring to puke," said Dave as he spotted Mike at one of the tables.

Mariela's smile widened as she turned her gaze on him. "Wait and see."

Seeing their approach, Mike gave a wave and stood to greet them with a firm handshake that threatened to dislocate Dave's wrist and a hug that deprived Mariela of oxygen.

"We were about to give up and head to the restaurant without you," said Mike as he looked for their server. "Sky's gone to powder her nose."

"Then we've got time for a quick one," Mariela replied, taking a seat as a young girl arrived to take her order. "A glass of whatever."

"In that case, three glasses of that red with the violet aroma," Mike said as he sat back down. "And what about you, Dave?"

"I'll sample one of Mariela's," Dave replied, adjusting his tie before taking a seat at the table. "And you are?"

"Hanna," the waitress replied, holding out her hand. "It's a pleasure to meet you. I can't wait until the movie comes out. Mike's told me all about it."

"I bet he has," Dave replied, shaking her hand as Mike fought to suppress a mischievous grin.

Mike frequently took advantage of Dave's innate ability to be one of those faces you recognize but cannot place to spin a tall tale when they were running late. On this occasion, Dave was the star of an upcoming rom-com about a merman that falls for a human princess.

"There you are," said Skylar, returning to the table as Mariela took the first sip of her wine.

"No," said Dave, raising his glass to Skylar. "We're not there, we're here."

"Uh-uh," Skylar replied, pouring herself a glass of water. "I'm here, and you're there."

"We're all here," Mike said before Dave could reply. "Okay?"

"Agreed," said Mariela as Dave nodded in agreement.

"But we should be there," said Skylar, gesturing in the direction of the restaurant with one hand as she raised her glass to her lips. "Drink up."

Dave chuckled, conceding the point to Skylar as he took a swig of his wine. Mariela emptied her glass as Mike gulped his and reached for his jacket. There was no enjoyment from drinking the wine so quickly, but the alcohol helped calm Mariela's nerves. Taking Dave's half-empty glass, Mariela downed that one too.

"Are you not finishing yours?" Mariela asked as Skylar finished her water and scooped up her jacket.

"Nah, I'll get a fresh one at the bistro. I need some food to settle my stomach before drinking any more."

"Suit yourself," Mariela replied, grabbing Skylar's nearly full glass of white wine and drinking it like water.

"Something you wanna share?" Skylar asked as Mike settled the bill.

More than you would want to hear Mariela thought as she held her hands out, palms up, and shrugged. "It's been a long day."

-40-

SANTA BARBARA COUNTY, CALIFORNIA
June 06, 2029

"Shit, Mar. That's rough," said Skylar as they entered the Bistro. "How'd she take it? No. forget I said that. Stupid fucking question. Tell Vasily and Brianna our prayers are with them."

A few eyes turned their way as Skylar and Mariela entered, taking in Mike and Skylar's leather-clad physiques with mild interest, but nobody commented on their attire. As with the wine bar, they were regulars at the restaurant and known by all the staff. All except one.

"Hanna?" Mike asked as a waitress arrived to take their order. It was easy to see why he would think so.

"Gemma," she replied with a smile. Even her dimples looked the same. "I take it you've met my sister."

"Yeah," Mike said as he settled back with his hands behind his head. "She didn't mention she had a sister. Why would that be? You two don't get along?"

"You're losing your touch, Michael," Mariela jumped in before Gemma could answer. "Fancy not learning Hanna has a twin."

"Triplets," Gemma corrected. "Although our sister isn't identical."

Mike chuckled. "Nice try, I'm not falling for that one."

Smiling, despite being caught out, Gemma took their order and bounded off to the kitchen. Despite their identical appearance, the two girls could not have been more dissimilar in their behavior. Gemma's youthful exuberance and boundless energy stood in stark contrast to the prim and proper nature of Hanna's behavior. This was more evident when she returned with the food as Gemma jittered with nervous energy and embellished her comments with exaggerated motion. A far cry from Hanna's more reserved range of motion as she stood, ramrod straight, and chatted with Mike.

As with so many meals, Skylar sat and listened to Mike talk and talk and talk as she ate. It wasn't just idle chit-chat either; Mike genuinely expressed interest in the things people had to say. Mariela seemed content to let Mike drive the conversation, which was hardly surprising. Skylar imagined she would be glad of the opportunity to shrink into the background if Jeremy or Alex dropped a bombshell like that on her.

Skylar barely knew Vasily, but Brianna went to college with Alex. It was wrong that someone so young could fall prey to such a terrible affliction. To think Brianna would be lucky to reach her thirties made Skylar shudder.

"I'm going to..." Skylar began, sliding from the booth and waving her hand toward the washroom.

Clamping her mouth shut for fear of what would come out, Skylar burst into one of the empty stalls just in time. Her body heaved as it purged itself of whatever had upset her. No amount of willpower was going to stop her from being sick. Chunks of half-digested pasta and macerated crab meat splattered against the porcelain as Skylar placed a hand on the cistern to steady herself. Her ribs ached from the strain, tightening around her lungs as another wave burst forth.

"Fu-" Skylar said, choking on the word as the last of her meal poured from her mouth. "-ck."

Straightening up, Skylar wiped the trails of spit from her chin as she leaned back against the door to the stall, unaware that it had swung open while she vomited. Grasping frantically for the door frame, she managed to arrest her fall and yank herself back into the stall.

"Shit," she muttered as she rested her head against the side of the stall.

Second time that night. What Skylar took for being too much wine on an empty stomach at the bar needed a rethink. After waving a hand over the sensor to flush away the evidence, Skylar exited the stall and checked her makeup in the bathroom mirror. Despite everything, she looked fine. Except for the bloodshot eyes. And her pale complexion.

"Everything okay?" Dave asked as Skylar returned to the table. "You look a little washed out."

"Too much wine," said Skylar, receiving a nod from Dave and a sympathetic smile from Mariela. Mike reached across under the table and gently squeezed her thigh as he spooned chocolate cake into his mouth.

"Speaking of which," Mariela said as Gemma returned to the table with another bottle and another woman.

"This is my sister Erica," Gemma said as she poured Mariela another glass. "I'll take that apology now, Michael."

Despite the hollow knot that left her drained, Skylar could not help but laugh as Gemma stood there, hands on hips, with a wickedly mischievous grin on her face. There was undoubtedly a family resemblance between the two girls. Enough to believe they were sisters.

"No, no," Mike replied, wiping away some crumbs of chocolate cake with a napkin. "I need to see proof. How do I know you aren't just a year apart?"

As if expecting such a comeback, both girls shot out a hand toward Mike's face, ID cards at the ready.

"No. I call fake."

"Mike, admit it. They got you beat," Dave said, laughing as Mike shook his head in denial. "It's possible to have triplets where only two are identical."

"Okay, okay," Mike relented as he pushed his empty bowl to the center of the table. "I'll let you have this one. But you better not have any other tricks up your sleeve for when we come back now."

Gemma rolled each of her sleeves up and waved both hands as Skylar poured herself a water and swished it around her mouth. The acidic aftertaste was making her feel sick again.

"Can I get you anything else?" Gemma asked, receiving the same negative response from each of them.

"I'm sorry I've been such a bore," Mariela said as Gemma left to process their check. "I'll make it up to you at the dinner party on Sunday."

"Oh shit, is it this week, Mar?" Skylar asked. "That came around quick. And nobody thinks you've been a bore. I'm surprised you came out at all after such a devastating piece of news. I take it you're heading straight home after this."

Mariela nodded. "Car's all programmed ready. We just need to jump in and go. One day, you'll realize the benefits of the tech and join us in the twenty-first century."

"Nope," Skylar replied as Gemma returned with the bill. "Give me a car with a gas pedal, a computer with a real keyboard, and a restaurant with traditional waiter service and I'll be a happy bunny."

"Don't be such a dinosaur," said Mariela as Mike handed Gemma his credit card. "You can't avoid the future. Join me in this brave new world."

"You do realize that's a dystopian novel, don't you, Mar?" asked Skylar as they hugged goodbye.

"The world is what we make it, Sky. Let's make it better."

"Okay, you two," said Dave as he linked arms with Mariela. "Save the tech talk for another day. We're going back to our comfortable home, and our comfortable bed, with our comfortable sheets. You enjoy the hotel."

"We will," Mike replied without a trace of bitterness or envy, grabbing Dave's hand and shaking it. "See you Sunday."

Returning to her seat while they waited for Mike's credit card. Skylar held Mike's hand and closed her eyes. Sleep beckoned.

"That's a beautiful pendant by the way," said Gemma when she returned with Mike's card, drawing Skylar from her half-sleep. "Simple but elegant."

Skylar took the pendant between her thumb and forefinger and lifted it to get a better look. "You think so?"

It was her oldest piece of jewelry, a copper disc she found when searching for buried Roman coins in the fields around Jeremy's home in Wales. There was nothing remotely special about it beyond a strange fold mark along the middle that reminded Skylar of the rolling surface of the sea before a storm.

"Here," Skylar said when Gemma nodded, lifting the long chain over her head. "It's yours. May it bring you luck."

"Are you sure?" Gemma asked.

"I'm sure," Skylar replied turning to Mike. "I've held it for long enough. In that time, I found the man of my dreams and the career I always wanted. It's about time I shared some of that good fortune."

VENTURA COUNTY, CALIFORNIA
June 07, 2029

At the sound of tires on the gravel drive, Jeremy closed his laptop and placed the device in his desk drawer. The network was quiet. Too quiet. After an event as monumental as the outbreak, Jeremy expected something. What that something would be, he could not guess, but the lack of action was unsettling. It was unlike the council to let an opportunity to test their boundaries go to waste. Especially Lukai.

Jeremy reached for a book as the garage door rolled back to allow Skylar and Mike access. He estimated he had five minutes before she burst into his office.

"Just leave it, Mike," Jeremy heard her say through the open office window.

Make that two minutes.

As he opened the book at the halfway point, Jeremy found himself wondering if he wanted the council to make a move. The last time Lukai tested his limits, the people closest to Jeremy suffered. Still, he could not shake the feeling that the council's inactivity was more ominous.

"Alex! Jeremy!" Skylar yelled as the front door swung open, the door nearly tearing from its hinges as it slammed against the wall. "Get your butts down here!"

Jeremy waited silently, listening to Skylar open the closet at the bottom of the giant staircase that dominated the hallway and hang her jacket before kicking her boots off. The gentle thud of them landing in the corner of the hallway was followed by the thud of Mike's boots landing next to Skylar's.

"Jeremy?" Skylar called again as she crossed the hallway. "Alex?"

Jeremy glanced at his watch. Sixteen seconds out.

"Hey, Uncle," said Skylar as she pushed open his office door. "There you are. What are you reading?"

"The latest Daniel Myers novel," Jeremy replied, closing the book and placing it on his desk. "What has got you in such a state?"

Beneath the light sheen generated by the evening sun, Skylar had a glow of positivity Jeremy had not seen in her since the quarantine was first announced. Virtually bouncing with excitement, Skylar could barely contain herself.

"I'll tell you in a minute," she replied, turning her head to look down the hallway to the kitchen. Where's Alex? I want him to hear this."

"By now, somewhere over mainland China, I would guess, Sky."

Skylar's head snapped back to focus on Jeremy. "What?"

"Somewhere over mainland China," Jeremy repeated as he stood and pushed his chair under the desk.

"I heard you the first time. I just didn't believe it."

"He left this morning," Jeremy said as if Alex had gone to the shops. "Backpacking around Asia. Something about wanting to take time out to discover himself."

"And you let him?" Skylar asked as Jeremy straightened the notepad he kept on his desk for jotting down ideas. "Have you forgotten his gap year?"

"The only person struggling to remember Alex's gap year is Alex."

After finishing college, Alex wanted to go back to the UK to visit some of the towns and cities. Ringwood, Witney, Bury St. Edmunds, Cardiff, Burton-on-Trent. It took Jeremy all of seven seconds to spot the connection between the places on Alex's list. His brewery tour lasted three weeks, one of which included a visit to a hospital to get his stomach pumped.

"Well, I hope he has fun after ruining my surprise," said Skylar, the disappointment in her voice making her words sound sour.

"He'll be fine," said Jeremy holding his hand out to indicate that Skylar should head to the living room. "He's a lot more responsible than he was back then, Sky. Besides, he deserves some fun. We all do after the start this year has given us."

To make sure Alex did not make a liar of him, Jeremy had contacted some friends in Asia to keep watch over Alex. If Lukai did decide to make a move, Jeremy wanted to be sure his loved ones would not be caught in the crossfire this time.

"True," Skylar conceded as they crossed the hallway to the living room. "I shouldn't be mad. He didn't know I had a surprise. Hell, I didn't know until this morning. I suppose I'm a little bit jealous. He has all this freedom to come and go as he pleases. I sometimes wish I could drop everything and go on holiday at the drop of a hat."

"You can," said Jeremy as Skylar dropped onto the giant lounge chair in front of the television and snuggled into the thick, fake fur blanket draped over it. "But you won't. You're not selfish enough to walk away from a crisis like this. That's what makes you so special, Sky."

"I am, aren't I?" Skylar said with a wicked grin. "If I wasn't so humble, I'd be literal perfection."

"I don't know about that," said Mike, entering the living room from the kitchen door. "I thought I was perfection."

"B minus," Skylar replied sitting up so that Mike could sit next to her.

"I'll take it," Mike said as he sat down, a glass of water in hand. "Have you told him? Or are we waiting for Alex?"

"No, I was waiting for you, Mike," said Skylar, placing her hand on his thigh. "Alex has buggered off to China."

"What? Why?"

"You're pregnant," Jeremy interrupted, not wanting to go over Alex's departure again.

"Jeremy!" Skylar yelled, pouting slightly that he stole her thunder.

"Well, that's a bit harsh," Mike replied with mock indignation. "I've put on a pound or two since the shoulder injury, but pregnant is a bit of a leap."

Sorry, Sky," Jeremy replied, taking a seat on the sofa. "You had something you wanted to tell me."

A child complicated things. It was bound to happen sooner or later, but Jeremy always thought it would be later. He wanted to see his adopted children enjoy life for a few more years before shattering their illusions and revealing the truth of their parentage.

"Yes, uncle," Skylar replied, her tone deadly serious. "We've decided to take action. We can no longer stand by and ignore the terrible damage being done to our planet. We've adopted a snow leopard."

Jeremy watched Skylar's stony expression crack as her resolve buckled under the weight of her excitement.

"And I'm having a baby!"

-42-

NEW TERRITORIES, HONG KONG
June 07, 2029

"Xander? Is that you?"

Alex looked up at the owner of the voice, wondering who would be calling him by his high school nickname in the middle of Hong Kong International Airport. He did not recognize the woman, with her powerful build squeezed into a short frock top and skinny jeans, or her Australian accent. There were only three girls he could remember with black hair, but none of them were Australian or athletic. At least, they were not athletic back then. It was nearly ten years ago.

"It is. Isn't it? Xander Zhang. From the football team. My sister had such a crush on you."

Alex's face retained a look of mild interest as he searched his memory for who the woman might be. Knowing her sister had a crush on him whittled down the possibilities, but not by enough.

"What brings you to Hong Kong?" The woman asked, leaning gently on the handle of the carry-on case beside her. "Sitting in the food court on your lonesome?"

"It's not by choice," Alex replied. A problem with Reika's flight resulted in a diversion to a remote Canadian airstrip. Judging from the background noise in the voicemail she left him, several passengers were far from happy about being stuck on a grounded plane in minus twenty Fahrenheit conditions.

"What? Being in Hong Kong or being on your own?" the woman said, fiddling with the cluster of earrings in her left ear.

"Being on my own. I'm sorry, but I have no idea who you are."

The woman smiled and shook her head in mock displeasure. "Julie. Maxwell. Eleanor's big sister. You must remember Ellie, yeah?"

"No," Alex said in surprise. He remembered Eleanor and her clique. They were the stereotypical mean girls of his year. "That would make you…"

Alex's voice trailed off as he realized what he was about to say.

"Nearly forty. Yep. Way to make a woman feel good about her age."

Alex felt his ears burning with embarrassment. "That's not what I meant. I mean…"

Julie placed her hands on her hips, waiting for him to finish, with an expression somewhere between annoyance and fascination. Held by her enchanting gaze, he struggled to find the words to express himself clearly, fumbling a compliment on her beauty.

"So, if I'm understanding you correctly," Julie replied as Alex rubbed his forehead to force some sense into his brain. "I can't be old because I'm beautiful. Would you like a bigger shovel? Or would you like a ladder to get you out of that hole you're digging?"

"No. I mean… Argh. Can we start again?"

"Relax, kid," said Julie, taking a seat next to him and pulling a bag of potato chips from a rucksack. "I'm just messing with you. Should have seen you squirm. Wish I'd taken a video and sent it to Ellie. She named her son Xander."

"Really?" Alex asked, placing his rucksack on the floor and shifting over to give Julie more room. "She barely said a word to me in school."

"Can you blame her?" said Julie, holding out the bag of chips only for Alex to decline. "You were the hot transfer student. She was the prom queen's lapdog. She may have acted like she was top tier, but there was no way she was going to risk upsetting the queen bee."

That made sense. Lynne Everett always was a complete control freak. It was easy to imagine that Ellie feared her as much as she wanted to be her.

"Anyway. Enough reminiscing. You look like a man in need of a plan, and it would be highly uncivilized of me to leave you here when I've got a spare room you can sleep in."

Alex turned to Julie with a look of suspicion. For all her talk of bygone years, he knew very little about her.

"What?" asked Julie, leaning away from Alex slightly as he studied her. "Have I got something in my teeth?"

Alex considered his options as Julie picked between her top teeth with her nail. As innocuous as she seemed, Alex had to assume the worst.

"Thanks for the offer, but I should wait here for when my friend lands."

Julie turned and looked back across the food court as if she expected Reika to come bounding out of the gate any second. That was not going to happen. The airline's best estimate was a twelve-hour delay with no guarantee they would continue to Hong Kong instead of returning to Newark. Given that Reika was supposed to land two hours ahead of him, that put Alex waiting at least ten hours in the airport.

"Well, I hope your friend doesn't keep you waiting too long," said Julie, rising to her feet and brushing non-existent crumbs from the front of her jeans before tightening the flannel shirt tied around her waist. "If you have time, I recommend Victoria Peak. If you think I'm pretty, you'll love the views from the top."

Alex nodded and thanked Julie for the recommendation. Sightseeing was not part of his plan, but he had no reason to rush back to California either. Extending his trip by a day or two was an option if his mother wanted to spend more time learning about her son. Alex could not picture Reika taking time out to smell the flowers or enjoy the view. It went against her strict, no-fun lifestyle. Worst case scenario if he wanted to make the most of the trip and see the best views of the island, he would have to go it alone.

Unimpressed with the notion of whiling away the hours on his own, Alex picked up his rucksack and scanned the airport for Julie. If he picked the right direction, he could probably catch up to her. Just as he was about to pick a direction at random, he spotted the combination of white cotton, grey flannel and blue denim that made up Julie's outfit as she disappeared into an elevator.

With nothing better to do with his time, Alex set off after her.

-43-

NEW TERRITORIES, HONG KONG
June 07, 2029

Julie stepped from the elevator and glanced at the signs to identify her next direction. Hoisting her rucksack onto her shoulder, she set off for the coach station, dragging her luggage case behind her.

"Hey, Julie," a voice called out as she crossed the airport. "Wait for me."

Julie turned and scanned the crowd, spotting Alex heading her way. Her mouth spread into a smile that slowly faded as she spotted a man in a red shirt. He was loitering in the food court while she spoke to Alex.

"Where are you going?" Alex asked as he caught up to her.

The man in red kept walking.

"Bus," she replied, gesturing in the direction of the coach station. "It takes longer, but it's the cheapest option. A taxi to Tsuen Wan is almost twenty times that."

"How much quicker is it?"

"Taxi's half the time," said Julie as she adjusted the weight of her rucksack on her shoulder. "Not including waiting around."

"That settles it. If you're giving me a place to sleep, I'm paying to get us there quicker."

"Really? Thanks," said Julie, glancing toward the coach station before setting off in the direction of the taxi ranks. "I admit, I wasn't looking forward to the bus ride."

They walked in silence, Julie casting furtive glances over her shoulder, until they got outside. Joining the queue for a taxi, Julie turned to Alex to disguise her search of the area.

"You didn't answer my question," she asked.

The man in red was back and loitering by the airport door.

"What question?"

"What brings you to Hong Kong?"

There was another man, six spaces behind them in the queue, that Julie saw loitering in the food court.

"Family," Alex replied as Julie swung her head back to face him. "I'm here to meet my mom."

"Cool," Julie said distractedly. "Don't look now, but I think that guy in the red is following me. He was loitering in the food court until I went to the coach station. He walked by me when you called. Now he's here."

"Maybe he didn't want to wait for a bus either," Alex replied as he shuffled forward to stand alongside Julie.

"And what about the guy six spaces back? He was in the food court too."

Alex turned to check his luggage, surreptitiously picking out the men Julie identified.

"What about him?" Alex asked as he straightened back up and faced the front of the queue again, edging closer to Julie. "We'll be out on the road before he gets a cab."

Julie shook her head and smiled. "I'm sorry. Being in a strange land always puts me on edge. I start imagining everyone is watching me."

"I thought you said you lived in Hong Kong," Alex said, turning to Julie with a puzzled expression.

"No," Julie said, handing the attendant a slip of paper with some Chinese writing on it as they reached the front of the line. "I said I had a spare room you could sleep in. The apartment belongs to a friend. I use it whenever I'm passing through Hong Kong."

Ushered into a waiting taxi, Julie surrendered her bags to the driver and jumped into the back seat, leaving Alex to tip the attendant as his bag joined hers in the trunk.

"English?" The driver asked, handing Julie the slip of paper with her address.

"Australian," Julie replied as Alex climbed in next to her and pulled at the seatbelt. "And an American."

"Sort of," Alex added, his seatbelt clicking into place. "I was born here but grew up in Britain before moving to America."

"Really?" Julie asked as the driver forced his way out into the traffic. "I always assumed you're American. Ellie never mentioned it. And you don't have a British accent."

Alex half turned in his seat, eyes watching the other taxis. Julie resisted the urge to check if the two men were still following them.

"I've lived in California for ten, twelve years now. My accent wasn't very strong anyway. What about you? Ellie's accent was proper valley girl."

"Oh, I know," said Julie, tucking the address slip into her pocket. "It drove mum nuts the way she Americanized everything. Mum was a proud Aussie. That's why I moved to Queensland after dad died."

"I'm sorry," Alex said, his attention on the cars behind them.

"Why? You didn't kill him."

"Good point," said Alex as he turned to face the front. "Change of subject. You may want to get out at a different address. That guy in the line is two cars behind us."

Julie nodded and took out her phone. If there was somebody following her, she was not about to take any chances. Bringing up an alternative address, Julie leaned forward and asked the taxi driver if he could take them there instead.

"Okay," he replied, giving the screen the most cursory glance possible. "Ten minutes."

The remainder of the journey was made in silence as Julie watched the scenery pass by, occasionally tapping out a message on her phone, and Alex studied the traffic.

Pulling up outside the shopping center Julie selected, Alex jumped out of the car and retrieved the bags from the trunk while Julie handed over the cash to the taxi driver. Guessing her intent, Alex was already making his way into the shopping center with the bags when their taxi pulled away.

"This way, quick," she said as soon as they were through the door. From the corner of her eye, Julie saw one of the men following her step from another taxi as she disappeared into the building.

Dashing to the right, Alex and Julie emerged onto the street crossing the one from which they entered the building. Stepping to the side, Julie peered around the frame of the large glass door to see her pursuer step into view and look around.

"There he is," she said, pulling back from sight. "Let's go."

Moving as swiftly as they could without drawing unnecessary attention, Alex and Julie crossed the street and headed for the apartment, sparing a glance as they rounded the corner of the building to make sure they had lost their tail.

"Well, that was a more adventurous start to my trip than I expected," Alex said as Julie opened the apartment door. "I could do with a drink after all that excitement."

"Local beer okay?" Julie asked, abandoning her bags as soon as they were clear of the door and heading straight for the kitchen fridge. "I got some lagers from a brewery on the island that opened last year. Haven't tried them myself yet."

"Sure, sounds good," Alex said as he looked around the room.

The apartment was more brown than any room had a right to be. The coffee carpet butted up against tan colored walls. Even the furniture was brown; A pair of khaki armchairs, and a two-seater sofa positioned beneath the apartment's only window.

"Take a seat," said Julie, opening drawers as she searched for the bottle opener. "Sorry about the color scheme. My friend likes dull and lifeless. I'm more of a cool-blue myself. Reminds me of home and the ocean at Port Douglas."

"I thought you said you were from Queensland," said Alex as he wandered the room before leaning on the countertop that divided the kitchen and living space.

"Port Douglas is in Queensland," Julie replied lifting the bottle opener from the fifth drawer in triumph.

"My geography is awful. I can't even drive into Downtown Los Angeles without a sat nav."

"Is that where you live, now?" asked Julie, dragging two bottles from the fridge and putting them on the countertop before levering the top off one and passing it to Alex.

"Santa Paula," said Alex, grasping the bottle by the neck and lifting it.

"To home," Julie said, flipping the second bottle top off and clinking her bottle against Alex's. "The place I lay my head to rest."

"Aye," Alex said before taking a swig of beer. "Home is where the heart is. Or so they say."

"I wouldn't go that far. How's the beer?"

"Good," Alex replied as Julie skirted the divider and dropped into the nearest armchair.

"If you say so," said Julie, waving Alex to the other chair as she grimaced at the label. "I won't be buying this one again. Drink up and I'll open the other one. It's not as strong, but hopefully tastes better."

Julie relaxed into her chair as Alex sat in the one opposite her. She could not recall the last time she sat and had a normal conversation with someone. Her entire life was consumed by work and managing her master's projects. Taking a moment to sit and chat made her feel almost human. Too bad it could not last.

-44-

LOS ANGELES COUNTY, CALIFORNIA
June 08, 2029

"What's the problem, Frank?" Chief Parker asked as Eckhart entered his office.

"Why do you always assume I'm bringing you a problem, not a solution?" Eckhart asked as he dropped into the seat opposite Parker.

"Because this shitshow has given us more problems than solutions."

"You mean the recruitment shortfall? That's not why I'm here. We have a visitor downstairs who claims to be a friend of Mrs. Sinclair-Blake. Refused to speak to anyone except the chief. Not even me."

"Was he legit? How much does he know?"

"Hard to tell," Eckhart replied with a shake of his head. "But if he is friends with Mrs. Sinclair-Blake, it could be a way of getting the case on her radar without direct action from us."

"How so?"

"Print a copy of your records. Put them in a folder with a copy of the official records." Eckhart stood and moved the spare chair from the corner of the office to the wall next to the chief's desk. "Leave the file on this chair."

"What? Why?"

"Bear with me, chief," Eckhart replied, dismissing the interruption with a wave of his hand. "When he arrives, ask him if he's here about the missing children. Even if he wasn't, he is now. Keep things vague but feed him enough to whet his appetite."

"Okay, but where does the file come into this?"

"It's a trap. Discreetly cover it with a coat or something during the

174

meeting. Not so discreetly that he misses the point but not so obvious that he thinks he's being set up. Make an excuse to leave the room partway through the meeting so he gets an opportunity to look at the file. Hopefully, the attempt to cover it will have sparked his curiosity. If I'm right, he'll go running back to Mrs. Sinclair-Blake, and you'll have the support you asked for without raising further suspicion from Mariela."

"Awesome, Frank. Truly inspired. Just one problem. I need to connect the laptop with the files to the network to print it. The entire reason for keeping it offline is to avoid any of Mariela's snoops from finding it."

Eckhart waved away the concern as he went to the door. "There's a non-networked printer in my office. Print quality isn't great, but it will do the job. I'll stall him for fifteen minutes while you get in position."

"But what if they don't take the bait?"

"Then we are no worse off and we'll re-examine our options. Better than throwing yourself on your sword."

It was a good plan. For the next ten minutes, Parker carefully staged the scene, even going so far as to leave the roller doors to his stationery cabinet open in case their would-be informant felt the urge to make physical copies of any of the documents. Like his worn chair, the stationery cabinet was a relic of Parker's earlier days in the department that he fought to keep. Apart from the labels used cataloging evidence, the entire department was paper-free, recording everything on portable electronics, but Parker felt an office was not an office without a stationery cupboard.

With everything in place, Chief Parker became anxious that their unwitting accomplice might not deliver the files to Skylar. What if he was a spy, sent by Mariela to test his compliance? Just as his frayed nerves were about to yield, urging him to call the whole thing off, there was a knock at the door. Too late to back out, the chief called the visitor into the office and encouraged him to take a seat, nervously glancing at the folder as the stranger sat down.

"I understand you sent a file on some missing children to a friend of mine," the stranger said in a strong but clear Scottish accent, ignoring the file as he tried to flatten down some of his strawberry-blonde hair. "I figured my expertise might prove useful, maybe shed some light on your situation."

"I'm sorry," Parker replied as he casually took his jacket off the back of his chair and placed it over the folder. "You are?"

"The name's Forbes. Kellan Forbes. I'm what you might call a private security consultant. I offer specialist services to politicians, companies and government agencies. Event security, personal protection, investigative services. That sort of thing."

"Legalized thuggery," said Parker, leaning back in his chair. "Well, I'm sorry you wasted your time. Your friend already sent across someone to investigate this for me. They didn't find anything amiss. Just kids killed by the outbreak."

"Look, I'm not going to dick around. Tate and Tanner are nice enough boys but they aren't experienced enough to handle a case like this. Now, do you want my help or not?"

Sitting forward in his seat, Parker sighed and gave Kellan the official story, that kids had gone missing but their bodies turned up as the outbreak progressed and more victims were found. To set the cat among the pigeons, he cited the case of Emma Brayford, a girl who had been reported as taken from her bedroom but found dead a few miles from her home, knowing that her case was in the original file. Parker had ensured her file was at the top of the new folder, complete with notes that shed doubt on the official story.

"Probably attempting to run away from home when the infection kicked in," Parker finished dismissively, eliciting no response from Kellan.

Throughout their conversation, Parker cast the occasional nervous glance at his jacket to raise awareness while looking like his intent was the opposite. Once he was convinced the trap was sufficiently baited, and Kellan had enough to begin picking apart the case, Parker excused himself from the meeting to take a bathroom break. Upon his return to the office, he was disappointed to see that Kellan had left, and the folder remained untouched.

"Well?" Eckhart asked, appearing in the doorway as Parker checked the photocopier in the corner of his office.

"So much for that plan," Parker replied confirming the photocopier had not been used. "It seems Kellan was just as easily deceived by the cover-up as the rest of them."

"Maybe," Eckhart replied, crossing the room to the stationery cupboard.

Dismayed that another chance to bring down Mariela had passed, Parker pulled a photograph of his daughter from his desk drawer, taken just days before she was kidnapped, and silently asked for her forgiveness.

"He didn't scan or copy the file?" Eckhart asked, drawing Parker's thoughts away from sacrificing his family to stop Mariela.

"Nothing in the print log."

"How many packs of paper did you have?" Eckhart asked, kneeling next to the copier and moving his hand over the casing.

"Five. No, four. I used one to print the files. Why?"
"The copier is warm, and you're missing a pack of paper."

-45-

LOS ANGELES COUNTY, CALIFORNIA
June 10, 2029

Mariela was fuming and needed to vent her anger, but there was no viable target. All the careful planning to ensure every child taken was accounted for, their disappearance easily explained away, and then Nikola ruined everything by trying to copy her methods in cities that were not suffering from the outbreak. Just when Mariela thought the whole operation had been neatly tied up with no loose ends.

The beauty of Mariela's scheme was that she had managed to turn an opportunistic snatching of a few hundred children into a mass harvest of over a hundred thousand. The number would have been much higher, but it had proven difficult to keep ahead of the infection. Despite the best efforts of her team, many of the children had fared no better than the victims in the hospitals and CDC field surgeries.

The premise was simple, grab the child and use the police to write that child off as deceased. Outbreak victims were cremated wherever possible, to minimize infection risk, so it was an easy task to ensure no physical evidence remained. Do that in a city like Seattle though, where there was no convenient cause of death, and the whole affair fell apart.

Mariela was stupefied at just how thoughtless Nikola could be on times. Her agents had rushed to scrub the evidence before the FBI got wind of the spate of kidnappings, a feat made possible only through Nikola's control of the upper echelons of so many intelligence agencies. The scant evidence that made it into the public domain was barely enough to make the whole thing seem like scattered conspiracy theories, feeding into the bureaucracy that hampered co-operation across state borders.

Nikola dealt in mistruths and conspiracy theories, making the earlier arrival at the house of one of her agents distressing. There was no uncertainty in his instructions; Mariela needed to rectify this mess and get rid of the reporters and agents that knew anything before the whole thing blew up in their faces. He even suggested that she invite them all to the gala she was planning and kill them then, in one fell swoop. Clearly, that was a message direct from Nikola that had not been sense-checked by one of her more considerate subordinates.

Mariela assured the agent there was no cause for alarm and none of the rumors would offer any hint of the true nature of what was happening, but he would not be swayed from his position. He even had the gall to suggest it was Mariela's fault. Fortunately, Nikola was not the most attentive of bosses. A brilliant mind, hampered by apathy. All Mariela had to do was create the illusion of results and her supposed master would lose interest. That was where Deputy Chief Eckhart came in. Dave had invited a small group of influential friends to dinner that night to discuss ideas for honoring the dead and supporting the survivors. Mariela had instructed Eckhart to arrive early so she could discuss alternatives to multiple assassinations.

"I need assurances, Frank," Mariela said as they entered the drawing room. "I have some very influential, very nervous people breathing down my neck."

"It's certainly a challenge," Eckhart stated when Mariela had explained the situation. "Obviously, any investigation into the events in LA will yield nothing of merit. Darren will see to that."

"Will he?" Mariela asked pouring herself a drink before returning to her armchair. Eckhart was still nursing the drink she poured him on arrival. "The man has hardly proven trustworthy lately. First, he lets one of his officers send a report to the FBI, then I find out he called them to follow it up. Now, these other reports detailing cases in other states emerge. If I didn't know better, I'd swear somebody was doing their very best to sabotage our plans. You can see how that may shake what little confidence I had in your chief's ability to keep a lid on this."

"That is an over-simplification. Yes, a report was sent to the FBI, but as I explained before, the officer responsible is no longer with us, if you get my meaning. Knowing how volatile such a report might be in the hands of a federal agent, the chief called Mrs. Sinclair-Blake intending to make it seem like the police were trying to get the FBI to do some donkey work for them. As you know, it had the desired effect and Mrs. Sinclair-Blake threw it straight back to the chief to deal with. No agents were assigned, just a couple of private detectives that the chief and I kept distracted for a week or so until we could dismiss them without suspicion. We've already been through this."

Mariela sighed. It was true that the chief's call had done more harm than good to the investigation, but she found it hard to reconcile his attitude with his behavior. He disapproved, that much was clear, and a report filed by another officer would be a convenient way of exposing things without direct involvement and the risk of harm to his daughter. Not that Mariela would harm Sophie, but there was no need to tell the chief that. Calling in support of the case would jeopardize his daughter so that made no sense. Calling to scupper the investigation also made no sense. The safest option would have been to do nothing and hope the FBI picked up the investigation.

"Also," Eckhart continued, sitting forward as he spoke, "you are aware that I too followed up with Mrs. Sinclair-Blake, just to make sure that the investigation did get buried. From what I know of Mrs. Sinclair-Blake, going to her with a plea for more support was bound to antagonize her and get her to switch off. Mission accomplished, as directed."

"Okay, but what about these fresh reports. The ones that include details from other states. My methods are known only to a select few. How were they replicated in other states?"

"I cannot speak for other states, Mrs. Michaelis. All I know is that we buried the Los Angeles investigation the moment the FBI dropped the case."

"I would prefer it was cremated," Mariela said, raising her glass to her lips, only to realize she had finished the whiskey while they talked. "No chance of somebody with a morbid curiosity digging it back up."

"I'll see what I can do," Eckhart replied, leaning back in his chair. "I don't believe eliminating anyone with knowledge of the case is necessary. Better to let the conspiracy theories remain just that. With the aid of your intelligence contacts, I can feed enough false evidence into the system that anyone wanting to validate them will quickly tire of running down dead ends."

Mariela sighed, a sound that paradoxically combined relief with tension. Having Eckhart manipulate the evidence to keep the conspiracy theories in a perpetual state of disarray would certainly be the most attractive option. It would do no harm to plan for the worst though and assume that using more drastic methods to follow through on Nikola's instruction would be unavoidable by the time the gala rolled around.

"Very well," Mariela conceded, rising to get another drink. "Do what you can. I want the tinfoil hat wearers to be the only ones talking about this by the night of the gala, or I will need to take action."

"How much time does that give me?"

With her glass refilled with the finest Tennessee sour mash, Mariela turned back to Eckhart. "I'm looking at mid-August, the invites are being printed this week so they should go out to everyone on the weekend. Now, enough business, I'm sure my husband would like to discuss sports or something with you. Let's head to the kitchen, shall we?"

"I'm sure he would," Eckhart replied, rising from his seat and heading for the door. "Daisy-Marie is probably talking his ear off about pies. She's become obsessed lately with pie recipes."

Mariela laughed as they exited the drawing room and re-located to the kitchen, where an earnest discussion was being had over the merits of using marshmallow mix in meringue. Daisy-Marie had struck oil as Dave was a major food buff and did all the cooking for the pair of them. The dinner party had been entirely Dave's idea, and he insisted on preparing all the food himself, forcing Mariela into exile from the kitchen. Not that she minded. Mariela had a rare culinary talent for burning water when left to cook for herself.

They remained in the kitchen, the conversation working its way around to sports for Dave and Eckhart and summer holidays for Mariela and Daisy-Marie, until more guests arrived. Rather than crowd the kitchen, Mariela moved the party to the dining room, leaving Dave to finish up with the cooking in peace. Inevitably, conversation turned from small talk to business and the purpose for gathering everyone.

-46-

LOS ANGELES COUNTY, CALIFORNIA
June 10, 2029

Despite Dave and Mariela's party having a limited guest list, Mike and Skylar arrived late enough that parking the Range Rover was a challenge, even in the spacious driveway of Dave and Mariela's.

The Michaelis house was the envy of their neighborhood. The ornate and stylish manor, with its winding cobblestone drive, had a fantastic view over the valley. Perched at the edge of San Vicente Park, looking down over Mulholland Drive, the house was designed by Mariela herself, custom-built to celebrate their fifth wedding anniversary.

Dave had already announced he was running for Mayor when construction began. The grand opening took place amid much fanfare and an elaborate gala just in time for their anniversary. That party secured Dave enough funds to see his campaign through and ensured Dave and Mariela made it onto the cover of several lifestyle magazines. Not that Mariela was a stranger to such things, having already written several articles regarding the latest trends in Los Angeles herself.

The building itself attracted vast amounts of attention, the pseudo-gothic architectural inspiration to the brick and sandstone edifice blending with the neo-futuristic in a way that sounded like it shouldn't work but somehow did. It was a testament to Mariela's boundless design talent that she herself dismissed in favor of her garden. Rising in tiers as it ascended the mountain, Mariela's garden was lined with fruit trees that sectioned off the areas for entertaining. A bocce ball court, hidden behind a row of persimmons, and a miniature golf course, down behind a row of plumcots, were some of the more relaxed activities.

The jokes about Mayor Michaelis always being on the golf course were inevitable, and Skylar prided herself on not going for the obvious riposte. Instead, standing in the courtyard that dominated the back garden, she had asked if that was where the globe of death was being installed. Rather than amused chuckles, Skylar received blank expressions from Dave and Mariela.

"That's what you get for trying to be funny," Mike whispered to her that first night at Casa Michaelis. "Read your audience."

Why she remembered that moment as Mike eased the car into the last available space, two wheels on the grass verge, Skylar could not say.

"Told you we should have brought the bikes," Mike said, as Skylar squeezed through the tiny gap between her door and the adjacent car.

"I told you, Mike, as soon as Dave installs a globe of death," she replied, identifying the trigger for the memory.

A couple of businessmen were talking shop in the hall as they entered the house. Their hushed conversation conveyed a sense of urgency regarding a series of late shipments. Sweeping through the hall with the grace of a swan, Mariela gave Mike and Skylar a warm welcome and ushered everyone to the dining room before Skylar could learn more.

Despite the sparkle of the fine bone china and the luxury of the silk napkins on the designer tablecloth, all bathed in the warm radiance of the soft light from the elaborate chandelier, the dinner felt cold and way too formal.

"When Dave said you were throwing a dinner party, I thought it would be, you know, a party," Skylar whispered to Mariela as some businesswoman outlined the city-wide benefits for investment in a memorial outside her shopping precinct. "Not some stuffy board meeting. I have my share of those in work."

"That's because Dave planned this one," Mariela said without dropping her hostess smile. "Right down to preparing the meals."

Dave outdid himself on that count. The food had an Asian fusion vibe and was some of the best Skylar had ever tasted.

"I would like to propose a toast," Dave announced as they neared the end of the meal, reaching into an ice bucket on a stand next to him and presenting the table with a bottle of champagne. "To rebuilding Los Angeles, and to all of our success and safety over the next few months!"

Not just the next few months, Skylar thought as he popped the cork and began pouring. The statement sounded short-sighted, an unusual slip for a man who was up for re-election next year.

"Are you all right, Skylar?" Mariela asked as she passed her glass on to the woman to her right. "You love the Veuve."

"Can't really drink right now," said Skylar, a smile spreading across her face as she put her hand on her belly, feeling the slight curve that would soon turn her marriage of two into a party of three. "I can eat for two, though."

Skylar expected Mariela to be overjoyed, even though it was still early in the pregnancy, but her expression barely changed. If anything, there was a hint of disgust in the way she looked down at Skylar's belly, like Mariela was expecting her to start gasping for air and collapse on the table as it burst forth from inside.

"Oh. That's great. Congratulations."

From across the table, Mike mouthed "are you okay" as, at the sound of her name, Mariela turned to someone from further down the table. Skylar nodded and waved her hand, indicating that she would explain later. Mariela's reaction stung. Brushing off a pregnancy announcement like that was uncalled for. At six and a half weeks into the pregnancy, Skylar's emotions were raging, making it difficult to know if she was overreacting.

"This is nothing compared to what the gala will be like," Mariela whispered, turning back to Skylar. "I'll need your help picking out a few things when you have time."

There was no evidence of an emotional reaction to Skylar's previous comment in her voice.

"Of course, Mar, whatever you need."

Skylar fidgeted in her seat as Mariela looked at her, no trace of joy or compassion in her eyes. It was like Skylar hadn't mentioned the pregnancy at all. She bit her lip, trying her hardest not to make a scene in front of Mariela and all her guests.

"Want to get some air?" Mariela asked.

Skylar nodded, glad of the opportunity to escape the confines of the dining room and the attention of its occupants. Feeling like all eyes were on her, she stood and followed Mariela out of the room.

-47-

LOS ANGELES COUNTY, CALIFORNIA
June 10, 2029

The sun was beginning its slow crawl beyond the horizon, turning the early June sky a soothing shade of orange as the two women stepped out onto the lit front porch. Solar-powered tea lights, placed on the planters lining the path leading around to the magnificent, three-tiered garden on the back hill, began to flicker as they fell into shade.

"So," Mariela said, looking out at the vast expanse of lawn, "how do you like what I did to the front?"

"It's lovely," Skylar replied through clenched teeth. Her anger was barely held in check and Mariela decided it was better to let the bull charge and step aside at the last minute than try to maneuver around it.

"I've been getting more hands-on with it and, if I do say so myself, my topiary skills are coming along nicely."

Mariela knew Skylar well enough that if she continued to talk about seemingly mundane things, like her decision to try a bit of gardening herself, she would eventually blow a fuse. It had started with a bonsai tree that Mariela had received for a birthday present last year. Taking care of that little tree awoke something in Mariela and she decided to start managing the garden herself. They still had a professional gardener come in once a week as Mariela's skills were still developing, and her time was too limited to manage the entire garden.

"What the hell, Mar?" Skylar interrupted as they walked to the outdoor bar and seating area to the side of the house where the true act would take place. "I just told you I'm having a baby, and you're treating it like some throwaway comment about the weather. What is your problem?"

"I'm happy for you, Skylar," Mariela replied, her smile fading. "I really am."

"Really? Because you're doing a magnificent job of convincing me otherwise."

It was tempting to reveal the whole sordid truth but Mariela did not want Skylar pitying her for the rest of her life. No, a lie that was close enough to be plausible would suffice. Sighing, Mariela put her face in her hands, taking care not to smudge her makeup needlessly, and let the darkness buried deep inside rise briefly. By the time she removed her hands and looked once more at Skylar, the tears were already welling in her eyes.

"Can I tell you something?" she asked, luring Skylar in with a wistful, melancholic tone. Skylar stepped closer and took Mariela's hands.

"Of course, Mar, always. What is it?"

"I can't have children. Dave and I found out last year. The doctor said that my eggs are defective and the chances of me having a baby are almost non-existent. We've been trying for so long, but nothing has happened."

"Mariela, I'm so sorry. I had no idea."

The sympathy in Skylar's voice was unmistakably genuine, confirming that Mariela's decision to only give a partial explanation was the right choice. Dealing with the darkness was bad enough without hearing that pitying tone every time they spoke. Mariela swallowed and pushed the darkness down, as deep as she could, fixing her mask in place once more.

"No, you wouldn't know. I'm sorry I wasn't happier for you when you told me. I really am thrilled for you."

"I know you are," said Skylar, giving her a hug. "That had to be difficult to hear, I totally understand."

One problem solved, but Mariela still had to deal with the investigation. With Skylar being pregnant, it was more crucial than ever that she not get involved in the kidnappings. If Nikola persisted in her demands for everything to be dealt with by the night of the gala then Mariela would need to work fast. Eliminating her best friend would be terrible but ultimately doable. Killing Skylar's unborn baby was a step too far for Mariela to entertain. As Skylar and Mariela walked and talked about the gala, going into far more detail than required on the lights and place settings, Mariela considered her options.

"Do you have a date for the gala yet, Mar?" Skylar asked as they linked arms and walked back to the house.

"October twelfth," Mariela replied after a brief pause. It would mean re-printing all the invites but it might just work. It would increase the amount of time Eckhart had to make sure there was no chance of Skylar getting involved and give Mariela enough time to think up an alternative plan. Yes, delaying the gala until October might just work.

-48-

LOS ANGELES COUNTY, CALIFORNIA
June 10, 2029

The dinner party was already breaking up into groups as people exchanged gossip or ideas on how they could contribute to the fundraising effort. Skylar roamed the room, eavesdropping on the various conversations, gradually becoming despondent about what she heard.

"Just think of the publicity."

"It would be a great marketing opportunity."

"If we push for those, your nephew's company could fulfill those contracts."

"It would be a considerable tax write-off."

It sickened her to hear those vultures talking about return on investment and marketing opportunities when the whole point of Dave's dinner party was to give back to a city that needed everyone to pull together. The donation Mike and Skylar were making was entirely unconditional. Listening to the conversations taking place, it sounded to Skylar like theirs was the only one.

"Have you heard some of the things people are talking about?" Skylar asked Mariela as she circled back to sit with her and Dave.

"I'm sure I can guess," Dave answered as Mariela shrugged. "ROI, marketing, publicity, promotion, perhaps even opportunities for sons and daughters to get some magazine coverage or experience for a resume."

Skylar stared at him, dumbfounded at the uncanny accuracy of his summary. He smiled, and that's when she remembered he came from that world, a shrewd businessman for over thirty years, before becoming mayor.

"Let them," Dave continued, his rosy glow indicating that the sip of Veuve Cliquot for the toast was not his first, or last, drink of the night. "If it means the city gets a few extra million in the budget, I won't begrudge them the opportunity to make a few of their own. The easiest way to get people like that to spend money is to make them think it will earn them more. What's important is that we get those donations."

"Speaking of important matters," Mariela interrupted, switching the topic of conversation. "How are things proceeding with recruitment? How soon can we expect the FBI to be back to full strength in LA? I hear Darren is crying out for some federal assistance."

Skylar took a sip of water as she searched her memory for requests from the chief.

"Not recently," Skylar replied, dragging out the words as she turned to Dave, her eyes narrowing in suspicion. If Mariela had intel on Parker's cases, it was likely Dave was her informant. His expression was one of bewilderment. "There was a missing children case he raised, but Eckhart told me that was closed. Unless you know something I don't know."

"That's the one," Mariela replied as she glanced around the room. "I'm glad to hear the chief managed to resolve the issue without burdening the FBI. You have enough on your plate as it is."

Before Skylar could press Mariela on what that comment was supposed to mean, she was confronted by the most out-of-place person at the entire party.

"OMG. I just heard the news, congratulations."

"Uh, thanks," Skylar replied, accepting, but not returning, the unsolicited hug. "And you are?"

"Daisy-Marie," the woman replied with a giggle. "You work with my husband, Frank. I am, like, so happy for you. And your husband."

Her head bobbed from side to side, scanning the room for Mike. The action caused some of her blonde curls to shake loose. Skylar had no idea if Daisy-Marie knew her husband by sight or was expecting him to be carrying a sign. Either way, she abandoned her search and focused her boundless energy on Skylar again.

"Boy or girl? Do you have a name yet? I love kids. You should call it Blake if it's a boy. That would be kinda cool, having the same first and last name. Flowers are good for a girl. My mom wanted to call me Daisy, but dad thought it sounded too much like ditzy. He wanted to name me after Elvis' daughter. So, they compromised on Daisy-Marie. It's better than Lisa-Daisy, don't ya think? That would have been tragic. But, also kinda funny. You don't meet many Lisa-Daisy's, do you? Oh, are you going to the gala? What are you wearing? I imagine you'll be showing a lot more by then. Apparently, it's going to be super glamorous. Not like this. No offense, Dave. I'm loving this. The food was excellent. I'll definitely be trying some of the tips you gave me when I'm in the kitchen tomorrow."

The pause as Daisy-Marie Eckhart took a swig of wine was the first opportunity she gave Skylar to comment on the barrage of questions and comments. Before Skylar could pick an item to address, Daisy-Marie was off again. This time, Mariela was the one facing the onslaught.

"This wine is awesome. Where did you get it? I'm more of a cider girl. Sometimes, Vodka. If I knew wine like this existed, I would have tried it sooner. There's a wine bar near us that does tasting sessions. I'll have to go and see what I like. Will you be having this wine at the gala? I'm going to make my own dress for the gala. I wanted to make wedding dresses when I was little and practiced sewing every day."

Tiring of the one-sided conversation, Dave dismissed himself and left Skylar and Mariela to listen to Daisy-Marie's outpouring. Her enthusiasm was infectious. By the time she finished talking, what seemed like a full ten minutes later, Skylar had grown to find her inoffensive and overly outgoing nature somewhat alluring. It was easy to see how Eckhart had fallen for her, despite his reserved and formal manner.

Unlike Daisy-Marie, the evening eventually wound down as people made their excuses and left. Toward the end of the exodus, Eckhart retrieved a drunk Daisy-Marie from the kitchen, and Skylar extracted her husband from a heated debate over rumors that one of the players in his fantasy football squad was going to quit next season. It was a conversation that was lost on her. Skylar's interest in sports did not extend beyond the compulsory support for local teams.

"Someone's popular," said Dave as Skylar passed through the kitchen on a final circuit of farewell hugs, her phone pinging to notify her of an influx of messages.

"It's Alex," Skylar replied, glancing at the list of notifications on her screen. "Bunch of text and picture messages."

"It's a bit late to be sending messages, isn't it?" Mariela asked, sifting through the bottles of wine on the counter to find one that was not empty. "What could he possibly be taking pictures of at this time of night? On second thoughts, pretend I didn't ask that."

"It's not late for him," Skylar replied as she opened a picture of a waterfall. "He's touring Asia, taking pictures of random scenery by the look of it."

"Good for him," said Dave as Mike made a point of examining his watch. "If he gets a chance, he should visit Okinawa. Beautiful place. I lived there for about eighteen months. Until the travel became too much.

Something you may want to consider with this job in Maryland. Especially with a little one on the way."

"It'll be a while before I have to worry about that," Skylar said as she placed a hand over Mike's watch. "This is a temporary fix until Jerry gets back. Besides, I'm still waiting on the paperwork for my position as ADIC here. You're not getting rid of me that easily."

"And neither would we want to," Mariela replied as she discovered a bottle with half a glass of wine left in it. "You make sure you find some time for your friends when you're top of the ladder. Remember, all work and no play-"

"Makes me very tired," Mike interrupted.

"Okay, point taken," said Skylar. "We'll see you two for the honors ceremony."

"If not before," Mariela called after them as Mike and Skylar made their way out of the kitchen and down the hall.

The honors ceremony was one of the few proposals that met with unanimous approval at the dinner party. Intended as a small event to honor the public servants that died defending the quarantine, it would serve as a reminder to the citizens of Los Angeles and the wider world of the sacrifices made in the name of protecting the people. After the social, political and media backlash over the national guard's heavy-handed tactics in New York, some positive coverage of the various law enforcement agencies in Los Angeles would be a big boost to Skylar's attempts to recruit new agents.

As Mike and Skylar headed to the car, away from the gossip and Daisy-Marie's distracting chatter, Skylar's thoughts drifted back to the snippets of business talk she overheard. Was there a difference between her motivation for agreeing with the honors ceremony and the profit-focused proposals of the business people around the table? At what point did siding with a proposal go from being in the interests of the public to personally motivated? Were the two mutually exclusive?

"What's wrong?" Mike asked.

Preoccupied with her moral quandary, Skylar was only half-listening to the tales he picked up at the party.

"I'm fine. Just a little disappointed with everyone tonight," Skylar said, shaking her head as she decided there was no such thing as altruism. "Nobody talked about the cause, they just focused on how it could help themselves. It was pretty pathetic, you know? When did everyone stop looking out for each other?"

-49-

NEW TERRITORIES, HONG KONG
June 11, 2029

Forcing his eyes open, Alex frantically tried piecing together the previous night's events. He remembered catching up to Julie and heading to her apartment. Details were blurry, but Alex was convinced he only had two beers before bedding down in Julie's spare room. That did not explain the hangover. Or the bindings on his wrists and ankles.

Adjusting to the glare of the industrial lighting above him, Alex was able to make out more of his surroundings. Bare stone walls on all sides allowed no natural light into the room, making the strip light above him the only source of illumination. The air on his naked body was cooler and less humid than outside but with a stuffiness that suggested he was underground. There was no sound of traffic, indicating he was far below ground or not in a populated district, and there was no echo of activity in a nearby room. The heavy-looking steel door in one corner of the room suggested industrial. A warehouse cellar.

There was no give in the bindings. Try as he might, Alex could not twist his way out of such secure knots. Alex allowed himself a moment of appreciation for the professional workmanship, despite his situation, before pulling as hard as he could on the ropes. The bedframe to which he was tied was sturdy enough to withstand Alex's best efforts. Temporarily out of ideas, Alex decided to conserve his energy until the door opened and he knew what he was dealing with.

Alex's mind drifted to Jeremy and the old man's paranoia. He could almost hear his uncle's voice tutting and telling him he was too trusting, asking what kind of boy he raised. Growing up, Jeremy pitted Alex and

Skylar against each other in his version of hide-and-seek, a variant on the traditional version that tested their ability to evade capture. As children, the game involved hiding in cupboards or behind curtains until Jeremy came and found them. As adolescents, the stakes became more severe, with television and internet privileges revoked if they were caught too quickly.

By the time Alex and Skylar were teenagers, Jeremy had enlisted their small group of friends as snitches, making it impossible to trust anyone while the game was in session. With only the hum of the electricity passing through the light to keep him company, Alex regretted not taking the game seriously and treating it as the training exercise Jeremy intended.

That was assuming this had anything to do with Julie. Maybe Alex was the victim of black-market organ harvesters. Perhaps Julie was in another cellar being sliced open, her lungs, heart and kidneys put on ice, at that exact moment. The words frying pan and fire sprung to mind as Alex considered the possibilities.

When Julie arrived, Alex was asleep. His first indication he was not alone in the room was the splash of water on his face that shocked him into wakefulness.

"What? Why?" Alex spluttered as Julie continued to pour, slowly emptying the glass over his face.

"I need you awake for this," Julie replied, grabbing Alex's face and holding his right eye open. All trace of warmth was gone from her voice, replaced by the disinterested tone of casual boredom.

Alex tried to blink as Julie shone a light in his eye, flooding his vision with white, but her grip was strong. He tried to twist away, but she placed a knee on his chest, pinning him down.

"It will be less painful if you stop resisting," she said, her voice sounding like she did not care if it hurt or not.

"Why are you doing this?" Alex demanded, continuing to struggle in vain.

Julie ignored the question, grabbing his wrist and studying her watch instead. Alex tugged at his restraints, her vice-like grip tightening in response until she released him, whatever task she was performing completed.

"I demand an answer!" Alex yelled as Julie left the room.

The reprieve was short-lived for Julie returned almost immediately, pushing a cloth-covered trolley. Having seen plenty of spy movies, Alex knew the significance of a cloth-covered tray and began tugging furiously at his restraints. Shaking the bedframe for all he was worth, Alex achieved nothing as Julie looked on with mild curiosity.

Exhausted from his efforts, Alex slumped onto the bedframe, the exposed bars pressing uncomfortably on his back, and waited for the torture to begin.

"It's no use," Alex said dejectedly as Julie pulled back the cloth to reveal an array of medical instruments. "I don't know anything."

"I'm not interested in what you know," replied Julie, taking a needle and vial from the tray. "I'm interested in what you are."

LOS ANGELES COUNTY, CALIFORNIA
June 14, 2029

Shay slid her cards to the edge of the table and lifted the corners. A two and a five. So much for diamonds being a girl's best friend.

"Fold," said Emma as she tossed her cards into the middle of the table.

"I'll raise you three buttons," said Alejandra, sitting back with a smug smile on her face.

It was the first time the three of them had spent any time together since the night at Carlos' beach house. Alejandra's training occupied most of her time while Emma was studying medicine to support their injured comrades. Although each of them had visited Carlos, individually or in pairs, they had yet to relive that night.

"Fold," said Shay, flipping her cards to reveal her lousy hand.

They were supposed to visit Carlos that night, but some last-minute emergency meant the base was on lockdown, leaving the three girls stuck playing poker for buttons. As wonderful as the promised future sounded, Shay could not help feeling that the equal distribution of wealth robbed the game of its excitement. Without stakes, poker was a boring game.

"You know, girls, you should really learn to bluff," said Alejandra, flipping her cards to reveal a two of clubs and a three of spades.

"I'm bored," said Emma, uttering the words Shay was too numb to speak. "Let's do something else."

"Like what?" Alejandra asked as she dealt another hand. "We can't go anywhere, the electricity is out, and the police are looking for us."

"The police don't even know what we look like," Emma replied snidely. "Besides, they are too busy sweeping the zombie brains off the streets."

Alejandra gave Emma a confused look as she picked up her cards. "What are you talking about?"

"Zombies," said Emma, scooping up her cards then throwing them down in frustration. "Amy said the outbreak was a bioweapon, and everyone infected turned into zombies. She said she went to visit her master, and when they went through a tunnel, there were zombies pressed up against the walls, peering in at her."

"From where? Through the concrete walls?" Alejandra asked as she threw five buttons into the center of the table.

"No. The tunnel walls were glass."

"Listen to yourself. Why would a tunnel be glass? Tunnels go underground! And you're training to be a field medic? Lord help us all."

Shay looked at her cards and folded. She was not going to win with a three and an eight.

"I'm just telling you what Amy told me."

"Play amongst yourselves," said Shay, tiring of Emma and Alejandra's back and forth. "I'm going for a pee."

"Fine," Emma said as Shay got to her feet. "But I want to play for more than buttons. Let's increase the stakes."

"Like what?" Alejandra asked as Shay walked away from the table.

The woman who entered Vasily's office just before the base went on lockdown had just left, and Shay wanted to know who she was. A stranger in the building was the closest thing to excitement in days. Alejandra was right about one thing. With the quarantine lifted, it was getting harder for the resistance to operate undetected. The influx of supplies had slowed to a steady trickle, and fewer reconnaissance patrols returned.

Wondering if they were losing the war for California, Shay climbed the staircase to the warehouse's mezzanine floor and Vasily's office.

"Hey, boss," said Shay as she knocked on the open door. "Can I speak to you?"

"Always," Vasily replied, looking up from his computer screen. "But don't call me boss. Vasily is fine. We are all equals here; we are merely burdened with different tasks."

Shay entered the room and took a seat as Vasily gestured to the wooden chair opposite his desk. One leg was slightly shorter than the others, causing Shay to wobble as she sat.

"I was curious. Who was that woman earlier? Is she one of our leaders?"

Vasily shook his head. "No, sister. That was the woman I wish to spend my life with. A wonderful woman. Intelligent, talented, and so very funny."

"That's good," said Shay, wondering if she would find somebody who spoke so highly of her.

"It is." Vasily's tone suggested otherwise, making Shay shudder. "But our political masters disagree. They do not want me to spend my life with Brianna. They want her to suffer, denied the medication she needs, and die in my arms."

"That's terrible," said Shay, trying and failing to match the contempt in Vasily's voice. "Why would they do such a thing?"

"For profit. Politicians, CEOs, activists. They all talk about making a better world while ascending on the trampled bodies of others. Brianna has terminal cancer. The CEOs won't lower the prices so we can afford the treatment. The politicians won't change the laws to make treatment affordable because they profit from the lobbyists. The activists will complain and stamp their feet but fail to elect the people that will change the laws. All they offer are empty promises. That is why we must take control of the government and force the change we want."

"But how will we do that?" asked Shay, waving her arm in the direction of the dormitories. "There must be half as many people down there as when I first arrived. Most of the recruits that go to fight don't come back. And those that do won't talk about it. Are we losing the war?"

"Ah," Vasily said as he stood and walked to the window overlooking the warehouse. "I always thought keeping you here was a bad idea. You analyze everything you see, but you don't understand what it means. I told them you needed to be taken away."

"What? No!" Shay cried, jumping up from her seat and backing up against the wall. "I won't tell anyone, I swear. Please don't send me away."

Vasily laughed and shook his head. "You mistake me. I meant you should be in our management training. You are a clever girl, but the lies they told you still cloud your judgment. Our leaders could mold you into a great leader one day. Your potential is wasted here."

Shay relaxed a little as Vasily returned to his seat and unlocked his computer. The idea of losing what she had kept her from being too enthusiastic, but the prospect of more was too tempting to ignore.

"Management? Me?" Shay asked as she sat back down, taking care with the wobbly chair.

"Why not?" Vasily replied without looking up from his screen. "You observe, you learn, and you adapt. Take that chair, for example. You nearly fell off the first time you sat on it. This time, you accounted for the shorter leg. Next time, you will be looking for the faults in the chair before you sit. You have a lot of potential, Lieutenant Bryant."

Shay stared at Vasily, unable to detect if he was mocking her. "Lieutenant?"

"It won't be easy, but I think you can handle it. What do you say? One of our senior leaders is coming to Los Angeles next week. I would like to introduce you as our latest management trainee."

"Yes," said Shay, the word bursting from her mouth before her brain had time to consider the offer. "Yes, thank you. What do I need to do?"

"For now. Nothing," Vasily replied as he turned his attention to Shay. "There are some forms I must complete to get you enrolled and assigned to a mentor. Until then, continue as you were."

Shay stood and made to go to the door. The sight of Alejandra ascending the stairs to the office made her pause. "Will I need to leave my friends?"

"Not for some time. You can continue living here until you are assigned a sector to manage if that is what you want."

Shay nodded and stepped aside for Alejandra. She wanted to hear what happened. It was hard not to snigger as her friend stood in the doorway, one hand over her bare breasts and the other over her naked crotch.

"Uh, Vasily. could I borrow some clothes, please?" Alejandra asked before turning to Shay. "Emma's a grifter. Never play cards with her again."

-51-

NEW TERRITORIES, HONG KONG
June 15, 2029

The sound of the heavy door swinging open woke Alex from his slumber. One of his wrists was free, but his other arm and both his feet were still chained to an iron ring in the wall. A rough piece of sponge served as a makeshift pillow, alleviating some of the discomfort of being on the floor, and he was granted the dignity of a dirty, cotton sheet to cover himself.

"You've got a text from your sister," said Julie as she approached Alex, phone in hand. "It says 'Nice view. And I don't mean the city,' followed by a winking emoji."

"How long has it been?" Alex asked, testing the length of his chains. There was enough slack for him to stand and move his legs, but he would not get far from the wall.

"Since when?" Julie asked, typing a response. "Since you arrived here? Or since you sent Skylar a picture of the blonde you climbed Victoria Peak with this morning?"

"Is that my phone?" Alex asked as he pulled himself upright. His legs wobbled, refusing to support his weight.

"You're malnourished," said Julie, sliding Alex's phone into the breast pocket of her flannel shirt. "The injections I've been giving you only go so far. I'll get you some rice, but first, you need to provide another blood sample."

"What? No. Not until you tell me what's going on."

"It will be less painful if you cooperate," said Julie as she removed a pair of latex gloves from the back pocket of her jeans and pulled them on. "Less chance of the needle snapping off in your arm."

Alex paused, lying on his side as his head swam. Julie came to him before. She took blood and hair samples and cheek swabs using the equipment on the tray in the corner. It lent credence to his organ harvesting theory that Julie wanted to check he was healthy. As she knelt beside him and grabbed his arm, he pushed feebly against her.

"Like I said, you're malnourished."

Alex watched, powerless to resist as the needle pierced his flesh. The vial was slow to fill, his body too enfeebled to pump the blood.

"One more," Julie said once the vial was full. "Let's try the other arm. See if I can get better penetration."

Alex snickered despite himself. In better circumstances, it was an opportunity too good to pass up. He barely felt the scratch of the needle as Julie found a vein in his other arm. The blood flowed more freely, filling the vial in half the time.

"That's more like it," Julie said as she pulled the needle out of Alex's arm. "I'll go get you some food. You'll need it."

As she left, Alex heard his phone ping. His sister had to see through Julie's subterfuge. But what then? She could trace his phone, but Hong Kong was outside her jurisdiction. Dave Michaelis still had connections in Asia. Skylar could go to him and get him to stir up the press. Local police would not want the media frenzy caused by the kidnap of a high-profile FBI agent's brother.

Julie knew his passcode. A thumbprint and facial scan were easy enough to fake when he was unconscious, but his passcode could only come from a deep personal knowledge of Alex. If she could circumvent his phone's security, Julie must know him well enough to be able to masquerade as him in a string of text messages. Provided Skylar didn't try to call him, an unlikely scenario given the time difference, Julie could keep up the pretense for months.

Alex pulled feebly at the chain. It was better than being strapped to the bed, but it did not help his situation. In his weakened state, having one hand free made little difference. Even if he escaped his chains, he had no idea where he was. For all he knew, he might not even be in Hong Kong. It was impossible to tell how long he was unconscious. In his windowless cell, Alex could not even tell the time of day. He guessed that was part of the design. Julie's comment about the messages to his sister might be part of a ruse to trick him into thinking more than a single day had passed.

There was still hope. There was always hope. When the drugs Julie slipped him wore off, his strength would return. The chain looked strong, but every chain has a weak link.

"Here, eat this," Julie said as she returned to the room with a bowl of rice and a glass of what Alex assumed was milk.

Alex shook his head as Julie placed the bowl on the floor next to him. There was nothing with which to eat the rice. Did she expect him to bury his face in the bowl like a dog?

"I'll be back in ten hours," said Julie as she covered the tray of medical instruments and began wheeling it out of the room. "Don't go anywhere."

VENTURA COUNTY, CALIFORNIA
June 16, 2029

The tune in Skylar's head was beginning to frustrate her. All morning, the same thirty seconds played on repeat as she organized her garage, all the while trying to work out which song it was. Which band would be a start. Humming the tune, Skylar flipped the lid off an old storage box and peered inside.

"Junk," she muttered, lifting out a handful of power leads from mobile phones and laptop computers long since recycled.

Hurling the leads into a large container for recyclable waste, Skylar reached inside the box and lifted out a small notebook. Mistaking it for an old diary, Skylar opened the notebook to discover it was filled with poor quality sketches. There was a time when Skylar wanted to be an artist and got Jeremy to buy her an easel and canvases for Christmas. The first painting went on the bonfire the following November. The second one was probably somewhere in the attic of Jeremy's estate in Wales, half-finished and gathering dust. Apart from a handful of pencil-drawn landscapes that were half decent, flicking through the sketches reminded Skylar that art was not her strong suit. She hesitated a moment, debating whether to tear out the few good pages, then tossed the notebook into the recycling, pages flapping wildly as it spun through the air.

"What are you doing?" Mike asked as he strolled into the garage.

"Clearing out the garage, Mike," replied Skylar, flicking through the DVDs at the bottom of the box.

"Okay. Why are you doing?"

"Clearing some space," said Skylar, giving him a peck on the cheek as he peered into the storage box. "I can't see us having the summer house ready this year so I'll store my gym equipment in here, for now."

"Is that your way of telling me you want the spare bedroom decorated?"

"Since you brought it up," said Skylar, putting the DVDs back in the box until she was certain there was no DVD player to go with them. "I was thinking more of getting those summer house plans finalized."

"I thought they were finalized. Is this going out?"

Skylar turned to see what he was poring over. "That's for donation. Stuff in the box is for the church. Stuff on the trailer is going to Mariela's for the auction. Her cousin is coming by later to collect it."

"Bit early, isn't it?" Mike asked as he wandered over to the trailer.

"Maybe, but I need to get rid," Skylar replied as she slid the storage box onto a set of shelves against the back wall. "Mariela's got the space."

Donations to the auction were not expected, but Skylar saw it as a great opportunity to offload some unwanted items passed down through the family, from one generation to the next. Mostly, the items Skylar picked out were old artworks and ornaments that probably appealed to somebody a hundred years ago but held no interest for her.

"Ew, that's one ugly dude," Mike said as he lifted the sheet covering the last portrait loaded onto the trailer.

"Yeah, some Carpathian tyrant or something. Lived to be a hundred and five, apparently. Great-uncle Ivan left it to me."

Skylar was glad to be rid of the portrait, along with the two expensive, but dull, landscape artworks that took up space in the garage. The way its eyes followed you around the room was deeply unsettling.

"What about this?" Mike asked as he tapped an old trunk with his foot. "Must be worth a bit?"

"Not mine," replied Skylar, putting the lid back on a box of Halloween decorations and walking over to the trunk. "I thought it was yours, Mike. You know, from that time when you bought a boat and went sailing for adventure on the big blue sea."

Mike shook his head and grabbed Skylar's rear. "Not my sort of booty."

"Don't I know it," she replied as she turned her body to his, pressing against his muscular frame. "But it will have to wait. I want to get this done so you can bring the training gear down while I'm in Virginia."

"Not Maryland?" Mike asked as he rattled the lock on the trunk.

"Nope. CIA wants to talk about interagency cooperation. Can't be done over the phone. I told you about this on Wednesday."

"Probably," said Mike, lifting the trunk and placing it against the back wall. "You're back and forth the east coast so much lately, I struggle to keep track."

"Twelve weeks, then Jerry's back, and I can focus on settling into my new office."

Skylar stepped back and examined the space she had cleared. If they bunched the bikes up a bit closer to each other, her training gear should fit. It would be tight, but it was not like she would be using anything much more than a yoga mat for the next few months.

"Are they any closer to swearing you in?" Mike asked as he picked up a broom and began sweeping.

"Not really. Too much focus on the outbreak," Skylar replied, her eyes drawn back to the trunk. "What do you suppose is in there?"

Mike stopped sweeping and followed Skylar's gaze to the trunk. "Dunno. Knowing Jeremy, some saucy, French lithographs. For historical preservation."

"Hmm. Remind me to ask him when I get back. For now, having a shower is more important."

"Need me to join you? Scrub your back? Rub your-"

"I'll manage, Michael," said Skylar, turning and flashing him a grin. "I may need some help in the bedroom in, say, twenty minutes?"

-53-

NEW TERRITORIES, HONG KONG
June 17, 2029

Alex woke to the smell of mashed potatoes and gravy. The smell made his shriveled stomach clench at his nose's betrayal. With no other means of exerting his free will, Alex refused to eat every meal Julie brought him, living off the daily glass of milk she provided. It was a simple tactic and the only show of defiance available to him.

"Morning, soldier," said Julie, waving a bowl of food under his nose. "Are you going to eat today?"

Alex tried to turn away from her, only to discover his wrists and ankles were once more bound to the bed frame. Delirious from hunger, Alex said nothing. At least he was propped up on some pillows this time.

"Suit yourself," said Julie, grabbing him by the jaw and forcing his mouth open.

Too weak to resist, Alex's attempts to break free of her iron grip were predictably doomed. His body tried to heave as Julie forced a tube down his throat, the sensation triggering every gag reflex he had, but there was no stopping her from bypassing his mouth. Resigned to his fate, Alex ceased struggling as Julie poured the liquefied potatoes directly into his stomach.

"Bring it up, and I'll pipe your next meal into your system," Julie said as she slowly removed the tube. "Refuse to eat, and I'll pipe your next meal into your system. Nod if you understand."

Alex mustered the energy for a solitary nod. The experience was enough to encourage him to eat whatever she put in front of him in the future.

"For what it's worth," Julie continued as she tightened a strap around Alex's arm, "Your commitment is impressive. I was tempted to let you carry on. Call it morbid curiosity, but I wanted to see how long until you snapped. When I've finished with you, maybe I'll let you starve yourself to death, just to see how much longer you would have lasted."

Unused to food, Alex's stomach rebelled at the presence of the meal, despite it being blended to the consistency of melted ice cream. As his body convulsed, Julie's hand clamped itself over his mouth.

"Swallow it," she ordered as his body forced the mashed potatoes to reverse their course.

It took several attempts for Alex to push the food back down to his stomach, each attempt less painful than the last. While he attempted to keep his meal down, Julie worked one-handed to hook him up to an IV.

"This should help you find your strength again," she said as she pressed the needle into his arm. "A simple Myer's cocktail to boost your system. Eight days without food takes its toll on the body."

"Why?" Alex asked when Julie removed her hand from his mouth, his voice barely a whisper.

"I told you, I'm interested in what you are," Julie replied as she loosened the strap around his arm and pulled a chair alongside the bed.

"And what is that?" Alex managed to say.

Holding his head up was too much work. Instead, Alex looked down the length of his nose as Julie sat down and put her feet up on the edge of the bed.

"Tell me, Alexander, when you see the suffering that takes place on this earth, do you ever wonder why God lets it happen?"

Alex closed his eyes. Julie had him tied to a bed in a cellar, and she wanted to talk about suffering? When he opened his eyes, Julie was still sat there, watching him.

"I waited patiently for the Lord," Julie began, reciting from memory, "and he inclined unto me, and heard my cry. He brought me up also out of a horrible pit, out of the miry clay, and set my feet upon a rock, and established my goings."

Alex stopped listening. If Julie thought quoting psalms was going to convince him she was chosen by God she was sorely mistaken. Whatever reason she had for chaining him in a basement, it was not divine. Alex would be the first to admit he was no saint, but nothing he did in his life warranted such barbaric treatment.

"If you're trying to teach me a lesson, it's not going to work," Alex whispered when Julie finished. "I can't learn from my mistakes when I don't know what I did to you."

"You didn't do anything to me," Julie said as she inspected the IV.

"If I didn't do anything, just let me go," Alex pleaded, not that he felt he could make it off the bed if she unchained him. "I won't say anything, or tell anyone what you've done."

"I can't do that," Julie replied, sitting back in her seat. "Not until I know if you can help me."

"Help you with what?"

"Finding answers."

"Answers to what?" Alex asked, lifting his head slightly.

"Life and death," Julie replied, closing her eyes. "I don't expect you to understand. I expect you to comply. It would be much easier on you if you did."

Alex did not doubt that for a second. Still, complying with Julie's demands felt like signing his own death warrant. Resistance may not be an option in his current condition, but he was not about to build his own gallows.

Alex turned his face away from Julie and closed his eyes to hide the tears beginning to form. He was still alive. That meant he still had options. There was no time for tears; he needed to figure out which option would secure his freedom.

-54-

VENTURA COUNTY, CALIFORNIA
June 22, 2029

The chair squeaked. Somebody was definitely in her office.

Skylar was already alert and in defense mode, having spotted the light in her office from further down the corridor. She knew for certain she had turned it off when she left. Whoever was in there was making no effort to be discrete. Reaching for her sidearm, Skylar ran through a mental checklist of who was on site. Drawing on a fellow agent was not a polite way to start the day.

Agent Omundson was in his office. Skylar passed Huffman and Armstrong on their way out to the yard as she arrived. Agent Stuart had yet to arrive, and she had heard Sheppard on the phone as she came down the corridor. If it was Agent Maxwell, Skylar would know from her incessant whistling. It would not be Agent Pellegrino either since he was running a training session with Agents Boecher-McCormick and Lehne, which just left Miner.

No, Agent Miner was in reception with Diana. Skylar had overheard her on her way in, talking about a coffee mug that had gone missing. It seemed trivial to Skylar, the break room had plenty of spare mugs, but she was not a coffee fiend like Meg Miner.

Skylar slid her gun from its holster and stepped closer to the door, convinced it was not one of her agents inside her office. Weapon at the ready, her back pressed against the wall next to the door, Skylar yanked the handle down and threw it open.

"Easy tiger, wouldn't want any accidents now," said the hulking figure sat at her desk as Skylar moved to check the room.

"What on earth are you doing here?" she asked, lowering her gun.

Kellan Forbes, gun for hire, was leaning back in her chair, grinning like he was expecting her to come in all guns blazing. His strawberry-blonde hair was matted and frizzed from the wind, giving him an appearance that matched his roguish charm. That charm was the only thing keeping him from getting a sound beating right then. Few people could break into Skylar's office and not feel the full extent of her wrath.

"I let myself in. Good thing you're not on high alert here," Kellan said as he picked up a mug of what Skylar assumed was coffee.

Holstering her gun, Skylar shut the door and dropped into the second chair, a guest in her own office. She let it slide, watching as he took a gulp of his coffee, exaggerated slowness in every step of the process.

"Courtesy of Agent Aycox," he said, answering her unasked question and nodding toward the ceramic lip. "Had to modify it, if you get my drift."

The meaning was not lost on Skylar. Kellan was the stereotypical Scotsman, forty percent alcohol by volume, and it was not a great leap to assume he had strengthened his coffee.

"It's not Aycox anymore, Kel. She got married back in February, goes by the name Miner now."

"Aye, I remember her dating some daft bugger from Massachusetts. Shame. Talented lass, that one. I could do with more like her working for me. Even if her coffee lacks any kick."

"Yeah, she's got spirit," said Skylar, forcing a grunt from Kellan at her pun. "You gonna tell me why your happy ass is in my chair then?"

"I heard you were having some trouble with some missing kiddies so I paid a visit to a friend of yours, to see what the fuss was about."

Skylar stared at him, incredulous, as he pulled open a pack that he had kept out of sight and hauled out a stack of papers at least twice the size of the case file provided by the LAPD.

"This needs to be one doozy of an explanation, boyo," Skylar said as Kellan slid the papers over to her.

"Chief Parker wasn't exaggerating how many missing children there were. He was downplaying it. Big time. Whole families of siblings are missing, their friends, everyone. The number is into the tens of thousands, and it's not just California."

"How do you mean?" Skylar asked, reaching over to open the mini-fridge next to her desk.

The fridge was a new addition, something to make the office seem less glum. Skylar pulled out two water bottles and tossed one to Kellan. He caught it, glanced at the label then set it down an arm's length away like it was some sort of poison.

"That's what I need to talk to you about," he replied, leaning forward and putting his elbows on his knees. "Something doesn't add up about the chief's reports. This file is only for California. I have contacts that are seeing similar patterns of disappearances in New York, Washington, Nebraska, and Wisconsin. Possibly others. This is an outbreak of its own."

"I was only informed of disappearances in LA. How did you even find out about this, let alone find time to do your own investigation?"

In all the years Skylar had known Kellan, she never suspected he would fly five and a half thousand miles and investigate a case she so casually dismissed. That was one of the perks of running mercenary contracts, the ability to pick and choose which assignments you handled. Still, Kellan did pick some strange cases for pro bono study.

"Wait. Did you swipe these from the chief's office, Kel?"

His mischievous grin told her everything she needed to know. It was easy to imagine Kellan performing some sort of sleight of hand, swapping out one file for another, as he pretended to assist in the chief's investigation. Kellan and Skylar became friends at university in England, when she tried out for the archery team, and he was forever working on these little practical jokes. It all seemed innocuous at the time. If it wasn't for his tendency toward selfishness, he would have made an excellent intelligence operative.

"There was a chair in his office with the reports sitting on it. Parker threw a jacket over the seat to hide them."

"Wait, what?"

"Just what I said. When I arrived at his office, the folder was there on a chair, plain as day. As soon as he spotted it was on display, he covered it up with his jacket. He tried to make it look all casual like he was simply throwing his jacket on the side and it just happened to cover the file, but I think it was intentional."

"That doesn't make any sense. Granted, I've only met the chief a handful of times over the years, and only once was it more than a nod as we passed each other, but he always struck me as being an honest, by-the-book kinda guy. Why would he be trying to hide this?"

"That's not what I meant. I don't think he was intentionally hiding the file; I think he was intentionally drawing my attention to it. What's the easiest way to make somebody want something?"

"Tell them they can't have it," Skylar said, nodding to show she understood. "But why?"

"Take a look."

Skylar opened the folder and began looking through the files. Emma Brayford, Michael Oliva, Natalie Martinez. The list went on. There was no obvious pattern to the kidnappings, the victims ranging across the entire spectrum of race, gender and social status. This collection, however, was far more detailed than the one officially submitted to the FBI.

"I know what you're thinking," Kellan said after she had studied the first few files. "The only common factor is that they're all eighteen or under. It's not obvious from that file alone, but the Chief's notes have these all marked as open cases yet official records have almost all of these children reported as casualties of the outbreak."

"That's possible," Skylar began, but Kellan indicated he had not finished.

"I made some inquiries. For some of these, there aren't any bodies to go with those medical files. The handful I did manage to trace don't match the descriptions here."

Skylar drew a deep breath. Did the chief suspect the official story? Perhaps she was too quick to dismiss him when he came to her for help.

No, Skylar thought. *This wasn't on me. None of this was in the file I was sent. There was no way I could have known.*

Skylar told Kellan as much.

"Skylar, some of these reports go back to the day you were notified. Did you ask for these files?"

"I was in the middle of coordinating the outbreak response. I told the chief to handle it himself."

"Well, there you go," Kellan said, settling back and taking another big swig of coffee. "This is how he handled it."

That made sense. If Kellan used her name to get the chief to provide access to the investigation, it followed that he would make a play to get the files under her nose again. It worked, but all this cloak and dagger behavior was frustrating. Why couldn't he just come to her with this in the first place?

"Okay, let's back this up a minute," Skylar said as Kellan drained his coffee mug. "We've got missing kids, reports that indicate they are dead, and a big, stinking question mark over the truth. Who signed off on the official records?"

"It varies, but two names frequently cropped up on the ones I looked at. Doctor B. Hung and Doctor D. Robe."

Skylar's incredulous stare was met with a mischievous grin. Just as everything was beginning to sound like some grand conspiracy, those two names made the whole thing sound farcical. No, worse than farcical, they sounded like the names of a pair of sex therapists in a low-budget porno.

"Or something like that," Kellan added. "I couldn't find any actual doctors going by the names on the reports. The point is, the precinct is officially closing those cases down."

As Kellan reached into his pack for another massive pile of papers, Skylar scrolled through her phone directory.

"Wagner," she said when her line connected to the Los Angeles office. "Is Bunton in the office with you? Good. Hand him your outbreak cases and head up to the Ventura office. I've got something I want you to cast your eyes over without entering it onto the system."

Kellan nodded in agreement as he pushed the second file across the desk. "These are for the other states. You won't find them in the system. Trust me. I am nothing if not efficient."

"You're a pain in the ass. This is one headache I really could have done without. I can't even begin to imagine how I'm going to fit this into my workload."

"No," Kellan said before she could ask for further assistance. His tone softened when he realized how drained Skylar was. "I got you those files as a favor. I can't be running around doing FBI work. You could always call her. I know you still have her number. And don't act like you don't know who I mean."

Skylar knew exactly who he meant. In the same way that he knew why it was not an option. Reika Pfeiffer was poison. Skylar wanted nothing to do with that woman after what she did to Alex. True, Reika's card was in her wallet, but that was to remind her she was never that desperate.

"I'll find a way," Skylar said, refusing to acknowledge his suggestion. "I always do."

"Don't be so stubborn. Call her."

Skylar shook her head. "She's out of our lives. I'm not giving her an inch. I dread to think what false hopes she could fill Alex's head with if I let her."

Kellan rose and stepped around the desk to hug Skylar. "Your choice. Just remember, you're not supposed to be scrubbing the carpets when you own the hotel. That's what subordinates are for."

Skylar reflected on the wisdom of his words as she wrapped her arms around him and squeezed, his cologne filling her nostrils.

"I'll see what ideas Wagner has," Skylar said as he released her from his iron embrace. "You're sticking around for a while?"

"Yeah, I'll be back in the area before you're done here. In that massive house of yours, I'm assuming there's a spare room available for me to crash in?"

"I'm sure we can find a patch of floor. You'll need to plant a tree to make up for all this paper though."

Skylar thumped the nearest stack to prove her point.

"Yeah, yeah. I know how fond you are of hard copy. I'll swing by before end of play."

Kellan grabbed his pack, much lighter now than it must have been when he arrived, then ducked out through the door. Shaking her head, Skylar looked down at the first report in the stack.

Emma Brayford. Fourteen. Never returned home from a slumber party. The names of five other girls were scribbled in the margin. Skylar was sure she would find reports on all of them if she searched the stack.

In that moment, Skylar hated herself for not having a handle on this. For dismissing the chief so easily. For being so curt with the deputy chief. She had allowed herself to be railroaded into cracking this outbreak case. Kellan was right. She was micro-managing, burying herself in the details of one case instead of delegating. That wasn't director level behavior. How many other things had she missed as a result?

-55-

LOS ANGELES COUNTY, CALIFORNIA
June 29, 2029

Vasily walked the length of the shipping containers, searching for the one that was not listed on his paperwork. The industrial internet of things ensured everything was recorded and traceable, and the Port of Los Angeles had one of the most sophisticated shipping systems on the planet. All incoming cargo, the intended recipients, and delivery schedules were churned through the port's massive digital infrastructure and converted into automated unloading, storage and distribution schedules overseen by just a small team of operators.

The automated system had taken years to develop and provided massive improvements to efficiency but so much data proved problematic for Vasily. It was not that he needed to understand it, the computers took care of all that, but detailed shipping manifests were a staunch enemy of smugglers. Making containers disappear was not easy.

As Vasily side-stepped a reach stacker barreling down the road between the containers, he contemplated how fortunate he was that it was not easy to make containers disappear. If it was then he would be facing stiffer competition.

Vasily had built a sizeable shipping company from the small logistics business his father had created, a greater achievement than any of his family for the last hundred years. All their achievements were built on family money, they weren't built from blood and sweat out of the backroom of a dry cleaner's. Getting cast out of the Malinovskyi dynasty may have forced Vasily's father to work hard just to get enough food for the following day, but he was all the stronger for it, and Vasily followed in his father's footsteps.

As it stood, almost nothing came through the port without Vasily's knowledge and no contraband left the port without him taking his cut. Vasily's influence and control meant he could easily live off the profits of other people's work, but that was not Vasily's style. The legitimate business operations more than provided for Vasily and his employees, leaving the criminal world's charitable donations free to advance Mariela's utopian dream.

"This one," Vasily said, stopping at a container that stood alone at the end of a row stacked three containers high. "We need this one empty and off-site before the morning."

The two thugs following him grunted, one of them going to fetch the truck they used for clearing items not in the system while the other cut the chain securing the doors of the container. He looked at Vasily expectantly, unsure what to do next as the sweat ran down his face, despite the cool breeze sweeping in from the ocean that night.

"Well, open it."

The thug nodded and grabbed the container door's handle. Vasily took a step back and watched the door creak open. From the darkness of the container, a hand reached out and drew the thug inside. The incident happened so quickly there was no time to scream.

"Welcome to Los Angeles. When you're done with that traitor, I have a fresher selection for you to try," Vasily called into the darkness of the container.

"Why should I wait?" came the reply from the darkness, a disembodied voice that dripped with malice. "I should tear out your throat for making me wait so long."

"It's been forty minutes. In a port this size that's nothing to track down an unregistered container. You're lucky I'm good at my job or you could have been here all night, wondering how you would manage when daybreak arrived."

The doors to the container swung open, revealing a lavishly furnished interior complete with television, games console, lounge chair and bed. It was instantly clear to Vasily that Lukai had spent the entire trip living up to the teenage stereotype of sleeping, gaming and precious little else. Just like a teenager he had also dumped the packaging his food came in on the floor, a small spatter of blood staining the plush, cream carpet that covered the container floor. The man would not be missed, a victim of his stupidity for thinking the cartel wouldn't spot their cocaine was short a few kilos.

"Had that happened, I would have made sure I survived long enough to tear out your heart, even if all the flesh was scorched from my bones and all that remained to do it was my sun-bleached skeleton."

Vasily laughed, a deep throaty laugh like granite slabs falling down a well, as Lukai adjusted his tie before collecting his suit jacket from a hook on the wall. It was hard to think that this sixteen-year-old child, play-acting as a high-flying executive in his tailored suit, was hundreds of years old and the most prominent player in a powerful undead oligarchy.

"I consider it fortunate that it didn't happen then," Vasily answered. "On a more positive note, shipments are back on schedule now that the quarantine has been lifted. We still have some of the cargo in storage but that will be cleared within a couple of weeks."

"Why so long?" Lukai queried as Vasily led the way to the car that was waiting to take him to the warehouse. "Does Mariela not control the authorities? Surely you can just move the product and have her fix the inspection reports later."

"Yes, but rushing everything would not impact on the overall timescales and would require interference that could be avoided. Much safer to do it over a couple of weeks and not risk undue scrutiny. We will still be in position in time to begin phase two. Mariela has diverted the children who do not freely give themselves to the cause to the mine works in Death Valley so we can cover more ground and hopefully reduce the delays there."

"Unacceptable," Lukai said as they turned a corner. "I want the timeline moved up. The sooner we are ready, the sooner I can go to the council and force their hand."

"I will make preparations," Vasily replied as he took out his phone and sent Mariela the message they both knew was coming. The reports Mariela provided took Lukai's impatience into consideration. None of their activities would change.

"What of the bloodlines?" Lukai asked as they reached the car.

"Dealt with," said Vasily, hoping his half-truth would not betray him.

VENTURA COUNTY, CALIFORNIA
June 29, 2029

"How are things with the baby?" Mariela asked as she settled onto a stool in Skylar's kitchen.

Everything was falling into place for Mariela. Dave's re-election bid was off to a promising start following a party endorsement, the agenda for the Los Angeles honors ceremony in memory of the outbreak victims was almost complete, and her plans to transform California into a haven for all decent, law-abiding citizens was closer than ever to becoming reality.

"Besides making me sober?" Skylar asked as she poured herself a glass of water.

Mariela chuckled gently. "I saw the scan on Mike's social media posts. Surprised you didn't post anything."

"Mike has enough accounts for the both of us," Skylar replied, sitting down and taking a grape from the bowl in the center of her kitchen island counter. "Besides, I'm trying not to think about it too much at this stage. Still too much work to do, Mar."

"You have three men living in this house, Sky. Get one of them to decorate the nursery."

Skylar chuckled as she took another grape. "Nursery is almost empty, and Mike's already agonizing over color choices. He'll need until at least Christmas to settle on a color. Good job the little one isn't due until January."

"Hopefully you won't end up sharing a birthday," said Mariela as she swirled her wine. "I guess you'll be off work by then."

"I'm thinking of finishing up for Christmas and returning around Easter."

Mariela studied Skylar's tired but determined expression with mild curiosity. Betting on Skylar handing over the keys to the office before the gala would have been the height of folly, but hearing she planned to return so soon was an interesting twist.

"Somebody has to keep our streets safe, I suppose," said Mariela, tiptoeing around the subject she most wanted to address, "but surely this recruitment drive you're on will allow you a little more time off than that."

"Oh, yeah," Skylar replied before taking a sip of her water. "It's not a staffing issue. We always planned for me to go back and for Mike to do the bulk of the childcare."

"That makes sense," Mariela agreed, gauging how best to nudge the conversation in the right direction without raising Skylar's suspicions. "You are the higher earner. Not that you need the money."

"It's not about the money, Mar. You know that. I want to do good in this world. I may not be able to bring about world peace, but I can make our cities safer. Starting with a review of how our law enforcement agencies can better cooperate. Too many of the structures and processes we have in place collapsed in the wake of the outbreak. We need to be better at responding to threats while maintaining order."

Mariela smiled to hide the disappointment in her heart. Skylar's words fell short of an outright admission that she was going to start digging into cases that needed to stay closed, but Mariela knew her well enough to read between the lines and safely assume the worst.

"There are many ways to make California a better, safer place," Mariela said before emptying her glass and pouring another.

"Oh, I didn't mean it like that, Mar. I've seen the work your charity does to get our youth involved in the community and steer them away from drugs and gangs. If anything, we need more projects like yours to do the things the state can't."

Mariela gave Skylar a wide smile. "I'm glad my work is appreciated, but I wasn't suggesting you thought otherwise. I meant there are things you could do besides working for the FBI."

"Like what?" Skylar asked as she stood and went to the fridge.

"You're wealthy," Mariela said as Skylar closed the fridge and went to the cupboard. "You could afford to strike out on your own. I don't know how you tolerate the bureaucracy that working for such a massive organization brings."

"Says the woman married to a politician," Skylar replied with a laugh. "It doesn't get more bureaucratic than that. I get your point though. Not sure how I could be more effective without the resources of the bureau at my disposal."

"Well, there is that," Mariela conceded as Skylar took a loaf of bread and hacked off a thick slice. "I couldn't go back to working for a big company again."

"Pros and cons," Skylar replied as she went to the freezer and returned with a pint of strawberry ice cream.

Mariela watched with undisguised curiosity as Skylar scooped several spoonfuls of ice cream onto her bread, followed by a handful of crushed walnuts, and topped the whole thing off with slices of cucumber and a dollop of mayonnaise.

"What?" Skylar asked through a mouthful of food as Mariela stared wide-eyed at her.

"Nothing," said Mariela, turning her attention to Cali as she padded into the kitchen.

Mariela learned long ago that to pet Skylar's dog was to spend weeks picking white hairs out of her clothes. As gorgeous as Skylar's husky was, Mariela begrudged the clean-up work after giving it any attention.

"I'm surprised you haven't moved to the city," said Mariela, turning her attention back to Skylar. "Traveling back and forth can't be easy."

Skylar shrugged as she took another bite of the monstrosity in her hand. If Skylar saw her position in the FBI as a balance of pros and cons, Mariela would ensure Skylar saw as many cons to a path that put them on a collision course as possible.

"It is what it is," Skylar replied as she reached for a glass of water.

"Well, I for one am glad we have such a dedicated, hard-working role model for our cities. You're a better woman than me, Skylar. I couldn't put myself through your paces when I could put my skills to use in my local community instead. Being so distant from my charity work would make me wonder if I was really achieving anything. I can see why Mike prefers being in the thick of the action. Don't you miss it when you're knee-deep in reports?"

"I do," said Skylar, licking ice cream trails from her fingers as she sat back at the counter. "But I know I'm making a difference to so many lives."

Mariela nodded in understanding. Better to drop a few seeds and let them germinate naturally than force the harvest. As long as Nikola kept her nose out, there was plenty of time to bring Skylar to the realization that her attention needed to be directed elsewhere.

"And long may that be the case," said Mariela, raising her glass. "To a better, safer vision for the future."

"To the future," Skylar replied, clinking her glass of water to

Mariela's wine glass.

-57-

LOS ANGELES COUNTY, CALIFORNIA
June 29, 2029

The drive to the warehouse was as mundane as could be, the ever-changing scenery outside the window offering Lukai no relief from the boredom. So much time spent traveling on business had dulled Lukai's interest and sense of wonder at the sights of foreign lands, not that he had held a great appreciation for sight-seeing when he was alive. The sight of the warehouse, however, aroused his curiosity.

"What is the meaning of this, Vasily?" He demanded upon entering the facility.

The warehouse looked more like an army barracks or austere orphanage, devoid of many of the comforts of civilian life with bunks filling as much of the space as was physically possible. Lukai estimated there must be close to a thousand bunks in total for a warehouse this size. It was a tremendous waste of space. Vasily could easily have crammed the same number of children into a much smaller facility had he used cages.

"Mariela's orders, none of the children are to suffer needlessly. I must admit I was skeptical at first but it has proven rather effective. Nearly half of the children have joined us willingly, and we have them on a cycle for blood donations that ensures they remain healthy enough to be farmed indefinitely. The rest are in the mines. Mariela was very impressive, the way she convinced so many to freely submit to what must have seemed like a truly terrifying prospect.

"Many of their families were killed in the outbreak and Mariela soon had the children convinced that the safety of the warehouse was their

221

best hope for survival. By the time the outbreak had died out and the CDC lifted the quarantine, the children were so indoctrinated that they continued to play their part."

Lukai was incredulous. "But all this blood is just sitting here!"

"Here and in twelve other warehouses around the city. Nearly fifty-six thousand children in total, providing us with more than enough blood for phase two. Had we gutted and drained the children we would need fresh supplies by the end of the year, but this system means we no longer need to take people from the streets. Our risk of exposure is the lowest it could possibly be."

Lukai suspended his disbelief at Mariela's methods in the face of her achievements. It was not how he would have dealt with the situation, but he had to admit there was a certain grace and style to her approach. Operating in the shadows was unimportant to Lukai, he was fully prepared to wage war against the humans should the truth be revealed, but not inciting war prematurely did have some advantages. There was one thing that Lukai did not understand though.

"Why are there so many empty beds?" He asked as the pair exited the dormitory space and entered the office space on the mezzanine floor.

As they sat, Vasily explained that some among the children freely offered themselves directly to the vampires in Los Angeles and the surrounding counties. Each child's openness to various activities was matched to the specific desires and fetishes of the vampires on the condition that no child would be forced to do anything against their will. It made Vasily feel something like a cross between a pimp and a matchmaker but it enabled the vampires to indulge many of their cravings and, once word got around of how erotic the act of being fed on was, there were plenty of volunteers signing up to some particularly sordid acts.

"Really?" Lukai asked when Vasily was done with his explanation. "So…?"

"Already on it," Vasily replied to the unasked question. "A selection of girls is being brought to you shortly."

-58-

LOS ANGELES COUNTY, CALIFORNIA
June 29, 2029

Shay checked her reflection in the mirror as she adjusted her tie. As much as she wanted to make a good first impression, wearing a tie felt unnatural.

"Here, you've got it wrong," Alejandra said as she stepped up to Shay and peered over her shoulder at her reflection. "Let me show you."

Shay pulled the material through the knot and yanked it from under her collar. When Shay agreed to enroll in the resistance's management training, Vasily sent her a set of clothes to match her new role. The baby-blue shirt and navy-blue jacket would not have been Shay's first choice, but they did give her that professional look that her uncle always had. As she fed the belt through the loops on her pants, Shay reflected on how much like her uncle she felt. After his second assault conviction, Shay realized that no amount of fancy clothing could turn a loser into a winner.

"Here," Alejandra said as she slipped the knotted tie over Shay's head and pulled it tight against her throat.

"Uncool," Shay snapped as she grabbed the tie and yanked the knot apart.

"Woah, sorry." Alejandra threw her hands up and took a step back. "It was just a joke about the stuffiness of corporate culture. You know? How the office life is so stifling it makes people feel choked by their suits."

The knot undone, Shay hurled the tie onto her bed and swept her hands in front of her, from her head to her feet, as if that was all the answer Alejandra needed.

"Uh, duh," Shay said when Alejandra's bewildered expression remained riveted to her face. "The triple K? Lynching? Hundreds of years of black oppression?"

Alejandra's expression shifted to shock as Shay placed her hands on her hips. "Wait. You think I pulled your tie too tight because I'm a secret white supremacist? Me? A Latina?"

Alejandra made a good point. When viewed in context, the idea that she meant it as a racial slur seemed outlandish. Even so, Shay was too upset to back down so easily. "Well, you need to be more careful about how your actions can be taken."

Turning away from Alejandra while she collected herself, Shay undid her top button and straightened her collar before sliding her feet into the formal shoes Vasily provided. He had offered her the option of high heels, but Shay felt that was going too far. High heels would have made her feel even more of a fraud, like a cheap hooker roleplaying as a corporate executive.

"Is that what you're wearing?" Shay asked when the silence between them became unbearable.

Alejandra looked up from polishing her boots. "Yeah, why?"

"We're meeting one of our leaders, not going on maneuvers."

Alejandra looked down at her khaki cargo pants and white vest top. "I was going to wear my flak jacket."

"That just makes it worse," Shay said as Alejandra finished buffing her boots and tucked the brush and polish under her bunk.

"If you say so," Alejandra said as she quickly tied her laces. "At least I'll be comfortable. You look like you're going to have a meltdown in that suit."

Shay folded her arms across her chest and tucked her chin in. She was self-conscious enough without Alejandra piling on. "Let's get going."

"Hang on," said Alejandra, reaching up and smoothing Shay's collar. "Keep your chin up. You need to project confidence. Show them you're the right person to take charge."

"I don't feel like the right person to take charge."

"Doesn't matter," Alejandra said as she placed her finger under Shay's chin and tilted her head up. "It's all about looking the part, not how well you can do the job. Name me a president in our lifetime that was any good at being in charge."

Shay thought for a moment as she fiddled with her belt.

"Precisely," Alejandra said before Shay could come up with a name. "It's all about looking the part. Knock 'em dead."

Shay drew a deep breath and nodded. Alejandra's words repeated in her mind as they ascended the stairs to Vasily's office, meeting a girl named Stephanie at the top of the stairway.

"About time you got here," Stephanie said as she gently tapped on the door.

Shay dried her hands on the seat of her pants as Vasily called for them to enter. Sat behind Vasily's desk was the most handsome man Shay had ever seen. No, not a man. Despite his suave appearance, Shay estimated he was no older than her.

"Allow me to introduce three of our most promising ladies," Vasily began as he stepped over to the girls. "Alejandra here is making a name for herself in our military. I see her becoming one of our youngest generals in a few short years."

The boy behind the desk slouched in Vasily's chair as Alejandra saluted. He barely cast a glance at Alejandra as Vasily described her aptitude for guerilla warfare. Similarly, his attention remained elsewhere as Vasily outlined Stephanie's achievements in scientific study.

"And finally, Lord Lukai, Shay here is our most recent promotion to lieutenant," said Vasily, giving Shay a proud smile as he stood before her. "Very perceptive, this one. An endorsement from yourself would mean a great deal in allocating her a mentor."

"That one," Lukai said when Vasily was done. "The rest of you can go."

Stephanie cast a cocky smile at Shay and Alejandra as she stepped forward. Having watched Lukai the entire time Vasily spoke, Shay was silently grateful that it was Stephanie and not her or her friend. The pang of nervousness at his indifference had grown into a knot of worry in her stomach. There was something off about him. He was unlike any of the other vampires Shay had met.

Despite his status, Shay saw Lukai as the youth he was, an arrogant, self-important douche who thought himself better than everyone else. When the girls first entered the room, his eyes had roamed over the girls like he was selecting a cake from the dessert buffet and wanted to make sure he picked the best one there. Not because he valued the cake, but because he wanted to make sure he had the biggest piece. His lack of interest in Vasily's words proved that.

As Vasily ushered Shay and Alejandra out, closing the door behind him to give Lukai and Stephanie some privacy, Shay saw him unbuttoning his shirt with one hand. His other hand was on Stephanie's head, pushing her to her knees before him.

Descending the stairs, Shay grasped Alejandra's hand and thanked her stars that it was not one of them that Lukai had picked.

-59-

NEW TERRITORIES, HONG KONG
July 08, 2029

Alex did not bother opening his eyes at the sound of the bolts sliding back. He made no effort to engage with his captor as the door swung open and approaching footsteps announced the next round of tests. The passage of time had lost all meaning in the underground bunker. It may have been weeks or months since he was captured. Alex no longer cared.

"Show me," an unfamiliar voice instructed, causing Alex to stir. Throughout all the tests and examinations, Julie was his only visitor. Another presence was a source of temporary distraction from the monotony of his internment.

Apart from her heavy-handed approach to quashing his resistance, Alex's interactions with Julie were remarkably civil. Granted a degree of comfort once he began eating, Julie provided him with some soft bedding and a proper pillow. He was still chained to the wall, but it was a marked improvement to being chained to the bedframe. After each round of testing, Alex expected the thumbscrews to come out and interrogation to start, but Julie made no attempt to question him. By now, Alex knew the drill.

Blinking away the afterglow of his eye examination, Alex tried to focus on the other man in the room. If he could, Alex would have rubbed his eyes in disbelief at the sight that greeted him.

"You should have told me you're a member of the foot clan, Julie," Alex said as she extracted another vial of blood. "I could have saved you all this trouble and told you where the turtles are hiding."

Julie paused, turning to her colleague for clarification.

"He mocks me by implying I look like the Shredder," the man explained with a slight Japanese accent. His explanation only served to increase Julie's confusion. "From the Teenage Mutant Ninja Turtles comics."

"Oh," Julie replied flatly before striking Alex across the face. "Such insolence in the presence of Akechi-sama will not be tolerated."

Alex recognized the name. There was a warrior in one of his video games set in feudal japan named Akechi. Mitsuhide Akechi, general of the demon lord Nobunaga. Alex presumed this clown was styling himself on the long-dead warrior. It certainly explained the theatrics of the samurai outfit.

"Pulse is strong," said Julie as she held his wrist. "No change in overall health over the last two weeks. The supplements have done their job. I see no reason not to proceed."

Alex balked at the revelation that over two weeks had passed since Julie's methods got him to eat the meals she brought him. His spirit sank as he realized that the odds of being found were terrible. Any possible trail leading to his location would be cold.

No. That was not true. Reika knew he was in Hong Kong. She found his mother, a woman living outside the system since Alex was born, with nothing to go on besides the name of the orphanage. As long as Reika was looking for him, there was hope.

"Proceed with what?" asked Alex, his voice flecked with defiance.

"Very good," Mitsuhide said, ignoring Alex's question and drawing a knife from his belt. "Fetch the generator."

Alex kicked out as Mitsuhide advanced. The man was strong, catching Alex's feet and pinning them to the floor. Without a word, Mitsuhide pressed the knife to the bottom of Alex's ribs, drawing a line of blood as he made a shallow incision. The cold steel made Alex flinch, the involuntary contraction creating a hook at the end of the otherwise perfectly straight cut.

"Why are you doing this?" Alex demanded as Julie returned to the room with a generator in tow.

"Ah, the classic villain monologue," Mitsuhide replied as Julie connected pipes and wires to the generator. "Is that what you're expecting? Sorry to disappoint. If it is any consolation, what you are about to experience is not personal, but I need to be certain."

"Certain of what?" asked Alex as the generator whirred into action.

"Ready when you are," said Julie, tying off a length of copper wire to the chains around Alex's wrist before handing Mitsuhide a length of electrical cable.

"Ready for-"

Alex's question was cut off by the surge of electricity through his body as Mitsuhide pressed the cable to Alex's abdomen. The contact lasted barely a second, but it left Alex craving the cold detachment of Julie's earlier visits. Before Alex could recover enough to respond to the torture, Mitsuhide pressed the cable to his abdomen again.

"I've already told you," Alex cried out in a break between shocks, looking to Julie imploringly, "I don't know anything!"

"And I've already told you, I'm not interested in what you know," replied Julie as she checked his pulse.

With a look of dismay, Julie turned to Mitsuhide and shook her head. If he thought it would end the pain, he would tell them anything. If only they would tell him what they wanted to hear.

"My name is Zhang Xing-Fu," Alex mumbled when the shocks finally ceased. Sweat was beaded on his brow, it hurt to open his eyes, and his tongue was made of sandpaper. If talking put a stop to the pain, he would talk.

"I came to Hong Kong to find my mother. Roses are red. I don't know who shot the deputy. I'm not who you think I am. I'm Batman."

Alex barely registered the light as Julie checked his eyes and reported his condition. "He's not responding. We need to let him rest if he is to be of any use to us. He's right about one thing. He isn't what we think he is."

"Collect samples. Blood, bone marrow, spinal fluid and semen. When you are done, turn him over to the doctor. Let us see if he has any luck with his experiments."

"My lord? Is that for the best? I can run more tests."

"Don't question me, Daryl. You have wasted enough time on this mongrel. There are other candidates out there."

Alex struggled to raise his head as Mitsuhide turned and marched from the room. There were so many questions. Tests for what? Who was Daryl? Who are the other candidates? Alex's head throbbed as he tried to commit the details to memory. He wanted to ask Julie for answers, for what good it would do, but all Alex could manage as she lifted his head and trickled water into his mouth was a spluttering gasp.

As glad as he was that Mitsuhide was gone, Alex doubted that his visit to the doctor was going to see an improvement in his circumstances.

-60-

VENTURA COUNTY, CALIFORNIA
July 08, 2029

"Thanks, Trish," said Skylar as she switched her phone off speaker and pressed it to her ear. "I'm in Maryland for a meeting on Thursday with Director Banks. Schedule a meeting with me, Houston and McGregor. My calendar should be up to date. Let's nail these bastards."

"Will do, director."

It was about time they had a result. The counterterrorism investigation was accelerating at a rapid pace as more pieces began to fall into place. Special Agent Patricia Gates had proven herself a competent team leader since Skylar decided to step back from micromanagement and let the team flex. Sighing as she took a seat at her computer desk, Skylar decided reassigning Agents Houston and McGregor to support Patricia would not be enough to remove the temptation to chase the case herself.

Opening her emails, Skylar tapped a message to Director Banks requesting additional agents. Although not conclusive proof, Patricia's discovery of a multinational terrorist group, combined with Agent Lovelace's latest assessment of the reports, was damning enough that it would be hard to refuse support for more surveillance of the conspirators identified so far.

Too wired to go straight back to bed, Skylar left her study and wandered down to the yard, the wind making her shiver as it lashed at her legs and tore through her nightshirt. Watching the leaves rustle from the comfort of her study, the breeze had not seemed that strong. The moonlight, sparkling off the waxy leaves of the trees, sent a coded message of reassurance. Even in the deepest darkness, the light would find a way. The victims of the outbreak would finally receive retribution.

With an end in sight, Skylar reflected on the events since that first call. Lack of sleep and the frustration of not finding a culprit had taken their toll. Finally, the net was beginning to close around the terrorists. With justice dealt for the damage the outbreak inflicted, Skylar assumed sleep would return. Just in time for the baby to arrive and deny her any.

"Couldn't sleep, Sky?" a voice called from the direction of the pool.

In the darkness, Skylar could not see Jeremy, but it was unmistakably his voice.

"For good reason, this time, uncle," Skylar replied, heading in his direction. "Took a call from one of my agents in Maryland. The case against her suspects is coming together nicely."

Jeremy was sat on one of the loungers alongside the pool, reading a book. How he was able to discern the words in the moonlight was beyond Skylar. Sharp was a wholly inadequate word to describe Jeremy's eyesight.

"That's good, Sky," said Jeremy, closing his book but leaving his thumb between the pages. "I'm glad there was a rational explanation."

"I wouldn't call an anarchist terrorist organization rational, uncle," Skylar replied as she took a seat on the adjacent lounger. "There's no excuse for slaughtering millions of people over political bias. No excuse at all."

"I meant there was a motivation rooted in human actions."

"As opposed to what, uncle? Don't tell me you thought that, somehow, this was a rerun of Sodom and Gomorrah?"

"Nothing quite so fanciful, Sky," Jeremy replied with a chuckle. "I meant that it was not some terrible force of nature against which we could not defend ourselves."

"Well, it was that," said Skylar, suppressing a shudder at how devastating the attack was. "But nature doesn't choose targets."

As the wind whipped across the yard, churning the surface of the pool into gentle waves, Skylar tucked her legs in tight and pulled her nightshirt over as much of her bare flesh as she could manage.

"Your preference for wearing a woolen waistcoat makes more sense at four in the morning, uncle."

Jeremy looked down at his corduroy slacks, dress shirt and lambswool waistcoat and shrugged. "I don't really notice the heat or the cold, Sky."

That was true. His wardrobe was virtually unchanged from the winter months he spent in Wales when Skylar was growing up to the summer months of California. The notable exception was his raincoat saw a lot less use after he retired to Santa Paula.

"Well, I do. And this wind is a touch too chilly for my liking. I'm going back indoors, see if I can snatch another hour of sleep before my phone rings again."

"Good idea," Jeremy said, flicking his book open again. "You need to look after the baby, not just yourself."

"Don't remind me," Skylar said, rising to her feet and putting a hand over her belly. "I never thought I'd miss a glass of wine with a meal so much."

"Not having second thoughts, are you, Sky?"

"God, no. I'm looking forward to it. Although, not as much as Mike. He's already scheduling football practices, choir rehearsals, and piano lessons."

"I don't blame him," said Jeremy, his usual, over-protective tone creeping in. "I'm sure your child will grow to change the world as we know it. But only if you get some rest."

"Alright, alright," Skylar replied with a chuckle. "It's past my bedtime. No more stories."

-61-

VENTURA COUNTY, CALIFORNIA
July 08, 2029

Mike was just nodding off again when the soft click of the door opening triggered that part of his brain clinging to the waking world.

"Was that Agent Gates?" Mike asked as Skylar crawled back into bed, snuggling into his arms.

Mike wrapped his right arm around her torso and slipped the other under Skylar's neck, bending his elbow to draw her back into his chest. Her body felt cold after her impromptu stargazing. He knew the night was Skylar's favorite time, had been since she was little, but he felt discomfited by her decision to wander outside after taking her call.

"Yeah, briefing me on her latest findings," Skylar replied, shifting to get as close to him as possible, sucking up as much of his body heat as she could to warm her shivering frame. "We should have enough to conduct raids soon. Waiting on the CIA to coordinate the overseas operations."

"What is it?"

There was no hiding how Skylar felt from him. Mike could read her like a large font book with words of no more than two syllables. That was the beauty of being married to a woman who was not just the love of your life but your best friend.

"Nothing, Mike. I'm just being silly. Jumping at shadows."

Fully alert, Mike reached down and began rubbing Skylar's thigh, massaging some warmth into her legs. The night air should not have left her feeling this cold. She turned and looked up into his worried gaze, giving him a reassuring kiss on the cheek.

"It's just, I dunno," Skylar began with a sigh. "I'm worried we're going to miss something. To pull off such a devastating attack would take unprecedented levels of coordination. There must be splinter cells all over the world."

Mike continued to stroke Skylar's thigh, her skin becoming warm to the touch again.

"Like I said, it's nothing," she added, the sigh more relieved than despairing this time. "We have to act on the evidence we have. I can't let the 'what ifs' prevent us from bringing those we know of to justice."

"It's a tough case. Don't be so hard on yourself. Trust Jerry's team to handle our side and let the CIA take care of the overseas stuff. I mean, that's the reason you're heading east this week."

Skylar nodded. Another Sunday flight to the east coast. Another week of meetings. There was no denying it was upsetting being stuck at home while Skylar disappeared for a week at a time, but at least Mike was back at work to distract from sitting in an empty house, even if it was only desk work. The management position he had avoided for so long was his future now.

"Tell you what, why don't we take a ride up through the canyons and let off some steam?" Mike asked.

"I'd love to," Skylar replied, the tension in her back and legs slipping away as he continued to run his hand along her thigh. "Just as soon as we get through this mess. No way I could leave the office at this stage."

"Name the time, and we'll go."

Skylar mumbled her assent as Mike kissed her neck. The feel of her supple body against his had stirred him from sleep. Working his hand up her thigh until his hand reached the fabric of her underwear, Mike nuzzled the exposed flesh of her collar. Nudging her nightshirt with the tip of his nose, he slid one finger under the elastic of her panties, feeling the softness of her neatly trimmed pubic hair against his skin. Skylar reached down, placed her hand over his, and guided it back to her thigh.

"Not tonight," she whispered. "I'm not feeling it."

"Sure," Mike replied, gently kissing her neck. "Another time."

Twisting her body to face him, Skylar pressed her lips to his, slow and firm. She parted her lips and traced his top lip with the tip of her tongue. Mike's mouth tingled with that kiss, and he pressed his body closer to hers.

"I love you," Skylar murmured, breaking the kiss and flashing him a smile.

Mike brought his hand up to rest on her hip as she settled back down. Her scent was intoxicating. "I love you too."

"I won't be offended if you disappear into the bathroom for thirty seconds to jerk off."

Mike chuckled. As tempted as he was to unburden himself, he did not want to leave her side.

"I'm so proud of you," Mike said as he settled back on his pillow.

"Why? For letting you masturbate? In that case, I'm proud of you too."

Mike laughed at her attempt to brush away the compliment. "I really am. So much gets dumped on you, but you just put your head down and take care of business like it's nothing."

"Well, it isn't easy, you know. I'm allowed to have my meltdowns like any other person. Especially when somebody won't let me go to sleep."

"Message received," Mike replied as she reached back and patted his thigh.

Skylar could face down any threat the world could throw at her, but one well-timed compliment and her take no prisoners attitude dissolved into passive-aggressive sarcasm. Closing his eyes, Mike tried to ignore the erection straining against his boxer shorts.

"Thank you," said Skylar after taking a moment to digest the compliment. "You have no idea how much I appreciate you saying that."

"Yes, I do. I'm a lucky man to have you in my life."

As Skylar's breathing slowed, her body drifting into a fitful sleep, images of Los Angeles played across Mike's eyelids. Scenes he would rather forget, but never would.

Too lucky, he thought, his mind recalling Claire's lifeless eyes as the flames engulfed her.

-62-

LOS ANGELES COUNTY, CALIFORNIA
July 09, 2029

Francis Eckhart adjusted his collar as he waited for the medical examiner to finish sowing the corpse back together. It was the second time Stephanie Walters was pronounced dead, raising concerns over how she made her way into the river. Mariela was supposed to have a handle on this.

"Anything?" Eckhart asked as the doctor removed his gloves and dropped them in the contaminated waste container.

Doctor Roh was bought and paid for by Mariela. If it was up to Eckhart, Roh would be serving time for his part in the morphine racket that rocked the city in 2025. The evidence that could put him behind bars was with Mariela as an insurance policy to make sure he cooperated.

"Jane Doe here drowned," replied the doctor, giving Eckhart a cold stare. "At least, that's what my report will say."

"I'm more interested in what it won't say," said Eckhart, folding his arms and scowling at Roh's attitude.

Like many involved in covering up the kidnappings, Roh was chafing over the extent to which Mariela's plans had reached. Eckhart was all too familiar with the signs of malcontent, but there was no benefit in rash action.

"Don't question the narrative," Roh replied as he sat at his desk and brought up Stephanie's file. "That's how it goes, isn't it? They tell us the lie, and we repeat it until it is true."

"Like how you don't have a drug problem?" Eckhart asked, his voice cold and empty. "How is your detox going, by the way? Wouldn't want

235

you slipping into old habits and overdosing, would we?"

Roh stopped typing and lowered his head. "Drained. Not a drop of blood left in her body."

Eckhart leaned against the door frame. When her body was recovered, Eckhart suspected the findings would confirm his fears. Emboldened by the success of their latest endeavor, the vampires were getting careless. "Anything else?"

"Hard to say. The girl was in the water for some time. Whoever dumped her there knew that the river would wash away most of the evidence. It looks like she had intercourse just before she died."

"Consensual?" Eckhart asked.

At seventeen, it was technically rape whatever the answer. If there was evidence of force, it might be enough to get Mariela to change course. At least Stephanie's death would count for something if it made Mariela realize there was no protecting the children from the vampires.

"Hard to say," Roh repeated. "Now, if you don't mind, I have a murdered child to make disappear."

Eckhart crossed the room and looked down at Stephanie's corpse. Her water ruined features made it difficult to identify her. Roh traced her dental records back to confirm she was one of the missing children.

"Write up your findings, the real details, and bring them directly to me," said Eckhart, turning and heading for the door. "Don't tell Parker."

The chief was becoming less reliable in his desperation to stop Mariela. Eckhart needed to manage the situation without getting caught in the crossfire. As volatile as the situation was, Eckhart's best bet was to nudge each of them to self-destruction then piece together what order he could from the remains.

-63-

LOS ANGELES COUNTY, CALIFORNIA
July 10, 2029

Vasily watched as Mariela inspected her grapevines, carefully removing small clusters from the burgeoning bunches. He had no idea what purpose her careful pruning served and no interest in finding out. Gardening was her hobby, not his. Steadily, she worked along the vines as if the news he brought her was as inconsequential as the day's rainfall in outer Mongolia. Vasily knew his cousin better than that.

Taking a seat in the gazebo as she diligently inspected the grapes growing against the trellis wall, Vasily took out his phone and continued searching for treatments that would help Brianna delay the inevitable. His fiancé was putting on a flawless performance of not letting her diagnosis affect her, but Vasily heard her sobbing at night too often to be fooled by her stoic appearance.

Tapping on the website for a research institute in the Czech Republic he had yet to try, Vasily scanned through the all too familiar prose about the fight against cancer, how medical science was improving survival rates, and the importance of continued research. There were only so many ways to politely tell someone their loved one was going to die before it sounded hollow. Vasily reached that point within twenty-four hours of receiving Brianna's news. Breaking through the sugar coating, Vasily picked out the one detail he was looking for, an experimental treatment he had yet to investigate.

Selecting the hyperlink to send the research institute an inquiry as Mariela stepped around to the next gazebo, Vasily rose and followed his cousin, typing his email as he walked.

"Where is he now?" asked Mariela, her seething rage nearly impossible to extract from her placid tone.

"Virginia," Vasily replied as Mariela snipped her way around the next set of vines. "He wanted to check that Nikola was upholding her end of the bargain."

Satisfied with the state of Mariela's operation, Lukai had left Los Angeles the day after his arrival. With no farewells, it was left to Erik, one of Lukai's foremost generals, to inform Vasily that his master was gone. Vasily presumed he took the girl with him until Stephanie's body was found in Ballona Creek.

"Erik informs me he will be back in the city by the weekend," Vasily continued. "He plans to check on the operation in Death Valley first."

Mariela nodded but remained silent as she continued pruning. Leaving Mariela to her grapes, Vasily wandered over to the house, finishing his email as he went. Selecting a reasonably heavy clay pot from a collection by the corner of the yard, presumably awaiting new occupants, Vasily returned to the gazebo and placed it on the small glass table.

"What's that for?" Mariela asked as she turned from the grapes.

"I think you know," Vasily replied as he took a seat and placed his left foot over his right knee.

Mariela looked back at the grapes and her increasingly haphazard pruning. Vasily could almost hear the ropes in her mind creaking against the might of the storm brewing in Mariela. Placing her secateurs on the table, Mariela ran one finger around the rim of the clay pot as she rotated her engagement ring with her thumb.

"You know me too well," said Mariela, picking up her secateurs and returning to the vines.

"Not as well as I thought. What do you want to do?"

"Nothing," Mariela said after a moment's pause. "We need him."

Vasily began silently counting as he waited for his cousin to continue, watching her twist her engagement ring as her other hand moved over the vines without cutting anything.

"For now," Mariela continued before Vasily reached five, lowering her secateurs. "Continue as if nothing has happened. I trust a cover story is in place."

"After meeting Lukai, Stephanie was so taken by the greatness of our plan that she tried to convince the decadent heathens of the error of their ways. Consumed by their greed, they saw her enlightened philosophy as a threat to their society and killed her. It's not the most original cover story, but that's what makes it effective. People killing each other over money and power is so commonplace it goes unquestioned."

Mariela sighed and placed her hands on the edge of the table. "I wish that wasn't true. Another crime against humanity we must put a stop to if our utopia is to flourish."

"It will," said Vasily, uncrossing his legs and sitting forward, his shirt pulling tight across his broad shoulders as he rested his elbows on his knees. "What do you want to do?"

"I just told you," Mariela replied as she straightened and turned her back to Vasily. "Nothing."

"That's what we're going to do. What do you want to do?"

Mariela folded her arms across her chest and stared out across the lawn. Vasily glanced at his phone while he waited for his cousin to weigh up her options. The notification on his screen was promising. Brianna had an appointment with a research lab in Tucson on Friday.

"What I want will have to wait," Mariela replied as Vasily sent a response to Brianna that they should make a weekend of it. "There are bigger things at stake than my selfish desires."

"The mark of a true leader," said Vasily, sliding his phone into his pocket as he stood. "Practice what you preach."

"Whatever the cost," said Mariela, her knuckles turning white.

"It will be worth it when the revolution is won, and the people are no longer slaves to the political elite. They are beginning to see that it doesn't matter which side wins, the people lose."

Mariela nodded but did not speak. There was no doubt in Vasily's mind that she was thinking the same thoughts he did when he found out about Stephanie. He imagined all the ways he would make Lukai suffer for what he did to that poor girl. Having the body of a sixteen-year-old boy could not hide the nearly five-centuries-old soul of a sadistic killer. Vasily then imagined all the ways Lukai would have him killed for trying to bring him to justice.

"I need to go to Tucson for the weekend. Brianna has an appointment."

Mariela turned, a melancholic frown forming on her face as Vasily made to leave. "That's good. Give her all my love when you see her. Leave Lukai to me. Brianna has to be your priority now."

Vasily nodded as Mariela gave him the slightest of hugs. "I'll let you know when I'm back."

"Take as long as you need," said Mariela, her cold, inscrutable mask sliding back into place. "Go. Be with Brianna."

Vasily hesitated, his concern for Mariela rooting him to the spot. For all her brilliance, Lukai's imminent return to Los Angeles worried Vasily. Accepting that there was nothing he could do against somebody like Lukai, Vasily turned and headed back to his car. The sound of clay smashing against the stone slabs of the yard as he disappeared around the corner of the house brought a smile to Vasily's face, his faith in his cousin restored.

-64-

NEW TERRITORIES, HONG KONG
July 14, 2029

Alex awoke to the sound of a man urgently shouting at him in Chinese. Had he been speaking English, Alex doubted he could have made any better sense of what the man was saying. It felt like a swarm of ants was busy colonizing his brain and his stomach was infested with termites. The man continued to speak anxiously as Alex rubbed the haze from his eyes and let out an anguished groan.

It took a moment for the sequence of events to register in his brain. As soon as the neurons fired to relay the significance of his actions, Alex bounded off the pile of blankets that substituted for a bed and grabbed the man by his collar. At least, that was his intent. Although he had been untied, Alex's body was unused to being in motion, turning his bound into a flop and his lunge into a pathetic flailing motion.

Yelling yet more Chinese syllables, the man thrust a phone to Alex's ear and pointed to his mouth.

"Hello," Alex said, his confusion making it sound more like a question than a greeting.

"Alex, Reika. Follow this man. Now."

Alex was so grateful to hear her voice that he obeyed without question. Pulling himself to his feet after weeks in chains, Alex was surprised to find his body could function beyond the two-foot length of chain Julie had granted him. It took a formidable effort to exert a modicum of control, but Alex managed to stagger to the door before the man yelled something at him. Nearly falling as he turned, Alex gripped the door for stability and looked where the man was pointing.

There, alongside the bedframe that Alex occasionally found himself strapped to, was Alex's clothes. After so much time stripped naked, the idea that he needed to put on clothes before venturing outside was slow to compute. Stood in the doorway, Alex considered leaving his clothes. He was so close to freedom, and the man looked unprepared to collect Alex's clothes for him. Deciding his coming reunion with the outside world was probably best done without revealing his wedding tackle, Alex staggered back to the bed frame and pulled on his pants and shirt. With shoes in hand, he took the phone and made his way back to the door.

"Reika," Alex panted, unused to such exertion. "It's good to hear your voice. Where are you?"

"Keeping watch," Reika replied. The faint rumble of a passing truck in the background was music to Alex's noise deprived ears. "Just follow Pi. He will lead you to us."

Reluctant to hang up on his link to civilization, Alex kept the line open and followed Pi down the corridor and up a flight of steps, almost dragging himself up the last few steps on his hands and knees. Whatever operation Julie and Mitsuhide ran, Alex was grateful it was unguarded as he emerged from the underground cell into a storage facility. Heavy gantry cranes shuttled back and forth, taking containers from a loading bay at one end of the warehouse and stacking them in neat rows. Taking a moment to catch his breath, Alex marveled at how little noise from the activity above him had reached his cell as an automated lift truck took the latest container to be deposited and loaded it onto a set of racking. After the prolonged isolation, the din in the warehouse was overwhelming.

"Where now?" Alex shouted, but Pi was already gesturing down a walkway between two rows of containers.

Unnerved by the ease with which they had made it out of the cell, Alex kept peering around every crate and checking behind him as they made their way across the warehouse. Never again would he mock Jeremy over his ultra-cautious tendencies. If only he had trusted Jeremy's teachings instead of going by his gut and thinking Julie was harmless, he would not be in this mess.

"How do I know this is really Reika?" Alex said into the phone's receiver, suddenly aware that he had no idea who Pi was or if it was even his real name.

"Your sister threw me out when I told you your father was dead. She called me a cold, heartless bitch."

Alex nodded and followed Pi for ten yards before stopping again. Julie had known details from his past that sounded authentic. He needed to be sure.

"How much do I owe you?"

"twenty-six thousand, five hundred and four dollars and thirteen cents. Now move. We don't have time for games."

It certainly sounded like Reika. "One more. So I know it's really you. Why four dollars and thirteen cents?"

"Because you still haven't reimbursed me for that chocolate bar last year."

Definitely Reika.

Hurrying along as best he could, Alex followed Pi to a door he hoped would lead to the outside. The desire to draw in a lungful of fresh air spurred his staggering frame onward until he grasped the handle of the door. Before Alex could yank the lever and escape, Pi grabbed his hand and held a finger to his lips. Sifting through the various sounds, Alex focused on a pair of voices outside the door. Flustered, he searched nervously for a place to hide. However, his panic receded when he realized the voices were getting quieter.

Pi kept hold of Alex's hand, preventing him from opening the door until the sound of a truck door closing cut off the voices. Only when the rumble of the truck's engine was no longer audible did Alex turn the lever and push the door open an inch to reveal the industrial estate beneath the late evening sky.

"We're at the door," Alex said into the receiver as he opened the door further. "Where are you?"

"Put your shoes on."

Alex glanced around, looking for Reika as Pi slipped through the door and crossed the yard between Alex and the next warehouse. "You can see me?"

"Water tower, west of you."

Alex squinted in the light of the setting sun as he tried to make out the water tower. After so much time underground, under the glare of the fluorescent tube, getting his eyes to adjust to natural daylight required conscious effort. Against the sun, he had no chance.

"On my way," Alex replied, slipping on his shoes.

Pi was already at the corner of the next warehouse by the time Alex began crossing the yard. Although the water tower was rendered invisible by the sun's glare, Alex assumed Pi knew its location. Second-guessing his guide at this point would be pointless. It was not like his situation was any worse than being in Julie's clutches. Relishing the feel of the sun's rays on his skin, Alex felt rejuvenated as they walked across the estate. Every instinct told him they should be creeping from one hideaway to the next, but Alex took his cue from Pi and strolled as if he had every reason in the world to be there. It made sense when he thought about it. Alex was far less likely to capture the attention of a casual observer with a purposeful gait than he was by sneaking around.

"Thank God," Alex cried with relief upon seeing Reika at the corner of the last warehouse.

Standing in the shadow of the water tower, Reika appeared as a beautiful blonde angel in a polyester suit to Alex's beleaguered eyes. Flanked either side by suited men carrying assault rifles, she was the epitome of stoicism as Alex threw his arms around her, weeping gently at the prospect of escape.

"Let's get you out of here," said Reika, prizing Alex off her as he pulled himself together. "There's someone you need to meet."

-65-

KOWLOON, HONG KONG
July 15, 2029

Alex smoothed down the collar of the new shirt provided by the Chinese gentleman outside his hotel room. After weeks in captivity, left to urinate and defecate in a bowl Julie left him, the act of scrubbing himself clean in the shower was tantamount to therapy. Freshly shaven, he felt human again, not an animal in a test lab.

Reika refused to explain who they were meeting, only that it was somebody important. Washed and dressed, Alex allowed himself to be escorted from his room to the hotel conference hall, all the while wondering what mystery would be revealed on his arrival. Reika was already waiting outside the conference hall as the elevator door slid open, granting Alex access to the third floor.

"Can you at least tell me if my mother is here?" Alex asked as Reika knocked three times on the conference room door.

"No," Reika replied without a trace of emotion.

"No, she isn't here or no, you can't tell me?"

"Yes," she answered as flatly as the first time.

Her obtuse answer was not intended as a jest but as a way of avoiding the question. Alex drew in a long, deep breath and slowly exhaled before marching into the room. Men and women of all ages filled the tables to either side of the long passageway to the front of the hall, rapidly typing on personal laptops. It reminded Alex of the gaming conventions he attended from time to time but with a sinister vibe. The stories he heard of bots and online adventure loot farmers sprang to mind.

Ahead of Alex was a raised dais guarded by heavily armed men. The doors, also flanked by armed guards, swung shut behind him as Alex and Reika proceeded to the stage. He could see Pi discussing something with a young woman in a long, sapphire cheongsam. Beside her was a girl of about ten years of age in what Alex assumed was her school uniform. Her expression was one of extreme boredom, not unlike the woman engaged in conversation with Pi. The only one displaying any positivity was the old woman sat at the center of the stage.

Presumably the leader of the assembled throng, the old woman had a slightly smug, entirely self-satisfied grin on her face as she sat with her eyes closed, listening to the steady clicking of keys. Alex assumed she was asleep at first sight, but the way her head shifted from side to side in response to the occasional cough indicated she was awake and studying the room by sound, not sight.

"Lady Sun," Reika announced, gesturing to the woman in the blue dress as Alex ascended the steps to the stage. "And her cousin, Sun Pi."

Alex bowed awkwardly in what he hoped was a gesture of respect. Pi gave him a quick nod before going back to his conversation with Lady Sun. Her dark eyes swept over Alex, but she made no move to return his greeting.

"Miss Chiu," Reika continued, indicating the sullen little girl in the middle.

Alex bowed again, receiving a venomous glare from Miss Chiu for his efforts. Up close, the similarity between Miss Chiu and Lady Sun was so striking Alex would have assumed they were sisters were it not for their differing family names. Both women had high cheekbones and a striking, angular jawline that made their scowls look all the more fearsome.

"And Madame Qiao," Reika finished, bowing to the old woman before stepping back and leaving Alex to face her alone.

"Why are you here?" Madame Qiao asked as Alex opened his mouth to speak. "For the same reason we are all here. Powerful players are making their move, and us pawns must play our part."

Madame Qiao opened her eyes and gave Alex a warm, reassuring smile that spoke of fleeting safety. Her words and the transitory joy in her eyes turned Alex's heart to ice. Here was a woman who knew that happiness was but a brief respite from endless toil and suffering. Years of pain and sacrifice were writ large in the creases of her forehead and sunken cheeks, but the optimism of her smile was defiant.

"I'm sorry," Alex replied, glancing at the others. Nobody was paying him any attention. "I have no idea what is going on. I just came to Hong Kong to meet my mother."

Madame Qiao nodded. "I was the one who found her. We have been watching Kendra for many years now, wondering who would come for her first. When your lady friend approached our organization for assistance, it came as a surprise to me. Our agent in California was supposed to inform us of any attempt you made to contact your mother. If she had, we may have been able to prevent your capture."

Alex looked at Reika, but her stony countenance revealed nothing. It was hard to imagine she was unaware of any surveillance that Alex was under. Equally, it was hard to imagine she would allow him to walk into a trap with the knowledge he was being watched. The secrets and counter-espionage were all too much. Madame Qiao snapped her fingers to summon another chair as Alex put his hand to his forehead.

"Why?" Alex asked as one of the guards placed a chair opposite Madame Qiao for him. "Why would you be stalking me? Why was Julie stalking me? None of this makes any sense."

"I don't suppose it does," Madame Qiao replied sadly as Alex took a seat. "Mr. Outteridge has always been too secretive for his own good. Where to begin? Where to begin?"

Alex glanced at Reika as Madame Qiao considered her next words. Her response was a meaningless shrug.

"The one you call Julie. She is the right hand of our second greatest enemy, Akechi Mitsuhide. As ruthless and cold as her master, she will stop at nothing to become the most powerful of us all. We know her as…"

Madame Qiao paused, turning to Lady Sun and speaking in Chinese. Alex watched the exchange, the scorn in Lady Sun's voice apparent despite the language barrier.

"Spawn of Siming," said Lady Sun, turning her attention to Alex. "A vile woman who seeks to control the balance of life. We are all playthings to her."

Alex nodded, understanding the sentiment far better than he would have liked. "You said second greatest enemy."

"I did," Madame Qiao continued. "As terrible as Akechi Mitsuhide and his attack dog are, there is a greater threat. You."

Madame Qiao waited as her words startled Alex's already drowning mind. He allowed Reika to lead him here in the hope it would bring answers. Instead, so many questions were vying for supremacy that Alex did not know which one to ask first.

"Okay," He said, leaning forward in his chair. "Let's back things up and start again. You had me followed?"

Madame Qiao nodded. "Since birth. Until my agent failed to report you leaving California."

"And you know my uncle, Jeremy?" Alex asked, receiving another nod. "And my mother?"

"You are a very interesting person, Mr. Zhang," said Madame Qiao, closing her eyes. "We needed to keep a close eye on you."

"Because you think I'm a bigger threat than the woman who captured and tortured me?"

"You and others like you. Descendants of the guardian knights. People like Jeremy, who has hunted our kind for centuries. All because you see us as monsters."

Even Reika's stern disposition slipped as Alex looked to her for reassurance. Her quiet, calm and unshakeable purpose gave Alex the confidence he needed to keep going. Seeing the doubt in her eyes as she stood on the stage with these strangers put him straight back to being at Julie's mercy. Fearing he may collapse as the waves of terror washed over him, Alex angled his body toward the exit.

The color, already preparing for evacuation, drained fully from Alex's face as Lady Sun clamped a hand on his shoulder, pinning him to the chair and preventing his escape. Her nails dug into his shoulder, cutting through the thin cotton of his shirt and drawing blood as she whispered an answer to the question he was too afraid to ask.

"Nosferatu."

-66-

VENTURA COUNTY, CALIFORNIA
July 15, 2029

"This is bullshit," Skylar muttered as the heel of her shoe finally slid over the back of her foot.

Skylar was sitting on her bed, hunched over, with her face pressed against her thigh, trying to fit her feet into a pair of heels. This was the worst part of attending the awards ceremony, forcing on a pair of shoes that were both glamorous and torturous in design.

"What a drama queen," Mike said as he walked into the room.

"What are you wearing?"

It looked like he was off to tune the bikes not getting ready to go to a swanky party. His cargo shorts were stained with engine oil, and his gym shirt was so worn it would be unsuitable for the gym. It reminded Skylar of the time he tried to take her out for dinner wearing a muscle tank and Bermuda shorts. She almost throttled him then, and her shoes were making her feel murderous enough to complete the job this time.

"I thought this was a casual thing."

"What part of 'black tie' says casual to you?"

"Well, my shoelaces are black, and they tie."

"Michael. Change."

He grinned as he slipped out of the room, announcing that he was going to go shave and didn't want to ruin his tuxedo in the process. Skylar smiled, a forced effort in the circumstances, as she tottered over to the bedroom vanity and eased herself into the chair.

After three weeks of searching, Wagner had found nothing to prove or disprove the kidnappings in the other states or link the missing children in California to anything other than the outbreak. With each report he brought her, Skylar began to question if she was delving down the same rabbit hole as the 9/11 conspiracy theorists. Were rumors and circumstantial evidence enough to justify having an agent conducting an unofficial investigation? More importantly, if she took it to senior management, would she have the confidence to demand an official investigation? Covering up a conspiracy large enough to explain away all of Parker's suspicions would require a massive, concerted effort at multiple levels of law enforcement. Was it not more plausible that the children died in the outbreak and the tales of missing children in other states were just rumors?

Filing the case in the part of her brain that handled tomorrow, Skylar opened the draw of her vanity table, determined to relax and enjoy this night. Rummaging through her makeup, Skylar found her mascara and applied a light amount, just enough to bring some definition to her lashes. Then a little more just to be sure. Stretching the muscles around her eyes, she sat back and examined her face from every possible angle, catching sight of Mike's reflection as he re-entered the room.

"Don't you look dashing," Skylar said with a smile, the tension in her temples easing as she watched him strike a pose.

"What do you think? Every woman at the party will be dying of envy when they see me in this."

Skylar laughed as he strutted around the room in just his tuxedo pants and a bow tie, bursting into hysterics when he turned his back to her to reveal the holes that he'd cut around his ass cheeks. It wasn't the only modification he made. Skylar turned around just in time for him to rip the trousers off, the Velcro stitched into the seams making the move seem effortless.

"At least those pants died for a good cause," she said as he stood before her in just his underwear. "Not sure the socks and briefs are a good combination though."

"Pfft. This is the height of fashion."

He finally walked over to his closet and pulled out his tuxedo, slipping the shirt on as Skylar teased a few of her blue-black locks into position before applying a little hairspray.

"How's my hair?"

"Going for the 'Wild Child' look, are you?"

"Maybe."

Her hair was looking a little eighties, but Skylar liked it. After this event, big hair would be back in fashion. Or Skylar would feature in the "what was she thinking" section of tomorrow's fashion editorials.

Unconcerned with her fashion reputation, Skylar picked up her blush, a warm peach shade to complement her soft skin tone, and tapped the brush on the apples of her cheeks. Slowly, she teased the color back and up, just enough for a little definition.

"You okay, sugar pop?"

Skylar started at Mike's words. In what seemed to be the blink of an eye, he was dressed and stood behind her.

"You haven't said a word in almost ten minutes."

"Uh, yeah," Skylar replied, slightly disorientated. "I must have spaced out, or something, Mike. Wondering if we're missing something in this outbreak case. You were saying?"

"I was wondering out loud what Alex was up to, and when he's getting back. It's been a while since you heard from him. Don't tell him I said this, but I kinda miss him dirtying up the place. That sink hasn't been left full of dishes in weeks."

"Three days since his last message," said Skylar, closing her eyes as she sat back in her chair. "He's probably getting cozy with that girl from the train. Not that I blame him, she was smoking hot."

"I can't say I noticed."

"Sure you didn't," Skylar replied, her voice becoming more lethargic with each passing moment.

"You know, we don't have to go. If you're not up for it, I mean."

Skylar shook her head, knocking loose the cobwebs as she dismissed Mike's suggestion. "I haven't cut off the circulation to my toes for nothing. And don't think you are getting out of wearing that tux. We're going."

"Before we leave," Mike said as he stepped up behind Skylar, "I've got something for you."

Skylar opened her eyes to see a beautiful pendant on a gold chain dangling before her eyes. The graceful design consisted of a simple wave motif through the middle of a circle. A trio of tiny diamonds studded the crest of the wave, and a garnet sat on the outer ring, suspended above the wave like the setting sun. Reaching up, Skylar turned the pendant around and read the inscription on the back.

"You are my light. The beacon that guides me through the stormy waters of life."

Skylar thought it the most beautiful gift Mike had ever given her. Not because of its physical form but because of what it represented. Placing a hand over her abdomen, Skylar revised her opinion to make the pendant the second most beautiful gift.

"It's wonderful," Skylar replied as Mike fastened the clasp.

Skylar stood and blinked away her sleepiness before holding out her hand. Smiling as Mike took her hand and led the way from the bedroom,

Skylar ignored the nagging feeling deep in the pit of her stomach that told her not to go.

67

LOS ANGELES COUNTY, CALIFORNIA
July 15, 2029

The grand opening of the Neuvo Bella Hotel marked the beginning of Los Angeles' restoration in the wake of the outbreak. Reduced to a charred shell during the quarantine, after it got torched during one of the sporadic outbursts of violence, the Neuvo Bella stood as a monument to the perseverance and fortitude of the inhabitants of the great city of Los Angeles; a sign that they would not yield in the face of adversity but rise from the ashes, stronger and prouder than ever before. That was what made it such a fitting venue for honoring those who helped Los Angeles through the nightmare of the outbreak.

"Everything's set," Dave said as he got off the phone to the front desk. The hotel rooms were not available for booking until the following day, allowing Dave and Mariela to use the third floor to get ready for the event. "Ovens are connected. Food is being prepared."

"Cutting it bloody fine," Mariela replied as she kicked off her shoes and unbuttoned her jeans. Empty since the start of the decade, Mariela restored the gutted building to a functioning hotel with barely an hour to spare. The entire second floor was converted into a conference suite without a hitch, but the restaurant renovation was delayed by a faulty oven that needed replacing.

"What now?" Mariela asked as a firm knock at the door forced her to rebutton her jeans.

Crossing the room, one of three apartment-style suites on the third floor, Mariela peered through the viewing glass to see Erik standing outside. Wondering why Lukai's general would be at the hotel, Mariela turned and asked Dave if he could give her a moment. Nodding, Dave headed to the bathroom to take a shower.

"What is it?" asked Mariela, opening the door just a crack to speak to Erik.

"Our master wants a word."

"Really? Now? Does he not realize we are hosting an awards dinner?"

Erik shrugged dismissively. "Does it matter?"

Mariela huffed with indignation. "It does if we are to turn this country into a land where every citizen is protected and cared for, and the wicked are not permitted to live."

Erik blinked slowly. If it were not for Mariela's knowledge of his true nature, she would think the man was sleep deprived. "That's your dream, not mine. If you want the master to honor his deal, you'd best get moving."

Mariela's eyes narrowed, her muscles straining to avoid scowling at the reminder that her vision was dependent on the whims of Lukai Golovkin. Mariela reached into her pocket to check she had the room key then slipped out through the door, following Erik to the end of the corridor.

"Master, you summoned me?" Mariela asked as she entered the room to find Lukai sitting in an armchair with a young girl sat at his feet.

Mariela recognized the dark-skinned youth in a blue suit as one of Vasily's lieutenants, but she could not recall the girl's name.

"Erik here will perform the ritual," Lukai explained before patting the girl on her head. "You will then need to feed. Which is where our young friend here comes in."

"You mean…" asked Mariela, her voice trailing off before she could finish the question.

"Nikola informs me you've done an outstanding job," said Lukai, examining his nails as he spoke. "She suggested turning you herself. That's a high honor coming from Nikola, she hardly ever does anything herself. I told her it would be an insult to the Golovkin line to have a Malinovskyi turned by a descendent of the House of Széchy. I can't have you being a thrall to the one you will ultimately replace."

Mariela rallied quickly at the news that her ascension to a position powerful enough to make her dreams a reality was imminent. There was just one problem. "You're not doing the ritual yourself?"

Lukai looked up from his fingers and gave Mariela a withering stare. "Every time a vampire creates another, they give a little of themselves. The more you make, the weaker you become. Erik here turns my most loyal followers on my behalf, so that I may remain stronger than the rest of the council."

Mariela could not help but be disappointed that she was not being turned by a council member, but Lukai's logic was difficult to argue against. She nodded her understanding and tilted her head to one side, awaiting the blood kiss. Her surprise when Erik took her arm, rolled up her sleeve, and injected a few drops of blood into her was impossible to hide.

Lukai laughed at Mariela's confusion.

"The blood kiss is an act of passion. This is a more clinical approach to inducting a friend into our family. I suggest you sit; in a moment you will become weak and suffer cramps. That is when you feed."

Mariela did not need to be told twice. She was already feeling a little light-headed as the blood traveled through her body, changing her from the frail human that was a source of disgust for so many years into something more. Someone who would never be abused, degraded or humiliated ever again. This was what she had aspired to since first learning of her family's pact with the Golovkin family; since she had learned about vampires. The years of manipulation and political maneuvering had finally paid off, and now she possessed the power to bring about real change.

Her heart suddenly stopped, the impact of the blood taking full effect, and forced Mariela to double over in pain as her stomach tightened. She felt her gums tear as her teeth mutated, fangs descending and piercing her bottom lip as her senses sharpened. The hunger overwhelmed her as Lukai pushed the girl forward. Mariela seized her. The craving was too much. Fangs sank into flesh, and Mariela heard the girl whimper as she fed. The hunger eased, the blood of youth sating her thirst.

As her spirit soared, Mariela released the girl.

"Shit," Mariela muttered as the girl fell to the floor.

Draining the girl was never part of the plan. All those who submitted to being slaves to their vampire lords did so willingly on the promise their lives would not be sacrificed. That was the rule and here Mariela was, breaking the rule she had implemented to prevent the exploitation of these children.

"It's just food," said Lukai.

Mariela clenched her fists at Lukai's inability to understand why she insisted on making such a big deal about the welfare of their followers. It was only because her results were impressive that Lukai allowed her to do as she pleased, as much as he disagreed with Mariela's methods. One day, it would be his undoing.

Ignoring Lukai for now, Mariela knelt alongside the girl and lifted her head. There was still life in her body, but it was weak and fading. With the awards dinner about to begin, there was only one thing Mariela could do.

"Give me the syringe," Mariela ordered, holding her hand out to Erik. He looked at Lukai, who shrugged disinterestedly, before handing Mariela the empty syringe he had used on her.

Grateful that she had yet to change into her evening dress, Mariela tore a strip from her top and tied it around her arm, pulling it tight with the aid of her teeth while clenching her fist over and over to make the veins more prominent. As Lukai and Erik watched, amused at Mariela's efforts, she filled the syringe with blood from her arm before injecting it into the girl.

"It's not working," Mariela cried. "Why is it not working?"

"She is drained. It will take longer for the change to occur," Lukai answered, stepping over the girl as her body lay cooling on the hotel room floor. "Erik will take care of her; you have an appearance to maintain."

Lukai was right. Ushered out of the door by her master, Mariela left the girl in Erik's care while she went back to her room to change. In a daze, Mariela slipped into her red dress and fixed her hair and makeup, barely noticing Dave as he stood and watched her, fiddling with his cufflinks and tweaking his tie.

"Need a hand?" Dave asked as Mariela adjusted her straps and reached for the zip at the back of her dress.

"Oh, yes," replied Mariela, turning her back to Dave and tipping her head forward. "Be a darling and zip me up, would you?"

"I was thinking more of helping you to remove it," said Dave, sliding the zipper up the back of her dress. "As good as you look in it, I'd rather see you out of it."

Mariela turned and smoothed the front of her dress with her hands, trying not to think of how sex would work now that she was undead. "Maybe later. How do I look?"

Dave stepped back and studied her for a moment. His eyes had roamed her body on so many occasions, but watching him study her now felt uncomfortable in a way Mariela immediately despised.

"I don't think I've ever seen you look so invigorated," Dave replied. "You make me proud to call you my wife, and my love."

Mariela's discomfort eased as she looked into his smiling eyes. She may have changed, but Dave was still her rock. Assured that their love was eternal, Mariela reached out for his hand. Drawing in a deep breath as he took her hand, Mariela led the way downstairs to the conference hall and their waiting guests. Breathing was important, it allowed her to blend in with the humans, and Mariela was surprised to find that her body had retained the instinct despite there being no need for it anymore.

Stepping up to the doors to the stage, Mariela turned and smiled at Dave. What came next would be her greatest performance.

68

LOS ANGELES COUNTY, CALIFORNIA
July 15, 2029

Skylar nudged Mike with the tip of her shoe as Mariela returned to the stage to give her closing speech. Like a high school musical or the Oscars, Dave's awards ceremony was two hours too long. The mini quiche and smoked salmon rillettes Skylar sampled during the pre-award drinks were a distant memory. Her stomach wanted more. In response to her gentle prodding, Mike slid his sleeve back for Skylar to read the time. Unimpressed, Skylar sipped her water and waited for Mariela's speech to be over.

"We should all take to heart the example of our honored heroes here tonight. Through selfless endeavor, we brought our city back from the brink. As a community, we will continue to thrive. United, we will be stronger. United, we will achieve greatness. United, we will win."

Despite a throbbing headache, her rumbling tummy, and the relentless pain in her lower back, Skylar found herself applauding enthusiastically at the close of Mariela's speech, and not because it was finally over. Her words were eloquently spoken, as always, and stirred a desire to pull together for the greater good with their impassioned delivery. With some minor adjustments, it could double as one of Dave's campaign speeches.

As soon as Mariela left the podium, Skylar was on her feet and heading downstairs for the buffet. Dave's political rivals tried to weaponize his decision for the awards ceremony to be held in the conference hall of the Neuvo Bella against him, citing Mariela's purchase of the hotel as a conflict of interest. That move backfired when the campaign team drew the media's attention to Mariela's offer to not only supply the conference facilities for free but to provide free food and donate any uneaten produce to the local homeless shelter. The resultant bump in the polls made his second term as mayor look like a foregone conclusion.

Despite her enthusiastic start, it seemed half the attendees made it to the buffet before Skylar. There were only one-hundred and eighty attendees, and Mariela would have put on a spread twice as large as needed, but Skylar could not help weaving through the crowd in as dignified a manner as her growling stomach permitted. Before she could get halfway to the food, a man in a light-gray suit stepped into her path.

"You're heading the wrong way, Mrs. Sinclair-Blake."

Despite making a bad impression on Skylar during that first call in March, begging for help with his case, Deputy Chief Eckhart redeemed himself by proving to be a useful, resourceful ally in Dave's restoration projects. Like all of those on the front line, the stress and strain of dealing with the outbreak took its toll on Eckhart. It was only once the pressure points eased that Eckhart was able to let his strengths shine through.

Eckhart's tendency to avoid waste was easily his dominant trait. Skylar found the meticulousness with which he approached tasks refreshing. On more than one occasion, Skylar had vented her disappointment to Mike that Eckhart's role in handling the outbreak was so minor. She could have done with more people like him and fewer clowns like Diaz on the quarantine team.

Skylar turned and looked in the direction Eckhart indicated to see Daisy-Marie holding a pair of plates. Each one was piled high with an assortment of items from the buffet.

"You, Daisy," Skylar said as she took a plate from Daisy-Marie, "are a lifesaver."

"Where's your award?" said Daisy-Marie, a small pastry raised halfway to her lips. "After everything you've done for the city, I expected you would at least get a mention. And with you-"

Eckhart's gentle touch against the back of Daisy-Marie's arm stopped her in her tracks.

"I mean, I'm surprised your name wasn't called," Daisy-Marie said with a slight nod.

Daisy-Marie's habit of not pausing for breath, a result of a nervous disposition around new faces, had eased somewhat as Daisy-Marie became familiar with Skylar. It was a vicious circle. She talked because she was nervous, making people apprehensive and standoffish. That, in turn, fueled her anxiety and made her talk more. Understanding her predicament, Skylar was able to work around it and get Daisy-Marie feeling comfortable around her. Mariela had also done an excellent job of coaching Daisy-Marie. She had a long way to go but, with the occasional nudge, Daisy-Marie was proving to be a quick study.

"I told Mariela if she called my name, they would never find her body," Skylar replied.

Daisy-Marie was taken aback, looking to Eckhart for guidance until Skylar broke out her most disarming smile. Skylar's dark humor was still a step too far for Daisy-Marie.

"She discussed it with me," Skylar continued, keeping her tone light to prevent Daisy-Marie from spiraling. "Mariela knows I don't like the pomp and ceremony, I'd rather be in boots than heels, so Dave's going to name a park bench after me."

"That's nice," replied Daisy-Marie. The conscious effort to not babble was noticeable in the way her head jittered slightly, her line of sight dropping slightly as she did so.

"I was hoping for a street," Skylar added before shoving a whole mini bruschetta into her mouth.

"Where's Mr. Blake?" Eckhart asked as he glanced around the room.

Skylar raised her hand over her mouth as she rapidly chewed her food before answering. "He went to talk to Dave about something. Hopefully, how much better Skylarwood sounds than Hollywood. What's Holly ever done for this city?"

"Who's Holly?" Daisy-Marie asked, eliciting a warm smile from Eckhart. "Wait, never mind. You're such a riot. Always making jokes."

"Speaking of riots," said Eckhart as Skylar plucked a cherry tomato from her plate and crushed it against the roof of her mouth with her tongue. "Mark Ewing is requesting a deal in exchange for providing names within the terrorist group. The CIA left a message with me earlier today to see what terms he's looking for. I haven't returned their call."

Skylar nodded as she bit down on a mini quiche. After what happened with Mike, Skylar hated herself for even considering a deal with Ewing. It was unlikely he would provide anything that her team had not already unearthed, but Skylar needed to consider all angles.

"Let's see what he has, Frank," Skylar said between mouthfuls. "But I want to leave that little shit with no wriggle room. Unless he can deliver me the devil himself in chains, I want a way out of any deal that gets struck. That fucker deserves to rot. I don't want him getting another early release."

Eckhart nodded, a wry grin spreading across his face. "Understood. I'm sure I can work something out. We'll make that piggy squeal then send him to the slaughterhouse."

As his smile faded, Skylar wondered if Eckhart knew anything about

Parker's secret file. If the chief was as paranoid as Kellan implied, would he have confided in his deputy? If so, would Eckhart confide in her? Skylar found another cherry tomato and bit it in half as she dismissed the thought. Until Wagner found something she could leverage, it made sense to stay quiet and let the conspirators believe they had her fooled. For now.

69

LOS ANGELES COUNTY, CALIFORNIA
July 15, 2029

"Oi, I need a word with you."

Mariela, back pressed against the stage doors, did not need to open her eyes to tell that Darren Parker was bearing down on her with the ferocity of a charging rhinoceros. She heard his footsteps long before he entered her field of vision. As he drew closer, the pounding of his heart, labored from the exertion, would have drowned out a marching band.

"You should take it easy," said Mariela, tilting her head back to stretch her neck, eyes still closed. "All that fast food will put you in an early grave."

"Don't lecture me on early graves," Parker snarled as he came to a stop before her. "Not when your pet monsters are putting children into theirs."

Mariela opened her eyes. Although Eckhart buried the findings, it was only a matter of time until the chief learned of Stephanie's demise.

"Walk with me, Darren," said Mariela, extending a hand.

Parker looked at her outstretched hand with undisguised contempt before stepping back and gesturing for Mariela to lead the way. Mariela could sense his hostility in the heat his body radiated as they set off down the corridor. Adjusting to her increased perceptiveness and aligning the new sensations with her old instincts was getting easier as Mariela became more accustomed to her vampire form. With each passing hour, she felt less like a stranger in her own body.

"How many children have died in car accidents in Los Angeles this year?" Mariela asked when it felt like Parker would explode from his pent-up frustration.

"What does that have to do with the girl we fished out of the river?"

"Last year, the figure was one-hundred and sixty-nine," said Mariela as they turned the corner and headed toward the front of the building. "Half-year estimates indicate a similar number this year if we don't do something. Of those deaths, ninety-nine percent involved a manually operated vehicle. The other one percent was freak accidents involving cars where the parking brake was not applied."

"What's your point?" Parker asked.

"My point, Darren, is that allowing people to drive cars resulted in the deaths of one hundred and sixty-nine children last year. Zero children were killed in accidents where exclusively autonomous vehicles were involved. To protect our children, it follows that the most sensible course of action is to ban all non-autonomous vehicles from the city."

Mariela turned and gave Parker a blank stare when he stopped. She knew what he would say, and he did not disappoint.

"That's not the same thing."

"Children were killed by human action," Mariela stated as she turned and continued walking. "Avoidable deaths. Or is a human killing a child somehow more acceptable than when a vampire is to blame? What about dogs? How many children were killed by dogs last year?"

"I don't know," replied Parker, his palpable aura of frustration clouded by confusion over Mariela's line of reasoning. "Why?"

"Vampires are beasts," said Mariela as they reached the staircase leading down to reception. From below, Mariela could hear the muted sounds of conversation from the restaurant. "You believe they should be exterminated for it. Dogs are beasts. Three children died last year as a result of injuries from dog attacks. Does that mean we should exterminate all the dogs in the city? Tell me, who gets to choose which creatures get to live or die?"

"That's-"

"Not the same?" Mariela interrupted. "Why is it not the same? If vampires are beasts, incapable of comprehending our moral code, then the analogy to dogs is apt. Or is it because vampires are capable of rational thought and moral judgment? If that is the case, how many children were killed by humans last year? Or are we separating the good from the bad when considering the human race but not applying that same consideration to other species?"

"Now, look here just one minute," Parker replied as he grabbed Mariela's arm to turn her to face him.

Mariela looked down at Parker's fingers, wrapped around her arm, then turned her venomous scowl to his face. His anger quickly dissolved, replaced by contrition at being so forthright, then fear as Mariela grabbed him by the throat.

"No. You look here," Mariela snarled as she lifted him off the floor. "I'm sick of you questioning me. This city is mine. I decide what happens. I decide who lives. I decide who dies. You live at my mercy. When the wheel turns, you can choose to join me in peace and harmony with those who believe in a just and fair world, or be crushed beneath it."

Parker gasped as Mariela released him, rubbing his throat where her fingers left red welts. "You… You're one of them!"

Mariela opened her mouth to reply, stumbling back a step as Parker's terrified face shifted out of focus. She squeezed her eyes closed to stop the room from spinning, but her body continued to sway as her sense of balance was overloaded. Reaching for the handrail, Mariela tipped to the side as her vision glazed over. Her foot hit the top step of the staircase, the force of the impact snapping her heel and throwing her further off balance. Panicking, Mariela grabbed for where she thought the rail was, her fingers closing around thin air as she fell.

70

LOS ANGELES COUNTY, CALIFORNIA
July 15, 2029

Skylar pushed her way through the crowd, yelling for people to make way for a pregnant woman until she reached the source of the ruckus. From the depths of the restaurant, the first indication Skylar had that anything was amiss was when people began filing out of the restaurant.

"I told you, I'm fine," said Mariela, pushing away a doctor she had presented with an award only an hour ago for his work in the field surgeries. "Which is more than I can say for these heels."

Mariela lifted her snapped shoe to emphasize her point, drawing a few awkward, relieved chuckles from the nearest onlookers.

"What happened, Mar?" Skylar asked as she broke free of the crowd and approached her friend.

Sat on the last step of the hotel's main staircase before it curled around to ascend to the second floor, her hair working loose from the elaborate, braided bun, Mariela was nursing her ankle. She did not appear drunk, but Skylar could make an educated guess of what happened from Mariela's position.

Mariela cast a glance to the balcony. "Stupid heel snapped as I stepped onto the stairs."

Skylar turned and studied the balcony, wondering what was out of place. Was somebody else up there when Mariela fell?

"Do me a favor and help me up," said Mariela, reaching up for Skylar's hand.

"It's probably sprained. Maybe broken," the doctor said as Skylar turned her eyes away from the balcony. Whatever secret it held, only

Mariela could tell her. "You should get an X-ray."

The crowd had thinned out, returning to their food now the drama was over, but a few stragglers turned back to see Mariela's reaction when the doctor spoke.

"I'm not getting an X-ray for a little fall. My bones are stronger than that."

"Your circulation isn't," Skylar replied as she hauled Mariela up. "Your hands are freezing."

An ice-cold wave of fear traveled along Skylar's spine as her arm tingled with an electrical impulse at Mariela's touch. Skylar had been on the receiving end of electrostatic discharges often enough to recognize the sensation. This was similar but unlike any shock she had ever experienced. The contact simultaneously burned and chilled Skylar, making the hairs on the nape of her neck prickle in response. Mariela pulled her hand away abruptly, almost as if she could sense what Skylar was feeling, and held it to her chest.

"Lack of food," replied Mariela, her face contorting with undisguised anguish as she turned and limped toward the restaurant's kitchen. "Didn't get enough to eat before the presentations."

The crowd ignored them as Skylar followed Mariela through a "staff only" doorway to the kitchen. Examining her fingers, Skylar leaned on one of the polished steel work surfaces as Mariela went to one of the industrial fridges and removed a selection of items.

"Drink?" Mariela asked as she uncorked a bottle of red.

"Can't," said Skylar, placing a hand over her belly. There was nothing there to inform the casual observer of her condition.

"Oh yes, of course," Mariela said. Her face hardening as she looked down at Skylar's torso. "How many weeks along now?"

"Nearly twelve weeks."

Mariela nodded, grabbed a knife and fork, and began sawing away at a piece of steak. Skylar knew Mariela was trying so hard to be supportive, but she could not shake the thought that being around Mariela did not feel right.

"Don't be silly, I'm looking forward to meeting the little one," she said when Skylar asked if her pregnancy was a problem for their friendship. "Why would you think that?"

"You hear of friends drifting apart when one gets pregnant," Skylar replied as Mariela took a sip of wine. "That, and you're eating raw steak."

Mariela looked down at her plate and gave an embarrassed laugh. "Guess I hit my head harder than I thought. Maybe I should have gone for a checkup after all. Pretend it's steak tartare."

Skylar made a retching noise as she placed two fingers in her mouth. "Can't be doing that shit. Raw steak and raw egg. No thanks. It grosses me out when Alex does his raw egg protein drinks. Medium-rare, at least, thanks."

"How is Alex?" Mariela asked as she brought another forkful of raw steak up to her mouth. "Haven't seen him in ages."

Before Skylar could tell Mariela he was enjoying the female attention in Hong Kong, the door burst open and Dave rushed in, Mike and Eckhart following close behind. As Dave grabbed Mariela by the cheeks and examined her head for injuries, Mike peered over at Mariela's plate, ever curious when it came to food, and gave Skylar a perplexed look.

"Are you okay?" Dave asked as Skylar shrugged and gave Mike a slight shake of her head. "Frank came and got me as soon as he heard. Where does it hurt?"

"I'm fine," said Mariela, taking hold of Dave's wrists and moving them to her sides. "Now that you're here. How's everything going out there?"

Although many people had left straight after food, there were still well over a hundred people in the restaurant, getting drunk on Mariela's dime. Skylar had to remind herself she was not jealous. Not even slightly.

"Well, I thought it was a great ceremony," Skylar said when Dave finished listing which public figures were well on their way to embarrassing themselves when they staggered out of the hotel, "but I am not sticking around for the fallout."

"Liar," Mariela said with the slightest hint of mockery. "You were bored shitless the entire time. Forget naming a bench after you, we'll have to put a sundial in Grand Park with your name on it, the number of times you looked at Mike's watch."

"I was just... struggling to come up with a good excuse?" Skylar replied to a chorus of smiles and chuckles. "Okay, I was bored. Next time you hire a Brit to host an awards dinner, hire one that's funny, not one that makes the lamest, most obvious celebrity jokes."

"Noted," Mariela replied. "What about you, Frank? Are you done for the night?"

"I am," said Eckhart. The man had not moved from the doorway during the entire conversation. "Daisy-Marie, not so much. We'll be here until the bar closes."

"In that case, I'll leave everyone in your capable hands," said Mariela, stabbing the last piece of steak with her fork. "It's been a long day, and I am not as young as I used to be. Staying out until sunrise doesn't appeal to me like it did when I was in my twenties."

Eager to be heading home, Skylar bid goodnight to everyone and ushered Mike out of the door as quickly as decorum permitted. Every fiber of her being was telling Skylar to leave. As much as she wanted to attribute her nervousness to the pregnancy, Skylar could not shake the feeling that she had somehow upset Mariela. Yanking her shoes off as soon as they were in the elevator, Skylar asked Mike if he sensed anything off about their friend.

"Not that I noticed," he said as he placed his hand on Skylar's outstretched hand.

"Keys," demanded Skylar, pulling her hand from under his and holding it out again.

Mike looked at her like he was going to insist he was sober enough to drive, despite their earlier agreement that she would drive home, but thought better of it when he saw Skylar's determined expression. She was in no mood for messing around.

"Maybe she bumped her head," Mike said as he pulled the key card from his pocket and handed it to Skylar. "Made her act strange."

"I still don't get how these radio ID things are more secure than a good, old-fashioned key," said Skylar, musing out loud as the elevator door opened onto the basement parking lot. "You're probably right about Mariela. She was lucky it was just a bump on the head. I really don't feel like going to the morgue to vouch for any dead bodies today."

Mike stopped in his tracks, blocking the door to the elevator. "That's not funny, Sky. Not after the rough start we had to the year."

Having buried so many colleagues in the wake of the outbreak, jokes about bodies still struck a nerve. With a few drinks inside him, Mike's tolerance for her morbid humor was lower than normal.

"Sorry," Skylar said, taking hold of his hand as they headed for the car.

"It's fine."

The slight shake in Mike's hand told Skylar it was anything but fine. He put on a brave face, they all did, but losing so many friends took its toll. It was weeks before he would talk about Claire's death. No matter how many times Skylar told him it was not his fault, that he could not help what happened, the question "what if" would occasionally crop up.

It was difficult to know what to say and when to say it when the mood struck him. Reminding him that Claire was a hero that knew the risks and signed up regardless sounded empty. All the usual platitudes, that the dead would want us to be happy so their sacrifice was not in vain, that every life is important and we should cherish what we have, felt equally hollow. Deciding to say nothing, Skylar unlocked the car and lifted her boots from behind the passenger seat.

Knowing that there was a possibility the man responsible for Claire's death may know something that would secure his early release made the drive home that much more uncomfortable.

-71-

LOS ANGELES COUNTY, CALIFORNIA
July 15, 2029

Mariela studied Dave's serene expression as the car made its way through the streets of Los Angeles. The worry lines in his forehead were less prominent as he sat there, eyes closed, leaning back with his hands resting on his stomach. It felt cruel to disturb him, but Mariela's change could only stay secret for so long.

"There's something I need to tell you."

Dave drew a deep, slow breath, keeping his eyes closed. "Good or bad?"

"Good," Mariela replied, but the waver in her voice made the statement sound more like a question.

Dave lifted his head and opened his eyes. He appeared to be forcing himself to concentrate on Mariela's words. That was disappointing. Midnight was nearly an hour away, and Mariela felt no such lethargy. The steak pushed back the worst of her hunger pains, leaving her with a desire for another form of physical gratification. First, she needed to come clean.

Jerking forward, Dave's sleepiness immediately vanished. Mariela had already heard the screech of tires, turning her head to the windshield as the van smashed into the side of the Range Rover ahead of them. Their car had been slowing in response to the lights at the intersection. The car ahead did not.

Mariela grabbed the door handle and pulled, forgetting that the car's safety system kept the doors locked while the vehicle was in motion, as Dave flipped open his phone case and dialed 9-1-1. As soon as the car pulled to a stop at the lights, Dave and Mariela threw the doors open and rushed to the wrecked vehicles.

"Driver's unconscious," Mariela heard Dave inform the operator as he reached into the van.

The driver's side of the Range Rover was wrapped around the front of the van, forcing Mariela to run around to the passenger door. Locked. Balling the skirt of her dress around her fist, Mariela struck the glass of the window, shattering it in a single blow. Without the reflection from the tinted glass, Mariela peered into the car, her suspicions confirmed.

"How are they?" Dave asked as Mariela gripped the door frame and pulled with all her strength.

The lock resisted Mariela's efforts for a second before yielding to an almighty heave. The door twisted and buckled as it tore free from the mechanism and swung open on its strained hinges.

"They're out cold," Mariela called out, checking Mike's pulse.

Mariela reached across and grabbed Skylar's wrist, frantically feeling for the tell-tale throb of life. Her vampire instincts told her it was too late. Blood trickled down Skylar's face from the gash on her forehead.

"She's not breathing!"

The sequence of events played out in slow motion for Mariela, everything seeming to take twice as long as it should as she unbuckled Mike's seatbelt and dragged him from the car. Crawling over the passenger seat, Mariela unclipped Skylar's belt and pulled her free of the wreckage. Laying her on the floor beside the car, Mariela pushed away the thought that Skylar's death here would immeasurably simplify her schemes and placed the heel of her hand between Skylar's breasts.

"Don't you die on me," Mariela muttered as she fought to keep Skylar's blood flowing until the ambulance arrived.

Mariela's stomach ached from the coppery tang of the blood on Skylar's face. Her gums ached where her fangs rested, waiting for release. It was an option. All Mariela needed to do was mix her blood with Skylar's and her friend would be saved.

"Van driver's awake," said Dave as he dashed around to Mike and lifted his eyelids.

Mariela retracted her fangs. "Good."

There was no way to be certain how Skylar would react if she turned her, but Mariela doubted she would embrace the change with open arms. As painful as it would be to watch Skylar die, it was a risk Mariela was unprepared to take. Dying as friends was preferable to living as enemies.

"Come on, you oaf," Dave said, slapping Mike's cheek as his eyes fluttered open. "Wake up."

Mike groaned, clutching his ribs as he tried and failed to pull himself upright. "What happened?"

"You ran a red light," replied Dave, placing a restraining hand on Mike's chest. "Ambulance is on the way. Sit tight."

"Where's Sky?"

Mariela opened her mouth to speak but could not form the words to tell him. "Everything's in hand."

Fortunately, Mike was too out of it to put up much of an argument. Flat on his back, he mumbled something about it not being her fault before closing his eyes. Mariela's restraint was already being tested to its limit; she could not handle Mike getting in her way.

"Do you want me to take over?" Dave asked.

Mariela shook her head as she continued administering chest compressions. She needed to do something to distract from the stench of blood, and her body was unlikely to tire from the exertion any time soon.

"Ambulance should be here soon," Dave said as he stood. "I'm going to check on the other driver."

Those minutes spent waiting for the ambulance felt like hours to Mariela as Skylar failed to draw breath. The sound of sirens barely registered as Mariela devoted every iota of her being to keeping Skylar's heart beating. Only when Dave pulled her away so the professionals could take over did Mariela realize her cheeks were stained with tears.

-72-

KOWLOON, HONG KONG
July 17, 2029

"What are you going to do?" Reika asked as she polished her glasses.

Alex stared at her, aghast that she could be so calm after what took place in the conference hall. His shoulder still burned where Lady Sun's nails had pierced his flesh.

"I..." Alex began, pacing around Reika's hotel room. "There's only one thing I can do."

For all Madame Qiao's promises of wisdom, Alex could not bring himself to accept the invitation to work with an organization led by vampires. He wanted to forget the details already revealed, not learn more. The revelations affected so much of his life that it would be impossible to go back to anything approaching normal. At least some things made sense.

The revelation that Jeremy was part of a secret society was not difficult to accept. That it was a society dedicated to fighting vampires not the gradual erosion of traditional values by the youth of today was harder to swallow. Madame Qiao's claim that Jeremy was centuries old, however, was near impossible to believe. To her credit, Madame Qiao made no effort to convince him of her words. There was no hard sell. The woman laid out the facts and told Alex to consider his options before coming back to her with a decision.

Replacing her glasses, Reika carefully folded her cleaning cloth as she prompted an answer. As with Madame Qiao, Reika declined to offer her own opinion on the correct course of action.

"I can't," Alex replied as he ceased pacing and sat against the edge of the desk. "It's too much. I-"

"Don't sit on the desk," Reika interrupted dispassionately as she walked over to the window and looked down at the passing traffic.

With a slight shake of his head, Alex straightened. Even when faced with the world-changing news that they shared a hotel with the undead, Reika maintained her stance on treating furniture with the proper respect. It was why Alex was prepared to follow her.

"I'm not one of these guardian knights. Qiao said so herself. I have the bloodline but not the power. Although, it sounds like that's a good thing. If Julie had-"

"Daryl," Reika corrected.

That the woman calling herself Julie was a fanatical scientist obsessed with dominion over life and death was an easy fact to accept. Daryl Metzger, the Spawn of Siming. As Alex understood it, Siming was a Chinese deity of life and death, balancing the yin and yang. It was a crude interpretation that Alex likened to being the grim reaper's accountant.

"If Daryl had found any trace of power," Alex continued, joining Reika at the window, "Pi would have been bringing you my remains in a bucket. Do you think we can escape out the window?"

"Is that what you want?"

Alex studied her eyes, filled with latent intensity, and wondered what made her so good at appearing unfazed. Alex was shaking with nervous energy, worried that another enemy in a war in which he wanted no part would burst through the door.

"How do you do it?" he asked, pacing back to the desk to hide his restlessness. "How are you so calm?"

"Why wouldn't I be?"

Alex stopped and looked at her, dumbstruck. This was the same woman that saw a vampire sink her talons into Alex's shoulder and announce that she was a bloodsucking monster. This was the woman who listened to Madame Qiao, a woman in her fifties, explain that she was a three-hundred-year-old vampire in command of a network of spies, cartels and creatures of the night. This was the woman who had recently discovered the woman she was paid to find was the mother of a living saint.

"Living saint is stretching it," she replied when Alex was done listing reasons to freak out. "Your ancestors were given magical powers to fight vampires. At best, you could pass that bloodline down and have a son with super strength. At worst, you live a boring life."

"I think you have that around the wrong way."

"Do I?" Reika asked, folding her arms across her chest as she turned her back to the window. "Let me put it in terms you can grasp. What would Bruce Wayne do? Would he buy himself a little plot of land and hide away from the world after his parents were killed? Or would he pull himself together and seek justice?"

Alex grinned. "Did you read a bunch of Batman comics over the weekend just so you could deliver a 'why do we fall, Bruce?' motivational speech?"

"No," Reika replied, dispelling the illusion that she was secretly a comic nerd. "I used my phone to look up Batman origin stories while you dithered. I thought it might resonate with you more than a choice between flight and fight."

Reika was not wrong. Burying his head in the sand was not a very heroic thing to do. Alex always thought that, when it came to the crunch, he would follow his idols and stand up to evil. It was an easy promise to make when the foes were human. Mutants, wizards and shapeshifting aliens were supposed to be fantasy. The pain in Alex's shoulder told him otherwise.

"Off."

Alex gave Reika a puzzled expression before realizing he was leaning on the desk again.

"It's too much," Alex said, taking a seat in the desk chair. "I came here for one thing, and that's what I'm going to do. Jeremy's secret fight club and Qiao's mystical fighting force will have to work out plans that don't include me. I have to put family first."

The slowly rotating desk chair came to a halt as Reika planted her foot between Alex's knees. "Is that your final answer?"

Alex hesitated as she loomed over him, all authoritarian and unyielding. Was she expecting a different answer? Did Reika want him to become a real-world caped crusader? There was no anger, relief or disappointment as she looked down at him. Her face was as unreadable as ever.

"Yes," Alex replied, summoning courage from deep within as he straightened up in the chair, meeting her commanding glare with resolute strength. "Take me to my mother."

"Okay," Reika said, straightening up and taking a step back. "I'll go inform Qiao Wei of your decision."

"Wait. What?" said Alex as Reika crossed the room. "Just like that? No argument or lecture about doing the right thing?"

Reika turned to him, hand on the doorknob, and shook her head. "I'm not here to tell you what to do. I'm here to complete our contract, bring you to your mother, and get paid. What you do after that is no concern of mine."

Alex stared after her in amazement as she marched out of the room, wondering what event in her life had made Reika Pfeiffer such a people person.

-73-

KOWLOON, HONG KONG
July 18, 2029

"So, this is it?" Alex asked, clenching and unclenching his fists in anticipation.

"It is," Reika replied. "The consequence of your decision."

Alex turned his gaze from the apartment building before him and gave her an incredulous look. She made it sound so final, like certain doom awaited them on the fourth floor. That Madame Qiao let them leave without argument still amazed Alex. When the vampiric mistress of south-east Asia asked him to pick a side, Alex did not expect her to accept "neither" as a response. There was a hint of sadness in her voice as she dismissed him that Alex did not expect. Unlike Lady Sun's apathetic gaze.

Too nervous to enter the building and ascend the stairs to his mother's apartment, Alex stood in the evening sun and examined his surroundings. Far from the tourist area of the city, Kendra's apartment building was strikingly less affluent than the steel and glass constructs of the city center. Seeing the poverty that was rightfully his made Alex appreciative of the comfort his life with Jeremy, Mike and Skylar brought. A comfort he had taken for granted for far too long.

Unmoved by the stark difference in possible lifestyles, Reika took out her phone and started scrolling through her news feed. For her, the challenge of the case was over and nothing of interest remained. Alex had long since abandoned the idea that she would derive any satisfaction from witnessing the reunion and accepted that Reika was a machine. The only reason she was here was that Alex requested her presence.

"Room 402," Reika stated after waiting five minutes for Alex to move.

"I know," Alex replied, wiping the back of his hand across his brow. "I'm building up to it."

"You're stalling," Reika replied, putting her phone away and putting a hand between Alex's shoulders. "I may be getting paid by the hour, but this is ridiculous."

Yielding to Reika's shove, Alex stepped up to the door and grabbed the handle. "What if-"

"If you don't drag yourself up those stairs, I will drag you before your mother with excessive force."

There was no anger or malice in Reika's words. No change in pitch or volume. That somehow made it more threatening, leaving Alex with no uncertainty that what she said would come to pass. If he was going, he might as well go willingly.

"Do you think it's a trap?" Alex asked as they ascended the stairs. "Letting us go, I mean."

"I don't pretend to know what games these vampires are playing, but she seemed sincere to me."

"Vampires," Alex said, turning the word over in his mind. "It all feels too surreal."

"As was lightning before we understood the science behind it."

"And you are far too calm about all this," Alex replied, stopping between the third and fourth floor to look Reika in the eyes.

"Getting hysterical isn't going to change anything," said Reika, gesturing for Alex to keep going.

Reika had a point. It made no difference how he felt about the situation, the facts remained the same. Positive action was required if anything was going to change. Glancing at each of the apartment numbers as he made his way down the corridor, Alex made himself a promise to change and become a better person, just like Skylar always wanted.

"What now?" Reika asked as Alex stopped.

Throughout his ordeal, Alex had not considered that he might not be the only target. If Madame Qiao was to be believed, Skylar came from one of the guardian bloodlines too. It made sense that Jeremy would take in two orphans suspected of being descendants of his order. The only saving grace was that there were no female guardians. Madame Qiao had no answer as to exactly why that was the case, only that there were no records of a female manifesting the guardian powers. Alex hoped that was enough to dissuade Mitsuhide from pursuing his sister.

"Nothing," Alex replied, knowing Jeremy would be looking out for

Skylar.

Arriving at apartment 402, Alex raised his hand and hesitated. "What should I say?"

Reika banged on the door with her fist. "Try, 'hi, I'm Alex' and see where it leads."

It was the moment Alex feared might never come. As a child, he convinced himself his parents were dead. As a teenager, he pretended they never existed and Skylar was his real sister. As a young adult, he assumed they would never be found. He glanced at Reika, eternally grateful for her work in creating this opportunity.

"Hi, I'm Alex."

The seconds ticked by with no answer as Alex repeated the line under his breath. After two minutes, Reika banged on the door again. It was the closest Alex had come to seeing her display anything approaching impatience.

"Out of the way," Reika instructed. "I'll pick the lock."

"You can't do that," Alex said, stepping aside despite his protestation.

"Think about it," Reika replied, setting to work on the lock. "You were targeted for being part of a bloodline. Who else is part of that bloodline?"

"What? You don't think…?"

"One way to find out," Reika replied to Alex's unfinished question as the door swung open. "Hello. Miss Williams?"

A wave of anxiety swept over Alex as he followed Reika into the room. The thought of encountering Daryl or Mitsuhide again turned his palms clammy and caused his stomach to knot. The room was messy but not in a ransacked way, suggesting there was no struggle. As far as he could recall, there was no struggle when he was taken prisoner.

"Since when did you carry a gun?" Alex asked as Reika pulled a sidearm from under her jacket.

Keeping the gun close to her chest, Reika moved forward into the room. There was a faint mustiness to the air, buried under the overpowering stench of cigarette smoke, and a smell reminiscent of damp towels left too long between washes. The ragged curtains blocked out most of the sunlight, shrouding the room in a muggy haze.

"Alex," said Reika, nodding toward an open doorway as she stowed her weapon.

Moving up to her position, Alex peered through the open doorway at the dark-skinned woman slumped on the bed. Looking to Reika for confirmation, Alex approached the bedroom door with a heavy heart. The gentle rise and fall of her chest indicated she was still alive as Alex carefully pulled the needle from his mother's arm.

"Heroin?" Alex asked, placing the syringe on the side and lightly shaking his mother.

Reika left this detail out of her reports. Alex wondered how he would have acted if he knew in advance that his mother was a drug addict. Disbelief? Anger? Would he have flown to Hong Kong if he knew? Would he have come to see for himself? With so many questions, it was easy to see why Reika had not warned him.

"Mom?" said Alex as his mother's eyes fluttered open. "It's me, Xing-Fu. Your son."

Kendra's gaze roamed the room before settling on Alex. In her drug-addled state, she struggled to form her words.

"It's okay, mom. I'm here. I'll get you help."

"No," Kendra managed, gaining a modicum of control as the grogginess of waking wore off. "No son. Drink."

Kendra pushed feebly against Alex's chest as she pulled a bottle of vodka from under the sheet next to her. After several attempts, she managed to remove the top and take a long swig straight from the bottle.

"We need to get you cleaned up," Alex said looking to Reika for support.

Reika stood in the doorway, arms folded across her chest, unmoved by the display before her.

"Do you have any?" Kendra said, clawing at Alex's shirt. "I need something for the pain. Just a little."

Alex looked into his mother's sunken eyes, alarmed at the sudden intensity in her gaze. Distressed by her shallow, labored breathing and emaciated frame, Alex tried to calm her with limited success.

"Please. Just something to take the edge off," Kendra pleaded, slipping her dress strap off her shoulder to expose her left breast. "I'll make it worth your while. I'll let you cum wherever you like."

"Mom! No," Alex cried shuffling back to put some distance between them. "I'm your son, Alex."

"You can fuck my arse," Kendra continued, her gaze going distant as she spread her legs and pulled her dress up to expose her bare crotch.

"No. Stop," Alex replied, grabbing Kendra's dress and pulling it back down over her. "What's wrong with you? I'm your son!"

"No," Kendra muttered, slumping back on the bed. "No son."

Alex heaved a sigh of relief as his mother ceased her attempts to coerce him into giving her more drugs. There was nothing he could do for her here. She needed professional help.

"Is there someone we can call?" he asked, turning to Reika. "A rehab center or…"

His sentence trailed off as he caught sight of the knife in his peripheral vision. He tried to pull back, but Reika was already in motion. Her foot came up, hitting Kendra's wrist as she lunged, shattering bone and knocking the knife from her grip. Stumbling backward, Alex knocked over a chair as the knife skittered across the floor. There was no sound from Kendra as the momentum of her thrust carried her off the bed. No cries of pain over her broken wrist or angry words about the attack. Slipping into unconsciousness, Kendra slumped to the floor like a dropped rag doll.

Alex scooped his mother up and placed her on the bed in the recovery position as Reika called for an ambulance. Even when unconscious, Kendra looked tormented. Her eyes fluttered beneath their lids as her body shuddered from the drugs burning through her system.

"Ambulance is on its way," said Reika, hanging up the call and straightening her jacket. "What do you want to do?"

-74-

KOWLOON, HONG KONG
July 18, 2029

It was late by the time Alex and Reika left Kendra's apartment. Purchasing food from a street vendor as they meandered across the city, Reika left Alex to his thoughts unless prompted for an opinion. After what went down, Alex could not have asked for a better companion than the ultra-stoic Reika Pfeiffer at his side. Her unflinching apathy kept him tethered. Without her, Alex felt he would break down in tears and surrender to the whirlwind inside him.

Disappointment over Kendra's behavior warred with anger that she would allow herself to become an addict. The rational part of him tried to contextualize the situation, highlighting that he knew not how she arrived at her predicament, but was overruled by the part of him that wanted to scream that Kendra betrayed the ideal of a caring mother. The cynical side of his brain told him that expecting a mother willing to abandon her child at an orphanage to show compassion nearly three decades later was the height of folly. Still, the optimist in him wanted to believe that the decision was out of her hands and she spent every day hoping he would get in touch.

It was a vicious cycle of guilt and anger. Guilt at being born. Anger at being abandoned. Guilt over not being there to stop Kendra's slide into addiction. Anger at being denied the opportunity to prevent it. And, worst of all, guilt for leaving after learning of her condition.

"This is all my fault," said Alex, tossing an empty soda can into a recycling bin as they entered a mall. "I should have been here, with her, not enjoying the perks of a comfortable life in California."

"Blame yourself," Reika replied, "but not for the actions of others. You didn't put yourself up for adoption. You didn't choose to grow up with Jeremy and Skylar. You didn't inject heroin into your mother's veins. You tried to find your parents. You tried to help her. Own your decisions, not hers."

"That almost sounded like a pep talk," said Alex, surprised when Reika grabbed his arm and pulled him toward a shop window.

"Simple logic," she replied, taking a moment to examine a pair of ornate dragons in the window before moving on, her pace slightly quicker than earlier. "Facts are independent of your feelings about them. The sooner you accept that, the sooner you can take rational and measured action."

It was that considered reasoning that made Reika so vital during Alex's attempts to reconcile reality with the imagined scenarios in his head. Whatever Kendra's reasons were, they were not his burden to bear. All that mattered was what he did next.

"Wait," Alex said as they exited the mall and turned left. "Isn't this the way to Madame Qiao's?"

"Well remembered," Reika replied, holding her phone up and taking a selfie as they waited to cross the road.

"Why would we be heading that way?"

After giving Madame Qiao his decision, Alex and Reika moved the few belongings they had to an apartment Reika had rented to keep a low profile. Although Alex had precious little need to return to the apartment, assuming his luggage was still in Julie's apartment, his desire to return to Madame Qiao's lair was substantially less.

"We're being followed," Reika replied, zooming in on the picture she took and handing Alex the phone. "We have been for about an hour."

"Are you sure?" Alex asked. There was nothing in the picture to indicate a tail, not that he expected somebody following them to be advertising the fact.

"I follow people for a living. Call it professional pride, but It takes more guile than this to sneak up on me."

Alex nodded and handed Reika's phone back. "Kendra's dealer?"

Reika shook her head. "Possible, but they wouldn't be as subtle. I think we'll be needing Qiao Wei's help before the night is done."

Alex shuddered at the implication, resisting the urge to turn around, and picked up his pace. As tempting as it was to run, they were still a long way from Madame Qiao's with no idea what lay between them and the hotel.

"Hey," said Alex as Reika suddenly linked arms with him and guided him down a side street. "Isn't the hotel back that way?"

"I don't want them guessing our route and cutting us off. If it is who I think it is, they already have people between us and the hotel. I would if the situation was reversed. Turn right ahead."

Alex did as instructed while thinking back over the route they had taken. Although their overall heading was east toward Kowloon Bay, what Alex could recall of their journey was gratuitously convoluted. It was no wonder they had walked for two and a half hours and were still so far from their destination.

"Doesn't that give them more time to prepare an ambush?"

"It would if they knew where to set it."

"I swear, Reika, I cannot keep up with your reasoning."

"Good. Hopefully, they can't either."

Continuing to zig-zag across the city, Alex and Reika eventually came within sight of Madame Qiao's lair. To Alex, the hotel looked just the same as when they left it, with no obvious signs of surveillance. Agreeing with Alex's assessment, Reika picked up her pace as the building loomed closer. Unable to resist any longer, Alex looked over his shoulder and spotted three men crossing the street a hundred yards behind them. Upon being spotted, they abandoned any pretense of discretion and started running.

Without words, Alex and Reika burst into action, sprinting for the relative safety of Madame Qiao's hotel. Ahead of them a trio of cars rounded the corner and aimed for the hotel, pulling alongside the building as Alex and Reika raced up the steps to the door.

"No," Alex cried as he slammed into the door, the barrier refusing to budge under the impact.

Reika spun and kicked out at the first man to ascend the steps, causing him to trip and fall as he dodged away from the attack. Alex rammed his shoulder into the chest of the second man, sending him sprawling back into the third, but more were stepping out of the cars.

"Inside," a voice from behind Alex called as the next assailant sprinted up the stairs. Reika deflected her attack, leaving herself vulnerable to the charge of the next woman to make it up the steps.

Alex glanced to the side as he fended off an attack to see Lady Sun stride across the top step, grab a man by his collar, and hurl him into three of his colleagues. Momentarily distracted by the new arrival, Alex's assailant left himself open to a counterattack. Sweeping out the man's legs, Alex sent his attacker rolling down the steps and moved to Reika's side.

Despite being outnumbered three to one, Reika was holding her own and giving as good as she got. Her nose was bloodied, her jacket ripped, and her glasses lost. Her elbow swung back and struck one of the women as Alex rammed a fist into the kidneys of another of her attackers. The interference was enough to turn the tide of the combat. With Lady Sun keeping the others at bay, Reika disabled one of her assailants with a savage kick to the knee and forced the other back with a chop to the neck. The lull in the fighting was enough to allow Alex and Reika to withdraw toward the hotel door.

From the safety of the hotel lobby, Alex watched as Lady Sun batted aside a lunge from one attacker, deftly sidestepped a second, and grabbed the wrist of a third. Using the man's momentum against him, Lady Sun pirouetted and hurled him down the steps to collide with two other assailants trying to get into the hotel. Alex counted eleven men and women in total, and Lady Sun was fending them off with an ease bordering on insulting.

"Upstairs," said Lady Sun, stepping back through the door and slamming it closed while the attackers regrouped. "We don't have much time."

Reika was already halfway across the lobby before Alex moved. Only when she rammed home the giant bolts that secured the entrance and turned to the stairs did Alex react to Lady Sun's instruction. As difficult as it was to trust the vampire, Alex had the mental acuity to know his chances were better with her than the enemy outside.

A voice from above made Alex look up. He had failed to notice that the lobby was two floors high and overlooked by the corridor of the next floor during his first visit. The grandeur of the lobby was obscured by the sight of Miss Chiu standing on the balcony rails and barking orders to a group of guards. Alex saw them level their machine guns at the door before the slate grey walls of the stairwell obscured his vision.

"This is your doing," said Lady Sun as they passed the second floor. "We have operated without invoking the warlord's ire for centuries. Protecting you has doomed us."

"I didn't ask for any of this," Alex replied, feeling that he had to say something to defend himself as Miss Chiu joined them on the stairs. "I never wanted anyone to go to war for me."

"This war is overdue," said Miss Chiu. "Let them come."

Shaking her head, Lady Sun pushed open the door to the third floor and marched to the conference hall. The evacuation was already in motion as Alex, Reika and their vampire escorts burst into the room and marched toward the stage. Alex marveled at the discipline on display as the assembled throng of people filed out in orderly lines through a set of double doors at the back of the stage.

"Just in time," said Madame Qiao as Alex jumped onto the stage. "This passage leads to the docks."

The distant roar of machine-gun fire signaled the door was breached. Worryingly, the gunfire stopped as abruptly as it started, leaving Alex wondering if he had imagined it. Several faces turned to the door as the guards on the stage dropped to the floor and flipped over the first row of tables to make barricades. Unperturbed by the interruption, Madame Qiao gestured for everyone to keep moving.

"We need more time," said Reika as Madame Qiao's army of hackers poured down the stairwell behind the stage.

"Time is something of which I have much experience," Madame Qiao replied pushing Reika toward the door.

Alex watched Lady Sun, her posture proud and dignified as she waited, and Miss Chiu, energized and impatient, as the crowd thinned. Turning to face Madame Qiao as she placed a hand on his arm, Alex saw that the last of her people was through the door. Her words were drowned out by the sound of the main doors slamming into the walls as they were thrown open.

"You have something that belongs to me," Daryl called out as she strode into the room at Mitsuhide's side.

The sound of Daryl's voice rooted Alex to the spot. Immobilized by fear, he watched as the guards positioned behind their barricades opened fire. Instead of cutting down their targets, the bullets scattered away from Mitsuhide and Daryl as if deflected by an invisible force. There was no second salvo. As Madame Qiao pulled Alex toward the door, the guards fell to the floor, steam rising from their bodies.

"What the…" Alex began, his question cut off by Miss Chiu's scream of rage.

Leaping from the stage, the young vampire dashed across the tabletops and launched herself at Mitsuhide. Horrified, Alex watched as Daryl stepped before her master, caught the girl by the throat as she descended, and drove her through the nearest table.

"Chiu Lixue!" shouted Lady Sun as Daryl lifted Miss Chiu's adolescent body from the wreckage.

Madame Qiao pushed Alex toward the door and grabbed Lady Sun as the woman stepped forward. For a moment, Alex thought Lady Sun would defy her elder and go after Miss Chiu. It would be an empty sacrifice. As Miss Chiu clawed desperately at her assailant's arm, Daryl kicked the broken table over and slammed her prey onto the jagged edge.

Leaving Miss Chiu's broken body impaled on the table, broken lengths of wood jutting through her chest, Daryl approached the stage. Shaken from his paralysis by the sudden and callous violence of Miss Chiu's death, Alex stepped through the doorway.

"Protect the boy," Madame Qiao instructed, pushing Lady Sun

through after him. "Get him home."

"No!" screamed Lady Sun as Madame Qiao closed the door on them, trapping Daryl and Mitsuhide in the conference hall with her.

-75-

KOWLOON, HONG KONG
July 19, 2029

Madame Qiao turned to face Daryl and Akechi-San as the blast door slid shut over the stage's double doors, sealing Alex and the others away from their reach.

"That was a foolish thing to do," Akechi-San declared as Daryl strode toward the stage. "Betraying me will be your last act."

"True," replied Madame Qiao, "but the boy will live."

Rolling her head to loosen up, Daryl stepped onto the stage and approached Madame Qiao, fists raised. Madame Qiao's eyes remained fixed on Akechi Mitsuhide. As great a threat as Daryl was, it was her master Madame Qiao needed to keep occupied.

"You would throw away all we have built for an empty vessel?"

Madame Qiao's eyes flicked briefly to Daryl at the sound of her voice. "We? I don't remember you being at Fort Zeelandia when we ended Dutch rule over Taiwan. I don't remember you fighting the British for control of Hong Kong. What about the Japanese invasion of Taiwan in 1874? And again in 1895? Or when the Japanese took Beijing, Shanghai and Nanjing? Don't lecture me on what we built. Your time on this planet is a speck compared to the years I have fought to protect this nation."

"I'll outlast you, you ungrateful bitch," Daryl replied as she inched closer to Madame Qiao. "Your dynasty ends where mine begins."

"Is that why you rebel?" Akechi-San asked as he stepped closer to the stage. He was in no hurry to support his lap dog. "A grudge over humans killing each other over invisible lines in the sand? I thought you were smarter than that, Wei."

Daryl struck before Madame Qiao could respond. She was faster than she had any right to be. Barely deflecting Daryl's palm strike with her cane, Madame Qiao stepped back and prepared for the next strike. She always suspected Daryl was supplementing her strength and speed somehow. There was no other explanation for a human rising to the top of the council's security.

A slight shift in Daryl's posture signaled her next attack. As her foot rose, striking at the space Madame Qiao immediately vacated, Daryl's shoulder gave away her intent. Ducking under her jab, Madame Qiao slammed her hand against Daryl's chest with blistering speed, hurling her across the stage. A blow like that should have shattered her ribs, but Daryl turned her fall into a roll and landed in a crouch, dropping her boxer's stance.

Akechi-San was taking his time joining the fight, approaching the stage as if he had all the time in the world. Using the brief distraction as Madame Qiao questioned whether Akechi-San's target was the boy, Daryl launched herself forward. Barely avoiding the ax kick she delivered, Madame Qiao was in no position to avoid Daryl's follow up elbow strike. Twisting away to minimize the impact, Madame Qiao took a glancing blow to the jaw.

As Daryl skipped back out of Madame Qiao's reach, Madame Qiao reassessed her situation. Her fate was sealed, but winning was never the plan. She needed to buy enough time for Lady Sun to lead the others to safety. Resetting her jaw, Madame Qiao questioned her ability to do that. If a glancing blow could do so much damage, it would not take many direct impacts to end this battle.

"What are you?" Madame Qiao asked, stalling for time. If she had an accurate measure of Daryl's power, every second gained would be crucial.

"I am Death," Daryl replied as she stepped to the side, attempting to turn Madame Qiao away from Akechi-San.

"She is the future," Akechi-San declared as Madame Qiao circled to keep them both in her field of vision. "The ultimate specimen of genetic evolution. Savior of this corrupt, decadent world."

"A soldier," Madame Qiao replied, painfully aware of how reductive the statement was but eager to keep them talking. "And a lab rat."

Akechi-San stopped, halfway to the stage, and tilted his head down. "They should be out of range by now. My gift to you for your years of service. Now, let us finish this."

Daryl swept in, closing the gap in a fraction of a heartbeat, and thrust her hand at Madame Qiao's heart. Striking her inner forearm to deflect the blow, Madame Qiao countered with a palm strike to the face. As fast as Daryl was, Madame Qiao was faster. Pressing her advantage, Madame Qiao stepped forward and drove her knee into Daryl's abdomen before grabbing her head and throwing her to the floor. Twisting from Madame Qiao's grip before she could capitalize on her position, Daryl rolled to her feet and backed away.

"You're fast, old woman," said Daryl as she circled the stage, visibly relaxed. "I can't remember the last time I felt challenged. This may be more fun than I thought it would be."

Madame Qiao ignored Daryl and shifted her focus to Akechi-San. "You're not here for the boy. Your attack dog said it herself, he is an empty vessel. You're here for me."

Raising his gloved hands, Akechi-San clapped, slowly, three times.

With teeth clenched, Madame Qiao turned her attention back to Daryl. The revelation that they were here to execute her, not recapture the boy, did nothing to the outcome. If Alex was safe, there was no need to delay the inevitable. Summoning the power of her chi, Madame Qiao raised her arm, elbow bent, until her palm pointed across her shoulders. Sensing the imminent release of energy, Akechi-San braced himself while Daryl adopted a defensive posture.

The shockwave as Madame Qiao dropped to one knee and slammed the heel of her hand to the stage threw chairs and tables across the room as it rippled outward. The boards of the stage splintered and cracked as plaster fell from the ceiling. Off-balanced by the shockwave, Daryl fell as the stage gave way beneath her, twisting as she collapsed. Akechi-san was unmoved by the show of force, but his resistance to the blast of energy unleashed by Madame Qiao would not protect him from the beam that dropped from the ceiling. Sidestepping the beam as it crashed to the floor, Akechi-san drew his sword and approached the stage.

As Madame Qiao summoned a second blast of energy, Daryl's hand reached up from beneath the stage and grasped the broken floorboards. Alert to the changes in the air, Akechi-san increased his pace. His leap onto the stage was timed to perfection, avoiding the blast that rippled out as Madame Qiao struck the stage again. Unfortunately for him, there was no place to land. The boards ruptured and fell to the floor beneath the stage.

Madame Qiao's attack did not end there. The blast of energy continued through the stage, splintering the beams of the floor and weakening the entire structure. Akechi-san's feet hit the floorboards as they collapsed into the room beneath them, the three combatants falling with the wreckage.

Madame Qiao lost sight of Daryl and Akechi-San as she landed on the floor beneath the conference room. Wherever they were, it would not take long for them to make their presence known. Pushing away a section of wall that had fallen upon her, Madame Qiao staggered to the door, hoping that Lady Sun was far enough away.

"Impressive," Akechi-san called, emerging from beneath the broken wood and crumbled plaster as Madame Qiao reached the door. Pieces of debris continued to rain down around them as the walls of the hotel began to topple. "You have gained much power since your rebirth."

Madame Qiao chose not to respond. There was nothing she had to say to the warlord that commanded Asia's vampire legions. She only hoped that her actions here would be enough for her true master to turn defeat into victory. Pulling herself to her full height she rolled her shoulders and slid her left foot forward, dropping into a cat stance. Akechi-san's blade was gone, giving her a fighting chance against him.

A section of rubble shifted as Akechi-san approached, undaunted by her readiness to strike. Madame Qiao would need to be quick if she wanted to finish this before the Spawn of Siming freed herself from the beams pinning her down. Making no attempt to adopt an attack position, Akechi-san strode into Madame Qiao's reach. Suspecting a trap, Madame Qiao ducked to the side and rolled away from the samurai.

"Do you wish to fight me?" he asked, turning to face Madame Qiao. "Or are we going to play games until this building buries us?"

Madame Qiao hesitated. His legs were straight, feet planted firmly beneath him, and his hands rested easily at his sides. No fighter would adopt such a weak position. Unless…

"So be it," said Madame Qiao as reality hit her. Nothing she did could threaten him. This was not a fight to Akechi-san. It was a slaughter waiting to happen. "At least I die fighting for my people."

Her first strike missed as Akechi-san pivoted away from her open palm. Her follow-up punch was deflected, the blast of energy carried in her fist sweeping out across the room, cracking the render. With embarrassing ease, Akechi-san caught her wrist as she struck again. Turning her momentum against her, he threw her to the wall. Madame Qiao was ready for it, kicking herself into a cartwheel and landing in a crouch instead. Her method was wrong. Attacking Akechi-san was wrong.

Rising to a crane stance, Madame Qiao thrust backward with her raised foot, striking the wall behind her. The wall cracked and fell into the hallway beyond. Skipping backward through the hole, Madame Qiao launched herself over the handrail and dropped into the hotel foyer below, summoning every ounce of her chi as she fell. The impact was deafening.

The foyer's tile floor shattered, erupting as the shockwave spread out around Madame Qiao. The glass of the doors blew out into the street, raining down over the hotel's steps. The columns supporting the balcony cracked and collapsed, bringing down the floors above them. Madame Qiao smiled as the rubble rained down around her, the weight of falling beams and concrete pressing her to the ground. If the hotel was to be her tomb, she would bury the warlord and his dog with her.

Her satisfaction was short-lived. The rubble pinning her down was thrown aside. Rough, bloodstained hands gripped her shoulders and dragged her from her grave.

As Daryl dragged Madame Qiao's broken body from the wreckage, Akechi-san strode forth from the cloud of dust that filled the space that was the hotel entrance. Focusing all her energy on repairing her severed spine, Madame Qiao turned her head to face her executioner.

"A brave attempt," he said, kneeling before her and grasping her throat. "But ultimately futile."

"What of my people?" Madame Qiao asked as he lifted her off the floor. There was nothing she could do. She put so much into her attack, there was nothing left to repair herself.

Akechi-san laughed as he carried her to the doorway. "Even in your crippled state, you try to bargain."

Madame Qiao heard the tearing of flesh but felt nothing as the splintered doorframe burst through her chest.

"I will let them live," Akechi-san replied as he proceeded down the front steps of the ruined hotel. "For now."

Impaled on the doorframe, unable to free herself, Madame Qiao thought of all the people under her care. She had risked everything to save the boy, and now she would pay for that gamble.

"Enjoy the sunrise," said Daryl as she limped past Madame Qiao's prone form.

Madame Qiao closed her eyes and waited for the sun's cleansing rays. If it saved her people, it was a price worth paying.

KOWLOON, HONG KONG
July 19, 2029

The journey to the tunnels beneath Hong Kong was made in silence. Only when the spiral stairway ended, opening into a wide corridor lit with the occasional emergency light, did anybody speak. With curt commands, Lady Sun marshaled her forces, sending people down multiple branches of the tunnel network. After witnessing the ease with which Daryl eliminated Miss Chiu, there was no doubt in Alex's mind that they were Lady Sun's people now. Despite barely knowing Madame Qiao, Alex felt a pang of regret that events had turned against her.

"What do we need to do?" Alex asked as he followed Reika and Lady Sun down the main corridor with twenty of her hackers.

"Don't die," replied Lady Sun as four people turned down a side corridor in response to a snap of her fingers. "Not until I complete Qiao Wei's orders."

Alex shook his head, a futile gesture in the dimly lit tunnels. "I meant for Madame Qiao. There must be something we can do? I can't let her risk her life for me and not do something about it."

Before he could react, Lady Sun's hand was around his throat, pinning Alex to the wall. Her eyes burned with ferocious anger but her voice was calm and measured. "There is nothing you can do. You are a weak, frightened child. I should kill you for what you have done to my family. Drain your corpse and leave nothing but ashes for the warlord and his dog."

The click of Reika flicking the safety off and pressing the muzzle of her gun to Lady Sun's head echoed along the corridor. "I can't let you do that. He hasn't paid me yet."

With a sweep of her arm, Lady Sun disarmed Reika and pinned her to the wall next to Alex.

"You, Mrs. Reika, have spirit," said Lady Sun as Reika kicked and scratched to break free. "I like that. Unlike your house cat."

"It's Miss Pfeiffer," Reika replied, balling her fist and striking Lady Sun on the temple.

Alex cringed at the thought of what would happen next. He imagined Lady Sun's retaliation would be swift and brutal. Braced for the sound of snapping vertebrae, he was surprised to hear laughter as she released her grip and let them both fall to the floor.

"If you harness that rage and direct it at our foes, you could be a formidable ally, Miss Pfeiffer," Lady Sun said with a smirk. "We should move. Too much time has been wasted."

Alex rubbed his throat as Lady Sun continued her march down the corridor. "Did she just call me a pussy?"

Reika glanced around the corridor in the hope of spotting her gun, but the poor lighting made the task too difficult. Accepting her loss, Reika straightened her jacket and moved down the corridor after Lady Sun.

"An accurate assessment," Reika said as they quick marched to catch up to the others, "but I suspect the pun was accidental."

Biting back a caustic response, Alex focused on keeping up with his guide. Although their pace was quick, at no point did they break into a run. As getaways went, Alex could not imagine a more civilized escape. More of Lady Sun's people peeled away from the group each time she snapped her fingers, following carefully rehearsed instructions unknown to Alex, until only Reika, Alex and Lady Sun remained.

"Through here," Lady Sun instructed stepping to the left when the main corridor reached a T-junction.

A colossal thud from behind made Alex turn as they walked down the left-hand corridor. Behind them, the corridor was sealed by a solid, brick wall.

"That explains the lack of urgency," he said as Reika glanced over her shoulder.

"It won't slow them for long," Lady Sun replied. "Our best hope is that they follow the wrong group."

What Alex had taken to be a carefully orchestrated attempt to get everyone to safety took on a darker twist as Alex realized that Lady Sun had sent her people to act as decoys. No doubt Reika agreed with the tactic. There was a cold logic to the plan, maximizing the chances of many at the expense of the unfortunate few that fell into Daryl and Mitsuhide's clutches, that she would appreciate. It shocked Alex that he was not more appalled at the idea than he expected.

Alex's heart sank as his mind rationalized Lady Sun's actions. More importantly, he felt no remorse for the people that would inevitably die. He did not need to imagine what torture Daryl and Mitsuhide would inflict upon them for the memories were burned into his consciousness. He only felt relief that he would be spared the torment. The revelation left him cold.

Continuing in silence, Alex wondered if it was worth the pain. He would not be sorry to leave Hong Kong, that much was certain. The city of his birth was not his home. Hong Kong would forever be a place of suffering for him. Not just the suffering he endured at the hands of Mitsuhide and Daryl, but the suffering he witnessed in Kendra's eyes. He could not bring himself to call her mother. She lost that right when she denied him as a son. Alex was able to overlook being abandoned at birth, the circumstances leading to that decision may have made sense at the time, but he could not forgive her refusal to acknowledge his existence.

Alex wanted to blame the drugs. He wanted to pretend that Kendra's addiction was responsible for her decision making. So deep in her spiral, the desperate need to satiate her cravings would be undeniable, but the fact remained that Kendra was a stranger. Skylar was his family. Jeremy was his family. A messed-up family full of secrets and cursed truths, but a family all the same. A unit built on love, support and friendship. More than ever, Alex wished he could see his family. His real family.

Wiping a tear from his cheek, Alex quickened his pace at the feel of cool air on his skin. The oppressive stillness of the tunnels had not registered until he had the reassuring touch of a breeze for comparison. The sense of confinement was suddenly overwhelming as Alex thought back to being trapped in Daryl's cellar. His hands began to shake as a cold shiver traveled the length of his spine. Feeling his stomach knot, Alex broke into a run, desperate to escape his confines.

A hand on his collar stopped him. In a blind panic, he lashed out at Lady Sun, hammering his fist into her elbow to make her release him.

"Alex, stop," he heard Reika say, but his brain refused to listen. "Stop."

He kicked out as another hand grabbed his arm, his foot contacting with flesh. With a mighty heave, Alex tore free of Lady Sun's grip, his apprehension lending him the strength needed, but she was relentless in her efforts to restrain him.

"Stop," Reika repeated. She sounded further away. "We're trying to help you."

"No!" Alex screamed at the darkness. The fuzziness of his vision made the dimly lit corridor seem black as pitch. "Let me go!"

Struggling for breath, Alex's vision swam as he fought to escape. His legs trembled as he pawed faintly at the hand gripping his shoulder. A fist collided with his skull, making the darkness complete as he collapsed to the floor.

-77-

SOUTH CHINA SEA, WEST OF TAIWAN
July 22, 2029

Alex woke to find his sense of balance seriously off. His head throbbed as he forced his eyes open to see the ceiling swaying gently. Fearing the blow he took had knocked something loose in his skull, Alex closed his eyes and waited for the room to stop spinning. His stomach rolled as he continued to rock from side to side, despite his best efforts to bring his body under control. Unable to fight his instincts, Alex rolled to the side and vomited.

"It's about time," said Reika from across the room. "I was beginning to think you were going to sleep the entire way to Taipei."

"What?" Alex asked, attempting to pull himself up only to be sick again. "What happened? Where are we?"

Alex used his sleeve to wipe his mouth as Reika outlined their escape from Hong Kong. Following his outburst, Lady Sun knocked Alex out and carried him the remainder of the way. The tunnel they had taken brought them within a kilometer of the docks where Lady Sun already had a ship and crew on standby, a response to the evacuation signal from the hotel, and they quickly departed Hong Kong.

"All in all, a fairly uneventful escape," Reika concluded. Stowed away in the hold of the ship, she had made herself comfortable on a chair built from sacks of flour. "Apart from your panic attack."

"It wasn't a panic attack," Alex said, a reflex response to the connotations of the term. "I thought we were taking too long is all."

Reika stared at him as he sat up, taking a moment to steady himself on the bed of sacks they had laid him on. It was a knowing look he had come to despise. There was no judgment or scorn in her eyes, but Reika had a way of making Alex feel stupid and childish for denying what she already knew.

"Okay," he conceded, looking around the room. "Maybe I panicked."

Sunlight streamed in through a porthole in the starboard wall, bathing the room in a warm radiance that Alex had not felt in a long time. He took a moment to drink in the calming effect of the ambiance, amplified by the oak paneling on the walls, and felt his stomach settle a little as he embraced the situation. Free of the dangers of Hong Kong, he felt a step closer to normality.

"What happened to Lady Sun?" he asked as he tested his legs.

"In there," Reika replied, nodding to a crate at the far end of the room. "Safest place for her until we reach Taipei."

Alex staggered as he adjusted to the rocking of the boat. "Why Taipei?"

Reika closed her eyes and settled back into her makeshift armchair. "Madame Qiao operated a private service out of the city's airport. Lady Sun has assured me we will be able to secure discreet passage back to Los Angeles. Assuming you're okay to fly."

Alex sat back down, fearing his knees would buckle from the shaking in his legs. "What do you mean?"

Reika gave him another of her looks as he fought to stop rhythmically clenching and unclenching his fists. His heartbeat was rising in response to the tightening he felt in his chest, and his throat felt dry.

"Focus on my voice," said Reika as she sat forward. "Ignore everything else. I'm going to count slowly. I want you to join in, but only on the even numbers. Are you ready?"

Alex placed his palms against his temples and shook his head.

"One," said Reika as she rose to her feet.

"Two," she continued as Alex began rocking back and forth.

"Three."

"Four."

Alex's panicked gaze darted around the room as Reika gently took hold of his hands. Thin, ragged breaths passed through his lungs as he searched for a way out. The door was so far away, and his legs were shaking so much.

"Focus on my voice, Alex," said Reika as she knelt before him. "Count with me. Five."

Alex locked eyes with Reika as she counted to six. Drawing strength from her placid demeanor, Alex nodded as she spoke the word seven.

"Eight," they said in unison. Alex's voice was hesitant. His eyes flicked to the side, taking in the crate that housed a monster. He was trapped on the ocean with a bloodsucking fiend.

"Nine," Reika continued. Her voice was flat. The emotionless delivery cut through Alex's scattered thoughts.

"Ten," said Alex, turning his attention back to Reika. He had to block out the chaos and focus on her voice.

Alex felt his chest relax as they counted. At twenty, Reika stopped counting the even numbers, letting Alex take the lead. The first time she skipped a number caught him off guard, threatening to skew his focus, but he persevered as they alternated their count. His breaths became more consistent as the numbers climbed into the forties, and the shaking in his thighs was almost gone by ninety.

"Do you think you can go above deck?" Reika asked after he reached one hundred.

Alex shook his head. "Not yet."

Although he felt like he was calling the shots, he did not want to chance another episode by forcing his mind and body to deal with more changes. The present scenario was taxing enough.

"What's the plan when we get to LA?" he asked as Reika unscrewed the cap of a water bottle and handed it to him.

"That depends on you," Reika replied as he gulped half the bottle down. "I'm a tracker. Reconciling the aftermath of my findings is not my strong suit. My advice… Seek help. I'm no psychologist, but it's clear to me that you have some issues to work through. And for good reason."

"I…" Alex began, feeling like he needed to say something but not sure what to say.

"Or don't," Reika continued, returning to her seat. "But you'll need to get better at lying if you hope to hide it."

"I don't know where to start," said Alex after emptying the bottle.

"You just did. Acknowledging you have a problem is the first step to fixing it."

Alex sighed and looked at the crate, wondering for what transgression he was being punished. To think that the biggest problem facing him at the start of the year was finding his parents. It seemed like such an impossible task at the time. No rational person would have predicted that his search would drop him into a supernatural civil war between vampires and whatever Mitsuhide and Daryl were supposed to be.

-78-

SOUTH CHINA SEA, WEST OF TAIWAN
July 23, 2029

The waves lapped gently against the side of the boat, creating a soothing environment as Alex stared out over the calm waters at the radiant but not quite full moon. Once, he would have laughed at being both literally and figuratively all at sea, but the reality of his situation made laughter impossible. Turning at the sound of the cabin door opening, Alex saw Lady Sun emerge into the night air. Pulling a long silk gown around her, she strolled across the deck to join him at the rail, her presence a reminder of how distorted his reality had become.

"I thought vampires couldn't cross flowing water," said Alex, turning his attention back to the sea.

"Superstition," Lady Sun replied, resting her forearms on the taffrail. "Rivers and streams are convenient borders. Think of how many rivers are used to denote boundaries on human maps. It is much the same for vampires. We do not cross into the territory of another unless invited. Or at war. Without a passport, you cannot legally enter a foreign country. That does not mean you cannot physically go there."

"True," Alex conceded, studying Lady Sun's face as she spoke. There was a sorrow to her expression and tone that Alex had not expected. "It's not all superstition though, is it? I mean, you hid in a crate from the sun."

"The line between superstition and reality is blurry. There is a rumor that Vlad, the father of all modern vampires, could walk in the sunlight. If it is true, that gift was lost for his children. As for superstitions like not being able to walk on hallowed ground or being burned by holy water, that varies from vampire to vampire. For example, I am a Taoist. I have no belief in the power of western gods. They have no power over me. A Christian vampire, like Vlad, would be fearful of the wrath of his God, making the cross and holy water useful weapons."

"Are you trying to tell me that vampires can believe themselves invulnerable?"

Lady Sun turned and gave him a pitying look. "Have you received no education on your foe?"

Alex shook his head. "I didn't even know I had a foe."

"Then your master is a failure. If this is what the Order of Solemn Guardians of Body and Blood and of the Holy Light has come to, it is no surprise the council pushes their luck. Much as a person who believes that dairy makes them sick will feel sick when they knowingly eat dairy, vampires can be harmed by those things they believe will harm them. And, just like somebody who is allergic to dairy, a vampire's belief cannot protect them from the things that will harm them. There is no placebo for decapitation."

"You're going to have to back this right the way up," Alex replied as he rubbed his forehead. "What is the Order of Bloody Guardians of Holy Light?"

"You," Lady Sun replied, turning to face him. "You are the Order of Solemn Guardians of Body and Blood and of the Holy Light. You, and your mother, and her father, and all their ancestors. Right back to the original guardians."

"Original guardians," Alex mused, struggling to wrap his head around the sudden history lesson. "That would be this Order of Heroes of Might and Magic, or whatever they called themselves? Like the Knights Templar?"

It was Lady Sun's turn to shake her head in disbelief. "If this is the training a neophyte guardian receives, we are all doomed. It is no wonder our mistress wanted you watched. What do you know about the guardians?"

"Only what Madame Qiao told me," Alex replied, turning his gaze back to the sea in embarrassment. "That I'm supposed to be one."

"How did I get this assignment?" Lady Sun asked the sea before turning back to Alex. "Short version. Forty-nine guardians were created using a magic potion in 1583..."

Despite himself, Alex chuckled at the mention of a magic potion, earning an irate glower from Lady Sun as she pressed on.

"...Forty-two died fighting the council to a stalemate. The council and the guardians agreed to a truce in 1763. The seven original guardians still alive became known as the Elder Monks of the Order of the Guardian Knights. They are the ones who should have told you all this.

Any offspring of the original guardians were trained to fight vampires. Some of those neophytes had powers and became guardians. Some, like you, don't."

"So, there's a whole bloodline thing in play?" Alex asked when it became clear Lady Sun thought that her history lesson explained everything. "But it's recessive. Like being ginger?"

"Or being left-handed," Lady Sun said with a nod. "But it never goes away. You can't breed it out like a bad gene. A descendent of the original forty-nine can become a true guardian, even if nobody before them had powers."

"Okay," said Alex, suddenly remembering he was talking to a vampire and surprising himself with how little it bothered him. "Let's back this up. If I'm the Typhoid Mary of guardian powers, how many others are there?"

"I don't know this Mary you speak of, but you can't infect people with guardian powers," said Lady Sun, leaning on the taffrail and looking out to sea again. "There were fourteen bloodlines from the original guardians. Four are still active. One of them is your family."

"Do you know who they are?" Alex asked, a glimmer of hope forming that Lady Sun might know other members of his family. "Brothers? Sisters? Cousins?"

Lady Sun shook her head. "Only you and your mother remain in your bloodline. Skylar is the last of her bloodline. Then you have-"

"Skylar!" Alex interrupted, grabbing Lady Sun's shoulder and turning her to face him. "Skylar is a guardian!"

The glare that Lady Sun gave him made Alex quickly remove his hand and back away. For the first time in their conversation, he felt afraid of the woman stood on deck with him. And rightly so. Remembering how she had lifted him by the throat, Alex shuddered.

"Skylar is a neophyte, like you," said Lady Sun as she adjusted her robe and settled back into leaning on the taffrail. "My mistress told you this already."

Alex gripped the handrail and closed his eyes, silently counting to ten before continuing. "That's not what I meant. Mitsuhide and Daryl were testing my blood. I didn't understand it at the time, but she said she was interested in what I was. If they didn't find what they were looking for in my blood, they'll be going after Sky next."

"We have long suspected that the spawn is experimenting on herself. She took you to obtain guardian DNA. If she could not extract it from you, she will not get it from your sister."

"Are you sure?" Alex asked, his voice tinged with anxiety. "Knowing I'm not a guardian didn't stop them coming to the hotel to recapture me."

"They weren't there for your blood. They were destroying the evidence. Anyway, women can't be guardians. Daryl needs an activated guardian."

"Then we need to warn the active guardians."

Lady Sun shook her head despondently. "There are no active guardians, only the original knights. None of the council would risk going after one of them."

-79-

ODESA OBLAST, UKRAINE
July 23, 2029

Iosif looked at his phone. Only a minute since he had last looked, but at least he got to see his daughter's smiling face again. It had been many years since he had seen Mariela in person and even more since he had seen her smile. The photograph on his phone's lock screen was from a happier time, a photo of a little girl that had suffered so much since.

Mariela's smiling face was both a welcome sight and a painful reminder, but Iosif would have done anything to see his daughter smile, genuinely smile, once more. Even on her wedding day, the last time Iosif had seen her, Mariela's smile was a carefully constructed mask intended to convince the audience that everything was awesome and nothing would spoil her big day. When he had looked into her eyes, Mariela's mask slipped briefly, showing Iosif that her pain was still there; a distant memory, but one she would never forget.

Iosif looked at his phone again. Another minute had passed. Regrets about what had happened would fix nothing now. The suffering his father had inflicted could not be undone so Iosif focused on the future and making sure nobody would be able to hurt his daughter like that again. If doing that meant killing this charlatan priest then he would do so without hesitation.

Although Iosif avoided direct involvement in the war between his master and the monks who oppressed them, Lukai's offer was too tempting to ignore. The monks were strong but not invulnerable, and Lukai had prepared an especially powerful poison to use on this monk.

The monks were members of an organization created by the church nearly five hundred years ago to fight the undead, that much Iosif knew. The tales of their ability to hurl fireballs or erect walls of solid air, however, were too fanciful for Iosif to take seriously. If they were as powerful as the stories made out then it was inconceivable that they would have failed to eliminate the vampires over the course of five hundred years. It was far more likely that they were just some artificially enhanced super soldiers.

Placing his phone in his pocket, Iosif thought of how the Malinovskyi family history might have been different, for Iosif was descended from one of those who had gone to Rome to become one of the monks. Alas, it had not been so. The tale of betrayal was one that had been told and retold through the generations, with each re-telling becoming more embellished. The version his grandmother had told him was of how brave and bold Pietr Malinovskyi went forth to Rome seeking to become a knight in a new order that was being created to push back against the forces of evil.

With the encroachment of Protestantism in his homeland, Pietr believed that having a local knight join this new knightly order would instill a sense of pride and solidarity in his community that they might better ward themselves against those who sought to undermine their faith. His ambition was to be thwarted, however, when he answered the challenge of an Irish bard who dared to put himself forward for selection.

Pietr had fought bravely and with honor, but the Irishman was a wily trickster who used magic and witchcraft to overcome his opponents. Aided by faeries and other spirit creatures, he was able to turn aside Pietr's blade, avoiding every thrust, before turning his magic on Pietr and felling him with an ensorcelled blow. Stunned, Pietr had demanded a rematch but the Irishman refused. Others attempted to defeat the Irishman but they too suffered the same fate, falling to sorcery and enchantment.

The confusion cast upon him by the Irishman lasted for the entire tournament, his spell causing Pietr to struggle against far less formidable opponents. Pietr raised objections with the church when it was revealed the Irishman was selected while brave knights like Pietr had been confounded by his magic and lost their opportunity. The church dismissed his claims that the Irishman cheated and told Pietr to return home and serve his community. When Pietr did return home, it was not with a message of hope from the church but a sorrowful story. From that day forward, the Malinovskyi family were sworn enemies of the order.

Adrian's book signing tour was in its final week when he arrived at Iosif's bookstore. If he arrived at Iosif's store. He was late, and Iosif was beginning to get agitated. Not because of the crowd, only three people had turned up to have their copies signed, a damning indictment of Adrian's literary success, but because Iosif got edgy when things did not go according to plan.

Twenty minutes after the agreed time, the little bell above the door tinkled to announce the arrival of an aging man in an old, tweed jacket. Instinctively, Iosif knew this man to be his target.

"I'm so sorry," Adrian apologized as he entered the store. "Today has been one problem after another. I'm so grateful to you all for waiting."

Iosif heaved a sigh of relief and showed Adrian to the area that had been prepared for his signing session. With the benefit of hindsight, Iosif would have made less of an effort to prepare an area for Adrian's fans. The seventy chairs that were arranged for Adrian to give a question and answer forum looked ridiculous with only three attendees.

"Would you like a drink?" Iosif asked as Adrian clumsily slipped one arm out of his jacket. The show of frailty was wasted on Iosif.

"A black coffee would be most appreciated," replied Adrian, unhooking his jacket from the other arm and placing it over the back of his chair.

Iosif nodded and disappeared into the small kitchen at the back of the store. As he waited for the kettle to boil, Iosif lifted the vial of poison from his pocket and held it to the light. To think an act as simple as pouring the dark liquid into the monk's coffee was all it took to propel his daughter into Lukai's upper management. Happy to be doing something good for Mariela, Iosif returned to the store with a smile on his face, setting the coffee alongside Adrian as he signed the books of the three teenage girls.

Adrian's novel was about an agent of the Security Service of Ukraine who discovers a conspiracy involving the kidnap of young adults by a coven of witches. It was riddled with plot holes, not least of which was the fact that there was no explanation of why the witches were even taking their victims. Even the explanation about why the local police were involved seemed contrived. Iosif found completing the book to be a chore. It was no wonder Adrian's signing tour had not generated much of a turnout.

"Will we find out what happened to Alexei after he was attacked by the Fomorian?" One girl asked.

"Oh yes," Adrian answered enthusiastically, taking a sip of the coffee. "I have plans to make this book into a thirteen-book series. I might even do some spin-offs that focus on some of the other characters and their histories."

Iosif groaned inwardly at the prospect of a whole series of these books. Worse still would be if they made them into a series of films starring some blank-faced, talentless actress in the lead role.

"As a priest yourself," another girl enquired with a boldness that suggested she had her argument all worked out before arrival. "Do you receive any criticism for what could be seen as a glorification of revenge and unbridled violence against those who do you harm? As a member of the church, shouldn't your message be one of compassion, tolerance and forgiveness? Would it not be more fitting for the sinners to find their absolution and repent of their unholy ways?"

Iosif revised his headcount down from three fans to two as Adrian attempted to explain his stance to the girl who had only turned up to criticize the author and his book in person. It was a rare thing to see the youth engage in intelligent debate instead of simply pouring out their scorn and derision on the internet. Iosif watched as the girl ran rings around Adrian, demonstrating an intellect beyond her years by quoting scripture that any true priest should have countered with ease and forcing the fake priest to become more flustered.

Adrian glanced at Iosif imploringly, hoping that Iosif would intervene and call the session to an end, but the more flustered he became, the more he sipped his coffee. Then, disaster struck.

To Iosif, the whole sequence played out in slow motion. Attempting to stall for time and come up with a plausible response to the girl's latest criticism, Adrian took another sip then placed the cup back down, catching the saucer at an awkward angle and forcing the cup to tip. He scrabbled to catch the cup, but it upended, spilling the remainder of the coffee. Iosif estimated that a quarter of the contents were now flowing across the desk and dripping onto the store carpet.

"I think that will be enough for today," Iosif called, bringing the session to an end as he grabbed some cloths and mopped up the spilled liquid. "Thank you very much for coming girls."

As the coffee soaked into the rags, Iosif wondered if it would be enough. Lukai had told him the poison was strong enough to kill a monk, but he had not told him how much a fatal dose was. The girls collected their belongings and left, providing Iosif with the opportunity to close the store.

"I'm sorry," Adrian said, standing shakily. "I'm not usually so clumsy. I don't know what has come over me."

The old man's pale face and bloodshot eyes made it clear to Iosif the poison was having an effect, but he had already decided he could not leave things to chance. For his daughter, he had to make sure the monk was dead. Lukai's threat was not an idle one. Against the monks of legend, Iosif would have stood no chance, but his opponent was an elderly man suffering from a dose of poison that was hampering his abilities. Stepping close, Iosif slipped the knife that he had kept concealed up his sleeve between the monk's ribs.

"Lukai sends his regards."

Despite his age and the poison coursing through his veins, the monk was strong and fought back against Iosif as he repeatedly jabbed with the knife. The struggle was brief but violent, ending when the monk collapsed back onto the table, blood coating his chest. Iosif had taken a few knocks as the monk fought to push him away but nothing serious enough to warrant medical attention. The monk's breathing became more labored with each rise and fall of his chest. Iosif knew it would soon cease but, for good measure, he plunged his knife into Adrian's chest once more, leaving it buried up to the hilt.

Iosif thought of Mariela as he wiped the blood from his hands, using the coffee-soaked rags, before taking out his phone and checking the time again. Lukai would be proud. Hopefully, proud enough to reward Iosif with the blood kiss. Becoming a vampire held no interest for Iosif, but it would grant him the strength to return to his daughter and make up for failing her all those years ago.

Iosif looked up from the phone as the building shook. Books fell from the shelves as plaster fell from the ceiling. Iosif glanced across at the monk as the shaking increased. Adrian's eyes were open, boring into the ceiling, and clouds of dust swirled around his body. Perhaps the legends of their magic were true, but there was no time to contemplate that now. Leaving the monk's crippled body to be crushed to powder by the collapsing building, Iosif dashed to the door. More plaster fell, bringing a section of the ceiling with it. Iosif dodged, cutting to the right and continuing to the door. Before he could make it across the room, a bookcase collapsed across the entrance.

The back door. Iosif turned and ran for the rear exit to the building, leaping over another bookcase that had fallen. The door was locked. Coughing from the dust, Iosif searched his pockets. Nothing. The keys must have fallen out of his pocket during the struggle. Iosif looked to where the monk lay, crushed under a fallen ceiling joist, as the building collapsed around him, his thoughts of Mariela extinguished as the roof came down upon him.

VENTURA COUNTY, CALIFORNIA
July 26, 2029

Using the two halves of the eggshell, Skylar separated the yolk from another egg and dropped it into Cali's dish. This weekend would be the last chance to take that canyon ride she promised Mike. After nearly dying, there was nothing that would convince her to delay some much-needed fun any longer.

"Where are we staying?" Mike asked as he slipped his boots on.

If Skylar was going to take the bikes out, it was not going to be a quick jaunt up to the canyons and back.

"We'll know when we get there," she told him as she sprinkled some chopped chives into the egg whites she was scrambling. "I just want to ride. Pick a new direction each day and go. No agenda, no place to be by a given time. No need to do anything, unless the mood takes us. One weekend of carefree living."

"Okay," he replied after a moment's thought. "Sounds fun."

"Awesome," said Skylar, sliding her scrambled eggs onto a plate and shutting off the heat. "Give me five to eat this and we'll head out."

"Don't you need to pack?"

"We'll buy what we need on the way. If I pack, I'll have to plan what I need, and that would be defeating the object. I've spent months worrying about who's doing what. It's time to let my hair down."

One plate of eggs later, Skylar was slipping into her leathers when Mike signaled he was ready with two engine revs in swift succession. Skylar liked to think of it as the motorcycle equivalent of military hand signals as Mike's V-Rod let out a mighty roar that her 1200 Custom swiftly answered. The ritual was so ingrained in their lives that no further dialogue was needed. On this occasion, there was something different about the signal.

Skylar zipped up the side of her boots and gave herself a once-over in the mirror. Satisfied no chives were stuck in her teeth, she tucked her pendant inside her shirt and strolled out to the yard.

"Thought you might have wheeled the Fat Boy out," said Skylar, tying her hair in a loose ponytail and tucking it under her jacket, so it wouldn't whip around while riding.

"It's been a while since the old girl had a spin," Mike replied, fastening the chin strap on his helmet before slipping on his gloves. "Is the Sportster good for you? Thought you might prefer something you knew was comfortable on long journeys."

Skylar smiled at Mike's devotion. As tempting as it was to take out one of the sportier bikes, Skylar wanted to know she would be able to walk after spending the weekend riding. Abandoning plans and freewheeling it did not mean sacrificing comfort.

Straddling her bike, Skylar flipped a coin to determine if they headed east or west, resulting in them heading for Santa Clarita. Turning north before they reached the city, their journey took them around Castaic Lagoon and up through the mountains to Lake Hughes. Guiding her bike along the mountain road, uncaring where the road would lead them, was a wonderful release. Skylar felt the year's accumulated stress begin to ebb away as mile after mile passed by under the scorching summer sun.

Granted the time to take stock, Skylar saw that her life had become consumed lately. Consumed by meetings. Consumed by phone calls. Consumed by deadlines and reports until she lost sight of the human element of it all and found herself thinking in terms of numbers and charts. Without realizing it, she had drifted toward being a cog in the bureaucratic machine. A well paid and highly respected cog, but a cog nonetheless. Was this what Mariela was trying to warn her about? Perhaps she was right; being out of the bureau might be a good thing.

After a brief coffee stop in Lake Hughes, Mike and Skylar turned north and took the 99 to Fresno. Skylar's thoughts on becoming a private investigator were interrupted as Mike pulled up next to her and waved before overtaking, pumping the air with his fist. Smiling at the routine of leapfrogging each other whenever they went out on an excursion, Skylar pushed thoughts of the future to one side and opened the throttle. With almost six months until the baby was due, there was plenty of time to decide what to do with her career.

Waking in the hospital after the awards dinner, Skylar's first thought was for the health of her baby. Distracted by Mike's distress and her own decision to offer a deal to the man responsible, Skylar missed the red light. From what she was told, it was a close call, but the baby was going to be okay. The doctors called it a little miracle that they both pulled through. The way Mariela retold the sequence of events, it sounded like Skylar was packing for a trip upstairs.

As her bike whizzed past Mike, Skylar wondered how much her near-death experience influenced her decision to live in the now. It was hard to tell. The whole thing sounded unreal to Skylar. Slapping the front of her helmet to banish thoughts of mortality, Skylar focused on the road in front of her.

"Steak for lunch?" Skylar asked over the headset as they approached the Fresno city limits.

"Sure," Mike replied. "Sounds good to me."

Traffic in Fresno had other ideas. Skylar's intentions of seeking out a great steakhouse were upended by construction-related tailbacks, complicated by an overturned trailer. Easing their bikes through the traffic was an option, but Skylar wasn't keen on ruining a, thus far, great ride fighting her way through a congested city.

"Fuck this. How about some fast food and back on the road?" she asked Mike as she inched her bike through the gap between two cars.

"Sure. Anywhere in particular?"

"As long as the food is more nutritious than the packaging. We can get some proper food when we stop for the night."

"I saw a pizza place about a mile back if you wanna swing around at the next junction. Puts us heading back to the 99 with less traffic."

Turning around at the next junction was easier said than done thanks to a city bus that blocked the junction, adding to the traffic chaos. Fresno's dedication to autonomous vehicles lagged Los Angeles' and resulted in the scene unfolding before them. The constant barrage of vehicles trying to squeeze past the bus had rendered it immobile as its sensors continuously registered a hazard.

"I have no intention of spending the rest of the day waiting for a bus," Skylar said as a gap appeared in the traffic.

Creeping forward, she began turning her bike back toward the 99. In her peripheral vision, she saw the bus lurch forward. Skylar's heart skipped a beat at the prospect of having her bike crushed beneath a city bus, not to mention her bones. Mangled in traffic was not how she wanted to depart this world. Mercifully, the bus only moved an inch or two as it momentarily registered a clear field ahead of it. The sensors arrested its forward motion, preventing the bus from turning her into paste as she slipped through.

"Regretting the 'wherever I may roam' decision yet?" Mike asked as they tucked into their first slice of pizza, a little over a half-hour later.

Skylar grunted in response as she peeled the melted cheese off and tossed the base back in the box. It wasn't worth risking life and limb for. It did, however, fill a gap. Mike seemed less concerned with the crappy quality of the food as he chatted with the waiter about everything and nothing.

Unable to focus on the conversation, Skylar pulled out her phone and fired off some emails. There was no harm in sounding out the idea of going into business for herself. Asking questions did not commit her to anything. Her attention was brought back to the present as Mike settled the bill and lifted his helmet from the chair next to him.

"Which way next?"

"Reckon we can hit San Andreas by nightfall?"

Mike gave Skylar a disappointed look. "I thought we weren't setting any targets of being someplace by some time."

"Good point. Let's head for San Andreas and see what happens," Skylar replied as she slid her jacket on and picked up her helmet.

Apart from the heavy traffic around Fresno, the ride north to San Andreas was reasonably smooth. Having eaten little of the pizza, Skylar's stomach was rumbling as they searched the outskirts of San Andreas for a suitable hotel. Avoiding the major chains in favor of something more characterful, they settled on a charming little place with a restaurant on the premises that also had live music.

"If you're interested in blues, our live act this evening will be on stage in about thirty-five minutes," said the receptionist, a spritely man in his late fifties, as he handed Mike their room key. "A charming lady from the United Kingdom. Highly recommended."

"Really? Which part?" Skylar asked. "I grew up in the UK."

"Stoking Trent or something. Can't say as I've heard of the place before, but I've never heard of a lot of places. Only once I ever left California. Didn't much care for it."

"Stoke-on-Trent," Skylar replied with a nod. "I've visited a few cities but not that one. Do we need to reserve a table or just turn up?"

"No reservations, sorry. First come, first served."

"That's fine," said Skylar, thanking the receptionist and heading to the elevator.

"Let me guess," said Mike, yawning heavily as they entered the elevator, "we'd be eating somewhere else if tables needed to be reserved."

Skylar smiled as she took his hand and rested her head on his shoulder. "Spur of the moment only. No reservations allowed."

The room was smaller than Skylar would have liked. Not that it mattered; all they needed was a place to sleep and shower. Emerging from the bathroom, having rinsed the dust of the road from her face, Skylar was disappointed to see Mike had drifted off to sleep. Stepping over to the bed to rouse him, Skylar paused, her hand an inch from his shoulder.

Unwilling to disturb the serene expression on Mike's face, Skylar dragged the thin blanket over him and headed for the door. Remembering the haunted look in his eyes whenever a conversation turned to the outbreak, Skylar hoped the change of pace and randomness of the day had given him the sense of release it had given her as she turned out the light and went to eat alone.

-81-

CALAVERAS COUNTY, CALIFORNIA
July 27, 2029

Having slept on it, Skylar decided to pursue her idea of setting up as a private investigator further. Given that Wagner had yet to discover admissible evidence of a conspiracy, she couldn't do any worse flying solo. Enthused by the prospect of a new challenge, her overactive mind could not wait to get stuck into the details. Rising before the sun, Skylar cursed her restlessness and decided she might as well get up and shower, washing the exhaustion from her body while she waited for Mike to rise.

As the water cascaded over her naked flesh, Skylar felt her energy levels rise. The warmth of the water, combined with the gentle pulse of the shower and the herbal fragrances of the shower gel, served to drain the tension out of her limbs and clear any lingering desire for sleep from her mind. Deliberating over what type of cases she would take on, Skylar ran her soapy hands over her body, wiping away the grime of yesterday.

There was something different. The warm air, filled with vapor from the shower, seemed to radiate with energy. Her skin tingled with a thousand electric shocks wherever the water landed. It was a strange but not unpleasant feeling, more like the sensation of a balloon held over the arm after being rubbed on wool than the sharp sting of touching an earthed object after walking over nylon carpet.

Skylar tilted her head back, allowing the water to play over her scalp and face, trickling down between her breasts, as her hand moved down over her stomach. The energy of life she felt in the air helped lower her inhibitions as her hand moved down, the air vibrating around her as she slid her middle finger through her pubic hair. Circling her clit, Skylar gently squeezed her breast with her other hand. Her knees began to quiver as she explored herself, the rush of endorphins as she sated her desire driving her onward.

Bracing herself with a hand against the wall, to avoid collapsing as her knees shook furiously, Skylar continued to pleasure herself until she neared climax. Throwing her back against the wall, she parted her legs slightly and grabbed the retractable showerhead with her free hand. Twisting the dial to produce a single, powerful stream of water, Skylar held her labia open and directed the stream against her exposed clit, shuddering as the jets of water, designed to provide a massaging effect, worked their magic.

Slowly, Skylar slid down the wall as an intense orgasm took control of her body. Dropping the showerhead, she ran her palm over her hair and down the side of her face as the waves of pleasure subsided. Her hand came to a rest on her chest as she drew short, sharp breaths. After a moment to recover, Skylar removed her other hand from her crotch and got back to her feet. Satisfied, she quickly rinsed herself and shut off the flow of water. Mike was still under the covers when she returned to the bedroom and got herself ready to face the day.

"Morning, sleepyhead," Skylar said when he raised his head, the sound of her getting ready stirring him from his half-asleep state.

"Morning, hun. Up long?"

"Could say that. Trouble sleeping," she said as Mike climbed out of bed and headed for the bathroom. "Been up for about an hour or so."

"Really?" He asked, stopping at the bathroom door. "You should have woken me. We could be on the road by now. What have you been doing all that time?"

Myself, Skylar thought, but the filter between her brain and mouth caught it. "Oh, this and that."

He nodded, a warm smile on his face as he stepped into the bathroom. "Okay, don't tell me. Give me five minutes to take a quick shower then we'll make a move."

Skylar heard the flow of water through the open door as Mike scrubbed himself clean. Scanning the room to make sure she had not left anything, she picked up her jacket and walked over to the bathroom.

"I'm going to go on down. Don't take forever. I don't want to be left waiting around by the bikes while you jerk off. And no pissing in the shower, either."

"Where am I meant to do it?" he shouted as Skylar turned and made her way out of the room, typing out a series of text messages as she went.

Given the hour, they decided not to linger in San Andreas and instead put some miles on the clock. After a brief diversion to buy new clothes as they skirted the edge of San Jose, Mike and Skylar picked up the coast road and headed south to Santa Barbara. With an entire day to kill and no specific goal in mind, they took their time and savored the fresh breeze sweeping in from the ocean as they rode.

With the bare bones of a plan in her mind, Skylar floated the idea of going freelance past Mike as they pulled off the main road south of Carmel and guided their bikes along a dusty road. He liked the idea of it being non-profit, as the expense of a private investigator was a barrier for many, but worried it might not be practical.

"Don't worry," Skylar told him as she turned off her engine and rested the bike on its stand. "I won't be taking on lost cat searches. I'm thinking of cases like the one Chief Parker brought me. Ones the police need help with when the feds can't spare anyone. It's not like I need the income from a regular paid job, just enough to cover expenses."

The more she thought about Mariela's suggestion, the more it made sense. Skylar's sizeable monthly stipend, left to her in her grandfather's will, was enough that she could live comfortably without working and would cover them until she came into her full inheritance on her thirtieth birthday. Getting out from the bindings of the bureau would also give her the freedom to pursue cases her way. She would not be able to cover as much ground without an office full of agents, but she could afford to be more selective, picking up the cases the FBI could not. Without having to answer to institutional higher-ups, she could make a more personal difference to people.

"Probably worth having a chat with Dave," said Mike, lifting the visor of his helmet as Skylar removed hers, "see if he can set you up with a contract for the LAPD."

"Maybe," Skylar answered as she hooked her helmet on her handlebars and wandered over to a tall, wooden gate barring the road. "I was thinking of staying local. Plenty of people needing help in the Santa Paula area. That's if I decide to go ahead with it. I'd be giving up so much that I've worked hard for."

The idea of a contract with the city was an intriguing one and worth further exploration provided she worked cases on her terms. It was the idea of being beholden to anybody that troubled Skylar. If she was going to do this, it would need to be with nobody calling the shots but her. That was a problem for another day. Today was about the ride and freedom from responsibilities.

"What are you doing?" Mike asked as Skylar began scaling the gate.

Skylar turned and looked back at him, hanging from the top of the gate with one arm, the tip of her boot barely able to fit onto the gate's central crossbeam. Growing up in Carmel, Skylar had heard stories that the old farmhouse at the end of the road they turned down was haunted. Abandoned when the last owner died at the beginning of the year, Skylar figured she was unlikely to get a better chance to find out for herself what spirits roamed the farmstead.

"It's private property," Mike reminded her as Skylar swung her legs over the gate and dropped to the other side.

"Don't be such a party pooper," Skylar replied as her phone pinged.

Opening her phone while she waited for Mike to join her, Skylar glanced down the road toward the farmhouse, hidden from view by the undulation of the road. Her friends in college and university used to tease her for believing in ghosts, but they were not attuned to the supernatural like she was. For as long as she could remember, Skylar fancied she could sense the presence of spirits. There were plenty of haunted houses in Britain, and her skin would always prickle when she visited one. If the connection to the spirit world was thin enough, her hands would begin tingling and her eyes would burn. Skylar was getting none of those sensations from the farmhouse ahead of them.

"Mariela's already offered to help me draw up a business plan," Skylar said as Mike landed on the road next to her.

"Not surprised. She doesn't like seeing you stressed any less than I do. Can we go now?"

"I thought you didn't want to see me stressed," Skylar replied as she grabbed Mike's hand and dragged him toward the farmhouse. "Seeing if this place really is haunted will help me unwind."

"I can't see there being many ghosts out this late in the morning," said Mike, putting up a token resistance as they headed along the road. "We should contact the owners and make arrangements to visit at night."

"The owner's dead, Mike. The place is being auctioned off next month. We need to seize the opportunity now."

Far too rarely Skylar lived in the moment. Even when it was a moment designed for that express purpose, like attending a party or hiking in the mountains, her mind was always too preoccupied with tasks and plans to truly cut loose. From deciphering the next piece of a puzzle at work to analyzing the social dynamics at a public event, there was always something occupying her thoughts.

"Told you," Mike said as they circled the building, Skylar peering into every dust-covered window she could reach. "All the ghosts have gone into town for brunch."

"You may be right," Skylar said as she stepped up onto the porch and rattled the door handle. "I'm not getting any ghostly vibes from this place."

"Does that mean we can go now?" Mike asked as he joined her on the porch.

"Aww, is my company not enough to keep you entertained?" Skylar replied in her most sarcastic tone.

"It's not you," said Mike, kissing her on the cheek as she stepped over to a swing bench at the end of the porch and ran her hand over one of its chains, "it's me. Boring old buildings don't do it for me."

"Hmm. Let me see if I can change your mind."

Without warning, Skylar pushed Mike onto the swing bench. Even with her holding onto one of the chains, it threatened to tip Mike onto the floor as his weight plonked down on the bench. It was far from a graceful landing, but he quickly gathered his composure as Skylar dropped to her knees in front of him and reached for his belt.

"What? Here?" Mike asked as she pulled the leather strap free from its buckle.

"Why not? The place is empty."

"But we're outside," Mike replied as she unzipped him and reached inside his pants. "At somebody else's house."

"Wouldn't be the first time," Skylar replied as she wrapped her hand around his flaccid penis. "At least your cousin won't catch us here."

Mike let out a soft groan as he responded to her touch. As much magic as Skylar's fingers worked that morning, the feel of his dick hardening in her hand made her throb with anticipation. Reaching down and unbuttoning her leathers, Skylar slowly lowered her head.

"What was that?" she said, pausing with Mike's penis only an inch from her lips.

"What?"

"I thought I heard something," Skylar replied, lifting her head and looking out over the farmstead.

"I didn't hear anyth-"

Mike's reply was cut short by the loud crack of a shotgun going off to the east.

"Okay, that I heard," said Mike, cramming his dick into his leathers as Skylar leaped to her feet. "Let's get the fuck out of here."

"No arguments from me."

Another blast caused splinters of wood to fly from the patio rail as they dashed for cover putting the house between them and their assailant.

"No good, thieving trespassers," a voice shouted from the field. "Get off my land."

"I thought this place was supposed to be abandoned," Mike said as they crept to the edge of the building and peered around the corner.

"It was," Skylar replied turning her head to the front of the house at the sound of the shotgun being reloaded. "We'll have to run for it."

Breaking into a sprint as they left the cover of the house, Mike and Skylar ran for all they were worth. There was no cover between the house and the gate, giving their assailant a clear shot if they did not crest the small rise quick enough. Feeling like the air was picking her legs up and making her movements effortless, Skylar hurtled up the slope. Mike was trailing behind her, unusual given his athletic prowess, so she slowed her pace to allow him to catch up.

"Jesus," Mike gasped as they crested the hill and began descending toward the gate. "Talk about speed of the puma."

Slowing slightly to look behind her, Skylar saw the roof of the farmhouse disappear below the ridge in the road. The gate was close, but there was no way of knowing if their pursuer was closer. Focusing on the gate, Skylar sped up, her legs pumping, and leaped.

"Sky," Mike said, panting as he dropped down from the gate and ran to the bikes. "How did you do that?"

Skylar shook her head as she threw her leg over her bike and grabbed her helmet from the handlebars. One second, she was jumping to grab the top of the gate, the next, she was rolling to avoid a botched landing, her leap having cleared the gate.

"Adrenaline, maybe," she said, thinking of the stories of mothers lifting cars off their children. "Now isn't the time to analyze it."

"Yeah, adrenaline. Maybe," Mike replied, his voice coming over the intercom as they spun their bikes around and headed for the highway.

Back on the open road with no sign of pursuit, Skylar smiled. The air rushing past as they continued to Santa Barbara radiated with energy. If this was what playing by her own rules felt like, maybe leaving the bureau and striking out on her own was the right thing to do.

-82-

TAIPEI, TAIWAN
July 29, 2029

Alex turned and looked out across the airport from the top of the steps leading up to Lady Sun's private jet. His stay in Taipei was only as long as needed to get a plane fueled and ready for boarding, not that Alex minded. After his experiences in Hong Kong, Alex had no taste for sightseeing. A new rucksack, some shirts, clean underwear, and a change of pants from a street market and he was ready to get back to California and his family. Lady Sun was already on board.

"Auf wiedersehen," said Alex turning his back on the city and ducking through the door of the plane as Lady Sun called for him to get inside.

Reika elected to take the next available commercial flight to Dublin to deliver a message for Lady Sun. With Madame Qiao no longer running a resistance network to keep Mitsuhide in check, Lady Sun feared for the stability of human-vampire relations. By that point, Alex's disbelief was saturated to the point that hearing her talk about it like an international trade deal barely fazed him.

Alex took a seat as the pilot locked the door and started the engines.

"You didn't have to come with me," he said as Lady Sun emerged from the showers at the back of the plane.

In anticipation of their arrival in Los Angeles, Lady Sun had ditched her Chinese dress in favor of a pair of blue jeans and a white T-shirt. Alex could not decide if the outfit made her more attractive or less attractive as she took a seat opposite him and towel-dried her hair. Her unwavering resolve terrified him, that much was certain, but he found her to be a curious creature.

"I will return you to your home then seek out the one that betrayed my sisters."

Alex opened his mouth to speak as the plane accelerated down the runway. Rather than shout over the engine noise, Alex waited for them to get airborne. The flight was going to be long enough that a minute's delay in replying would hardly make a difference.

"When you say sister," Alex said when they were off the ground, "you don't mean it literally, do you?"

Lady Sun shook her head. "We become sisters when we join our mistress' cause. The sisters sent to watch you were Americans."

"Vampires?"

"One vampire, one human," Lady Sun replied as she tossed the wet towel onto another seat. "We needed to watch you at all times. For my sisters to fail, the enemy must have killed them."

Alex looked out of the window as the clouds obscured the lights below them. "Or they switched sides."

"Possible, but unlikely."

Alex sat back in his chair and closed his eyes, silently running through the breathing exercises Reika taught him.

"Do you want me to put you to sleep?" Lady Sun asked, her casual tone sending a shiver down Alex's spine.

"That's not helping," Alex replied as he opened his eyes. Lady Sun looked thoroughly disinterested in his situation. "Besides, this isn't like the tunnels. I know where I am, here."

Lady Sun said nothing as she continued to stare out of the window, no doubt making the most of the night before she was forced to take refuge at the back of the plane. Switching his attention from his reluctant host, Alex surveyed the interior of the plane. He was so concerned with a safe take-off that his mind barely registered the plush cream carpet as he boarded. Peering along the aisle, he could see there were only twelve seats in the cabin, each one having ample legroom. The seating configuration reminded him of the trains he rode to college in Wales, with half the seats facing the rear. Beyond the seats was a fully stocked bar. Beyond that, the showers.

"What's your name?" Alex asked, growing bored of the silence.

"Lady Sun."

"I meant your given name."

"I know."

There was no shift in her expression as she spoke. No trace of humor creased her eyes. No flicker of anger furrowed her brow. Alex was used to emotionless responses from Reika, but they never felt personal. Lady

Sun's indifferent attitude felt targeted.

"I guess this is going to be a longer flight than I thought," Alex said as he searched for his seat controls.

After pressing each of the buttons to see what they did, Alex reclined his seat until it was almost horizontal, the footrest rising and extending to support his legs. All he was missing was a hot towel and a glass of champagne.

"Sun Ling Fang," Lady Sun said when Alex finished making himself comfortable.

Alex folded his hands over his chest and ignored her. His journey would be over soon enough if he shut out the world and slept his way back to California. His sister would welcome him home with open arms and a joke about him traveling halfway around the world to avoid doing any work. Mike would complain about how much messier the house would be now he was back, and Jeremy would pretend like nothing happened. That would make for an interesting conversation when Alex revealed the extent of his ordeal. If he revealed it.

"I'm nearly two hundred years old," said Lady Sun after another long pause. "Orphaned by the Taiping rebels, I was raised by Madame Qiao's handmaiden. I owe my life to our sisterhood. It's all I've ever known."

Alex raised his seat until he could look Lady Sun in the eyes. "Is that why you hate me?"

"I don't hate you," Lady Sun replied as she turned to face him. "I hate what you represent. You, and Daryl, and the order, and the council. An endless war, each side waiting for the opportunity to exterminate the other."

Alex stared at Lady Sun, wondering how such an impassioned speech could be delivered so dryly. The seething torrent of emotion Alex witnessed when Daryl ended Miss Chiu's life was dried up, leaving an empty riverbed of hopelessness in Lady Sun's heart.

"Well, I have no plans to exterminate you, if that's what you're worried about."

Lady Sun gave an amused scoff at Alex's comment, proving there was hope for her yet.

"What's so funny?" she asked as Alex smiled and shook his head.

"Nothing. Just thinking how bizarre this is. Sitting on an airplane with a vampire, wondering how I can cheer her up. It's a different world to the one I knew."

Lady Sun turned her attention back to the night sky outside the window. "The world is the same. The only thing that changed is that you've seen more of it. Me? Only revenge for my sisters will cheer me up. Are you willing to help me with that?"

Alex smirked mistaking her question for a joke. "Wait, you're serious? I wouldn't know where to start."

"Neither do I."

Alex shook his head. He just wanted to go home and pretend this whole thing was a bad dream. The longer it took, the more he learned. The more he learned, the harder it was to deny that things could never be like they were.

"I suppose I could ask Jeremy."

"No," said Lady Sun, a brief flare of anger behind her eyes. "You must not tell him what you learned. If he suspects, he will turn the order on us. I will not let my people be exterminated to get the bad. We deal with our own. Promise me you will not say anything to anyone about this."

"I can't do that. My sister needs to know the truth."

Lady Sun shook her head. "Not until our enemy is exposed. If you tell her now, we risk a war."

Alex took a deep breath and held it. Keeping this secret from Skylar felt wrong. He looked into Lady Sun's eyes and the fear that resided within. The change was disturbing, striking terror into Alex's soul.

"Okay, I promise," he replied, unable to imagine what moved Lady Sun so badly. Whatever it was, he did not want his sister to experience that fear.

-83-

VENTURA COUNTY, CALIFORNIA
July 30, 2029

Alex stared up at the house as the taxi pulled away from the wrought iron gates to Skylar's drive. In the past, he would have given the driver a one-star review for doing the airport to Santa Paula journey with broken air-con. Now, it felt like a waste of Alex's time and effort. Everything felt like a waste of time and effort.

"You managed before," Alex told himself as he entered the code to unlock the gates on a keypad to his right. "Like she said, the world hasn't changed."

Lady Sun's words were hard to disagree with and harder to live by. Some sights could never be unseen. Some knowledge could never be unlearned. That the world was home to black and white movie monsters was a truth Alex could not ignore. As the gates swung open, Alex's mind returned to the problem of living with his newfound knowledge. Lady Sun's instruction to say nothing echoed in his ears as he trudged up the driveway and grabbed the front door handle.

Locked.

Stepping back and looking over the front of the house, Alex ran his hand over his head. He was not expecting a welcoming party, but he figured somebody would be home. None of the windows were open.

"Balls," Alex muttered as he followed the path around to the side of the house.

All the windows were shut, denying him that ingress option, and the back door was also locked. Although he had bought a new phone from the first store he found, Alex could not remember anyone's number to put in it. Despite several shout outs on social media during the ride home, his family had yet to reply. Dropping the pack of clothes he acquired in Taiwan by the back door, Alex dragged one of Skylar's sun loungers from beside the pool into the shade and took a seat.

"Hey, Sky. How's things?"

His words sounded false. If he greeted her like that, her first thought would be to ask what's wrong.

"Hey, Sky," Alex repeated, his words sounding flat. "Hey, Sky."

Alex repeated the phrase until it sounded natural, buoyant, and free of any lingering despondency. He doubted telling the truth would be any easier. Exactly how one raised the notion that vampires were real without sounding crazy was beyond the limits of Alex's acting classes. Adding that Alex and Skylar were the children of vampire hunters sounded worse. Alex had no choice but to believe his own eyes, but Lady Sun's claim that there was a centuries-old bloodline of anti-vamps was a pill too large to swallow. That did not stop Daryl and Mitsuhide from believing it.

"You'd better be right, Ling Fang," Alex said as he stood and crossed the back garden.

When he left, the site of Skylar's summer house was virtually untouched, a couple of posts and a piece of string marking the perimeter of the proposed site. Now, a four-foot-deep trench dominated the far corner. Alex looked over the excavator parked alongside the ditch, but the keys were safely locked away.

Shame, Alex thought as he stepped down off the tracked wheels.

The distraction of clearing some soil would have been most welcome. Instead, Alex pulled off his top and threw himself in the pool. Dragging himself up the ladder after only two lengths, Alex flopped on the floor and let the sun dry him. Staring up at the clear, blue sky, his chest heaving from his brief bout of activity, Alex felt alive for the first time since waking up in Daryl's cell.

The sound of his phone drew Alex's attention from the heavens. It took him a moment to realize the ringtone was his. Once his brain caught up, Alex pulled himself up, wandered over to the sun lounger, and opened his notifications to see a message from Phoebe.

Glad ur home safe. How did ur meeting go?

Alex looked around the yard. His quest to find his mother had given him purpose. For the first time in years, Alex was unsure what to do next, but he knew who was worthy of his time.

Found my answers, he replied. *Taking some time to process before getting back to reality*.

Alex watched his phone as he contemplated what that reality might be. As much as he tried not to think about it, going back to the gym and cruising through life grew less appealing with each passing hour. There was always the option of taking Lady Sun up on her offer. Exactly how he could help her find out what happened to her sisters, Alex had no idea, but it was better than doing nothing.

Alex's phone beeped again. *Ditto. Been a strange few months. Are you going to the park today?*

Alex pursed his lips and sighed as he looked up at the empty house. *Sure. I'll be there around six.*

Whatever his new normal looked like, it could wait.

-84-

VENTURA COUNTY, CALIFORNIA
July 30, 2029

Alex flicked open his notifications at the now-familiar tone. Since announcing his return to California, a move Lady Sun had once again assured him was not a risk when he called her on his way to the park, a steady stream of likes and questions had rolled in.

"Penny for your thoughts?" Phoebe asked as she strolled over and took a seat on the wall next to him.

Alex looked over and smiled as he typed a reply to Tanner confirming he would be in the gym on Wednesday. He had almost given up hope that Phoebe would arrive after waiting nearly an hour beneath the cross. The sight of her in a pair of denim shorts and a floral top set his heart racing.

"Just the boys asking if I'll be working out on Wednesday," he said as his phone pinged again.

"And… are you?" Phoebe asked as Alex closed his inbox without reading the message from Kim.

Alex nodded. "It'll be good to get back into a routine."

"Things didn't go as well as you hoped in Hong Kong?"

Alex looked over at Phoebe's concerned expression, his jaw tightening in response. "Is it that obvious?"

"You don't sound like a man who has just been through a heartwarming reunion."

Alex sucked in a deep breath as he stared out over the Pacific, reminded of Reika's comment about learning to lie. Saying the right words wouldn't be enough. If he was to keep Lady Sun's secret until she uncovered the spy, he needed to sound convincing.

"I talked to her, but the only thing we have in common is biology. It's my fault. I built it up in my head that there would be a tear-filled reunion with her telling me how she missed me and regretted her decision. I didn't consider that, maybe, she never wanted to be a mom. I did have a mind-blowing holiday though. Saw some interesting sites. Met some interesting people. Once in a lifetime experience."

Alex watched Phoebe's reaction to see if his confident delivery was convincing. It helped that the words were true, even if the context was misleading.

"Yeah, I saw."

Alex frowned at the apprehensive tone of Phoebe's reply. Daryl had posted enough photographic evidence to his social media to make the lie believable.

"It looked like a beautiful place," Phoebe replied, her tone lifting as she smiled again. "I always imagined Hong Kong to be nothing but skyscrapers, but some of those parks you visited were beautiful. And the view over the city? That was awesome."

Alex smiled as the lie took root. "It was. A woman at the airport told me I had to go there before I left Hong Kong."

Phoebe's eyebrows furrowed, briefly, her nose and lips pinching together. "Was that the woman in your photos?"

There was that tone again. Disappointment tinged with concern.

"No. That was Lucy," Alex replied, using the name of the first Asian actress that came to mind to describe the woman on the train that had also appeared in a few restaurant photos. "She worked for the hotel. I mentioned that I wanted to go somewhere that wasn't the usual tourist trap and she offered to show me some traditional sights on her day off."

Phoebe looked away, tucking her hair behind her ears. "She was very pretty."

Alex nodded and looked back out over the ocean, convinced that Phoebe's tone had nothing to do with the lie. She was not the only one to get jealous scrolling through his news feed. Looking at all the things he could have been doing instead of suffering captivity made his stomach knot and his hands shake. He was unsure if the questions that would be raised if he deleted everything Daryl posted would be any more tolerable.

A sharp kick to his upper arm forced Alex back to the present. Before he could react, Alex found himself flat on his back, pinned down by a knee on his chest and a boot on his head, forcing him to turn his face to Phoebe or have his nose crushed.

"Is this layabout bothering you, miss?" the assailant asked as Phoebe jumped from the wall, fear written across her face.

"N-no," she stammered clutching her hands to her chest to shield herself, fists clenched tight. "We were just-"

"I know exactly what you were doing, and I'm here to save you from this despicable excuse for a man."

"Kellan, you Scottish sack of shit," said Alex, wriggling to free himself. "Get your fat ass off me."

"I prefer the term well-equipped," Kellan replied as he stood up, giving Phoebe a wink as he did so.

Alex conceded the point as he rubbed some feeling into the dead arm Kellan gave him. Kellan was stockier than Alex but in a powerful, athletic sort of way. There was no doubt Alex could surpass Kellan in a straight test of strength, but Kellan would excel in an iron man style contest. At least, Alex assumed he would. He had never seen Kellan exert himself physically.

"You two know each other?" Phoebe asked, hands still in front of her chest.

"We do. Now scram," Kellan replied as he waved her away. "We've got business to discuss. You'll have to suck his cock another day."

"What?" Phoebe cried out, her voice suddenly going shrill. "How dare you speak to me like that? I am a good Christian girl. See this? This is a purity ring. It shows that I am pure and chaste until the day I marry."

"I don't care if the ring on your finger is your boyfriend's arsehole. Get."

Phoebe stared at Kellan, her mouth and eyes wide open in incredulity. "Never in all my days have I been spoken to like that."

"Well that's a lie," Kellan replied taking his phone out of his pocket and glancing at the message. "I spoke to you like that just a few seconds ago."

"Okay, Kellan. That's enough," said Alex, before the banter escalated further. "Phoebe's a friend. I expect you to treat her with some respect. She isn't used to dealing with oafs like you."

"Forgive me, ma'am," Kellan said, feigning a posh English accent as he bowed a proper old-school bow, one leg out behind him and a hand across his chest, that went so close to the floor Alex was tempted to step on his back. "My dear papa was but an uncouth innkeep, void of manners and a scoundrel to boot. I am wont to forget that such behavior is uncivilized. Woe, I am beside myself with shame for you see, my lady, a rose so fair my eyes doth see. A rose fairer than any other in the land, and it makes my heart beat faster, stirring the vile beast residing within this man. This wicked man."

Phoebe looked from Kellan to Alex with the cutest look of perplexity, unsure how to react to such unusual behavior.

"Okay," Alex said as he shook his head and sighed, "now you're just taking the piss. What's crack-a-lacking?"

"I'll tell you in the car. Your sister needs us."

-85-

VENTURA COUNTY, CALIFORNIA
July 30, 2029

"Who's the blonde?" Kellan asked as they made their way to the car, leaving Phoebe to contemplate the meaning of life.

"Just a girl from the area," Alex replied, glancing back to see Phoebe staring up at the cross. "She's harmless enough. You should try being nice to people. You might find that out for yourself."

"What do you know about her? Who does she know? What does she know?"

"She's just a girl I met in a park. It's not a big deal."

Kellan stopped and rounded on Alex. "Everyone is an enemy until they prove themselves. You'd do well to remember that."

Alex huffed to hide his anger at learning that lesson from Daryl. "In your world, maybe. The day I live by that philosophy is the day I die inside."

The words sounded sincere enough to convince Kellan that day had yet to arrive. A part of Alex mourned that he would never again look at a stranger as a friend he had yet to meet.

"That day may come sooner than you think if you don't buck up your ideas. I didn't become the man I am by sitting in parks with pretty girls. I survived by not getting taken for a ride."

"And what kind of man is that, Kel? A dour, lonely, cynical, grumpy Scotsman? Way to shake off the stereotype."

A grin broke out on Kellan's face as he continued toward the van. "Aye. You've got me there. Just, be careful."

"What? Like, wear a condom?"

Alex unclenched his fists as the snappy banter eased the knot in his stomach.

Kellan's grin turned into a chuckle. "Aye. That too."

Alex glanced at Kellan as the lights of a black van flashed in response to a press of his key fob. "Could you find a more suspicious-looking vehicle? What's Skylar got us running? Drugs or guns?"

"Never underestimate the usefulness of a good van," Kellan said as he opened the door. "They've got me out of, and into, some tight places in the past."

"Aye, I bet they have."

Alex climbed into the passenger seat and gave Kellan a knowing grin as his mind flashed back to having sex in a service station car park in the back of a musician's touring van when he was in England. As Kellan smirked and pulled out of the parking lot, Alex reached for his phone. There was nothing to indicate that Skylar had seen the messages he sent. Not surprising considering his sister's erratic use of social media. Drawing a deep breath, Alex summoned the courage to ask the question he wasn't sure he wanted Kellan to answer.

"Was Sky alright when she called?"

Kellan flashed Alex a questioning gaze before looking back to the road. "As far as I can tell. Why?"

Alex glanced into the back of the van, unsettled by what he saw. "No reason. She was so stressed before I left. Where is she? Nobody was home when I got back."

"She's in the canyons between here and Simi. Have you not called her?"

Alex held up his phone as he turned to the window. "New phone. Don't have her number."

The serious tone of Kellan's voice dissuaded Alex from asking further questions. He was almost as bad as Skylar at drawing out secrets with innocuous questions. Instead, he turned to Mike's social media for clues. There were pictures of his bike, food, and Skylar trying to hide her face from the camera, but nothing to indicate anything was amiss. Was this what it was like for them, watching his social media and seeing a life nothing like the one he was living?

"I have to ask," Alex said, turning to look into the back of the van again. "Why is the van lined with plastic sheeting?"

Kellan glanced over his shoulder as if the detail had escaped him. "You don't have to ask. And I don't have to tell you."

"My sister has asked you to cover up a murder, hasn't she? This is a murder van."

"If you say so," said Kellan as they began winding through the canyons south of Santa Paula. "I wouldn't know what a murder van is."

"Then what did she call for?"

Kellan's response was interrupted as he swerved to avoid a dirt bike hurtling through the canyons. Alex fancied he heard and felt a bump against the side of the van, but the bike and rider were gone, a blue streak vanishing around the corner before Alex could get a decent look.

"Did you get the plates?" Alex asked as Kellan brought the van back under control.

"At that speed? I'm lucky I didn't get the bike. Which is why your sister called. Mike's bike broke down. We're going to load it onto the van and take it back to the Blake Estate."

"Which explains the plastic sheeting."

"Yes," Kellan said, dryly. "That is one hundred percent the reason for the sheeting."

Alex shook his head and scrolled further through Mike's posts. Trying to get an accurate read on Kellan was a fool's errand for which Alex did not have the patience. The mundanity of a breakdown did nothing to alleviate the tightening of his chest at the memories of his capture.

Tearing his eyes from the picture on his phone, Alex tapped out a message to Lady Sun.

Skylar's pregnant. Will Daryl go after the baby?

"What the-" Alex began as the phone flew out of his hand before he could hit send, the result of Kellan's sudden braking.

There, in the middle of the road, disheveled and splattered with blood like the villain of a horror movie, stood Skylar.

LOS ANGELES COUNTY, CALIFORNIA
July 30, 2029

Shay picked at a loose thread on her pants while she waited for her mentor to arrive. Her arm itched where the needle went in, an ever-present irritation that she struggled to ignore when idle. Dropping her head back onto the armchair, Shay stared up at the drawing room ceiling and stretched her lower jaw as her fangs slid down. Despite the pain, a sensation she was told would fade with time, she could not stop sliding them in and out.

"My cousin speaks highly of you, Miss Bryant," Mariela said as she entered the drawing room.

Shay stood to attention as her mentor ran her finger across a selection of bottles on a drinks trolley before lifting out a half-empty bottle of golden liquid. As the leader of their glorious revolution, Mariela commanded a show of respect.

"Do you drink?" asked Mariela, waving for Shay to be seated.

"I'm seventeen."

Mariela gave Shay a look of disbelief as she unscrewed the cap and picked up a glass. "So, that's a yes."

Shay nodded. "But I'm nearly eighteen."

Mariela poured the alcohol into her glass and took a seat in the armchair across from Shay. Her expression was cold and critical as she watched Shay over the rim of her glass. Shay shifted under her gaze, unsure what to do with her hands as Mariela slowly drained her glass.

"If you're going to lead, you need to stop fidgeting," Mariela said as she lowered the empty glass to her lap.

"You do it."

The words were out before Shay could stop herself. Shrinking as Mariela raised one eyebrow, Shay wanted the armchair to swallow her whole. It was easy to see how Mariela came to lead the revolution. Without a hostile word or threatening gesture, Mariela was able to radiate an aura of menacing authority.

"Vasily was right," said Mariela, laying her hand flat on her thigh to avoid fidgeting with her rings. "You're an astute individual."

Shay did not know what astute meant but guessed it was a compliment from Mariela's relaxed tone. Sensing the immediate danger had passed, Shay allowed herself to sit a little straighter.

"Let me be clear," Mariela continued, "our cause has no room for egos. We work for the betterment of society, and each of us has a role to play in shaping a fairer world. You are no more important than the person sweeping the streets or the person running the country. That being said, we each have our unique skills and talents. Not everyone is suited to lead, just as not everyone is suited to fighting against those who seek to profit at the expense of others. What makes you think you can lead?"

Shay folded her hands in her lap and straightened up. It was a question she had asked herself without receiving an answer. Sometimes, answers were overrated.

"What makes you think I can lead?"

Mariela lifted her hand and traced the outline of her lips with her thumb as Shay returned her curious stare. A slight smirk spread across Mariela's face as Shay, unable to maintain the staring contest as long as her mentor, raised her hand and rubbed the corner of her eye with her middle finger.

"What do you want from life, Miss Bryant?"

Shay thought for a moment, convinced Mariela was testing her. "What does anybody want from life, Mrs. Michaelis?"

Mariela turned her eyes to the fireplace, gazing at the logs stacked ready for winter. Given the modern look to the rest of Mariela's house, the fireplace looked out of place to Shay. Especially since there was no evidence of it ever being used. The poker was as bright as the day it was made, and the bricks that formed the fireplace were untarnished by smoke and heat.

"It was never about me," Mariela whispered. "It was always about the greater good."

Shay waited, unsure if Mariela's words were intended for her or if she was reminding herself. There were rumors that her husband left her after she became a vampire, but Shay did not believe them. True, Mayor Michaelis was not home, but that was because he was on official business in Sacramento. Hearing Mariela talking about the greater good made Shay reconsider the merit of such rumors.

"Mrs. Michaelis?"

Mariela turned back to Shay, a flicker of confusion in her eyes that suggested she had forgotten Shay was there. "Sorry, my mind was occupied by a little problem I'm having. That's the reason I agreed to take you on as my apprentice. With everything falling into place here in Los Angeles, I need to delegate some of my duties. You are aware of our operation in Death Valley, yes?"

Shay nodded. Vasily had briefed her on the massive underground network being excavated beneath the mountains. Legend had it that an ancient vampire was buried somewhere beneath the shifting sands of the desert, but no such discovery had been made by the excavation teams working around the clock to build their new sanctuary. The idea of building a vampire hideout in the hottest part of the country sounded crazy to Shay. Perhaps that was what made it so brilliant.

"I need somebody I can trust to run the operation when we begin phase two," Mariela continued as she stood and poured herself another drink. "Are you interested?"

Shay rose from her seat and straightened her suit. "When do I start?"

"Not so fast," Mariela replied as she raised her glass to her lips. "Your enthusiasm is commendable, but we'll start small. With Brianna needing medical attention that our corrupt, self-serving friends in the pharmaceutical industry refuse to provide, it would be unfair of me to expect Vasily to continue doing all he does for the cause unaided. I want you to use your experience with Carlos to overhaul the way we run our entertainment services."

Shay nodded to hide her surprise that Mariela knew about her visits to Carlos. "I can do that. I won't let you down."

Mariela emptied her glass and poured another drink. "It's not me you'll be letting down if you fail to serve, it is everybody that relies on us to ensure peace and prosperity for all. A brave new world beckons. We shall lead humanity into a new age of unity and cooperation, where nobody is left behind. If we, the people who can lead, ignore the plight of those who cannot, who is left to give hope to the masses? If we deny the people their freedom and humanity, we lose our own. We are not monsters, Miss Bryant. Never forget that. We are arbiters of justice, champions of equality, and leaders of and for the people."

Shay nodded but said nothing. Prosperity for all was easy to say when you lived in a multi-million-dollar mansion. If that was what it took to gain freedom and equality, Shay would become a leader, just like Mariela.

EPILOGUE

FAIRFAX COUNTY, VIRGINIA
July 31, 2029

Nikola's eyes flicked to the notification in the corner of her display. The slightest of twitches pulled her copper eyebrows together as her attention shifted back to the images projected against the wall of her living room. Flicking crumbs from the sofa with her bare foot, her fingers danced across the keyboard balanced across the top of her thighs as she swiped her mouse across the cushion next to her. The image pivoted left and up, catching the wings of a dragon as it passed overhead.

"I need healing," a voice boomed over the speakers built into her living room walls and ceiling as Nikola reached into a giant bowl of snacks and pulled out a handful of potato chips, popcorn and pretzels.

A wave of light radiated out from Nikola's character, healing her teammates as she crammed food into her mouth. Spamming her powers as they exited cooldown, Nikola watched her health bar yo-yo from half to full as she chewed, distracted for a second by another notification in the corner of her display.

Heaving a sigh, Nikola reached down the back of the sofa for her phone. Ignoring her teammates' demands for healing, she typed a response and tossed the phone onto the cushion before returning to her game. Two of her team were dead.

Shoving the keyboard off her lap, Nikola closed her eyes and let her head fall back onto the cushion behind her. She could continue healing, keeping the team alive indefinitely, but the damage her surviving teammates were dealing meant the dungeon crawl would take another six hours.

Smiling at her teammates' curses as they quit the team, leaving her half-elf healer in a pool of blood beneath the dragon's claw, Nikola reached out for another handful of snacks. Opening her eyes when her fingers failed to close around any food, Nikola looked up at the armored face of Mitsuhide, upside-down in her field of vision.

"I thought you'd be in Russia by now," said Nikola, a cruel smile forming on her lips, "begging Lukai for a seat at the table. Or down in California, fawning over your plaything's latest prize."

"Yet you do not appear surprised to see me."

Nikola shrugged and held her arms out to her sides. "What kind of spy would I be if I didn't know where my allies were at all times? That and you triggered the house's security system."

Mitsuhide turned his head from left to right, taking in the white-walled, wooden-floored room and the clutter within. The pizza boxes stacked on the table next to Nikola's sofa were a strong breeze away from being on the floor, and the residue in the collection of coffee mugs on the table in front of her was approaching sentience.

Mitsuhide made no effort to hide the disdain in his voice. "When was the last time you cleaned?"

"What day is it?"

"Tuesday."

Nikola smirked. "What week?"

Mitsuhide drew a deep breath and handed her back the bowl of snacks. Picking out some pieces of popcorn, Nikola watched as he strolled over to the other side of the room, her display reflecting off his lacquered armor as he stepped between the projector and the wall.

Events in California had taken an exciting turn when Nikola discovered the Sinclair girl was pregnant. For the first time in twenty years, there was something worth watching in the world. That Mitsuhide was the one to jump the gun and go after the child caught her off-guard. Nikola anticipated Lukai acting impetuously and had taken steps to guard against his interference, but not Mitsuhide's.

"What is it you want?" Nikola asked when Mitsuhide was done inspecting her home.

Nikola watched him stride over to the window and look out over the city as she shoveled more popcorn into her mouth.

"One of my minions has sided with the enemy. I need you to track her down and make an example of her."

Nikola exited the dungeon and returned to the character select screen, scrolling through her save list until she found her half-orc warrior. "Why is that my problem?"

"She is in your territory."

Nikola shrugged and readied her mace, eager to take out her frustrations on the first group of bandits she encountered. Nothing like the sleek weapon that felled her brother, Zsigmond, at the siege of Belgrade, caving in his skull as he fought to repel the Ottoman invaders, the video game weapon was an oversized monstrosity designed for aesthetic appeal.

"I expect you to deal with threats within your borders," Mitsuhide continued as Nikola charged into a bandit camp.

"Fine," she replied as she began spamming her powers, cutting a swathe through the bandits. "I'll have one of my agents deal with your upstart. What about the Sinclair girl? You know going after her was a bad idea."

"The attack was staged to look like an accident. Outteridge has no reason to suspect otherwise."

Nikola raised her eyebrows as her eyes swiveled toward Mitsuhide. "That won't stop him from jumping to conclusions. All for a little blood."

Mitsuhide turned from the window to stand in front of the projector, a move Nikola knew was intended to provoke her. Resisting the bait, she plucked a chip from her snack bowl and waited for Mitsuhide to speak.

"The blood of a guardian is worth a little suspicion. Sinclair lives. Feathers will be ruffled, but the status quo will remain if you keep Lukai in check."

Nikola grinned. "I knew you didn't come here because of a lost minion. What do you want me to do about him?"

"Keep him on a tight leash. Distract him until this blows over."

Nikola smirked as she picked an un-popped kernel from between her fangs. "Now you're talking my language."

With a nod, Mitsuhide strode out of the house as silently as he had arrived. No longer interested in the respawning mobs, Nikola slid the fingers of one hand under the waistband of her sweatpants, cradling her grumbling belly as she grabbed more chips.

The next twelve months would prove to be very entertaining.

ABOUT THE AUTHOR

Blood of a Guardian was written by Tyrone L. Williams, a.k.a. Atsie Newt, writing as M. J. Harper, and is the first book in the Cursed Truths series, created by Cynthia Strachan, Katrina Easley and Tyrone L. Williams.

Made in the USA
Monee, IL
17 June 2021